'A real treat ... [Meaney]
company and comfort
Sunday Ind

'Meaney can excavate the core of our human failings and
present it to us, mirror-like, on the page ... Which makes
her utterly credible, utterly authentic, utterly irresistible'
Irish Independent

'Warm and insightful ... Roisin Meaney is a skilful
storyteller' Sheila O'Flanagan

'Meaney weaves wonderful feel-good tales of a
consistently high standard. And that standard rises with
each book she writes'
Irish Examiner

'This book is like chatting with a friend over a cup of tea –
full of gossip and speculation, and all the things that make
life interesting' *Irish Mail on Sunday*

'An addictive read with engaging, flawed characters and a
unique writing flair that pulls you into the plot from the
very beginning and keeps you entranced to the very end'
Books of All Kinds

'A delightful read about relationships and the complexities
associated with family life ... A cosy read for any time
of the year, be it in your beach bag or sitting curled up in
front of the fire' *Swirl and Thread*

'It's easy to see why Roisin Meaney is one of Ireland's
best-loved authors ... Should you spot this on a
bookshelf, grab a copy' Bleach House Library

Roisin Meaney was born in Listowel, County Kerry. She has lived in the US, Canada, Africa and Europe but is now based in Limerick city. She is the author of numerous bestselling novels, including *The Anniversary*, *The Reunion*, *One Summer* and *The Last Week of May*, and has also written several children's books, two of which have been published so far. On the first Saturday of each month, she tells stories to toddlers and their teddies in her local library.

Her motto is 'Have laptop, will travel', and she regularly packs her bags and relocates somewhere new in search of writing inspiration. She is also a fan of the random acts of kindness movement: 'They make me feel as good as the person on the receiving end.'

www.roisinmeaney.com

@roisinmeaney

www.facebook.com/roisinmeaney

ALSO BY ROISIN MEANEY
It's That Time of Year
The Birthday Party
The Anniversary
The Street Where You Live
The Reunion
I'll Be Home for Christmas
Two Fridays in April
After the Wedding
Something in Common
One Summer
The Things We Do For Love
Love in the Making
Half Seven on a Thursday
The People Next Door
The Last Week of May
Putting Out the Stars
The Daisy Picker

Children's Books
Don't Even Think About It
See If I Care

Roisin
MEANEY

The
Restaurant

HACHETTE
BOOKS
IRELAND

First published in Ireland in 2020 by HACHETTE BOOKS IRELAND

First published in paperback in 2021

1

Cataloguing in Publication Data is available from the British Library.

Paperback ISBN 9781529375169
Ebook ISBN 9781529368246
Audio ISBN 9781529331400

Typeset in Book Antiqua by Bookends Publishing Services, Dublin
Printed and bound in Great Britain by Clays Ltd, Elcograf, S.p.A

Hachette Books Ireland policy is to use papers that are natural, renewable
and recyclable products and made from wood grown in sustainable
forests. The logging and manufacturing processes are expected to
conform to the environmental regulations of the country of origin.

Hachette Books Ireland
8 Castlecourt Centre
Castleknock
Dublin 15, Ireland

A division of Hachette UK Ltd
Carmelite House, 50 Victoria Embankment, EC4Y 0DZ
www.hachettebooksireland.ie

For Mike O'Grady, sadly missed, never forgotten

But what can stay hidden?
Love's secret is always lifting its head out
from under the covers,
'Here I am!'

RUMI

Emily

EMILY FEENEY, TWENTY-NINE AND STILL IN pyjamas, flings wide her bedroom window on a Thursday and tilts her face to the early-morning sky, the better to inhale the fresh, hopeful scent of April. She loves beginnings of days, particularly at this time of year, with the vigorous bloom of spring not yet spent, and the promise of summer in every burst of birdsong, every drift of cherry blossom, every budding geranium.

A sound in the street below catches her attention. There is Vinnie Corbett, reliable as the dawn, emerging from his house across the way. She watches as he slips a key into his pocket and pulls the red front door closed behind him. She sees him tap with his fingertips, like he always does, on the adjacent kitchen window before moving off. Saying another goodbye to Angie, who will have filled the yellow lunchbox that's tucked under his arm.

'Hey, Vinnie,' Emily calls softly.

He lifts his head and finds her, and sends her up a smile. 'Morning to you, Emily,' he says. 'Lovely day.'

'Sure is.'

After he's vanished around the corner, off to his barber's shop two blocks away, Emily turns her attention back to the street that's been her home for the past two years, give or take. A short ramble from the town's main shopping area, it's a pleasing undulation of one and two storeys, and a happy juxtaposition of commercial and residential, with little alleys scooting between every two or three buildings, and a line of trees – rowan, maple, willow, cherry – running along the edge of the wider pavement on Emily's side.

No chain stores are to be found here. There's the carpet shop owned by Karl, whose name is different in his native Syria, and who's lived in Ireland long enough to curse as fluently as any local. There's the launderette run by cousins Sheila and Denise, source of glorious wafts of fragrant cottony air each time its door is opened. There's Pauline's crèche, and Joan and Frank's secondhand bookshop, and Imelda's minimart, and Barbara's chemist, and Tony and Charlie's hardware store. All the businesses of the street scattered about – and nestling between them are the homes. She knows everyone. At various stages she's fed everyone.

She watches by the window as the place comes

slowly to life. Vans arrive and slot into alleys, shop shutters are rattled up, workers and schoolgoers emerge from houses, car engines sputter on.

At twenty to nine, James appears. He props his bicycle against the painted wooden bench outside Emily's front window and takes a bundle of mail from the canvas bag that sits in his large wire basket. A second or two later she hears the rattle of her letterbox. 'Thanks, James,' she calls.

He looks up and grins. 'Hello, you. Not a bad morning.'

'Not bad at all.'

At length she leaves her position to shower and brush her teeth and get dressed. The swirly pink skirt she's in the mood for today, a crisp white shirt above. She wriggles her feet into slippers and dabs colour from the same small pot onto her lips and cheeks. She runs a wide-toothed wooden comb through her curls and goes downstairs, fingertips skimming the ridges of the wallpaper in an ashes-of-roses shade that has hung there for decades, and that she sees no need at all to change.

A cream envelope lies face down on the hall floor. She knows before she turns it over that it will have a Portuguese stamp on it, and her mother's slanted handwriting. She takes it unopened into the restaurant kitchen, where she sees Barney sitting on the sill outside, waiting to be let in. At the sight of her he gets to his feet and presses his way along the glass, tail high, mouth moving in silent, hungry mews. She leaves the kitchen and opens the back door to let him into the corridor. Strictly no animals in a commercial kitchen, she was told by the health inspector before she was given the go-ahead to open the restaurant, and she obeys.

Down he bounds, graceful as a ballerina. 'Good morning, best boy,' she says, crouching to scratch between his ears. He butts his head against her hand; she feels the vibration of his purring. 'Come on,' she tells him, 'your breakfast is waiting.' They travel together up the stairs. He pads eagerly towards his filled bowl and begins to eat.

Back in the kitchen she washes her hands before weighing ingredients – flour, salt, yeast – into a large bowl. She scoops out a crater and dribbles in oil and tepid water and coaxes it all together. She tips the soft, warm dough onto a floured worktop and kneads, the comfort of the familiar movements allowing her mind to wander away, to touch on half-remembered snatches of conversation, to hum a song about a wandering minstrel that has snagged lately on a corner of her mind, to think ahead to the evening's dessert ingredients. Lemons and eggs for the tarts, bitter chocolate for the mousse.

When she's worked the dough into a shiny elastic ball she sets it by the window to rise and starts another loaf, and after that another, and another. She halves olives. She chops marjoram and thyme and rosemary. She spoons seeds – pumpkin, caraway, sunflower, sesame – into a small bowl. Minestrone and cream of tomato the soups on today's lunch menu, accompanied by slices of crusty bread, herby olive or seeded.

She returns upstairs to find Barney washing himself. She crouches to gather up the usual small scatter of his food pellets on the tiles, and return them to his bowl. So small he was when she found him, not a fortnight after moving here. Abandoned in the alley between the launderette and the bookshop, his tiny high cries caught her attention as she walked by on an evening stroll, her head full of the new direction her life was taking. She halted and peered up the alley, straining in the muddy twilight gloom to find the source of the sound – and there he was, clambering unsteadily over what she first took to be a little heap of rags, but which turned out to be the limp bodies of two others, presumably his siblings, lying half in and half out of the plastic bag they must have been transported in.

She stooped and gathered him up without thinking. She tucked him inside her coat – how he trembled! – and returned home with him, where she warmed milk and poured it into a saucer. He spluttered and choked, drenching his face and paws, too small to manage. She tried feeding him from a teaspoon. Here he fared slightly better, but still the process was messy, with more milk ending up on his face than in his tiny stomach.

She lined a pudding bowl with one of her scarves and deposited him there, and returned for the other two casualties. She wrapped them in an old tea towel and dug a hole for them in the shrubbery at the end of her narrow garden – but what was she to do with the survivor? With many splatters and splashes she coaxed a few more mouthfuls of milk into him, wondering if it was the right food for this helpless little creature, or if she was doing him more harm than good.

She returned him to his bowl and placed it next to her pillow, and spent the night straining to hear the small sounds of him. She listened to the fierce little rapid breaths and imagined his tiny lungs working frantically to keep him alive. She heard his snuffles and scratches and mews as he clambered his unsteady way around the bowl, her heart in her mouth in case all his noises stopped.

The following day she brought him to the vet, who told her that he was a he, and roughly a month old. 'You'll need to bottle-feed him for a couple of weeks,' he said, and gave her a bottle hardly bigger than her thumb, a funnel and a carton of kitten milk. She filled the bottle and wriggled its teat into the small mouth; her charge sucked at it greedily, like a baby, and grew round and tubby within a fortnight. After each feed she brought him out to the garden and set him on a patch of earth. Tiny as he was, he burrowed out a little hole and squatted over it.

Two years later, look at him. 'My big boy,' she says, and he runs a licked paw over his ear again and again and ignores her. He is her first pet, the first animal she has ever owned – if anyone can truly own a cat. By night he prowls the rear gardens and yards of the street, returning at dawn to his windowsill; during the day he sleeps a lot, curled in a corner of the sofa on one of Gran's old cushions that Emily hadn't had the heart to throw out.

Most of the time, apart from his morning welcome, he exhibits little evidence of fondness for her. He'll shy away from an attempted caress, making her feel that he looks on her purely as a source of food and shelter – but every now and again, when she's tapping on her computer or engrossed in a book, he'll leave his cushion and butt against her leg, demanding to be lifted and stroked and scratched before settling in her lap to purr and doze. She cherishes these unexpected episodes, this evidence that he holds her after all in some affection.

Grooming over, he leans unhurriedly into a stretch with the same fluid grace that accompanies all his movements. It ripples along the length of his body, elongating his limbs, pulling everything taut as a piano string. Watching him, she feels her own muscle groups flexing in response. He bounds onto the couch and gives a few exploratory prods of his cushion; the prelude, she knows, to his first snooze of the day.

She cuts a slice from a lemon and drops it into a cup and covers it with hot water. She spoons thick Greek yogurt into a bowl and eats it drizzled with pale yellow honey from the market and scattered with a teaspoon of toasted flaked almonds. She watches a pair of thrushes flitting about in the little back garden below, checking out the rowan hedge for a possible home. Be careful, she tells them silently. Watch out for Barney if you settle there. Keep your wits about you. Keep your babies safe.

As she dries her bowl she remembers her mother's letter, abandoned on the worktop in the restaurant kitchen. She retrieves it and slits open the envelope. She pulls out the single page and leans against the sink to read it.

Hello there!
Hope all's well with you. Patrick cut his foot on a rock a few days ago and had to have two stitches and a tetanus jab. He's fine but he loves a fuss, so I'm pretending it was far more serious. One of our students won quite a big swimming competition at the weekend, great excitement! We had local press at the school, so we were all in our Sunday best. What else? A neighbour fell off a ladder and crushed a vertebra, or slipped a disc, something painful anyway. I felt obliged to visit him in hospital, although he's a cranky so-and-so. He was asleep, which was a relief, but he looked about a decade older in the bed, and not half as fierce in his pyjamas. I left a bag of oranges and sneaked away. I might look in again in a few days, if only to make sure he knows who left the oranges!
Must go – we've been invited to drinks, it's

my yoga teacher's silver wedding anniversary.
Patrick did his best to wriggle out but I wasn't
having it. He sends his love, by the way,
Dol xx

Dol for Dolores. Never Mum, or Mam, or any of that.
Dol and Patrick they were called, by their children
as well as by everyone else. Was that why, Emily
wonders, they always seemed more like amiable
guardians, people who'd been entrusted with two
children and instructed to see them safely into
adulthood, rather than the parents who'd conceived
them?

Not that Emily and Daniel were neglected,
nothing like that. Never slapped or shouted at either.
On the contrary, they grew up in a state of comfort,
well dressed and well fed. They were brought on
holidays like everyone else, and encouraged to do
well at their very respectable schools, and driven
to or collected from friends' houses when they
requested it. But from the time she was old enough
to notice it, before she had learnt enough to put it
into words, Emily was aware of some disconnect,
some short circuit in the emotional current that
flowed between them.

Their infrequent embraces struck her as distracted,
as if they were following convention rather than
demonstrating affection. Their greetings and goodbyes
were breezy; their words of comfort when mishaps
occurred sounded formulaic rather than heartfelt.

Even their censure lacked conviction, as if whatever offence had prompted it – a negative comment on a report card, a complaint from a neighbour about loud music, a breaking of curfew at the weekend – didn't really bother them all that much.

The harsh truth of it, Emily finally concluded, was that her parents were more interested in each other than in their children. Individually they were happy to spend time with Emily and Daniel, but the instant they came together, their focus changed. They gloried in the other's company. They were enough for one another, with Emily and Daniel being the afterthoughts, the by-products of their union. The tolerated baggage.

Hard not to draw that conclusion, when they had packed their actual bags at the earliest opportunity. Their duty done, it felt like. Their preferred unencumbered lives ready to resume.

We're moving to Portugal in September, they said, the summer that Daniel, younger than Emily by three years, had got his first job. We've been offered positions in an international school. You'll both be welcome to visit anytime you want, as soon as we're sorted with accommodation.

But you have work here, Emily said. They taught in separate secondary schools; Dol's subjects were English and French, Patrick's science and maths.

We've resigned, her mother replied. We thought this was a good opportunity: if we left it much longer we'd be too old for anyone to want us.

So arrangements had been made, without any consultation with their children. Hard not to feel abandoned, even if you were twenty-two and earning a fair enough salary, even if you were still going to have a roof over your head – the house is yours and Daniel's, they were told, for as long as you need it. Hard all the same not to feel that they were making their escape.

And you'll have Gran with you, Dol said. Gran, Patrick's mother, lived in town, in the flat above the hat shop she'd opened after handing over the family home to her son and his new wife, twenty-five years earlier.

She's finally ready to retire, Dol went on. We've asked if she'd like to move back here, to live with you two.

Another decision taken without Emily and Daniel being consulted – but this was one Emily was all in favour of. Gran felt like family, real family. All through her teens Emily had so often dropped into the hat shop after school, to sit behind the counter and watch Gran with her customers, or to climb the stairs on days the shop was closed, to drink tea and eat Garibaldi biscuits.

She'd never known her builder grandfather: he'd fallen to his death from scaffolding when Emily's father was still a toddler. I worked from home while Patrick was growing up, Gran told her. I was always handy with a needle so I did alterations, and made hats to order. When Patrick announced he was getting married it gave me the push I needed – I'd been dreaming about opening a hat shop for years. I was thrilled when I found this little place with accommodation upstairs. It was perfect.

The shop was an Aladdin's cave to young Emily. There was a large room to the rear where Gran made her hats, with a big trestle table covered with rolls of fabric and bundles of lace and stacks of felt, and two giant glass-fronted cabinets whose presses and drawers held her various trimmings and threads and tools, and a large family of pin-cushions that put Emily in mind of hedgehogs.

In the main shop the hats were displayed on tiered shelving, with their curving magnificent feathers, their tulle veils and delicate lace edging, their ribbons and buttons and sequins and flowers. It was a place riotous with colour, and glorious with shape and texture. There was a small dressing table with a mirrored triptych, in front of which frowning customers would tilt their heads this way and that while Gran kept up a running commentary, and sometimes reached out to tip the hat further to the front, or an inch to the side. There! she would exclaim, beaming, clasping her hands. That's made all the difference!

I'm leaving it to you, she told Emily once, during one of their conversations. This place. It'll be yours after I'm gone – and Emily, shy and sixteen, couldn't imagine having the confidence to run a hat shop, or any shop, could only protest at the unconscionable thought of Gran not being around any more. She'd pushed the remark to the back of her mind and it hadn't been mentioned again – and thirteen years later here she is, three and a half years after the unthinkable happened, and Gran left them. Here she is, living in the apartment that was Gran's home, proprietor for the past two years of the restaurant that used to be a hat shop.

Here she is, after the future she'd planned fell apart, forcing her to create a new one.

She folds the letter and slips it into the left dresser drawer with all the others. Her father doesn't write: he phones every Monday evening, and they spend ten minutes in the kind of amicable but empty conversation people make when they aren't close enough for anything deeper.

She must remember to ask him about the injury to his foot; that'll use up a minute or two. She can tell him about the young couple who've moved into Frances Cooney's house, along with their small baby and several cats – Daniel thinks five, but it could be more.

Frances, childless and unmarried, lived next door to them all through Emily's growing-up years, behind net-curtained windows that were never opened. Her rear garden, for as long as Emily could remember, was home to her various discards: a rusting fridge, an assortment of woebegone kitchen chairs, the tangled skeletal remains of several umbrellas, numerous bicycle wheels and frames, a lopsided wardrobe missing its door. Frances, tatty and friendly, collapsed and died without a murmur on her way into the supermarket on the morning of her seventieth birthday.

Emily spends the next few hours at her computer, stopping only to return to the restaurant kitchen and attend to the intermittent demands of her bread. At length, the warm, wonderful scent of the baking loaves begins to drift up the stairs as it does every working morning, causing Barney to purr happily in his sleep. Emily drinks vanilla chai and types on.

At eleven she hears the sound of Mike's key in the door. She saves her file and flips the laptop closed, and goes downstairs to greet him, and to begin the lunchtime preparations in earnest.

'Toothache,' he says, when she enquires if all is well. 'Kept me awake half the night. My own fault, been nagging me for a while. Should have done something about it.' Hanging his jacket in the narrow press behind the door, reaching for a clean apron, securing it about his waist.

'Oh, poor thing – you should have phoned. I could have got Daniel to give me a hand.' Her brother has stepped in on a few occasions before. Daniel doesn't have Mike's flair, but he's not a bad cook. Between them, he and Emily manage when they have to.

Mike rolls up his sleeves and washes his hands at the small corner sink. 'I'm grand, the painkillers have kicked in. I've got the dentist booked for a quarter past two – only time he could take me, so I'll have to leave you with the tidy up, I'm afraid.'

'No worries.'

'I'll pay it back.'

'You know you don't have to.'

'I know.'

But he will, of course. First person she's ever employed, and she doubts she could have found a more dependable one. For the next half hour they chop and fry and season and stir as the kitchen grows warmer and more fragrant. While the soups bubble and the breads cool, Mike cuts lemon and orange slices for water jugs and Emily goes to the garden for primroses, a reawakened Barney padding after her. The sun is weak and pale but it's there, the sky a patchwork of washed-out blue and pillowy white. She sniffs the air, damp and fresh from last night's rain.

Beads of water cling to the velvety flower petals: she tries not to dislodge them as she snips stems. She arranges them in four little rinsed-out spice jars and takes them through to the restaurant. She checks place settings and straightens a fork and pulls out a tweak in the tablecloth. Ten to midday.

Upstairs she dabs fresh colour on lips and cheeks, and scent behind her ears. She pulls her hair into a ribbon that will definitely come undone before lunch is over, but elastic of any kind, once secured in her hair, becomes a prisoner of her curls. She checks her reflection in the bathroom mirror and reminds herself, as she does every day, how lucky she is. Healthy and solvent – just about – with a business she loves, and a sideline that helps pay the bills, and friends and family who care about her. Not much to complain about.

Back on the ground floor she pokes her head into the kitchen. 'Ready?'

'Ready.'

She walks through the silent restaurant as church bells three streets away chime for the Angelus. She unlocks the front door and throws it open. As she glances out to check on the street, a man rises from the bench outside the window, shaking out the jacket that was resting on his lap as he runs a hand through straw-coloured hair that's every bit as unruly as her own.

She smiles at him. 'You're early.'

'The boss is away,' he says. 'I snuck out. Don't tell.'

Bill

HE CHOOSES MINESTRONE, BECAUSE LAST
Thursday he picked cream of tomato, and variety
is the spice of life. He wonders if he'll meet any of
the other regulars today. Sometimes their paths
intersect, sometimes he's surrounded by strangers.
He doesn't mind either way: people come here to
chat, to mix, so conversations strike up easily. Today
he's the first to arrive.

After taking his order, Emily lingers. 'Bill, I know
you always tell me you don't mind when I ask you to
do something, but if you ever feel like I'm becoming
a pest—'

'Never. What do you need?'

'One of the kitchen taps is dripping. There's no
rush, it's not major.'

'I'll come Saturday afternoon, if that suits.' He'd
go to the moon on a bicycle if she asked.

'Would you? Thanks a million, you're a star.'

When she's gone he selects a slice of olive bread from the basket she set before him, and spreads it with too much butter. A minute on the lips, an inch on the hips, Rosie Doyle would say if she saw it, arthritic finger prodding at the softness around his middle – but he's fairly sure an extra inch or two on him would go largely unobserved. Long time since anyone looked at him with enough interest to notice stuff like that. He's no George Clooney, with his tangle of hair and pointy nose, and mouth too big for its surroundings. Still got all his own teeth though, and the hair is as plentiful as it was in his twenties. Small mercies: he's thankful.

The bread still holds the last of its warmth. He chews slowly, relishing the generous chunks of olive he encounters. He was twenty-two before he tasted an olive; he remembers biting into its crinkled black flesh, not knowing what to expect. The surprise of his teeth hitting the stone: he'd been thinking little pips, like a grape.

Greece they'd gone to, he and Betty, less than a year into their marriage, and just a few months after her mother died. A little holiday, he'd said, trying to pull his wife's mind away from her grief, trying to distract her with sunshine and bougainvillea and chunks of tender lamb on wooden sticks, and houses so dazzlingly white he'd had to squint at them.

Fragments of crust scatter with each bite onto the tablecloth. He swipes them into his hand and drops them back on his side plate. He reaches for the little glass jar closest to him and dips his head to sniff the primroses. He runs a finger lightly along a petal to marvel at its softness. He was never one to coax flowers from the earth – Betty was the gardener, and Christine had an interest too – but the sight of them never fails to gladden him.

The door opens to admit two women. He guesses mother and daughter. Right ages, same chins. Mother shorter, daughter thinner. They nod at him and take seats at the far end of the table. Came for the food maybe, happy keeping to themselves. He doesn't remember seeing them here before, but this can't be their first visit. New people always do a double-take when they walk in.

Emily reappears with his soup. She presses his shoulder briefly as she leans in to deposit the bowl before him. '*Bon appétit,*' she says, like she always does. She turns her attention to the other two, leaving him with the echo of her touch, the soft, powdery trail of her perfume. He likes her in pink; she suits pale colours. Then again, he can't remember seeing her in a colour that didn't flatter her.

He tells himself to cop on, and lifts his spoon.

Over the following few minutes the table fills rapidly, as it generally does. People enter in ones and twos, seats are chosen, names exchanged with neighbours, handshakes across the table, conversations ensuing. Bill soon finds himself chatting with a holidaying Norwegian, who tells him that a barman recommended the restaurant to him the night before. 'It is different here,' he says.

'You travelled to Ireland on your own?' Bill enquires.

'Yes. I like it, more interesting' – but Bill can't imagine heading off anywhere without a companion. Not for him, never for him. Took him long enough to work up the nerve to walk into this place by himself. For weeks he'd dithered, getting as far as the door and then walking on by, cursing his cowardice.

It's your first time, Emily said, when he finally made it across the threshold. The situation plain, with him hovering on the sidelines like a red-faced fool, having missed, in his botheration, the sign that told him he could sit wherever he chose. I'm Emily, she went on, putting out her hand to clasp his. You're very welcome. He told her he was Bill, and she seated him next to a tiny old woman with a head of sparse snow-white hair, whom she introduced as Astrid. One of my regulars, she told him, doing her best to put him at ease.

Over the course of the forty minutes or so that he spent in her company, he learnt that Astrid had been born in Austria, but had lived in Ireland for most of her life.

We got out just as the war was starting, she said, her accent barely discernible, the 'r's softened, the 't's sharp. We were lucky: my father had contacts in high places. We came to Ireland because it was neutral, and he thought we would be safe here, and so we were. I married an Irish man but I'm a widow now, and we were not blessed with children.

Bill told her he'd been widowed too. He mentioned a daughter but didn't dwell on her. She has her own life now, he said, and left it at that, and thankfully Astrid didn't probe. He has since come to recognise and appreciate the sensitivity that allows her to understand what isn't always articulated.

Emily comes and goes today, greeting known faces cheerily, keeping an eye on lone diners who look a bit lost. Bringing steaming bowls to new arrivals, keeping bread baskets filled, asking if anyone wants second helpings.

As he gets up to leave, Bill spots the two women he noticed earlier, in conversation with a pale, freckly man whose wire-rimmed spectacles perch on the bald dome of his head. As he talks, the man tears a slice of bread into pieces and floats them in his soup. He glances in Bill's direction and catches his eye briefly before Bill lets his gaze slide away, afraid that a smile might come across as mocking the bread islands.

'Always good to see you, Bill,' Emily says, taking his money, and his name on her tongue sends warmth through him.

'I'll be back on Saturday,' he replies, but if it wasn't Saturday it would be Sunday, or soon anyway. He can't stay away, is the truth of it. He feels compelled to return, like Astrid. This place is like home for me, she told him that first day. I come here two, sometimes three days a week – and now it feels like home for him too, and he's become one of the regulars that Emily entrusts with the shy newcomers. He drops in nearly every other day for lunch, and on Sundays he sometimes treats himself to evening dinner here.

But it's not just the food that pulls him back, or the company of his fellow diners. The pathetic, laughable truth is that his foolish smitten heart insists on his returning, again and again. Another encounter, it commands. Another chance to look at her, to listen to her. Another chance to do your level best to make her laugh.

A light mist begins to fall as he strolls back to the nursing home, the blue all but chased from the sky now, his hair frosted with tiny wet beads when he runs a hand over it. Still, they got the morning dry. Focus on the positive, Betty would say, and let the rest go – and it helps a bit, it does, when he can manage to do it. The bread and soup have left a pleasant fullness in his belly: he'll only want something small this evening. An egg, maybe; fry it up with a tomato.

'Bill,' Mrs Phelan says, 'the sink in Rory Dillon's room is blocked up.'

Always he hears a small edge of impatience in her voice, leaving him with the faint suggestion that he's somehow a disappointment to her. Una Phelan she said, the first time they met, him done up in his only suit for the job interview, not that he's ever had the courage to call her Una. Even in his head she's Mrs Phelan.

But the residents are well looked after – you can't fault her there. Three decent meals a day, cups of tea in between if they want it, milk and a biscuit before bed. Bill could eat there too – it was mentioned at the interview. Lunch included, they'd said, but he prefers to get out. Feels more like a break if he leaves the premises.

He climbs the stairs to the first floor, and makes his way along the corridor to Rory Dillon's room. 'I don't know why it happened,' Rory says, peering anxiously over Bill's shoulder at the little puddle of cloudy water that sits unmoving in the sink. 'I only ever wash my face, that's all I ever do, and rinse out my teeth at night.'

'Could happen to a bishop, Rory. Don't worry, I'll sort it.'

The job is easy for him. He's always been handy around the house. Plumbing was what he was trained for, worked at it since he was eighteen in Hennessy's Builders. Never saw the end coming: Declan Hennessy gave them no warning. The doors locked when they arrived for work one Wednesday, coming up on four years ago. No sign of Declan, nobody at all around but a young lad in a grey suit and a crew-cut, telling them the place had gone into liquidation. Don't shoot the messenger, he said. Nothing to do with me, I'm only passing on the news.

Bill wasn't as badly off as some of the others, with his mortgage paid and his child gone to the dogs and his wife buried, but still it was a blow. Gainfully employed one day, surplus to requirements the next – and who'd want to hire a man in his forties if a younger fellow was willing to do the same work for less money? Who'd want to hire a plumber of any age, with the building trade still only picking itself up after the bust?

So he tipped away at odd jobs wherever he could find them, and then he heard that the nursing home was looking for a caretaker. He decided to chance his arm, and they took him on. The work is mostly undemanding, and it pays the bills, and he's grown fond of the residents – who look on him, he suspects, as a kind of adopted son. He buys them cards for their birthdays and takes their letters to post, and gets a tin of butter cookies and a new board game for the day room at Christmas. For some, for quite a few of them, the nursing-home community is the only family they have left; he's only doing what anyone with a heart would do.

From time to time he spots Declan Hennessy, still driving around town in his fancy car, pretending every time not to see Bill, who refuses to let it bother him. What's the point in harbouring a grudge? What's the good of letting something fester away inside him? No good at all, so he wishes his old boss no evil.

Not that he'd take a job with him again though, if

one was ever offered. He's not a complete fool – or not in that respect anyway.

The afternoon passes. He lets on to pump the tyres again on Rosie Doyle's wheelchair – they never need it when she asks, but it keeps her happy – and replaces a cracked plug on a toaster. He does his weekly check on the smoke alarms in every room, and on the carbon-monoxide ones in the communal areas.

He cleans two of the big dining-room windows, inside and out. He hoses down the nursing-home minibus and does what he can under its bonnet. He reckons the vehicle is about a decade past its best-before date, but it's going to have to soldier on for another while. Keep it going as long as you can, Mrs Phelan told him, so he changes the oil every so often and keeps an eye on the brake fluid and the plugs and points, and tops up the air in the tyres. He does whatever he can think of to prolong its life, and crosses his fingers after that.

At five to five he gets out of his overalls and packs up his tools. He washes his hands and makes his way to the day room where his audience is waiting, the dozen of them or so who enjoy this last bit of the afternoon.

'What'll it be?' he asks, pulling out the piano stool, and they call out names to him. 'Just A Song At Twilight', and 'As Time Goes By', and 'The Tennessee Waltz', and 'How Are Things In Glocca Morra', and 'We'll Meet Again'. He plays every one of them, bum notes and all. He's no pianist, never could get the hang of reading music, but he can plink out his own homemade version of a melody, and he can make up some class of harmonies as he goes along, and they're not fussy.

As he works his way through the tunes, Gloria McCarthy closes her eyes and sings. Her voice has grown a little wobbly with age but is still perfectly pitched. Nobody minds if the words don't always come out right, and everyone chimes in with the choruses. Rory Dillon taps out the rhythm of each song with a slippered foot, and Rosie Doyle fishes a tissue from her sleeve and dabs at the tears the music always prompts in her.

When Bill plays the opening bars of 'The Tennessee Waltz', Kate Greene and Jenny Burke get to their feet, as they always do at some stage in the proceedings, and shuffle slowly around the floor together – Kate thinking, Bill suspects, of Diarmuid, the husband who waltzed with her for fifty years. Elsewhere in the room heads nod along, and arthritic hands clap in time to the livelier tunes, and for half an hour they travel back through their stories and their songs, and remember.

He can't recall how it started, what chance remark prompted his first performance, more than a year ago it must be now. Someone mourning the fact, was it, that the piano was sitting there idle, no current resident able to play? Someone reminiscing maybe about the dances or showbands they used to love in days gone by. For whatever reason, Bill sat down one afternoon and gave them a spontaneous rendition of the first thing that came into his head – 'A Bicycle Made For Two' it might have been – and the gratifying reaction this received kept him there for a few more numbers, and saw him return to the day room the following afternoon when his shift was over, and again the day after that. Now they wouldn't let him miss it, this bookend of his working day.

The teatime bell is his signal to finish. He lowers the piano lid and helps them gather up their bits and pieces, and tells them he'll see them tomorrow as they move off in the direction of the dining room. Not a bad life for them, he supposes – although he privately hopes to end his own days under his own roof.

The plan isn't working out. The plan was for him and Betty to make their way into old age together, looking out for one another as the years moved on – with maybe Christine playing some minor role in their welfare, although he'd never have wished either of them to be a burden on her. But the plan isn't to be, not any part of it.

He leaves the building through the rear door, turning up his collar against the continuing heavier rain. Left his umbrella at home again. If he'd thought of it he could have taken one from Emily's – there's half a dozen poking from a painted metal holder just inside the restaurant door. *Help yourself if you need one*, the sign above them reads. *Drop it back next time you call.* No matter, he's homeward bound. He'll shower and get into something dry, and have his bite to eat in front of the telly.

Or maybe not.

He sees her as he nears the house, squatting by the front door, hood up, head bowed. She could be anyone, with her face hidden like that, but she's not. He wonders if any of the neighbours have spotted her. If Mrs Twomey has, she'll find an opportunity to say it to him over the next few days. I saw Christine, she'll say, watching his face like a hawk. Poor thing, you'd have to feel sorry for her, she'll say, and he'll make some noncommittal response and walk away before he says something he'd regret.

Christine lifts her head at the sound of the gate opening. She rises to standing and watches him silently as he walks up the path. No smile, never a smile from her now. He can't remember the last time he saw it, can't recall the change it makes to her face. Finds himself completely unable now to summon his own smile on seeing her.

He nods a greeting. She continues to regard him wordlessly. He recognises the tatty green parka, shoulders darkened now with the rain, and the brown cord trousers with the knees of them worn thin, but the suede boots are new – or new to him. What he can see of her hair beneath the hood is lank and uncombed. Her lips are dry and split, with a cold sore in one corner.

Her left cheek is grazed; the skin surrounding the eye on that side is pink and puffy. He doesn't ask about it. He's not able for what the answer might be.

'Hello, Christine,' he says finally.

'Hello.' She hasn't called him Dad in years. As she lifts an arm to bat away something on her face, he catches a glimpse of the bitten unpainted nails. He remembers how she used to mind her nails once upon a time, how she used to file them and paint them, and her mother's too. He recalls their lowered heads, the words travelling quietly between them, and how they'd take no notice at all of him when he walked into the kitchen. He used to love to witness that closeness they had.

He turns away from her and makes a business of taking his key from his pocket, his limbs feeling suddenly stiff and useless. He opens the front door and steps aside, and after a second she enters. He gets a waft of her unwashed odour as she passes him, and his stomach clenches in protest. He remembers the long baths he and Betty would give out about, the hot water gone, the bathroom smelling like a field of flowers or a mountain forest when she finally surrendered it.

He follows her in. He shrugs out of his wet jacket and drapes it on the end of the banister. He walks past her down the hall to the kitchen – and as he opens the door Sherlock bounds out, tail pumping, butting against her, whining his greeting, like he always does.

Traitor.

No, not a traitor: Sherlock is faithful. Apportioning no blame, accepting her exactly as she is. Giving her the same unconditional love she always got from him. 'Sherlock,' she whispers, sinking to her knees and burying her face in his neck, giving the same love back to him. Easier to show it to a dumb animal than to her father.

In the kitchen Bill rubs the worst of the rain from his hair with a tea towel and rakes his fingers through it. He plants his hands on the edge of the sink and looks out at the lawn as he listens to her continued soft murmuring to the dog. Three weeks, around that, since her last appearance, two or three weeks she generally leaves it between visits. Going that long without a proper wash, without a decent meal in all likelihood.

First time she turned up was around two months after she'd moved out, taking the contents of Bill's wallet with her. When he saw her standing on the doorstep he'd thought, in his innocence, that she'd come to her senses, that she was turning her back on drugs and returning home. Christine, he said, opening his arms to take her in, ignoring the unkempt appearance of her, willing, more than willing, to forget all that had gone before – but she stayed out of reach of his embrace. I just wanted a wash, she said, not raising her gaze higher than his chest. I thought you might let me have a shower – and he lowered his arms and opened the door wordlessly and let her in, and the pattern was set.

At length he goes through to the utility room. He opens a press and retrieves the clothes she wore on her last visit, laundered and ironed. He returns to the hall and she rises to her feet to accept the bundle. Her wrists, thin as twigs, break his heart.

'Towels in the hotpress,' he says, as ever.

'Thank you,' she whispers, and climbs the stairs.

'Come on,' he says, and Sherlock pads after him to the kitchen and is fed. Bill opens the fridge door and peers in. If he had a bit of notice of her arrival he could pick up a cooked chicken or a lasagne or something on his way home, but when she turns up unexpectedly like this he's forced to work with whatever he has to hand. Today he finds sausages and eggs, so he pulls out the frying pan and gets the bottle of olive oil.

Not that it matters what he puts before her. Whatever it is, she'll show little interest in it, she who always loved her food. These days it no longer holds the attraction it did, her body craving something different now. He'll press it on her anyway; he'll guilt her into eating at least some of it.

When he hears the shower starting up he climbs the stairs and retrieves the small heap of her clothing from outside the bathroom door. He brings it down and loads it in its entirety into the washing machine, not brave enough to sort through it. He pours in detergent and softener, and switches it on.

Although it's still raining he flings open the big kitchen window. He turns on the hotplate under the pan and sets the table for two. He fills a jug with water that she won't drink, and puts out a can of Coke that she will.

Sherlock scratches at the back door: he lets him out. He stands by the cooker while sausages sizzle, and listens to the churning of the washing machine, and imagines it lifting the dirt of the street from her clothing. He pushes the sausages aside and cracks eggs into the pan. When they're as done as they need to be he lowers the heat and sits.

He props his elbows on the table and sinks his head into his hands. He wishes himself back in the nursing home, plinking at the piano keys or pressing the end of a sweeping brush into the red test buttons of thirty smoke alarms one after another, or rubbing a smear from window glass. He wishes himself anywhere but here.

He has failed Betty, is how he sees it. He has failed to keep their only child safe. He is heartbroken. He is broken of heart, his only solace a restaurant designed to comfort the lonely, where he feeds from the company of strangers as much as from the proffered dishes, and where he loves a woman who will never love him back.

He risks conjuring up an image of Emily, smiling and pink-cheeked, her beautiful coppery curls eternally escaping from their ribbon as she tends her customers, as she nourishes souls along with bodies. Emily, who is a million miles out of his reach. Emily, who finds her way into his dreams.

He feels a small rush of happiness at the thought of Saturday afternoon. He loves that she comes to him when she needs help – he'd happily do her repair jobs for nothing but she insists on paying. He treasures the times they meet outside opening hours, when he doesn't have to share her with all the other customers. She'll be there for the half hour or so it'll take him to fix the dripping tap, putting together whatever dessert is planned for the evening. She'll send him home with some treat along with his payment, a wedge of cake or a trio of cookies.

At length he hears the shower cutting off. He gets to his feet and returns to the utility room, where he takes a toilet bag from a shelf. He unzips it and checks the contents, the same things he always puts in. Toothbrush and paste, box of tampons, deodorant, pack of emery boards, shampoo, bar of soap, comb, Chapstick, tube of antiseptic cream, card wallet of plasters. He has no idea if she uses any of them, but he fills a toilet bag between each visit because it's something he can do for her. He'd buy her underwear if he wasn't clueless about sizes. He'd do anything for her, if only she'd let him.

He opens his wallet and takes out the bundle of tenners, five of them, that he keeps at the ready, wrapped with an elastic band so he won't spend them. They'll be used to feed her habit: he knows this, he's not a fool. They'll be slipped one by one into a hand in return for a few hours, or maybe a few days, of oblivion, or happiness, or whatever she gets from it. He has little knowledge of how her life works now, and no desire to know.

Would you let me organise for you to go somewhere? he'll ask her, like he always does, sometime during the meal that neither of them wants. I'll help you, he'll say. I'll pay whatever it costs. I'll bring you there, you won't have to do it alone.

He lives in hope. It's a lonely place to be. She's said no every time he's asked, but he'll ask again. He has to ask again, has to go on asking until she gives the right answer. He must keep believing that one day she'll say yes: the darkness would swallow him without that belief.

On days like this, he feels every one of his forty-eight years.

He turns on the radio. He's not interested in it, but it will fill their silences. He leafs through the local paper as he waits for her, skimming the news items: a planned parish trip to Lourdes, an accident on the dual carriageway that put three in hospital, the opening of a skateboarding area in one of the parks.

He turns the page and sees *Dear Claire*, the agony-aunt column he normally bypasses – but something makes him stop this evening. He reads the problems, and the responses. He sees an email address, and an invitation to get in contact.

How could a stranger be of any help to him? What could anyone suggest that he hasn't already tried?

Nothing to lose though. Everything lost already.

Might open a new email account, make up a name to go with it, and give it a go.

And later that evening, after he's said goodbye to Christine, he does.

Dear Claire,

I've never written to someone like you before. I'm not entirely sure why I'm doing it now, only you always seem to have the answers, and I could do with a few.

My wife died eight years ago, when our only child, our daughter, was sixteen. After her death, our daughter's behaviour changed. She'd never given us any trouble, she was always a happy girl with lots of friends, and she had a good relationship with both of us, but in the weeks and months that followed her mother's death she became quieter and less inclined to talk to me like she used to. I put it down to grief and assumed it would pass, but instead it got worse as time went on. She'd be late home from school without an explanation, and if I questioned her she'd get on the defensive and accuse me of bullying her, and I'd back off because I didn't know how to handle it. When I spoke to my workmates, who were all men, they said it was typical teenage behaviour and she'd grow out of it. I hoped they were right.

One day I noticed money missing from my wallet. When I asked my daughter about it – not accusing her, just thinking she might have needed a loan – she flew into a rage. She denied taking it, but I knew it had to be her. She became even more moody and unpredictable after that, to the point where I was afraid to say anything in case she blew up. There was terrible tension in the house whenever she was there. In desperation I asked my sister to speak to her, thinking she might do better than me, but my daughter refused to have a conversation with her. My sister said the same as my workmates, that it was probably teenage moodiness, so I resolved to endure it in the hope that they were all right.

One day, a little over a year after my wife died, I got a call from my daughter's school asking me to come in, and when I did, the principal told me her teachers were concerned about her, that she was missing days and not doing homework, and showing aggression when they questioned her. She'd always been a good student, and she was in her Leaving Cert year, so this was very worrying. When I went home I tried to talk to her, tried to reason with her, but she told me to mind my own business – and then, a few days later, I got a visit from the mother of one of her friends, who told me that my daughter had offered her daughter drugs.

It came as a terrible shock. I was convinced she must be mistaken, that my daughter would never do such a thing – but the more I thought about it, the more sense it made, the easier the jigsaw became to assemble. I figured that my daughter must be taking drugs herself, must have been for some time, and was now turning to selling them to feed her own habit. What others had put down to teenage moodiness was, I decided, something far more serious.

I had no idea what to do. I confronted her when she got home, but I didn't handle it well – I hadn't been sleeping for quite a while, and spoke more sharply than I'd intended – and she ended up storming out of the house, and staying out till the small hours.

Sorry, I didn't mean this to be so long, but you may as well have the full story. Basically, I lost her that day. She began staying out more and more, and ignoring me as much as she could when she did show up. I stopped answering phone calls from her school, too cowardly to hear what I knew they wanted to tell me. I was losing her, and the prospect was terrifying. I rang phone numbers that offered help for families affected by addiction, I rang every place I thought might tell me what to do, and I was told by pretty much everyone that if she didn't ask for my help, I couldn't give it. Basically, I could do nothing apart from join one of those groups for families affected by drug abuse, which I didn't. The thought of sitting in a circle and baring my soul to a group of strangers held no appeal.

One night, she didn't come home at all. The following day I reported her missing. She was a few months off her eighteenth birthday, so technically still a child. The guards found her easily enough, sleeping rough with a few others in a vacant house. They brought her home and I tried to reason with her. I said I'd do whatever it took to help her. I thought I'd got through to her; she agreed to let me help. She went to bed in her old room, but the following morning she got up early and made off with the wallet I had foolishly left in the pocket of a jacket that was hanging in the hall.

That was six and a half years ago. She dropped out of school, so she didn't do her Leaving Cert. She's twenty-four now and still living on the streets. I've seen her begging. It is not a sight any parent should see. The first time I saw her I approached her, but she left without giving me a chance to speak, so now if I come across her I walk on by. I have no idea what else she does to make money, and it's probably best that I don't. She turns up at the house every so often, and I feed her and wash her clothes and let her have a shower.

Day and night I feel haunted and guilty. I am broken-hearted that her life has become so hard. I've failed her as a father, and I've failed her mother too. Is there any advice at all you can offer me, any wisdom you can share that might help us out of this purgatory?

Regards,

John

Emily

WHEN EMILY FEENEY WAS TWENTY-FIVE SHE took from their packaging two white nylon stockings that had cost a scandalous twenty-seven euro. She lifted the first and shook it out, and unrolled it slowly and carefully up her leg. She did the same with the second, wondering how long it would take for their elasticated tops to become an irritation.

She fastened around her wrist the silver charm bracelet she'd owned since her twelfth birthday (something old) and put on a sleeveless ivory dress made of silk (something new) that fell like liquid to her ankles. She attached her grandmother's drop earrings (something borrowed) to the lobes of her ears. She pulled taut a garter bought for her by her bridesmaid (something blue) to bring it slowly up her leg without once making contact with the stocking. She stepped into shoes whose thin satin straps fastened with mother-of-pearl buttons, her insides all the time fluttering as wildly as bunting on a gusty day. *It's here. It's come. This is it.*

She touched hair that had been gathered up and pinned into place earlier that morning by a stylist from the salon where Emily worked as a receptionist. The stylist had sprayed it to keep it from wandering: it felt stiff and unfamiliar now to Emily. She dotted on perfume and touched up her lip colour for the umpteenth time. When all her preparations were complete her father Patrick, home with her mother Dol from Portugal for the occasion, drove Emily and her bridesmaid to the church in a rental car.

Her mother, slim and tanned, stood waiting at the church gate in her lavender dress with its matching coat. She approached the car as it pulled up. 'Drive around,' she told Emily's father. 'Don't come back till I call you.'

'Isn't he here yet?' Emily asked, but her mother stepped back as she waved them away with her silver clutch bag, and didn't answer. It was half an hour after the ceremony should have begun, which was when Emily had been advised by her married friends to arrive. You need to be fashionably late, they'd said, but he'll be nervous, so don't leave him waiting too long.

Her father skirted the perimeters of the town for twenty minutes as Emily's bridesmaid talked about hangovers and punctures and traffic jams, and Emily looked through the car window at houses and hedges and playing fields, and told herself that nothing at all was wrong. It was a blip, no more. They'd laugh about it this evening, when they were husband and wife. She'd say she'd been fit to kill him for nearly giving her a heart attack; he'd sweep her up and twirl her around and tell her for the thousandth time how sorry he was, and he'd swear never to keep her waiting again as long as he lived.

Any minute now her father's phone would ring, and it would be her mother summoning them back to the church. This time tomorrow Emily would be on the plane to France, sipping Prosecco because Champagne gave her heartburn. She'd let it slip to the friendliest member of the cabin crew that they were on honeymoon. It might be announced over the intercom; they might get a round of applause from the other passengers.

And all the time she was thinking this, all the time she was forbidding her mind to go elsewhere, something cold and hard was lodged behind her throat, butting up against every breath she took, and her bridesmaid held her hand so tightly that her engagement ring pressed painfully against its neighbouring fingers.

Eventually her father pulled in to the side of the road and phoned her mother. Well, he said, and there was a long pause while he listened, and, Right, he said then, and it was clear by the careful way he said it that Fergal hadn't shown up. He ended the call and started the car without looking at Emily.

We'll go home, he said, and wait there, and she knew she wasn't getting married that day.

He'd been in an accident. Not a serious one, nothing that threatened his life, just bad enough that he couldn't contact her. She'd get a call later on from one of the hospitals. He wanted you to know, they'd say. He's fine, he'll be absolutely fine, but he can't talk right now. She felt another stab of pain from her squeezed ring: she eased her hand from her bridesmaid's and regarded the small perfect diamond he'd bought for her.

I'm sure there's an explanation, her bridesmaid said. I'm certain, Em.

Shh, Emily replied, and Gran's earring was cold against her neck as she turned to look up at the pale grey sky, and she wished she could disappear.

When they got back to the house there was a white envelope on the hall floor, with her name and no stamp on it.

Emmy
I'm so sorry. I can't do this. I'll regret hurting you all my life. I won't ask for forgiveness as I don't deserve it, but please try to forget me.
F xx

He must have been waiting somewhere until the coast was clear. He must have watched her drive away to her wedding with her father and her bridesmaid. She imagined him walking up the path, slipping the envelope through her letterbox while she joked with her bridesmaid about pairing her up with the best man, in blissful ignorance of the calamity that was about to unfold.

She read and reread the letter that told her nothing, that explained nothing. I can't do this? Why not? Why couldn't he? She sat through the storm that followed, as first her father and then her brother promised to hunt Fergal down and kill him. She listened on the phone later that evening to his mother's tearful assurances that he'd said nothing to her, that she'd been as much in the dark as Emily.

He left for the church before me, she wept. You must believe me, Emily. I couldn't understand why he wasn't there when I arrived, I was sick waiting for him to show up. I came home to a letter, just like you. He's gone away, he's gone to Canada. He's left the two of us, Emily.

If he was already gone to Canada this wasn't a spur-of-the-moment thing, a last-minute-nerves kind of thing. This had taken planning. He had to have bought an air ticket, had to have packed his passport and his belongings. She pictured him sneaking from the house the previous night with his suitcase, slipping it into the boot of his car after his mother had gone to bed. While Emily was thinking about the seating plan and the photographs, he was calculating what time he'd need to be at the airport.

She endured the rumour that spread through the town not long afterwards, and that her bridesmaid eventually shared with her: that he'd gone to

Canada to be with Therese Ruane. Therese who'd
been his girlfriend before Emily, Therese who'd
finished with him and emigrated to Canada a
month before he'd walked into the salon where
Emily worked, and asked to make an appointment
for a cut. Therese who'd returned to spend last
Christmas with her parents, who'd bumped into
him and Emily one evening. I hear you're getting
married, she'd said, looking at him instead of at
Emily. Congratulations.

Rise above it, Gran said, when Emily's parents
had returned to Portugal, and Daniel had forgotten
about his promise to kill Fergal, and her friends had
got tired of asking her to come out to the pub with
them, and Emily finally felt safe enough to let out
the tears. Rise above it, my darling. Don't dwell on
it. Don't allow him to make you bitter. And don't
judge all men by him: you were just unlucky this
time. The next will be better, wait and see.

But Emily had already decided that there would
be no next. She'd learnt her lesson: hearts were better
off kept in their owners' possession and surrendered
to nobody. She'd stay single, and eventually she'd
sleep through the night like she used to, and one
day she might even experience happiness again, or
something approximating happiness. She would
mend her heart as best she could, and keep it safe.

She said nothing of this to her grandmother,
who'd been complaining of backache, and who
had taken to staying in bed till noon, and who still

looked worn out at the end of a day. Gran would only argue, she'd try to dissuade Emily, and Emily's mind was made up.

The backache turned out to be cancer of the spine, which had been quietly spreading its shoots to other parts of Gran's body. By the time it was discovered, three months after Emily's aborted wedding day, it was too late for anything but morphine – and just weeks later, Gran floated away without a fuss.

And as she had promised, she left the hat shop and the apartment above it to Emily.

The premises had been unoccupied since Gran's return to her marital home three years earlier. I should let it, she'd say every so often, it's a shame to have it lying idle like that – but it had never happened, tenants had never been sought for it. It took Emily almost a year after Gran's death to return to it, to turn the key in the back door lock and walk through the dark, dusty rooms with their boarded-up windows, and wonder what came next.

She wasn't looking for her own place: she was perfectly content living with Daniel. She could do what Gran had never got around to doing, and put it up for rent. It would need a little work, a little renovation to make it liveable again, and then she could simply hand it over to someone else and collect the rent each month.

But even as the thought occurred to her, it felt like the wrong thing to do. Gran letting it was one thing, but now it had become Gran's parting gift to her, and passing it on to a tenant would feel ungrateful, like she didn't really want it.

So she must do something with it herself – but what? She was trained for nothing. After school she'd gone straight to work at the salon, thanks to the older sister of a classmate who worked there. She could operate a cash register and take appointments over the phone. She could put magazines into neat stacks and make coffees and teas if called upon, and she didn't object to sweeping hair from the floor when the place was busy.

It wasn't exactly an extensive skillset. It didn't equip her to run her own business, any kind of business.

'Open a bakery,' Daniel said. 'You like to bake, and you're good at it' – but Emily thought of the hours she'd spend producing the loaves and cakes and whatever else, and the other hours she'd spend selling them, and she dismissed the idea. It was true she loved to bake though: maybe she could find some way to incorporate it into a business idea.

Maybe she could find a chef, and open a restaurant. She could bake, the chef could cook. That might work.

She walked through the place again. The problem was the size of it. It had been ideally suited to Gran's little hat shop, with never more than half a dozen people in it at any given time, but a restaurant was out of the question. The back room would make an ideal kitchen, but the front space only had room for three or four tables at the most, and they'd be cramped at that. It wouldn't do.

Unless she had a single table in the centre of the room, one long table – or maybe a round one. Yes, round was a more sociable shape, and might fit better into the given space. She stood at the door, trying to picture it, trying to decide how many chairs would fit around her imaginary table. A dozen, she thought, or thereabouts. Twelve or fourteen diners she could accommodate at the most – which was all very well if she was guaranteed a large booking every time she opened, and no good at all for smaller gatherings. No good for individuals, or couples, or families of three or four.

Hang on though. Did they have to know one another, the people who came in to eat her food? Couldn't they become acquainted over the course of the meal? Couldn't she feed those who would have nobody to eat with otherwise, people like herself who for whatever reason found themselves alone at mealtimes? Couldn't she open a place that offered company and companionship as well as food?

Over the following days and weeks she thought about it, and the notion began slowly to form and grow. She could keep it casual, with no reservations; people could simply drop in, and sit wherever they wanted. She could open for lunch and dinner, say two hours at lunchtime, three in the evening. The menu could be simple: two or three choices, no more. It could change daily, but the weekly menu could remain unaltered for a month, say, so, over time, people would come to know what to expect and be reassured by this.

And the food on offer could be the best of comfort food, the kind that cheered as it satisfied. What was more gladdening, more heartening, than a bowl of nourishing homemade soup served with freshly baked bread? What could lift spirits like a roast stuffed chicken, or pasta in a rich, creamy sauce? She could offer food made with love, food that solitary hearts hungered for.

And she'd stay open at weekends, which could be the toughest time for people with no other halves. She could close on a couple of the weekdays instead, say Monday and Tuesday, when most people didn't think about going out to eat.

The more she thought about it, developing and fine-tuning the idea, the more substance it took on, and the more eager she became to do it. She'd have to find a course to teach her how to run a small business. She'd have to find the finance to get the place renovated, and then she'd have to source the right chef, someone who'd embrace the thinking behind her idea. She'd have to hunt down a big table, and equip a proper kitchen, and stock up on lots of crockery and cutlery and the like.

She wondered if people would take to the idea of eating in a communal setting, and striking up conversations with strangers. Had it been tried elsewhere? She'd never heard tell of such a place, never come across one in her travels. She asked her friends what they thought, and they all had differing opinions, some more positive than others, so in the end she decided she wouldn't know until she tried.

She felt it was worth a try.

Of course, there was also the question of financial survival. She wondered if a venture so small could earn its keep. With such limited seating, even if the place was full every day, it was hard to see it as a money-maker. She thought of all the outgoings, the ingredients for the dishes, the chef's wages, the rates she'd have to pay, the insurance and utility bills and whatnot. It seemed miraculous that a restaurant operating on such a limited scale could possibly cover all that, let alone make a profit.

To survive, she'd probably need another job. Something she could do in her own time, something that would slot into the hours the restaurant was closed. But again, with her lack of qualifications and narrow set of skills, where on earth was she to find something like that?

And then, quite by chance, it found her.

I'm in a fix, her uncle said, ringing from the next town over where he lived and worked. One of my regulars has gone out on sick leave, and I need someone to fill in for her. I was wondering if you'd be interested.

Doing what? she asked, and he told her. You could work from home, he said, as long as you met your deadline. It will probably only be for a couple of weeks.

It wasn't something she'd ever thought of doing. Never once in all her growing up years had the notion of choosing such an occupation crossed her mind. There was responsibility going with it, a lot of responsibility – but her uncle seemed to have confidence in her, and it was just a temporary thing, so she crossed her fingers and said yes. And she found, once she started, that she quite liked it.

And a couple of weeks turned into several, and eventually her uncle told her that the employee she was covering for wouldn't be back. Will you stay on? he asked, and Emily said she would, because the job had grown on her, and had become important to her, and her uncle seemed to think she had a flair for it. You're a natural, he told her. They love you – the feedback is great.

And in the meantime she learnt how to run a business, and her parents gave her the money to do what renovations and installations were necessary, and when the workmen moved out, she and her brother and a few friends painted walls and sanded floors, and scoured charity shops for chairs and lamps and paintings, and tablecloths and crockery. She visited a Men's Shed in the town and got a retired carpenter to fashion an oval table, which an architect friend had told her would be the most efficient use of the space.

After that she found Mike, fresh out of cookery

school, and she hired him because he brought a slice of homemade pizza to his interview – blatant bribery, he admitted – and because he seemed to get the thinking behind the kind of restaurant she was planning. Together they devised a simple weekly menu, something to get them through the first month.

And finally, her heart in her mouth, more than two years after the wedding that never was, she opened The Food of Love. They started by offering dinners only, one tentative step at a time. On the first evening three people showed up, two of whom left after reading the minimalist menu. Hey, don't beat yourself up, the third said. You've just opened, it's gonna take time – and I'm tickled that I'm your very first customer. Which one of those main courses should I go for?

So Emily rang her two best friends, whom she'd asked to stay away in case there wasn't room for them. They arrived within ten minutes and made the acquaintance of the restaurant's one and only diner, Heather from America, over bowls of beef tagine with fruity couscous and thick Greek yogurt.

Listen, Heather said, setting down her fork, communal dining isn't for everyone. We got it in San Francisco so it's no big deal for me, but it'll take time to catch on here. Just keep putting the word out, and the ones you're aiming at, the ones who need you, will find you.

Emily could have hugged her.

And half an hour later, after thirty minutes of waiting and wishing and hoping for more diners, Daniel looked in with his girlfriend of the day, Just to see how you're doing, they said, and they ended up staying for chicken pie, which Heather from America asked to sample too – because I gotta see if it's as good as the tagine – and declared to be very good indeed. And Emily tried not to be disappointed that on her first night of business she had precisely one paying customer – whom, in the end, she didn't charge, because how could she take money from the very first person who'd put her faith in the restaurant to feed her?

And when everyone had had enough helpings of the main courses, Mike emerged from the kitchen with the summer pudding Emily had made earlier, along with a bowl of softly whipped cream, and after that they all had coffee, and some of Emily's lemon and ginger cookies.

And at the end of the evening, Heather from San Francisco, who it turned out had been living in Ireland for years – I got a kid who's nearly six, she's never been to the US – left Emily a generous tip, only slightly less than she would have paid if Emily had charged her, and said it was the best food she'd had in forever, and promised to come back. And she did come back, she does come back: she's become one of the regulars. I was her very first customer, Emily has overheard her declare many times.

And happily, over the days and weeks that followed, there was a slow and steady blossoming. The residents of the street showed up, driven by curiosity to come in. A positive review appeared in the local paper from a journalist who'd eaten there incognito. Comments on social media were mainly good. The same faces returned, saying they'd told others about it. And every night when she'd finished serving, Emily would sit and join whoever was there and eat dessert with them, so that another chair would be filled.

And one evening, about six weeks after opening, there came a night when there was no room at the oval table for Emily, when three people had to be turned away because the place was full. It's time, she thought, listening to the buzz of conversation, the spatters of laughter as she removed empty plates. We're ready, she thought, so they began offering lunch as well as dinner, and in time that took off too.

It isn't always easy. Every so often there are diners who look for something that's not on the menu, and who sometimes take umbrage when they don't get it. There are others who assume they're coming to some sort of dating event, and who aren't pleased to discover otherwise. There have been those who have slipped out without paying while Emily was in the kitchen, and a woman once who claimed to have burnt her tongue on the soup, and who took a case against the restaurant. Thankfully, these instances aren't commonplace.

Mostly what happens is that people come in and eat, and exchange chat and stories. Mostly what happens is that Emily feels she's doing something right, something worthwhile. Mostly what happens is that friendships are born around the big oval table – and yes, maybe romantic love has ensued now and again. It wouldn't be inconceivable, given the circumstances, but it doesn't concern Emily.

With her ticking-along business, and her other job that makes up the financial shortfall, and her rescued cat, and the regulars she's come to count as friends, and the street that has become home to her, with its community of neighbours who look out for one another, she can't say she's unhappy. Most of the time she's too busy to be unhappy.

And if there are moments, late at night maybe, listening to the rain tapping on the window, or in the middle of an afternoon, reading her book before Mike arrives to set up for the evening, if there are moments when she feels a pang of loneliness, she nudges it aside.

She has enough. She won't look for more.

Astrid

'CAN YOU PASS THE BUTTER?'

She looks across the table and regards the speaker. Forty at the most, she thinks, although the older she gets the harder it's becoming to tell. Mid-brown hair streaked with paler shades, cut short enough not to need a comb. Gold stud passing through his right eyebrow, for goodness' sake. He should know better at his age.

May I please have the butter, she says in her head. Manners not a priority for some: every day it pains her.

'Certainly you may,' she replies, handing over the butter dish, and he gives her a look that tells her he thinks she's gaga, and she realises that her response was out of sync with his request. Not gaga though, far from it. She may be in her ninety-third year, but thankfully she's as sharp as she always was. She remembers everything, when there is so much she would rather forget.

She allows her gaze to roam about the table, and counts ten seats filled. No Bill, which is a shame. She likes it when she and Bill coincide. She senses the quiet sadness beneath his cheery exterior, and doesn't seek out its cause. Let him choose to confide in her, if he ever wants to.

So lost he seemed that first day. So unsure as he stood in the doorway, looking like he might turn and bolt at any second. She was glad when Emily brought him over to sit with her – and now Astrid sees him doing what she did for him that day, making diffident newcomers feel at home in this special place.

Her own discovery of The Food of Love, over a year ago, happened entirely by chance. She'd been wondering where to find an out-of-print poetry book when she'd seen a small ad in the local paper for a secondhand bookshop. Worth a try, she'd thought, so she'd written down the address and taken a bus to the main street, and made her way on foot from there, stick tapping along the pavements. The book wasn't to be found on the shelves, but the shop and its owners were charming, and Astrid emerged with two substitutes stowed in her canvas bag.

But the walk from the main street, and the standing in the bookshop, had tired her. With her ninety-second birthday approaching, her energy was seeping away with the years. Tasks that she'd carried out without thinking now needed to be carefully planned, with rests in between. She scanned the street in both directions and spotted an orange bench on the path, four or five doors away: that would do. She reached it and sank down thankfully, settling her bag beside her, and took stock of her surroundings.

She'd been on the little street before, but not for quite some time. Nice neighbourhood feel to it, a mix of private homes and unassuming shops. Nothing flashy, nothing higher than two storeys – and the trees, parading down the length of it, were a bonus.

A few people passed. Astrid smiled, and was smiled at. The August day was mild and a little grey, but no rain had been mentioned on the forecast that morning. She heard a church bell chime noon – and directly afterwards, the metal *thunk* of a bolt being pulled across, and a door opening behind her. She turned to see a woman with beautiful burnished copper curls standing in the doorway.

You don't mind my sitting here? Astrid asked, and the woman assured her she didn't mind at all, and enquired if Astrid would like a glass of water, or a cup of tea. Taken by surprise, Astrid said yes please to the water and no thank you to the tea – and when she was alone again she turned her head to scrutinise the building she'd hitherto taken scant notice of.

A restaurant it was, or a café, its name in cursive

lettering above the window, painted orange to match the bench. The Food of Love it was called, which caused something to stir in Astrid's memory, something about music and the food of love. Maybe this place featured a pianist, playing quietly in the background as people ate.

Have you been open long? she asked, when the woman returned.

Coming up for eighteen months now. It was my grandmother's premises, and she left it to me. She had a hat shop here for over twenty years – maybe you remember it.

Astrid searched her memory, and thought she recalled the little premises, although a shop selling hats would never have tempted her. Some people had heads for hats and others didn't, and she was definitely among the latter. A big change, she said, from hats to food.

The owner smiled: a dimple popped in her cheek. It certainly is. I could probably bake a loaf of bread blindfold, but I couldn't make a hat to save my life. Would you like to have a look inside?

Funny now, when it's become such a familiar place, to recall her surprise that day on seeing it for the first time. She did a rapid count of the mismatched chairs around the large egg-shaped table and got fourteen. One table and fourteen chairs: clearly not the setting for a potentially romantic first dinner date – but maybe it happened here in a group. Maybe it was a place where singletons got together, seven men and seven women, hoping to find love over the boeuf bourguignon, or whatever. And maybe, since nothing was taboo now, there were occasions when the diners were all female, or all male.

She took it all in slowly. The cream cloth that covered the table, the little glass jars of colourful blooms dotted about, the blue butter dishes, the water jugs with floating lemon and orange slices. *Today's soups: chicken and mulligatawny* written in yellow chalk on a large blackboard affixed to the rear wall, hearts instead of dots topping the two 'i's. *Today's breads: granary and poppy seed.*

She turned back to her companion. Fourteen chairs, she said, and one table. This is not a typical restaurant.

Indeed it's not. Another smile, another dimple. With so little space I didn't really have much choice, so I opted for a place that offered company at mealtimes for anyone who wants it.

And there it was, as simple as that. No organised blind dates; no motive other than to feed people who preferred not to eat alone. The food of love, for those who might feel the need of it.

Astrid thought of her own situation, her main meals for the entire week arriving each Monday morning in their foil containers. Which do you want left out? Pat would enquire, and she'd pick, say, the chicken stew, and he'd store the rest in her freezer. His offerings were competently put together if a little unimaginative, lacking the spices and herbs

Astrid loved, a small shortcoming she forgave him in return for the convenience. Not too pricey either – she went for the mini option, which was more than enough to satisfy her diminished appetite.

Pat had been a find, a leaflet thrown in her door around the time she was falling into the habit, in her mid-eighties, of opening a tin of beans or poaching an egg when dinnertime came around. *Nutritious meals delivered*, she'd read. *Reasonable weekly rates, friendly service* – so she'd phoned the number on the leaflet and made the acquaintance of Pat, who'd put his full brochure in the post for her. She'd chosen two meals from it to try out – introductory offer, he said, the first order half price – and she'd been satisfied enough to stick with him, and in seven years she has hardly used a saucepan.

But with her few remaining friends gone to nursing homes, or taken in by their children's families, she found herself eating alone, always alone. She didn't mind the solitary breakfasts – somehow the first meal of the day seemed to suit the silence, when her mind was still unfolding after sleep, when her limbs were warming up for another day of movement. The other times were more of a challenge, the lone midday and teatime meals. Sometimes, sitting by the electric fire in winter with a tray on her lap, or at the kitchen table during the softer months, every tap of her fork against the plate, every soft shake of the salt cellar, every bite and chew and swallow would drive home her solitariness.

She looked around the little restaurant again. You're open now?

That's right. Our hours are twelve to two for lunch, and seven to ten for dinner. We're open five days a week, and closed Mondays and Tuesdays.

And you serve ... just soup?

Just soup at lunchtime – we like to keep it simple. A choice of two every day, and two different breads to go with them. Everything made fresh this morning.

Astrid had no objection to soup. Today's offerings, wafting through the air, smelt more tempting than the slice of Pat's quiche she'd taken from the freezer last evening. She must come here one of these days, try it out.

Or ...

Do I need to book?

No – we don't take bookings. We prefer people just to show up.

In that case, can I stay? For lunch, I mean. Now.

You'd be most welcome, the owner told her, extending her hand. I'm Emily, and very glad to meet you.

Astrid, she replied, and that was that. She had a bowl of chicken soup, and made the acquaintance of three young Australians on a tour around Ireland who'd heard about the restaurant from someone in their hostel. The soup was a flavoursome broth with a peppery kick and hints of garlic, basil and parsley, and a generous amount of shredded chicken. The poppy-seed bread was thickly cut, and tastier by far than the supermarket loaves she'd turned to when baking had become too challenging. She spread it with a little butter and ate every crumb, dipping the crust into the soup to soften it.

On her second visit, three days later, Emily greeted her by name. Come and sit here, she said, placing her next to a large woman in her twenties wearing jeans and a blue shirt, her black hair pulled into a tight ponytail. I think you should meet Heather, Emily said. My very first customer.

Potato and leek soup she chose that day, sundried tomato bread to accompany it. I'm a Jack-of-all-trades, Heather told her, in an accent that to Astrid's ears could have been American or Canadian. I wash cars and clean windows, and lots of other stuff besides. I'm a single mom with one daughter, who's wonderful. She's at school right now.

I'm a widow, Astrid told her in return, which was the truth. I have no children, she said, which was also true. My family left Austria before the war and came to Ireland, she said, which wasn't the truth – because what really happened wasn't the kind of story people wanted to hear over a lunchtime bowl of soup.

I ran away from home when I was sixteen, Heather said. Never went back. Haven't set eyes on my parents since. What do you think of that?

Astrid didn't quite know what to think of it. Are you in touch with them?

Oh yeah – we talk on the phone. They got over it. She chuckled, showing good teeth. She was pretty, Astrid thought, but unaware of it – or aware, and unaffected. No make-up, no need of it. Clear skinned, bright eyed. Confident, not bothered by what others thought of her. Someone you could depend on, Astrid decided.

My windows, she said, could do with a clean – and Heather immediately produced a phone and took her address. Since then she's been turning up once a month to wash the seven windows of Astrid's little bungalow. It's a business arrangement, but they've found time, over cups of green tea once the work is done, to become friends.

In The Food of Love, conversations across the big table tend to remain casual, even if the same diners find themselves once again sharing lunchtime and a chat, like Astrid and Bill and Heather frequently do. No significant confidences are exchanged over the soup bowls, no real intimacies shared. Astrid respects that: isn't everyone entitled to keep to himself what he wishes not to be known? Hasn't she as many secrets as anyone?

Today she's surrounded by strangers, which never bothers her in this safe, familiar space. She exchanges a few remarks with the slender, beautiful woman on her right, who tells Astrid that she lives in Limerick, but that her daughter Pauline runs a crèche a few doors down the street. 'I like to pop in here when I'm up for a visit.'

'I've been coming for over a year,' Astrid says. 'I'm a regular.'

'You're not Irish though,' the woman says, lifting an eyebrow, smiling to take any sting out of the observation. Such minefields conversations have become, everyone terrified now in case they say the wrong thing, and offend.

'I'm from Austria,' Astrid tells her, like she's said so many times. Baffling how she still sounds foreign to Irish ears, after living here for almost seventy years.

'Austria? I was there at Easter.'

It's the man across the table, the one with the earring in his eyebrow. Shoving himself into their conversation, whether he's wanted or not. Astrid makes no response other than a small nod of acknowledgement, hoping he'll take the hint and leave them alone.

He doesn't. 'Holiday with my kids,' he says. 'My daughter's fluent in German, languages come easy to her. We had a week in Tyrol, doing a bit of hiking, then on to Vienna for a couple of days. What part are you from?'

'Vienna,' Astrid replies. Impossible to ignore a direct question.

'Nice place, bit pricey but great cakes.' A grimace then, a shake of his head. 'That Holocaust memorial, though – if you don't mind my saying so, bit of an eyesore. I mean, don't get me wrong, I go along with the whole never-forget thing, but this is like a giant cement block, isn't it? No style about it.'

Something tightens down low in Astrid. Something twists and clenches, making the rest of her soup impossible. She sets her spoon onto her side plate. Quietly, no drama. She raises her napkin and dabs her mouth. 'I wouldn't know,' she replies, as lightly as she's able. 'I've never set eyes on it.'

Another lie. A sort of lie. She hasn't seen the stark edifice in the square in which it sits, hasn't made a pilgrimage to it, like so many others. She hasn't reached out and placed her hand against its cold blank greyness, or stood before the huge double doors that don't open. She hasn't lowered her gaze to see the Star of David that's carved into the ground before the door, and flanked by three versions – German, Hebrew, English – of the same dignified, terrible statement.

She hasn't walked around the structure to read the list of places inscribed on the sides and the back of the plinth, the hellholes where the lives of sixty-five thousand Austrian Jews were wiped out. To this day she can't hear the names of those places without feeling her insides rise up and threaten to spew out.

She hasn't been to see it, but of course she's aware of the monument. How could she not be, with photos of it splashed all over the papers, accompanied by column inches of description, when it was unveiled twenty years ago? Didn't heads of state from everywhere come to view it? Didn't Pope Benedict himself pay it a visit – and offer up a Christian prayer, no doubt, for all the Jewish souls who had found their way too soon to the World to Come?

You want to go there? her husband had asked, not knowing much because she had never told him much, and Astrid had said no, and it was never mentioned between them again.

She turns to her companion, the mother of the crèche owner. 'Excuse me,' she says, getting up, careful not to look in the man's direction. Emily is at the far end of the table, refilling bread baskets. 'I'll be off,' Astrid tells her, handing over payment.

'Everything alright, Astrid?'

Something must be showing in her face. 'Yes, everything is fine, thank you. See you again soon' – but when she emerges from the restaurant she hails the first taxi she sees, instead of walking back to the bus stop on the main street as she always does. Straight home she goes, no wandering into a shop or two today while she waits for her bus.

Outside her house she pays and thanks the driver, and lets herself in. She sits by the open kitchen door, coat still on, gazing out but seeing nothing of her garden with its out-of-control shrubs, its weed-choked flowerbed, its straggling hedge, its lawn patched with moss that normally fills her with frustration. Today her head is too full, after a chance thoughtless remark, of what she hasn't managed in over eighty years to forget. Today she finds herself pulled back into memories that clamour once more for her attention.

Instead of the neglected garden she sees her brother Gerhard coming home from school in tears one afternoon, his bare legs streaked red from having been whipped with ropes by a gang of Aryan boys who had lain in wait for him, or for any Jewish boy unlucky enough to fall into their path. It was the spring of 1939, a year almost to the day since German boots had marched onto the streets of Vienna, and Adolf Hitler had declared Austria to be part of the Reich, and life as Astrid knew it had begun to change.

The arrival of the Germans had been followed by a spate of violent acts in the city, the news of them spreading in frightened whispers. Houses attacked, shops vandalised, sudden angry eruptions on a pavement, often in broad daylight, that could leave a person – man or woman, or even child – bleeding on the ground. An old man pushed from a moving tram one afternoon, a girl set upon by others on her way home from school, her uniform torn, her hair hacked off with a knife.

Why? Astrid had asked, and her parents had told her that some people just didn't like Jews. It had bewildered and unsettled her, the idea that a person could be resented simply because of his or her religion. It had caused a quivering inside her. Could people know, she'd wondered, just by looking at her, that *she* was Jewish? Might her family be targets? Might they too be attacked on the street?

And then had come the Saturday when her father had announced that they would no longer be visiting the synagogue. From now on, he'd said, we will pray in the homes of our friends, or they will pray in ours. Hearing this new development, Astrid felt a sense of relief – walking into the synagogue each Saturday, clutching Mutti's hand tightly, she'd felt terribly exposed, knowing the action proclaimed loudly their Jewishness to anyone who might be watching – but she also recognised the new erosion it signalled, the further crumbling of the familiar, another step into the unknown.

It had added to her paranoia. Each night she would find it harder to fall asleep. Each morning she would walk to school with a sense of foreboding, sensing that she was being watched, sized up, hated. Every day it felt like she was waiting in dread for the next bad thing.

And the next bad thing never took long to arrive. I'm not allowed to talk to you, Birgit Greiser had told her in the schoolyard. My mother says I can't hang around with Jews any more. Others had followed suit – Birgit was popular – forcing Astrid and the other Jewish girls to form their own circle. Pushing them out, making them feel as if they'd committed a crime – but they weren't criminals, they were innocent children.

The weeks and months had passed. People Astrid knew had begun to disappear. Dr Taubmann, who'd seen her and Gerhard safely through the usual childhood illnesses, had been replaced unexpectedly with another doctor. Her father's friend Oskar, who was also his lawyer, had closed his business abruptly and moved away with his wife and young child. The local pharmacy had changed hands, and the Neumanns who had owned it were suddenly gone, all seven of them. Jutta Peckel, a classmate and friend of Astrid's whose father was head librarian in Vienna's largest library, had also vanished, along with her entire family.

They moved to America, her father had told Astrid when she'd asked about the Peckels, but Jutta had said nothing at all to her about this. Why would they suddenly go without telling anybody? Why would they leave no forwarding address?

New notices had kept appearing in public places, forbidding Jews to hold bank accounts, to own businesses, to attend the cinema, to go to university. Every week, it seemed, to be Jewish was to have the world more set against them – and then had come the monstrous, terrifying night in November, the night of breaking glass and shouts and running footsteps and smoke, when Jewish shops and synagogues had been raided and ransacked by angry mobs, when buildings had been set alight and their occupants beaten or chased away, or worse.

After that, the fear had been everywhere. Astrid had seen it in the eyes of her parents and grandfather, had sensed it in the hurried muttered conversations that would break off as soon as they noticed her nearby. And now it was the spring of 1939, and Astrid was eleven, Gerhard a year younger. Their father Wilhelm worked as a hotel cook; their mother Monika was in demand as a piano teacher in the homes of wealthy Austrian families, Jew and Gentile alike. Opa Josef, Astrid's maternal grandfather, had moved in with them after Oma Ursula had died, four years earlier.

A week after Gerhard's attack, her father was dismissed from his job. I'll find another, he promised them, cooks are always needed – but Astrid saw his forced smile, saw the defeat in her grandfather's face, the helpless anger in her mother's. That evening there was more murmured dialogue. Astrid sat on the stairs in her nightdress, knees drawn up, arms wrapped tightly about her, and strained to hear sounds she couldn't distinguish, her throat aching from the effort of keeping in the scream that wanted so badly to come bursting out.

The next morning, over breakfast, their father told them they were to leave Vienna. It's important, he said, hands cradling his coffee cup, that you say nothing to others, not even your good friends. We must keep it our secret.

When will we go? Gerhard asked.

As soon as possible. As soon as we can arrange it. The end of the week, I hope.

End of the week. Three more days. Where? Astrid asked.

Her father spread his hands. Wherever we can. Wherever will have us.

She searched his face, looking for comfort she didn't find. Couldn't we go to America, like Jutta and her family?

A long moment passed, during which her mother rose abruptly to her feet. Maybe, he replied finally, while Mutti gathered plates noisily and didn't look at him.

It was Tuesday, the day Astrid went from school to her ballet class. She lived for Tuesdays, for the single hour that she could lose herself in arabesques and pirouettes and pliés with her companions, when her biggest concerns were the positioning of her feet and the placing of her arms. This Tuesday though, the class didn't work its usual magic. Concentrate, Astrid, her teacher scolded, but concentration was so hard, with her father's announcement cranking up the fear. She couldn't think beyond the upheaval that was to come, the new and surely dangerous path they were to embark on in just a few days.

Come straight home afterwards, her mother had said, and Astrid did. It was past four, the scent of newly bloomed apricot flowers sweet in the air, but as she scurried through the streets she was oblivious to all save the urgent need to get home, to reach a place of safety. She passed a jeweller's shop whose brickwork had been freshly defaced: red paint dribbled like blood from the uneven letters of *Juden raus*. In her state of fright, every person she met seemed to glare at her: she expected, any minute, to feel the impact of a clenched fist against the back of her head, the slap of a hard palm on her cheek. What had they done, what had any of them done, to merit such hatred?

Her destination, her refuge, drew closer. Two minutes and she would be home – but as she approached her street, a large dark green truck emerged from it and turned in the direction of the city centre, away from her. She instinctively ducked into a shop doorway and peered out until it had disappeared, fingers tightening on the handle of her satchel, heart beating so hard it hurt her chest.

The bell above the shop door pinged behind her: she fled, not turning to see who was coming out. She raced the rest of the way home, scrabbling frantically with her key at the front door of their apartment building, half falling in her headlong rush up the three flights of stairs, her panic increasing with each tumbling step. She reached the third floor and stopped dead, panting heavily as she took in a new and freshly appalling sight.

Their apartment door was wide open.

It was never left open. Never.

For long minutes she remained rooted where she was, too afraid to move for fear of what she might find. She stared into what she could see of her home: a portion of the hall, the sitting room and kitchen doors, also open. She strained to hear anything, any noise that might offer a clue, but no sound issued from within. No sound came either from the other two apartments on their floor, in which the Kerns and Frau Bauer lived.

Her breathing gradually calmed, but her terror didn't abate. She could taste it at the back of her mouth; she could smell the cold metallic ooze of it. After what felt like a lifetime she took a slow trembling step towards the doorway, and another, everything standing to attention in her, every muscle poised to run again.

At the open doorway, she stopped. Should she knock on one of the neighbours' doors? Should she check with them before going further, see if they had any information, ask one of them to come with her into the apartment?

No. The paranoia of the last several months kicked in. The Kerns and Frau Bauer weren't Jewish: she tried to recall recent encounters with them, searching her memory for any slights she might have overlooked, any indications that they had crossed the same invisible line as her classmate Birgit Greiser, and were now her enemies. Had Herr Kern's greeting of a few days earlier been colder than usual? Had Frau Bauer looked strangely at her the last time Astrid had held the front door open for her?

She couldn't risk it. She couldn't involve them.

She forced herself to cross the threshold. She lowered her satchel noiselessly to the hall floor, slipped out of her shoes. Mutti? she called – but it wasn't a call, it was a whisper. Knowing, already knowing, that nobody was there to answer.

Papa?

Gerhard?

Opa?

She walked through the empty apartment in stockinged feet, every creak of her weight on the floorboards sounding obscenely loud. She saw Gerhard's school coat thrown across his bed, her mother's apron hanging from the stove rail, her father's boots by the fire escape, one standing sentinel, the other tipped onto its side.

She narrowly avoided stepping on her grandfather's spectacles, lying just inside his bedroom door, one lens shattered into tiny pieces as if stamped on. She stooped and collected the glass slivers with trembling fingers, and tipped them into his waste bin. How would he see without his spectacles? How would he read his beloved books?

She returned to the hall, her head spinning. She pressed her face to her father's coat, pulling the smell of his pipe tobacco into her lungs. She took his hat from its hook and inhaled the citrus tang of his hair oil. Where were they? Where had they gone, without leaving her so much as a note?

Astrid!

She started violently at the hissed word. She swung around to find Frau Bauer standing in the doorway, a hand holding her black cardigan closed.

They were taken, her neighbour said in the same low, urgent tone, not fifteen minutes ago! You must leave, child – you must leave now, immediately!

Taken? Her heart falling, dropping, stopping. Fright batting like a trapped butterfly against her ribcage. Who took them?

The Gestapo, the soldiers – quickly, Astrid, you must leave this place! Go!

Without waiting for a response, Frau Bauer wheeled away and scuttled back into her apartment, shutting the door quickly behind her. Astrid stood stunned, shocked, wanting to cry but unable to. Her family, taken by soldiers – as the Neumanns must have been, she realised suddenly, the knowledge landing with a leaden thump inside her. And her friend Jutta, and all the others who'd disappeared so abruptly. Not gone to America, not moved to begin a new life but snatched away – and now Mutti and Papa and Gerhard and Opa had been taken too.

The truck: she knew without a doubt that they'd been in the green truck she'd seen. She'd missed it by minutes – but now she was alone, with no clue what to do, and no idea when her family might return. You must leave now, Frau Bauer had said, you must leave this place – but where could she go, with danger suddenly looming monstrously all around her? Her other grandparents, Papa's parents, had fallen victim in their forties to a deadly flu that had swept across Europe in the wake of the Great War, both of them gone before Papa was a teenager. Her only uncle, Papa's older brother Stefan, had died in a skiing accident a year after Astrid was born. No aunts, no cousins, no other family that she was aware of.

She was eleven years old, and more afraid than she could ever remember being. Her mind raced, searching for inspiration, hunting through everyone she could think of to find someone who might help her. Not her classmates, not the Jewish girls she hung around with at school, for they must be in as much danger as she was, or soon would be – and not the others, not the Birgit Greisers who shunned her and her kind, and who couldn't now, in this new and terrifying world, be trusted not to do worse.

And then, out of nowhere, she thought of Herr Dasler, one of her mother's music students, who insisted on driving Mutti home after each lesson. Herr Dasler, who wasn't a Jew, but who seemed to bear them no ill will when Mutti would invite him in for a cup of coffee. Herr Dasler, who hadn't abandoned Mutti like some of her other Gentile students over the past weeks – hadn't she given him a lesson only a few days before?

That's where Herr Dasler lives, Mutti had said, some Sunday when they were out on a drive – maybe their last Sunday drive, before Papa had decided to put a stop to it – and Astrid had taken in the big house flanked by trees behind wrought-iron gates. He must have lots of children, she'd said, and Mutti had laughed and told her no children, nobody at all.

He lives alone, she'd said, and Papa had made some joke and called him Mutti's boyfriend, and Mutti had slapped his leg, but not in anger.

Astrid would go to him. He was her only hope, the only one she could think of. She would wait until darkness and then she would find his house, and beg him to help her. She would offer to work, to clean for him, to scrub his floors in exchange for sanctuary until this horrible time was past, and her family were home again.

She closed the apartment door quietly and went to Gerhard's room. She crawled under her brother's bed and clutched one of his tennis shoes she found there, and lay on the dusty floor in a tight tense ball as the bedroom darkened with unbearable slowness. Every sound, every small movement filled her with fresh terror, convinced her that the soldiers were returning to find her, were about to burst in and drag her from her hiding place.

She tried not to think about her family, and where they were, and what might be happening to them, but her traitorous mind kept returning to the stories of violence against Jews, kept imagining the worst possible outcomes. Let them be safe, she prayed silently. Let them be safe. Let them come home. I will work harder in school, I will be good if you spare them. I will help Mutti more. I will wash up after every meal without complaining. I won't fight with Gerhard. I won't be cross when he takes my pens for his projects and leaves the caps off.

She grew cold and stiff as the minutes and hours crawled by. She had no idea what time it was: her watch, a tenth-birthday gift from her parents, was in her satchel. She'd removed it for the dance class and stowed in the front pocket as she always did, and left it there afterwards in her haste to get home. She was hungry, nothing eaten since her lunchtime sandwich. She closed her eyes: it was possible that she slept a little. Maybe, despite the cold and the terror, or maybe because of it, her mind shut down for a short while.

Later, much later, a lifetime later, she emerged from under the bed and got slowly to her feet, trying to coax movement into her protesting muscles. She felt her way through almost total darkness to the kitchen, listening intently for a sound, any sound, that would send her hastening back. Her searching fingers closed on a loaf of bread: she tore pieces from it and chewed rapidly. On its own it was dry and hard to swallow, but she was too afraid to rummage for anything more, or to turn on the tap for water in case someone heard.

In the hall she found her coat and put it on, and buttoned it with trembling fingers. In the gloom she made out the pair of pen-and-ink prints of birds on the wall, reduced now to muddied grey squares; the long slender cylinder of her father's umbrella, still propped where he always left it in the corner behind the door. She found the dark bowl of her mother's good hat on the hallstand: the curved, barely visible wisp of its feather, the jauntiness of it, seemed obscene in this horrifying new order.

She could smell the mix of shoe polish and wood that she knew so well. The bread she had eaten too quickly lodged like wet sand in her stomach. Leaving the only home she had ever known, leaving on her own like this in the darkness was so dreadful a prospect she could hardly bear it. When would she return? When would they all be together again under this roof?

As well, perhaps, that she didn't know the answer.

On the point of opening the door, a new thought struck her. She tiptoed back to her parents' room. Gently, gently, she coaxed out the bottom drawer of the big mahogany chest and lifted away the folded sweaters until she found the jewellery box. Not a very good hiding place, Papa had said, but Mutti had kept it there anyway. Astrid fumbled it open and rummaged silently through the necklaces and rings until her fingers touched the smooth round coldness of the pearls.

These will be yours one day, Mutti had told her, years ago when Astrid was six or seven. I got them from my mother, who got them from hers. They will pass to you, and from you to your daughter, or your son's wife if you have no girls.

The necklace was rarely worn; her mother saved it for special occasions like Rosh Hashanah and Yom Kippur, and wedding anniversaries and significant birthdays. Astrid let it pour from her fingers into her coat pocket. She was looking after it, that was all. She was keeping it safe for Mutti. She replaced the jewellery box and returned to the hall.

Now what? Now to get out of the building without being detected – for besides Frau Bauer, how did she know who could be trusted? – and through the streets in her search for the house whose location she only vaguely remembered. They'd passed the hospital, she thought, but she'd been playing a word game with Gerhard as they drove and paying scant attention to their surroundings. Had they gone in the direction of the park after that? She fancied they had, and then around by the library. Yes: she remembered the red and black flags fluttering above the library windows. His house was on a road beyond the busy streets, one that headed for the city outskirts. Maybe.

No doors opened as she tiptoed down the stairs, no shouts to stop erupted behind her. She emerged onto the street and began a slow run, heart hammering, keeping her gaze averted from the few people she encountered. The full darkness she'd thought she was venturing out in hadn't yet been achieved, with the spring sky holding on stubbornly to the last of the light, but shadows were deepening, buildings and trees morphing into near-black hulking shapes.

After half an hour or so she reached the hospital, and after it the park. She slowed to a more sedate pace, out of breath, her resolve weakening, her apprehension increasing the further she went. Even if she defied the odds and found his house, he could still slam the door in her face – or worse, report her to the authorities and hold her until they got there. It was a chance she would have to take: she had no choice but to throw herself on his mercy.

Astrid, he'd said, the first time they met. My mother's name, he'd said, his hand clasping hers warmly. She clung to the memory as she sped on, searching streets after she passed the library for the big house with the trees and the gate. Bent on success, refusing in her desperation to countenance anything else.

It was properly dark now, car headlights seeming to glare more brightly as they swept past her, pedestrians becoming fewer as she left the cityscape behind. Still she trudged on, peering through gates, hoping for something she might recognise from her one brief glimpse of the house where he lived.

And finally, on the point of giving up, her feet aching, her stomach cramping from the bread she'd bolted, she found it.

It was the right place, she was reasonably certain. The same aspect she remembered, the trees that flanked it the same – yes, it must be it. It *must*. The gate was locked: without stopping to think she clambered over it, her dance exercises making her nimble, even swaddled as she was in her winter coat. She thought *guard dog* as she landed lightly on the gravelled driveway – but no dog came running and snarling, no security lights flashed on to pinpoint her in her trespass. He would surely be angry that she'd in effect broken into his grounds, but she had to hope he'd take her circumstances into account, and forgive her.

Her shoes crunched across the gravel, each step seeming as loud as the boom of a gigantic drum. Heart in her mouth, she climbed the wide stone steps to the front door. A soft yellow light burned in the hall: she saw it through the glass of the fanlight. Without giving herself time to think, she reached up on tiptoe to lift the knocker and let it drop heavily. Please, please, please, she thought, her petrified brain incapable of more. *Bitte, bitte, bitte.*

With a slam of her heart she heard a sound from within: someone was approaching. She shuddered in a breath, let it out. She curled her hands into fists and pressed her lips together. She pushed her feet hard into the ground. The skin on her face felt icy. *Bitte, bitte, bitte.*

Who is there?

A male voice. She couldn't remember what he sounded like.

Astrid, she replied, her voice cracking. Astrid, she repeated, more loudly, as loudly as she dared. Astrid Finklebaum.

Silence followed. Would he simply ignore her, was he already lifting the receiver of his phone to call the police? Should she tell him about Mutti, remind him who she was? As she searched for the right words, a bolt slid across and the door was opened.

His face was in shadow, lit from behind. He looked shorter than she remembered, and heavier. He wore a dressing-gown. His feet were bare. A large lit cigar sat between the first and second fingers of his right hand.

Astrid, he said wonderingly, his voice low. Little Astrid Finklebaum. Monika's child. My God. He lifted his gaze to peer over her head. But how did you get in?

It was him. The relief brought sudden heat to her eyes; she blinked hard to banish it. I – I climbed over the gate, she whispered. I'm sorry. Every word with a shake in it, her mouth so stiff with fear she could hardly move it.

You climbed over the gate, he repeated, surprise rather than anger in his voice. He took a step past her to survey the garden. Cigar smoke drifted in his wake, wafted about her, smelling of burnt caramels. His feet must be cold on the stone.

He turned back to inspect her again, and she saw his features more clearly. Yes, there was the round ball of his nose, the hamster plumpness of his cheeks. But where is Monika? he whispered. Where is your lovely Mutti, hmm?

Gone, she said, tears accompanying the word, streaming out of her, freeing her tongue as they spilt down her cheeks. The soldiers took them all, she cried. I was at my dance class. Everyone was gone when I got home. I have nobody to help me.

A look of concern spread now across his face. Shhh, he whispered, darting another look behind him. Not so loud, my child. Dear me, he went on, poor Monika, and poor little Astrid. All alone now. He put his free hand on her shoulder and gestured towards the hallway with the other. We had better go in then, hadn't we?

And with her tears still falling, with terror still filling her heart, she stepped across the threshold of her saviour.

And the other Astrid, who is ninety-two years old and sitting on a kitchen chair at her back door, with the taste of Emily's soup still in her mouth, bows her head and cries too.

Emily

'NOW,' SHE SAYS, RETURNING THE LAST soup bowl to the press, tossing the damp tea towel into the laundry basket by the washing machine. No dishwasher in the restaurant kitchen: she prefers to do it by hand with lots of hot sudsy water, taking pleasure from the satisfying squeak of clean wet crockery, and the view from the window beyond the big sink as she soaps and scrubs and rinses. May well advanced, summer colour unfolding in the garden, shrubs in full leaf, tiny green apples on her two dwarf trees, birdsong loud and busy and cheery.

She unties her apron and adds it to the laundry basket. 'Done and dusted,' she says. Talking to herself today, since Mike has headed off for round two of his root canal treatment. Poor Mike. She'll pick up a few bananas for him when she's out. He'd live on bananas if he could.

Upstairs she washes her face and frees the last of her hair from its lunchtime ribbon, and dabs on fresh lipstick. 'You'll do,' she tells her mirrored self, although she'd prefer longer legs, and a less nondescript eye colour, and better-behaved hair. Daniel got the good hair in the family, same russet shade as Emily's but enviably curl-free and silky, the sort of hair beloved of stylists, the sort that falls perfectly into place after it's washed.

Daniel. Yes. Time to hunt him down, to find out why her calls to him over the past couple of days have gone unanswered. She puts two sour-cream coffee buns from her tin into a brown paper bag. 'See you later,' she tells Barney, and sets out.

Just fourteen minutes' brisk walk from her current home to her previous one, but a world of difference between them. The house is situated in a residential part of town, no businesses within a quarter-mile or so, apart from a single corner shop and a small hair salon. It's the end house on a quiet cul-de-sac of semi-detached homes, boasting as a result a more generously proportioned garden than its companions. Emily makes her way around to the rear and sees the border of colourful shrubs, the bank of green spears of montbretia and crocosmia – overcrowded: she must thin them out – the vivid patch of nasturtiums, the climbers on the rear wall. In the years since Emily's departure from the house, the garden her grandfather planted in the months before he died has become considerably more ragged around the edges, but his hardy perennials are hanging on, and his roses bloom and clamber about as faithfully as they always did.

The rest of it is showing its age too. The rusted basketball hoop Daniel requested one long-ago Christmas; the equally discoloured swing set outside the dining-room window that he and Emily played on. The wooden table with its bench seating, where the four of them used to eat dinner on warm evenings, is rickety and weatherbeaten, and possibly hazardous for anyone foolish enough, or brave enough, to surrender their weight to a bench.

She raps on the back door and opens it without waiting for a response. 'Em,' her brother says. Barefoot and bare-chested, leaning against the sink, his mouth full of whatever is in the bowl he holds. 'Did I know you were coming?'

'No. You would if you ever answered your phone.'

'Sorry, saw a few missed calls, was going to get back to you. Not up long.'

It amazes her that he can, and frequently does, stay in bed until well after midday, and still make enough from his freelance copywriting to afford the Jaguar outside the gate – second-hand and some-what ramshackle, but still – and the succession of girlfriends he seems to have no trouble in attracting.

'You look bonny,' he says, leaning in to brush her cheek with a kiss. 'Everything OK?'

'Fine. I just thought I'd drop over. Haven't seen you in a while.'

'Yeah, a few rush jobs came in. All done now though, back in circulation. I'll swing by in the next day or two for sure.' Most of the time he's a faithful supporter of the restaurant, calls in for lunch or dinner once or twice a week, sometimes alone, sometimes not. She tries to remember who his current girlfriend is, and fails.

'Before I forget,' he says, placing his empty bowl on the draining board, adding it to the other dishes that sit there, 'post came for you. I was going to bring it, next time I called.'

'Post for me? To this house?'

'Hang on.' He turns to riffle through a stack on the table. 'From Canada,' he adds, tossing it out like it's nothing.

Canada. The word sends a *whump* through her.

It can't be him. Why would he write to her?

It must be him. She doesn't know anyone else there.

'You want it?' Daniel asks, holding a blue envelope between finger and thumb. 'Or will I bin it? I would have, only I felt I should ask you first.'

She swallows. 'When did it come?' Not that it matters.

'Few days ago.' When she makes no move to take it, he sets it on the worktop. He puts his hands on her shoulders and squeezes. 'Em, don't sweat it. You needn't even open the bloody thing. Put "return to sender" on it – or better still, just chuck it in the bin. Don't give that scumbag another thought.'

Almost four years since she saw him. No word of him in the meantime, no news at all. He may as well have dropped off the edge of the world. She doesn't know if he's been home. She doubts that any of her friends would mention it if they saw him – and his mother Sarah, on the rare occasions that she and Emily encounter one another, just says hello and keeps on walking. They used to be close – don't make a granny of me too soon, she'd say to Emily – but Fergal put paid to that.

Why is he getting in touch now? What could he possibly have to say to her after four years of silence, other than a belated apology that she doesn't even want any more?

She picks up the envelope and turns it over. There is a picture of a waterfall on the stamp. Her name in his handwriting causes a small tremor within her. His address is in the top left corner. She's heard Vancouver is lovely.

She should tear it up, rip it into tiny shreds. She shouldn't give it a second's attention. Or put a *return to sender* message on it like Daniel suggested, so he'd be sure she'd seen and ignored it. Yes, that's what she'll do.

She slips it into her bag. 'I'll send it back to him.'

'Good for you. You want coffee? I'm making a pot.'

'Better not, thanks. I promised Mike I'd do his dinner prep. He's at the dentist this afternoon.'

There's time enough for coffee with her brother –

half an hour wouldn't make a difference – but suddenly she feels the need to be alone. She hands over the buns she brought, and gets a hug in return. He repeats his promise to see her soon. 'Don't let him get to you, Em – he's not worth it.'

Easier said than done. She walks home by the canal, trying to keep her thoughts from the envelope in her bag, and the puzzle of its appearance. She pauses by a bridge to watch a pair of swans glide under it, serene and beautiful. Faithful for life, aren't they, once they make their choice? No last-minute changes, no second thoughts.

She recalls his final letter to her, or note, more like, on what should have been the happiest day of her life. She'd kept it for months, pushed down in a drawer under her sweaters. Her wounded heart couldn't part with it, that was the foolish truth. Horrible as it was, it was still the last thing he'd written to her, the last contact they'd had. Eventually, of course, she'd torn it up. She'd brought the pieces out the back to the big blue recycling bin, and scattered them in among the flattened boxes and cartons and junk mail.

She carries on to the fruit and veg shop, where she buys rhubarb and oranges and lemons, and Mike's bananas.

'Rhubarb crumble and marmalade,' Greg behind the counter says.

'Close,' she tells him. 'Rhubarb and custard pie, and citrus cheesecake.'

'Yum.'

Greg visited The Food of Love in the early days, along with his wife Clodagh. Since then they've both returned several times, separately and together.

Back in the restaurant kitchen, Emily assembles the cheesecakes and slides them into the fridge before turning her attention to the second dessert of the evening. She lines three pie dishes with shortcrust pastry. She wipes and chops the rhubarb and tips it onto the pastry. She beats eggs and adds milk and sugar and the seeds from a vanilla pod, and pours the mixture over the fruit. Simplest dessert in the world, and one of her favourites.

While the pies are in the oven she scrubs and pricks potatoes and assembles them on a baking tray. She chops vegetables for the ratatouille, and poaches chicken breasts in stock for Mike's chicken and bacon lasagne, one of their most popular dishes.

Busy, but not busy enough.

She'll read the letter before sending it back. She'll steam open the envelope over a basin of hot water, and close it again so it looks like its contents were untouched.

No – she won't read it. There's nothing he could say now that she wants to hear, nothing that could possibly be of interest to her.

She won't return it either – why go to that bother? She'll bin it as soon as she goes upstairs, and leave him guessing, like he left her guessing.

She won't bin it, she'll burn it. She'll destroy it completely, leave no trace.

But …

She's curious, of course she is. Why is he getting in touch out of the blue like this? If she doesn't find out, it'll prey on her mind. It'll eat away at her, churn everything up again. Maybe she should just read it quickly to satisfy her curiosity. Nobody need know, least of all him. Then she can destroy it, and never think of him again.

She takes the pies from the oven just before Mike arrives. He attempts a grin that comes out lopsided. 'I'll have to smile on the inside,' he tells her, 'until I thaw out.'

'All done?' she asks. 'Torture over?'

'All over. How're we doing here?'

'Good – your prep's all done.'

'You're a star. Go and put your feet up for a bit.'

In the apartment she finds Barney awake and demanding food. She refills his bowl and takes a shower, and puts on her white dress splashed with yellow lemons and green leaves. She pushes two clips into her hair and dots foundation on her cheeks while cooking smells begin to float up from the kitchen.

She checks the time. Twenty to seven. Do it now.

She takes the envelope from her bag. She lifts it and sniffs. Nothing: a papery smell only. She traces a finger along the path his pen has taken on the front. She holds it up to the light, but can see only the outline of the folded notepaper within. Open it, a voice in her head commands, so she eases her little finger through the gap at the side and slides it quickly across. She pulls out the single sheet through the ragged slit. She sits on the couch and takes a breath.

Does she want to do this?

Yes, she does.

She unfolds the sheet and skims its contents, eyes racing as fast as her heart.

Dear Emily,

I'm sure you'll be surprised to hear from me. I hope you open this letter and read it, although I couldn't blame you if you didn't. I know I hurt you badly, and my behaviour was despicable. I've beaten myself up about it often enough, believe me. I was a coward, and I took the coward's way out instead of telling you face to face that I couldn't go through with the wedding. I was all mixed up; I didn't know what I wanted. I hated hurting you, but I thought it was better than marrying you when I wasn't sure if it was the right thing to do, and hurting you more later on.

I'm writing now to tell you that I'm moving back to Ireland in a few weeks, at the end of May. My work is transferring me to Dublin so I'll be based there, but I'll be calling home first to see Mum, and to collect my things, and I'd really like to see you too. I don't know if you'd be willing to meet me, and maybe you'd be right to tell me to take a running jump, but if you would be open to a meeting I'd be very happy. I heard from Mum that you've left the salon and you run a restaurant now – that's unexpected, but great. I hope you're happy, and that you've found it in your heart to forgive me. I've been a prize idiot, but you're a far better person than me, so I have hope that you're not holding my bad behaviour against me.

I'm assuming you have the same number. I'll ring you when I get back, but I'll understand if you don't answer, and I promise I'll take the hint and leave you alone after that.

I'm so sorry. I just want to clear the air and make it up to you. Please allow me that chance.

Ferg x

She reads it through a second time, more slowly, and then she sets it aside.

He's coming back to live in Ireland. He wants to see her. He gives no indication as to whether he's alone, or if he's spent the last few years with Therese Ruane, or with anyone.

He knows about the restaurant, so he must have asked Sarah about her. She doesn't imagine that her name would have come up casually in their conversations.

He's coming home at the end of May. It's the third week of May now, twenty days after the date at the top of his letter. Her phone will ring some time soon and his number will show up on the screen. Not his name – that was deleted from her list of contacts ages ago, but she'll recognise the number, assuming he held on to his Irish SIM card, and she'll know it's him.

And what then?

She knows what Gran would tell her. Have nothing whatsoever to do with him; don't give him the time of day. Daniel and her parents would say the same, and so would her friends, every one of them outraged on her behalf after his desertion. Nobody would think it a good idea for her to pick up her phone and press the answer key and say hello.

She looks at Barney, curled on the couch beside her. What would it be like, meeting Fergal again after all this time, or even having a phone conversation with him? She can't imagine it, with so many unknowns and uncertainties. There would be nothing to fear from an encounter though, she's sure of it. She's over him: she's made a new and happier life for herself, and she's stronger and more independent because of what happened.

Granted, the arrival of his letter threw her, but only because it was so totally unexpected – and wouldn't it be good in a way to show him how well she's doing now, how completely she's recovered from his jilting of her?

Or would it be looking for trouble, having any kind of contact at all with him? Would she run the risk of unravelling the last four years? Would he still have the power to hurt her, to upend all her carefully packed-away emotions?

'Emily?' Mike's voice, calling up the stairs. 'Five to seven.'

'Coming.'

She won't talk to him. She won't see him. It's not worth the risk of making her vulnerable again. She'll cut off the call when it arrives, and that will be the end of it. If they meet by chance in the street sometime, as may well happen with him back in Ireland, she'll greet him civilly and walk on, like Sarah does to her. He's in her past and she'll keep him there.

She opens the restaurant on the dot of seven. At ten past, Heather walks in, wearing her usual jeans and shirt.

'I like your dress,' she says to Emily. 'Very pretty. Very cute.'

'Thank you. Why have I never seen you in a dress?'

Heather gives her dark chuckle. '*Me?* That'll be the day. Dresses are for ladies like you.'

'Oh stop that – you'd be lovely.'

She *would* be. She's got the full feminine figure that the right style of dress – fitted on top, flared skirt – would celebrate. Emily sees her in sky blue to match her eyes, whose thick dark lashes need no mascara. And if she pulled that black hair out of its tight ponytail and let it tumble loose, she'd be magnificent.

The table begins to fill. People arrive in ones and twos and take their seats. Introductions are made, and the usual tentative conversations ensue. Some gather momentum, others stutter along heroically. Heather's laugh erupts every now and again: impossible to miss it. At half past seven, as Emily brings lasagne to a pair of Spanish au pairs who appear once a month or so, a man enters whose face she recalls from a few lunchtimes ago, mainly because of the eyebrow piercing.

'I'm glad to see you back,' she says. 'I didn't get your name the last time,' and he tells her Shane.

'Come and sit with Heather,' she says, spotting a free chair next to the American. 'She'll make you feel right at home.'

Heather

OH, FOR GOD ALMIGHTY'S SAKE. FOR CRYING out loud. She ducks her head, willing Emily to bring him someplace else, anyplace else – but over they come to ruin her evening.

'I'd like you to meet Heather, my very first customer,' Emily is saying as they approach. 'Heather, this is Shane.'

Cornered, Heather looks up. 'We've met,' she tells Emily flatly. 'Our kids are in the same class at school.' Deliberately avoiding his gaze. Not even trying to pretend that his appearance holds any pleasure for her.

A beat passes. Emily's smile falters. 'Oh – that's nice.' There's a second or two of silent awkwardness before he pulls out the chair beside Heather and sits.

'So … do I get a menu?'

He's going to brazen it out. Of course he is. Never a hint of embarrassment when they encounter one another at the school gates, or elsewhere. On the contrary, he always makes a point of smiling at her, while she's busy making a point of pretending not to see him.

Emily tells him the two dinner choices as Heather resumes eating: she'll be damned if he's going to ruin her dinner. He chooses the ratatouille and Emily scuttles off – delighted, no doubt, to escape from whatever's going on.

He flips his napkin open. 'This place is different, isn't it?'

Heather gives a curt nod. Can't talk with food in her mouth: one of the few things all her nannies agreed on.

'How's the lasagne?'

For Heaven's sake. She makes him wait, takes her time chewing and swallowing. 'Good.' She forks up the next load before he can get another question in. Bet he talks with his mouth full, bet it doesn't cost him a thought. If she gets a move on, she'll be finished before his arrives. She can get Emily to pack up her dessert, enjoy it in peace at home.

'I think I made the wrong choice,' he says.

She ignores him.

'For dinner. I think I should have gone for the lasagne.'

Not a question, no response necessary. She continues eating.

'So how long's this place been open?'

OK. Enough is enough. She swallows, takes a

drink of water. 'Listen, I don't want to sound rude' – she doesn't give a damn how rude she sounds – 'but I sure would appreciate less of the small-talk while my food's hot.'

He lifts his hands in mute surrender. She resumes eating.

And then he sort of leans in her direction. 'Look,' he murmurs, 'I'd like to say something, just for the record. All you have to do is listen.'

For the love of Moses.

'It's clear you're angry –'

And that's all it takes. 'Is it? Is it really?' she hisses. 'And I suppose you don't have the smallest idea as to *why* I might be angry!' Calm down, she tells herself. You're at Emily's, you're in public – but she may as well try to yank the tablecloth off without disturbing the plates. She stabs again at her lasagne and chews furiously, but all the pleasure has gone out of it.

'For what it's worth, I'm sorry.'

She feels a fresh wave of rage. She drops her fork with a clatter, causing a couple of heads to turn. 'Oh – you're sorry? Really? You're sorry about what – kicking me and my baby out on the street? Making it impossible for me to claim what was left to me in your father's will? What *exactly* are you sorry for?'

'I'm sorry about all of it, about everything that happened. None of it was my doing.'

She throws him a look of disbelief. 'Really?

It wasn't your idea to give me a week to find someplace else to live? You didn't hide behind your wife's skirts and let her drop the bomb instead? Gee, I wonder how I could have got *that* so wrong!'

'Look, I can understand —'

'You understand *nothing* – and by the way, you're welcome, because I'm sure you meant to thank me for returning your father's house after he left it to me!'

'You didn't have to return it —'

'Like hell I didn't, with you planning to contest the will – you think I had the energy for that, with a tiny baby to look after?'

He gives an impatient sigh: it's more than enough to crank her fury up a notch. 'Well, pardon me if I'm *annoying* you – pardon me if I'm giving you some inconvenient truths, Mister!'

'Listen,' he throws back, anger flashing in his eyes now, 'just *listen* for a second, would you? I'm trying to explain that none of it was my doing, I didn't *want* any of that —'

'So you're telling me you're such a weakling that you were powerless to stop your big bully wife from throwing us out of *your* father's house? Is that really the best you can do?'

In response he gets abruptly to his feet, scraping his chair loudly across the floor and narrowly avoiding a collision with Emily, who steps hastily out of his way. He mutters something – an oath? an apology? – and keeps going, and only after he vanishes through the doorway does Heather become aware of the dead silence in the room, and every pair of eyes fixed on her.

'What on earth is going on?' Emily asks quietly, dropping into his vacated chair, still holding his bowl of ratatouille.

'I'm really sorry,' Heather replies, her anger dissipating as quickly as it rose. 'We had a bit of a row. I didn't mean for it to go public.'

'Are you OK?'

'Yeah, sure. Look, I'll call you tomorrow and explain, when you have time to listen.'

Emily knows nothing, or very little. Heather's told her only the bones of her story, left out most of the flesh. Time for full disclosure now, after this.

Par for the course, his stalking out tonight. No wife to hide behind, so he takes off. What was he doing anyway, out on his own? Maybe he and Yvonne had a bust-up – maybe she told him to get someone else to make his damn dinner.

She considers all the acrobatics she's had to perform since Lottie and Jack ended up in the same class – worse, since they decided to become buddies, despite Heather's best efforts to steer her child in other directions. All the lies she's had to spin to prevent after-school encounters, determined never to have anything more to do with that family. All the day trips she organised on each of Lottie's birthdays, purely to avoid a party to which Jack would inevitably be invited. All the times she cajoled another parent to bring Lottie to Jack's parties, to spare Heather having to encounter either Shane or Yvonne – and now, when she puts it up to him, when she finally challenges him on how they treated her, he ducks all responsibility. 'None of it was my doing': what a load of horse manure.

She finishes her meal as conversations resume around the table. The place is filling up early tonight – not yet half past seven, and just three empty chairs. Heather loves the place, loves the fact that they all share a common space. There's something cool about the changing faces, the never knowing who she'll end up meeting here.

And even though it's not that kind of a place, it's not about picking someone up, or being picked up – who knows? Maybe one day someone will take the chair beside her, and they'll fall into conversation, and discover how much in common they have. And they might, they just might want to take it further. She'd be open to that possibility, is all.

One thing's for certain: if she ever finds herself in that situation again, it won't start on a phone screen. Oh sure, clicking on someone's profile and setting up a date in the comfort of her living room seemed like a nice easy way to meet a man, once she'd recovered from Lottie's father doing a runner as soon as she broke the happy news to him that he was to be a dad. Took long enough for that itch to need scratching again, almost three years before she felt ready to give love another go.

But once she did, she went for it. She sorted a babysitter for Lottie – plenty of volunteers in the neighbourhood – and she fooled around on dating apps until she had a date sorted with George, who was thirty, and single, and looking for fun.

Sadly, George turned out to be a lot closer to forty, and not that single either, with a divorce still pending – and not really taken anyway with Heather. She figured, judging by the glances he kept throwing at other females in the vicinity, that he was more into having fun with women who had less flesh on their bones. After George came Denis, who lost interest the minute she mentioned Lottie, and after Denis she arranged to meet Frank, but he must have lost his way because he didn't put in an appearance, and didn't contact her again.

She persevered, kept agreeing to dates with new contacts, kept showing up – and now and again things seemed to be rolling along nicely, and she had a bit of fun along the way, but ultimately all the promising starts petered out. If it wasn't Lottie, it was something else that eventually put them off Heather: her accent, her appearance, her independence, her whatever – or sometimes she was the one put off, by their lack of deodorant, or their fondness for drink, or their poor dental hygiene, or the wives they forgot to mention until something gave them away.

In the end, she got tired of trying. I don't need a man, she told Madge, her chief babysitter. I can manage without one.

Of course you can – but everyone needs a night out. Everyone your age, anyway.

So she still went out, one or two nights a week, with a rotating schedule of sitters. Every Tuesday, and some Saturdays, Heather would feed Lottie chicken nuggets and garden peas before Madge or Carol or Paula or whoever arrived to take over.

Heather would change one shirt for another and spritz some Calvin Klein behind her ears and set out, always with the slightly delicious feeling that she was somehow engaging in illicit activity, like a kid playing truant from school, or a hoodlum on her way to rob a liquor store.

Going out alone didn't bother her in the least: from an early age she'd learnt to be content with her own company. It wasn't for want of friends now: she had piles of them, Madge and Joseph and Carol and Paddy and Ernie and Paula, and all the others in the neighbourhood who employed her to do whatever needed doing – cleaning, painting, collecting kids from school, walking dogs, you name it. She always made friends with everyone she worked for: that was just how it went. Be a friend, and you'll never run short of them, Josephine used to tell her – and like everything Josephine had said to her, it was true.

Trouble was, all her employers were either married and settled, or too old, like Madge, to fancy a night out. Not that Heather was ever planning to stay out till the small hours – she liked her sleep too much for that ever to have appealed, even in the days before Lottie. No, her plans usually involved finding food she didn't have to cook, served on dishes she didn't have to wash up. That, or maybe catching a movie – or occasionally, if she was feeling in the mood, she'd take a chance on a play.

For food she steered clear of McDonald's, which was Lottie's eatery of choice on any special occasion. McDonald's was fine for a kid's treat, but Heather's idea of a good meal wasn't a burger parcelled up in paper, or a cardboard box of pale skinny fries. When she paid someone to cook her a meal she wanted real food, on real plates.

She checked out the town's restaurants and found a few she liked. An Italian, a Thai, a pancake house. Dining alone wasn't an issue – let the couples and groups of friends gawp all they wanted – but she did find herself wishing, as she twined tagliatelle around her fork or cut into a pancake to release its chilli filling, for someone, anyone, sitting across from her. No big romantic commitment necessary, just someone to chat with as she ate.

And then Madge told her about The Food of Love, one morning as Heather was packing up her stuff after cleaning the windows. There was a bit in the paper, Madge said. A new restaurant opening on Holland Street, something about bringing people together. Might be worth checking out.

Bringing people together sounded suspiciously like some brand of blind dating, and Heather had no intention of revisiting that particular scenario. But her usual favourites had begun to pall a little: she might just check out the new one, see what made it tick.

Where's Holland Street?

Not far from here – go by the canal and turn up after the fishermen's cottages, and then it's first or second right. There's a little minimart on the corner.

And on her very next night out, Heather found it.

It was tucked between a carpet shop and a narrow house built of red bricks, behind whose single upstairs window a little brown and white dog yapped soundlessly at her. It was small, with a wooden bench painted tangerine outside the single window, and a wicker basket full of trailing flowers suspended from a large hook by the door.

She wasn't immediately won over. She stood on the pavement and regarded it dubiously. The Food of Love did sound like the venue for some sort of matchmaking – or at the very least, a kind of romantic hideaway, some type of refuge for furtive lovers. There was every danger she'd find nothing but couples inside.

No menu was posted on the wall. She knelt on the bench and peered through the window, but the evening had reached that crepuscular, softened-edge stage where shadows and shapes became interchangeable, and eyes could no longer be fully trusted. A tumble of fairy lights on the inner windowsill was all she could be sure of: beyond that there were only vague yellow glows of candles or lamps, and humps of indeterminate furniture.

The door was open. She left the bench and stepped closer. She inhaled. Oh my: was that the golden-brown nutty scent of baking pastry? Was there a *pie* in there? She imagined its buttery crumbliness, the way the crust would yield to the smallest pressure of her teeth, surrendering the savoury contents within. She sniffed again – Lord, now she was getting spices, hot and dark and tantalising. Tender marinated beef, or maybe lamb. She could almost taste the fiery tease of it in her mouth.

Her stomach, empty since lunchtime, an age ago, rumbled in appreciation, in anticipation. To hell with it: what did she care if she was surrounded by lovebirds? Let them gaze into each other's eyes all they wanted: she needed to be fed.

She made for the doorway – and almost collided with two women, roughly her own age, who were hurrying out.

'What's it like?' she asked.

'Not for us,' one replied, and her companion tittered, and they kept going. Not for them could mean anything: Heather decided to see for herself, so she stepped inside.

And inside, she found nobody at all but a woman with glorious tumbling hair, wearing a pretty blue dress and looking on the verge of tears. At the sight of Heather, her face changed. Hello! she said, her voice as falsely cheerful as her smile. Welcome to The Food of Love – it's our opening night.

You're kidding! How come there's no sign outside? No balloons, no banner?

You sound like my brother, the woman said. He's in advertising – but I wasn't sure if I wanted all that stuff.

Heather took in the single big table covered with a cloth, and the shiny cutlery and polka-dot placemats, and the tea lights in little glass jars dotted here and there, and all the empty chairs. No indication of anyone having been fed yet. Opening night, and nobody there.

One table, she remarked. Communal eating.

Yes. The space is small, so this was the only option that worked. It's aimed at people who don't have anyone to eat with, who'd like a bit of company at mealtimes. Or just … if people wanted someone different to talk to.

Right. And the other two ladies, the ones who just left – this is what scared them off? The one table, I mean.

The woman's smile faded. I think it was more the menu, she said, indicating a blackboard affixed to the rear wall. I have just two options. I thought I'd keep it simple, but they wanted more.

Two options sounded fine to Heather, who ate everything. Written in big chalk letters on the board she read *beef tagine with fruity couscous*, and *chicken pie*. Hearts above the 'i's: all about the love in here.

Beef tagine and chicken pie, she said. Yes and yes. I may have to have a helping of each. Seriously.

The woman laughed. That would be no problem. Which one would you like to start with?

You got a wine licence?

Yes, but we keep just one of each, an Italian white and a Spanish red.

Heather grinned. You sure do like to keep it simple. I'll have a glass of red to start with then, and the tagine to follow. I'm Heather, by the way.

Emily. Delighted to meet you.

They've come a long way together since then, Heather and Emily and The Food of Love. Lots of meals, many conversations – and Emily by now is every bit as much a friend as a host. All good.

Heather finishes her lasagne, resisting the impulse to lift the plate and lick it clean. That cheese sauce is so damn good. Not for the first time, she wishes she could kidnap Mike and chain him to her stove at home.

'Another spoonful?' Emily enquires when she reappears.

No mention of the earlier incident. Like it never happened, bless her. Heather shakes her head and hands her the empty plate. 'Tell Mike he's going from best to even better, but I need room for dessert.'

'Fair enough. Citrus cheesecake or rhubarb and custard pie?'

Heather sighs happily. 'Make it one of each – and pack up the cheesecake to go for Lottie.'

'Will do. And decaf?'

'And decaf. Thanks, honey.'

The pie is a wonder. Soft chunks of rhubarb, just tart enough for the custard to provide the perfect sweet creamy contrast – and the pastry is its usual glorious beast. Nobody does pastry like Emily.

It's early when she leaves, not yet half past eight. The evening is dry, if a little chilly. She'll take the longer route home, down by the canal, work off some of those calories. It might be quiet at this time, but she never feels vulnerable. She's a big gal, and strong with it. More than a match for any would-be troublemakers.

As she approaches the point where she must turn off the road she spots a figure hunkered down on the path, hooded head bowed, paper cup sitting in front. Another paid-up member of the spare-change gang.

At the sound of Heather's footsteps the head lifts to reveal a familiar white face, and two unfocused eyes. Strung out, and looking for cash already to finance the next trip to Paradise. Hard to put an age on her, rough living probably adding years. Often begging at this spot.

Heather drops to a squat, notes the few copper coins in the cup. Wonders how much has already been pocketed. 'Hi. You hungry?'

A shake of the head, eyes closing briefly. High as the proverbial.

'You gotta eat.' Heather lifts the tinfoil package

from its small carrier bag. 'I got cheesecake.' What Lottie doesn't know won't hurt her.

The other looks at the package but makes no attempt to take it. 'Spare change,' she says, in a dead monotone. Her breath is bad. There's a cold sore in a corner of her mouth, the dark stain of what might be a bruise on one cheek. Her hair is hidden beneath the hood of the jacket that looks like it belongs on a far bigger person.

'Here,' Heather says, easing the foil open to show the cheesecake. 'You should eat this, it's so good. Come on, just take it.'

The girl takes the package and sets it beside her on the path. Her nails are bitten right down. Heather remains in her crouched position.

'Will you eat it? Will you promise me?'

'Yeah.'

But there it sits, and chances are it won't be eaten, or not by her. 'You got family?' Heather asks. 'You got people who care about you?'

Another shake of the head.

'Nobody? No one at all? No Mom or Dad?'

At that, the girl grabs the paper cup and pulls herself clumsily to her feet. Heather watches her stumbling off, bumping against the wall every few steps. Off to find a new place to beg, somewhere she won't be interrogated, or forced to eat cheesecake.

Heather retrieves the rejected dessert. No point in wasting it. She pinches the tinfoil closed and returns the package to its bag. She resumes her journey, wondering if it's too soon to have the drugs conversation with Lottie – could a seven-year-old comprehend that danger, or would the ugly truth traumatise her? That pitiable creature can't be more than twenty-something – there's every chance that at least one of her parents is still alive. Imagine seeing your daughter in that state.

Then again, maybe the parents aren't without blame – who knows what home the creature came from? Some families have a lot to answer for. As she strides along by the canal, looking down into the darkening water, Heather thinks of her own childhood, and the house in San Francisco where she grew up.

On the face of it, she was the girl with everything. The privileged only child of moneyed Californians, her mother's family one of the major tech players in Silicon Valley, her father with his string of vineyards in Napa. To anyone looking in, theirs must have seemed the perfect home, but from the inside it was a very different story. It was the story of blazing rows followed by loaded silences, and frequent lavish parties that went on all night, and her father's abrupt unexplained absences. Business trip, her mother would say, in a voice that didn't encourage questions.

It was the story of Heather, who was largely ignored by a couple whose tempestuous relationship left little room for the daughter they handed over to a succession of nannies, none of whom could stand the chaotic atmosphere for long, until it was Josephine's turn.

Josephine, whose name even now, all these years later, conjures up a small wash of grief. Josephine, who became more of a mother to Heather than the woman who'd given birth to her. Josephine, who had summed up the home situation within days, maybe hours, of her arrival, who had looked beyond ten-year-old Heather's sulky defiance and seen right through to the unhappy, neglected kid she'd been employed to look after.

Tell you what, she said, in the accent that sounded so foreign to Heather's ears, the first truly Irish person she'd had any real contact with, let's try to be friends and see what happens. And what happened, once Heather stopped acting like a brat and decided to give it a go, was nothing short of magical.

Josephine, who didn't drive, would be waiting for her every day at the school gate, and every day except Friday they'd walk the three blocks home together. On Fridays they'd take the bus – the bus! – in the other direction, all the way across town to where Josephine's son Terry and his family lived, in a far humbler house than Heather had ever been in.

The house had just one bathroom, with towels as hard as sandpaper that didn't match, and a single television for everyone to share, and no carpets anywhere, not even in the bedrooms. Heather would be given the job of looking after their two chattering cheery little girls in the backyard – one swing, a small sandpit, a tilting umbrella, a huddle of plastic chairs and no pool or barbecue – while Josephine and her daughter-in-law Karen, also from Ireland, prepared dinner.

It was a noisy, crowded affair when they were summoned to the table – there was an older brother, Seamus, who appeared for meals and bolted afterwards – but it was also full of laughter and good-natured teasing, and rather than asking for anything to be passed, people simply reached across the table and grabbed what they wanted. Sometimes tumblers got overturned, and forks were dropped, and food landed occasionally on the floor – but whenever any of this happened, nobody shouted or got impatient.

And Heather wished, so many times, that she'd been born into such a family.

After dinner, Josephine and Heather would take the bus back, and on the way Josephine would talk about Ireland. Heather heard about the husband who had died in a hardware store when a washing-machine tumbled from a shelf and fell on him, and the offer that had followed from their son who'd moved with his new wife to America a few years previously.

They'd just had Seamus, Josephine said. They told me I could be his nanny, probably to make it sound as if I was the one doing them the favour. I said I'd come for a few months, she said, looking through the bus window but seeing, Heather thought, something very different from the streetscape outside. I only intended to stay until I stopped feeling lonely – but look at me, still here, nearly twelve years later. I'm not quite sure how that happened.

Will you ever go back to Ireland? Heather asked, afraid as soon as the words were out that the answer would be one she didn't want to hear. Afraid she might lose the only person who truly seemed to care about her.

Oh yes, Josephine replied, the certainty in her voice causing Heather's heart to droop. Yes, I'll go back home. I'll go back when the kids are old enough to come for a visit. I want to live out my days in Ireland.

Do you still have a house there?

No, that's gone, that's sold now, but I'll get a little place. I have money from Ray's accident, I never spent that. It'll get me an apartment or something, in one of those developments for the elderly, where there's a caretaker to keep an eye out and someone to make your meals if you need them to. That's what I'd like, that kind of arrangement.

She caught Heather's expression then. She put an arm around her, and squeezed. Don't worry, pet – I'll be here for a long time yet. When I move back you'll be all grown-up, and you can come and visit me too, whenever you want.

It sounded wonderful. Heather imagined flying across the ocean, waiting to see the expanse of green below her that Josephine said would tell her she'd reached Ireland. She pictured taking a bus or a train from the airport to the town where Josephine lived, and meeting lots of families just like Josephine's happy, noisy one.

But she wouldn't just visit: she'd stay. She'd find a home of her own, close to her old nanny, and she'd become someone's nanny too. She'd live out her days in Ireland, just like Josephine. She'd be happy there: she knew it.

That was the plan, but the plan didn't happen – or not in the way Heather had envisaged it. The plan fell to pieces one cruel morning when Heather was almost fourteen, and Josephine was in a shopping mall, and a man with a gun shot dead four people who were strangers to him, and one of those was Josephine.

Her mother it was who broke the news to her, her mother who came to pick her up after school instead of Josephine. Climb in, her mother said. Where's Josephine? Heather asked, and her mother, instead of replying, pulled the car out of the parking space, and Heather was too afraid to ask more, in case her parents had decided she was too old to need a nanny, and Josephine had been fired.

She'd go to her, she vowed silently. She'd find her way to Terry and Karen's house – she'd take the bus when she got a chance. Even if Josephine was no longer her nanny they could still meet up, still spend time together.

And then they got home, and her mother filled a

dish with ice-cream in the kitchen, and said, putting it before Heather, You must be strong. And still Heather thought that the worst thing she was going to hear was that Josephine wasn't to be her nanny any more, and the ice-cream melted into a puddle as she heard words that couldn't possibly be true, as she shouted at her mother to stop lying, as she screamed that Josephine was alive, she was *alive*, that Heather would know if anything had happened to her.

But she was wrong. She'd never felt a thing as a bullet, or maybe lots of bullets, had torn a path through Josephine's skin and flesh and bones and muscles, and stopped her heart beating. Working it out later – sneaking the newspapers to her room to learn about the shooting, feeling compelled to know everything, everything, even as every word she read made her feel sick – she figured it had happened during math class. Josephine's blood had spread over a supermarket floor while Heather, all unaware, was working out the square root of something or other.

Her father took her to the funeral service, on her tearful insistence. She wept her way through it, unable to speak to Josephine's family, unable to approach the closed casket.

There was no talk of a new nanny. Her parents must have figured, after all, that Heather had gone beyond needing one. Just as well, since she'd have been obliged to hate anyone who tried to replace Josephine.

For months she was inconsolable. Her routine carried on, school and home and school again, but inside she was dumb and deaf and blind with grief. She pulled away from friends; she turned down party invitations and studied just enough to keep teachers off her back. Part of her yearned to visit Josephine's family across town but she never did, fearful of how sad it would be without the woman who'd brought them together. She was sad enough.

Her grades, never high, began to plummet. Her parents, at a loss, sent her to a shrink, who told her it was unhealthy to obsess about death at her age. Take up a sport, he said. You need to get out in the fresh air, find something you're interested in. What about basketball? Might help shift that puppy fat too. She endured three sessions before telling her folks she would slit her wrists if they forced her to keep seeing him.

I'm OK, she lied, I'm feeling a lot stronger – so the sessions stopped, and in time she learnt to fold away her sadness as she plodded on through the weeks and months that followed.

And inevitably, she flunked every one of her end-of-year tests, which resulted in her having to repeat grade nine, and her folks coming up with a new scheme.

There's this college in England, her mother told her, a week after the damning report card arrived. Well, it's more a finishing school. It's for sixteen- to eighteen-year-olds, to prepare them for university.

It's got a great reputation – all the top families in Europe send their kids there, royalty and diplomats and whatever. We'd really like you to go next year. We think it would be good for you to meet a bunch of new people. The right kind of people, you know?

A finishing school in England, miles from her parents, miles from the friends she'd already abandoned. A year or more of being surrounded by what her mother considered the right kind of people. She couldn't imagine being any happier there – but wasn't England close to Ireland? She looked it up, and discovered that the two countries were near neighbours, an hour apart on a plane.

And slowly and quietly, she made a new plan.

In August of the following year, at the age of sixteen, she was put on a plane for London, where a representative from the school was scheduled to meet her at Heathrow airport and ferry her to her new surroundings.

Text us when you land, her father said, and Heather tried not to imagine their reaction when a very different text from what they were expecting dropped into their phones. Make lots of friends, her mother said – already, no doubt, imagining the marriage to the crown prince of somewhere or other, and the royal grandchildren who would follow.

In the arrivals hall at Heathrow she walked right past the tall blonde woman holding up a board with her name on it, and found her way to the terminal where flights to Ireland were departing. As she was queuing to board the flight she'd booked to Shannon airport a month before with her credit card, she heard her name being called on the tannoy – and when she saw, an hour after that, the carpet of green spread out below her as the plane broke through the clouds on its descent, she wept for Josephine, who had never got to live out her days in Ireland, in a little apartment with a caretaker to keep an eye on her, and someone to cook her dinner.

I've left you a letter, she texted in Shannon, as she waited for her bags to appear on the carousel. *It's under my pillow. Please don't be mad.* Ten minutes later, at twenty past six in the morning California time, her phone rang, and she read *Mom* on her screen. Here it came.

You're in *Ireland*? How could you? How could you do this to us?

I'll be OK, she said. This is just something I've got to do. I'll be careful.

You're sixteen years old! You're still a minor! You're still our responsibility!

Still their responsibility, when all her life they'd passed her on to someone else to be looked after. Mom, I can handle this, I can look after myself. I just need you to let me do it, just for a while.

For a *while*? Exactly how long are you planning to stay there?

I don't know, maybe a few months. Maybe forever, a small voice in her head added.

A few *months*? What about your education? You can't just stop studying!

Of course she could, but she didn't say that. I'll take classes here. I'll find someplace.

Where will you even stay? Who will you stay with?

I've booked into a hotel. It wasn't a hotel, it was a hostel: her mother didn't need to know that. I'll be OK, Mom. I'll be fine. Thanks to you and Dad I have plenty of money, so if you keep putting my allowance into my bank account, I'll manage.

And *this* is how you repay us? By sneaking off to Ireland?

Repay them. She closed her eyes. I'll keep in touch. I'll call in a few days, OK? Don't worry, Mom.

She hung up before anything more could be said, or demanded, or threatened. She turned off her phone and collected her bags, and caught the bus to Josephine's town with some of the euros she'd bought in London. The day was warmer than she'd been expecting, and drier. Everyone around her on the bus spoke in Josephine's musical way. The snatches of conversation conjured up her old nanny's face: it was saddening and comforting at the same time. It made her feel like she wasn't quite so alone – but oh for the sight of Josephine, sitting once more in the seat beside her.

In the town she kept asking people for directions until she found her hostel. She went straight to bed in her tiny room, even though it was the middle of the afternoon. Lying fully clothed on the thin mattress, looking at the sink in the corner with its single tap, the hook on the back of the door, the kitchen chair by her bed instead of a locker, the weird stains on the ceiling above her, she wondered what on earth she'd done.

She was technically still a child, and thousands of miles from home, without a single friend or acquaintance. Josephine had mentioned family members in Ireland, cousins, a sister – but Heather had no names, no addresses. As long as her allowance continued she'd have enough money to get by, but her parents could pull the plug on that at any time. They could also take it into their heads to come and look for her, or hire a private eye to find her, but she didn't think they would. As long as she kept up contact, and kept making it sound like she was OK, they'd probably leave her alone.

But even if they kept funding her, she'd go mad with nothing to do. The problem was that she was qualified for nothing, experienced only in babysitting and dog-walking and cutting folks' lawns.

She decided to focus on the positive. She was in Ireland, in the town where Josephine had grown up and raised her family. She'd already walked streets that Josephine must have walked many times. She'd formed a plan and made it happen. She was where she wanted to be – and here she still is, coming up for nine years later, older but probably not much wiser. Little dreaming, that first day in the hostel, of the ups and downs that lay ahead in the country she'd chosen to live out her days.

Good now, though. Good mostly now.

She makes her way home with her cheesecake gift, as darkness begins to elbow the day aside.

Emily

'EARTH TO EMILY.'

She blinks. 'What?'

Mike adds sliced lemons to a water jug. 'You're miles away. I asked if you saw the *Great Irish Bake-Off* last night.'

'Sorry … No, I missed it. Any good?'

She's a mess. Running on automatic, unable to focus properly on anything. Jumping every time her phone rings, because his letter said he'd be back at the end of May, and June is two days away.

His letter, the cause of all this upheaval. Forcing her each time she lets down her guard to wander back across the years, revisiting events she'd vowed never to think of again.

I'm best man at a wedding, weekend after next, he'd told her the first time they'd met. *The bride has warned me to get a decent cut for it.*

Nice smile, she thought. He wasn't exactly what

you'd call handsome – his face had a peaky look to it, all jutting cheekbones and long nose – but the smile was good, a small tilt to the right with his mouth, eyebrows lifting to lend it a whimsical quality. It was the kind of smile you wanted to return.

When were you thinking? she asked.

Early next week, anytime after four.

She checked the appointments book, wondering what kind of job left him free at four. Teacher or shift worker, or his own boss and able to dictate his schedule.

How's Tuesday at four thirty?

Perfect. He pulled a phone from his pocket, tapped keys. Reminder, he told her, otherwise it gets forgotten. Another smile: yes, definitely his best feature. She flicked a glance at his left hand and saw no ring. Not a sure sign of anything, but still.

Name?

Fergal Kelly.

The first Fergal she'd come across. Where's the wedding? she enquired, wanting to prolong the conversation, and he named a hotel, country-house kind of place, a few miles outside town. Oh, that's a lovely venue – I was there for a birthday party a few months ago.

Can't say I've ever been myself.

Is this your first time to be a best man?

He nodded. Not a clue. Still have to put my speech together.

Good luck with that.

It was nothing, a few sentences, but she found herself looking forward to seeing him again. On Tuesday she wore the sea-green top everyone admired on her, and light grey trousers beneath. He wouldn't notice, but she'd feel more confident.

He noticed. Suits you, that colour.

She felt herself blush. Thank you. She kept him in her line of vision as he sat in the waiting area, scrolling through something on his phone. At one stage it rang, and he held a short conversation. When his appointed stylist approached, Emily watched the smile that accompanied his outstretched hand, felt an answering smile form on her own face.

What d'you think? he asked, returning to the reception desk half an hour later. Will I pass the Bridezilla test?

Definitely. All you need is a nice suit – and a speech, of course.

He groaned. God, the speech: don't remind me. I've made a hundred starts, all equally shite – excuse the language. He took his wallet from a pocket and produced a debit card. Don't suppose you'd like to give me a hand with it, would you?

She felt a little hop inside her. Give you a hand?

With the speech. I'm really clueless – I need some help. Would you do your good deed?

She laughed. She knew, right at that minute she knew that something was beginning. Some tiny spark was waiting to burst into flame. She slipped his card into its slot, tapped keys. Well, I'm not sure

I have much of a clue myself about writing speeches, she said, handing the unit to him for his PIN.

But we could give it a go, he said.

We. Already they were a we.

OK, if you really need help that badly.

Great. The smile was back. What time do you finish? If this evening is OK, I mean.

And that was how they started, two years and three months and one week and five days before he stood her up at a church and shattered her heart.

She snaps out of it and brings Bill his leek and blue cheese soup.

'Thanks,' he says, picking up his spoon. 'Looks good. Smells good. All good.'

She loves to see him coming in. He keeps her grounded, so steady, so decent – and funny too, with his terrible jokes that he knows are terrible. Bill would never abandon someone on her wedding day. He'd never be that cruel. If only she'd fallen for someone like him.

'Bill thinks he might know someone,' Astrid puts in, seated on his left. 'To do my garden, I mean.'

Emily has no memory of Astrid mentioning her garden, or anything about it. 'Oh, that would be good.'

'I'm not sure,' Bill says, shaking out his napkin. 'She might turn it down. I know it's been a while since she did any of that stuff. I don't have a number for her, but I'll ask her next time I see her.'

No sign of Heather today. She phoned Emily as

promised, the afternoon following the row she'd had with Shane. As promised, she explained the reason for it.

You know my first job in Ireland was as a live-in home help for Gerry, who'd suffered a stroke.

Yes, you told me that.

And I lied about my age, told his family I was eighteen.

That too.

Well, Shane was his son. It was he and his wife who gave me the job.

Ah.

And when I got pregnant with Lottie a few months afterwards, and the father did a runner when I told him, I had to come clean to the family about the baby, and they wanted to sack me there and then.

Shane did?

Shane and Yvonne, his lovely wife – boy, was she a piece of work. Luckily, Gerry put his foot down and insisted I stay, but he died when Lottie was just three months old, and the day after his funeral I was given a week to find someplace else to live.

But I thought Gerry left you the house in his will.

He did – I found that out later – but in the meantime I was evicted.

So where did you go?

Back to the hostel I'd stayed in before I got the job. I tried to figure out what my next move should be. I couldn't get another job with Lottie to care for, so I just hoped like crazy my folks wouldn't stop my allowance until I began earning again. I'd kept in touch with them, we spoke on the phone once a week, but I'd never been back home.

So what happened?

Two things. First, I heard through a solicitor that Gerry had left me the house.

How did he find you?

I'd told Yvonne where I was going. I said it was in case mail arrived for me, but it was really to make her feel bad. Probably didn't work – that woman was made of stone.

So you were left the house. That must have felt good.

Well, I was truly amazed – I mean, Gerry and I had always got on real well, but I'd no idea he was planning this huge thing – and while I was still trying to take it in, the solicitor told me Gerry's family was planning to contest the will, so I should prepare for a battle.

You mean …

Exactly. Shane and Yvonne strike again.

So what did you do?

Nothing. I wasn't interested in battles. I'd witnessed enough of them between my parents, and the last thing I wanted was to involve myself in a new one. I told the solicitor they could have the house, and I hung up. I stayed in the hostel for about three months after that, and then I happened to spot the house in the window of an estate agent.

And then?

Then I called my dad and asked him to loan me the cash to buy it.

And did he?

Surprisingly, yeah. He hit the roof a bit when I told him I was planning on staying in Ireland, so I may as well own property there. But when he heard the price, he totally calmed down. It was a drop in his ocean – I told you they're stinking rich, right?

You may have mentioned it.

So I bought it. You've seen it, you know how humble it is—

It's lovely. It's cosy.

It's all we need, me and Lottie – and it reminds me of a house I used to visit back home, full of happy Irish folk. And my dad never asked me to repay the loan, which I'd kinda figured would happen.

Right. And when did they come over?

Who?

Your parents. They must have come to see Lottie.

Emily, they don't know about her. I've never told them.

What?

I told you Dad hit the roof when I said I was staying here: imagine what he'd have been like if he knew I'd become a single mom. They'd have disowned me.

Oh, come on—

No, seriously. You don't know them, Em.

Heather, however they might have failed you

as parents, they deserve a chance to be grand-parents. I can't believe you haven't told them. And Lottie should know them too – it's an important relationship. I was really close with my gran.

Yeah … I'll probably get around to it sometime. Anyway, that's me and Shane. Sorry for losing you a customer. Can't see him paying a return visit any-time soon.

Her story was a momentary distraction for Emily, no more: ten minutes after the call, her mind wandered back to the letter, and all the questions and memories it threw up. And now, a week later, she's all over the place.

That evening, after Mike has left and she's finishing the last of the washing up, the call she's been waiting for, and dreading, finally arrives. She wipes her hands on a towel and looks at the familiar number on her screen, imagining him with the phone pressed to his ear, waiting for her to pick up.

The ringing continues.

Answer it. Ignore it. Pick it up. Leave it.

And then she snatches it up and presses the answer key, because ignoring him has suddenly become impossible.

'Hello.' Her voice sounds amazingly normal. Her skin prickles all over.

'Hi, Emmy. It's me.'

Emmy.

What has she done?

She should hang up, cut him off. She doesn't.

'Thanks for answering,' he says. 'I was afraid you mightn't. It's not too late, is it?'

'… No.'

The same. He sounds exactly the same. With her free hand she slides a casserole dish silently into the sink, which is still full of hot, soapy water.

'You're not in the middle of anything? Are you still working?'

'… No.'

'Good.' Pause. 'How've you been?'

'OK.' She looks through the window at the night. He's out there somewhere.

'It's good to talk to you,' he says. 'It's good to hear your voice.'

Maybe he's in town, at his mother's house. Twenty minutes or so from where she stands.

Another pause. She can hear his breath, the familiar small asthmatic catch of his inhalation. 'How's the restaurant doing?'

'OK.'

'I was surprised when Mum told me. Big change for you. You never talked about …' He lets the rest of it drift off, maybe sensing the danger of going back into the past.

She shifts weight from one hip to the other. 'Why are you calling me?' she finally finds the courage to ask.

He makes some sound, a kind of verbal click, a tap of teeth on tongue maybe. 'I, er … I just … Look,

Emmy, could we meet, do you think? Would that be something you might consider?'

Could they meet? What is she to say to that? 'I don't know. I don't know if I want to.'

'Just for half an hour, I promise. Just a face-to-face chat. It's … difficult over the phone.'

Silence falls between them. She hears an animal sound outside, a low growl. Barney, maybe, defending his territory. Well able for the neighbourhood interlopers. She searches the darkness and sees nothing, no pair of shining yellow rounds to give him away.

'We could meet wherever you want,' he says. 'I'm in town for another few days.'

He's here. 'I don't—'

'How about the little park behind the cinema? It would be quiet there.'

She presses the disconnect key, suddenly unable for any more. Why? Why has he come back into her life? Why has she allowed him back?

She ignores the phone when it rings again. She keeps scrubbing the casserole dish, more vigorously than it needs. She's *not* allowing him back. That's not going to happen.

But maybe that's not even what he wants. For all she knows, he's married with children, and just looking to touch base with her again, for old times' sake. Then again, you wouldn't be touching base casually with someone you'd treated very badly. You'd have to have a good reason, wouldn't you, to reconnect with them? An apology then, for what he did. A clearing of his conscience, so he can finally enjoy his new life. She probably should have agreed to meet, to let him have his say, whatever it is.

It's good to talk to you. It's good to hear your voice.

And, if she's completely honest, it was good to hear his. She imagines her friends' horror if any of them knew that she'd spoken to him. And Daniel would be most disapproving. She told him she was going to return Fergal's letter, but she didn't. Hopefully he's forgotten about it.

Daniel has a new girlfriend. He brought her to The Food of Love for dinner three nights ago. Nuala, was it, or Noreen? A few years younger than him, like all the ones that went before her. Nice girl, though. Can I help you to tidy up? she'd asked Emily. Sweet.

When everything has been dried and put away she checks the blackboard where she and Mike write up items as they fall into short supply, and copies the list into her notebook. Tomorrow is Monday, the first of their two closed days. Emily will spend the morning giving the kitchen a thorough clean before driving to the cash-and-carry to replenish the store-cupboard items. She'll have lunch afterwards with two friends, and meet another later on for coffee and a chat.

Around five her uncle will ring, the one she works for in her spare time. He likes to check in with her every week, to give her any feedback he's received from her efforts and make sure she's happy to go on doing what she's doing. You're a wonder, he'll say, as he always does. You're a natural. I don't know how we'd manage without you.

She'll scramble eggs for dinner. She'll stir a little smoked salmon into them to dress them up, and accompany them with a tomato and spring onion salad. For afters she'll have some leftover bread and butter pudding from tonight's dessert menu. She makes it with brioche, and sprinkles toasted almonds on top. Two helpings left tonight – she packaged the other up for Mike.

Later, around nine, she'll take the usual Monday evening call from her father in Portugal. She'll tell him about the snapdragons in her garden that are coming up again for the third year in a row, and about the diner from Portugal a few nights earlier who told her that he comes from the same small town where her parents now live. She'll make no mention of the fact that Daniel has a new girlfriend: let him tell them if he wants to. She'll ask about the boat trip that they were to take with friends during the week.

And all the time, every single minute of tomorrow, and however many days follow tomorrow until she forgets about his phone call, she'll do her best to stay in the moment, and leave the past where it belongs.

As she turns off the kitchen light, her phone rings again. She looks at the screen and sees his number.

She presses the answer key.

'Sorry,' he says immediately, before she has a

chance to speak. 'I shouldn't have pushed you. If you'd rather we didn't meet, that's OK. If you'd rather I left you alone, I will.'

'I … I don't know. It feels …' She can't finish.

'Why don't you think about it? I won't ring again, I promise. I'll leave it to you, if you want.'

She stands by the door, a slice of light from the hall cutting into the darkness of the room, picking out the toes of her shoes, making the side of the stainless steel recycling bin gleam. She doesn't want to think about it: she can't take any more uncertainty. She has to say yes or no to meeting him. She should say no.

She doesn't want to say no.

'I think … we could. Meet, I mean. But just for a short while.'

'Really?'

She catches herself nodding. 'Yes.'

'Great, thank you. Half an hour tops, I promise, whatever time suits you, any day between now and Wednesday. You pick the time and the place.'

Is she wrong to do this? He makes it sound like such a small thing, such a minor event.

'When and where, Em?'

She should say tomorrow, or the day after. With the restaurant closed, Monday or Tuesday are the obvious choices. But now her nerve is failing her. It's too soon, it's happening too fast. She needs more time to get her head around this.

'Wednesday,' she says. Wednesday afternoons are usually quiet, with Tuesday her weekly deadline for the other job. 'Three o'clock.'

'Will we say that park, the one behind the cinema?'

It's small and quiet, and located far enough away from anyone she knows. 'OK.'

'I'll see you by the gate then. Thanks, Emmy, look forward to it.'

Emmy. The word jabs at her heart. He was the only person to call her Emmy: she's Emily or Em to everyone else. I'm Ferg to my friends, he said, the first time he took her out, so he became Ferg to her too.

Emmy and Ferg. Ferg and Emmy. Whichever way she said it, it had always sounded right.

'Goodnight,' she says, and he echoes it, and she ends the call and closes the kitchen door and climbs the stairs, thinking, *Two days. Three if you count Wednesday.*

Monday and Tuesday crawl past: hard to believe they contain the same twenty-four hours as all the rest. Again and again she retraces their two short conversations, alternately berating herself for agreeing to meet him, and hopeful that their encounter will turn out to be casual, unemotional.

By Tuesday evening she realises she has to find someone to confide in, or go mad.

She rings Heather. 'Can you talk?' Because Heather, never having met Fergal, never having heard the story of him, might be the only safe person to talk to.

'I can. Your timing's excellent – Lottie's just gone to bed. What's up?'

'I don't know where to start,' she says.

'Try the beginning,' Heather suggests, so Emily begins four years earlier and ends with the two phone calls, and Heather listens without interruption.

'Oh, sweetheart,' she says, when Emily finally comes to a halt, 'I don't believe he left you on your wedding day. That's one mean and nasty thing to do. Lord knows I'm no expert on men – I wasn't five minutes with Lottie's father, and there's been nobody important since – but it seems to me you maybe should've torn up that letter when you got it, honey.'

And everyone else would tell her the same. Emily feels suddenly despondent, defeated. She sits back on the couch, closes her eyes. She shouldn't have agreed, shouldn't have answered his call.

'Hey, like I say, what do I know? You've decided to meet him because you're sweet like that – good for you. When's it happening?'

'Three o'clock tomorrow. In a park.'

'Broad daylight, neutral ground, that's good. So I would say just be careful here, OK? Wear your pretty yellow dress so he'll realise what an idiot he's been. Stay casual, and let him see that you're happy with your life now.' Pause. 'You *are* happy, right?'

'Of course I am.' Of course she is. 'Very happy.'

'And you're not in any danger?'

'What do you mean?'

'Of falling for him again. Of everything starting up again.'

'Oh, no. No danger of that at all.'

'Then you've got nothing to worry about. I'd like to come to lunch tomorrow, give you another boost, but I got a painting job across town, so best of luck. I really hope it goes well, sweetie.'

'Thank you.'

'Let me know, OK? Give me a quick call afterwards.'

'I will.'

She hangs up, drops her phone onto the couch. What should have been the fourth anniversary of her wedding, their wedding, is just a few weeks away. The date, every year it recurs, never fails to subdue her, to cause private tears. She wonders if it ever crosses his mind, or if the twentieth of June is just another number on his calendar.

If they'd married, she might be a mother now. She imagines a tow-headed toddler, a rascal with his father's smile and her dimple. Birthday parties with cakes and candles, miniature clothing flapping on the line. Photos sent to Portugal, her brother rising to the challenge of being an uncle. Skinned knees, a tricycle in the back garden. Visits from the Tooth Fairy, holiday resorts with kiddy camps.

The following day the hours crawl along again, slower than treacle. In the morning, while her dough is proving, she writes a letter to her mother.

Everything is fine here. Business is good, thankfully, lots of tourists. Mike's sister had a baby girl on Sunday; they've asked him to be godfather, which he pretends to scoff at, but I suspect he's charmed. Daniel was in twice last week. He's talking about changing his car. The weather's improved, no rain for three days and lots of blue sky. My neighbours across the road have gone to Achill for a week; I'm watering their window box.

All the trivia she can come up with, leaving out the one thing she can't stop thinking about.

Lunchtime is blessedly busy, keeping her moving from kitchen to restaurant for most of the two hours, forcing her mind to focus on who wants what, and who has yet to be attended to, and who needs more bread, or a water jug refilled. Astrid appears, but Emily has time only to take her order and deliver it, and accept payment when it's offered.

'You're up to your eyes,' Astrid says, upon leaving. 'Isn't it wonderful?'

'It certainly is. Sorry we hadn't more of a chat. See you soon, take care.'

And before she knows it, lunchtime is over and the place is empty, and it's suddenly a quarter to three, and she's left Mike with most of the washing up, and a promise to pay him back.

Something is doing somersaults in her abdomen as she pulls the front door closed and sets off to meet the man who broke her heart. Wearing not the yellow dress that Heather suggested, because she put it on and thought it looked like she was trying too hard. Instead she's in comfy old jeans, a pale blue hoodie and her pink canvas shoes, with her hair pulled back into a big clip and her heart thudding painfully in her chest.

All the way to the park, she calls herself a fool. Every step she takes, she questions her decision to meet him – and yet something draws her on, some force propels her towards the little park behind the cinema. Half an hour, she tells herself. Not a minute, not a second longer.

And there he is, standing by the gates.

'There you are,' he says, sliding his phone into a pocket. Weightier by a few pounds, face a little fuller. Hair shorter and blonder, skin tanned. Check shirt, chinos. Smiling.

'Hello, stranger,' he says. Keeping hands in trouser pockets, not attempting to hug her. Not doing anything she could possibly object to. 'You look great.' Tiny new lines crinkling the skin at the outer corners of his eyes. 'Thanks for coming.' Teeth whiter against his tan.

'Hi,' she says. She attempts a smile. Is it evident on her face, the confusion, the mix of emotions the sight of him is causing? She feels the possibility of tears, and prays fervently that they don't fall. Maybe Heather was right: maybe she should have dressed up, spent a bit more time making sure she looked her best. It might have given her more confidence now.

He takes his hands from his pockets then and spreads them in a gesture she remembers. The movement sends her a waft of his cologne, or aftershave. It's not one she remembers. 'Which way do you want to go?' he asks.

Over his shoulder she sees a few little children with their parents in the small playground, and a runner making her way around the path, and an older couple in matching raincoats seated on a bench. Nobody familiar. 'This way,' she says, striking left along the path, and as they set off the sun slides out from behind a cloud and pours light onto the grass of the playing field off to their right.

'So,' he says, 'a restaurant.'

'Yes.' It's surreal, being in his company again. It makes her tongue-tied, stiffens her gait. She keeps her gaze directed straight ahead. She doesn't know what to do with her hands. 'It was Gran's shop.'

'I didn't know she had one.'

Didn't he? He met Gran lots of times. He called her Mrs Feeney until Gran said, It's Bridie. The first time Emily brought him home to meet her, he presented her with a box of Thornton's chocolates. Mum got them for me, he admitted, when Emily praised him.

'She had a hat shop for years.' She glances at him. 'She died. Did you hear?'

He nods. 'Mum told me. I'm sorry. I know you were close.'

She remembers wondering at the time if he'd get in touch. Wanting him to make contact, wanting Gran's death to bring him back, to bring them back – but he didn't. Sarah came to the funeral: she'd met Gran when Emily and Fergal got engaged. She lined up with the other mourners to shake Emily's hand, but she didn't quite meet her eye.

'So what's it called then?'

From the playground a wailing erupts. Emily halts to look across, sees a woman scooping up a toddler.

'The restaurant,' he says, stopping too, but ignoring the sound. 'What did you call it?'

The woman rocks and shushes the child, who bawls on. He must know what it's called: Sarah would surely have told him. 'The Food of Love,' she says, the words bringing heat to her cheeks. She resumes walking, quickens her pace. Wills him not to laugh.

He doesn't laugh. 'The Food of Love,' he repeats. 'It's different. I like it, though. What sort of food do you serve?'

'We don't have a particular ... We've got a small menu, just a few dishes.'

Silence. She wonders if he's wondering about the 'we'. Their steps have become synchronised, like marching soldiers. They always held hands when they walked: in cold weather he'd draw hers into his jacket pocket. His hands were always warm, even on the chilliest days.

'Listen,' he says then, 'Emmy, I need to say something.' The sun is sliding in and out of the clouds, washing the park with light, pulling it away again. There's a vacant bench twenty feet ahead of them. 'Could we sit?' he asks.

She doesn't want to. All at once she doesn't want to hear what he needs to say, but she's here, so she must. She lowers herself onto the end of the bench, shoulders tight, palms flat on her thighs. He adopts a sideways position, facing her, so she feels compelled to look at him. At his face, at the space between his eyes.

'You must hate me,' he says, and stops. She waits, makes no protest. 'I don't blame you. What I did was unforgivable, and … I'm not sure that I can explain it.' He takes a breath, gives a bleak smile. 'Jesus, that sounds like such a cop-out.' He runs an index finger beneath his mouth. Another remembered gesture.

'Look,' he says, 'the truth is, I panicked, Emmy. I just – panicked. The morning of the wedding I was putting on my suit, and I – I came out in the worst cold sweat. I thought I was going to throw up the full Irish Mum had insisted on making for me.' He spreads his hands again. 'It was a panic attack, Emmy. I knew it was, even though I'd never had one before. I just knew – I knew I couldn't go through with it.'

Couldn't go through with it. He makes it sound so terrifying, like leaping from a plane with a parachute on his back, or diving off an eighty-foot cliff into the sea. What was so frightening about spending the rest of his life with the woman he'd professed to love, the woman he'd asked to marry him sixteen months earlier?

Unless he had never loved her. Unless it had all been a lie between them.

She thinks of something else. She frowns. 'But it wasn't on the spur of the moment, was it? You went to Canada, right afterwards. You must have made plans. You must have bought a ticket.'

He grimaces. 'No, I didn't. I mean, I didn't go right afterwards. I went to Dublin, and stayed with friends for a week while I got organised.'

'What friends?'

'… I don't think you know them. Gary and Jean. I was in college with Gary.'

The name doesn't ring a bell. Neither of them does. Oh, what does it matter, why rake up the past? All that matters is that he left her.

'Why?' she asks then, finding the courage finally to look directly into his eyes. 'Why did you propose to me?'

'Because … I thought it was what I wanted. What *we* wanted.'

'And then you realised that it wasn't. *I* wasn't what you wanted.'

'You were,' he insists. 'My feelings towards you didn't change. It was marriage, Emmy. That was what scared me.'

'So why didn't you just tell me that? Why did you have to disappear?'

He sighs, shakes his head, rakes a hand through his hair. 'I couldn't have that conversation, not on what was supposed to be your wedding day. I bottled it. I couldn't face the reaction from everyone. I was a coward, and I took the coward's way out.'

'And in four years you never once made contact, never tried to explain.'

'I – I wanted to, but the longer it went on, the harder it became. And I thought – well, I assumed you'd want nothing more to do with me, and I couldn't blame you.' He looks at her imploringly. 'Believe me, I've beaten myself up over it so many times. I've been a fool, Emmy. A stupid, prize fool.'

She thinks of Therese Ruane. *I hear you're getting married. Congratulations.* She recalls the rumour that went out about him following Therese to Canada. She wants to ask if it was true, but she can't find the words. Her pride doesn't allow her to find them.

'I'm so sorry,' he says. 'I'll be sorry for the rest of my life. Do you think you can possibly forgive me?' He searches her face. 'Do you think you can, Emmy?'

So this is what he's come for, after all: to be told he's forgiven, for his slate to be wiped clean. Can she do it? Can she grant him absolution? Does she want to?

She's over it, over him. She's made a different life for herself, and it's fine. Her heart has mended: the fracture he caused has knitted back together. This encounter is unsettling, certainly – but once it's over she'll forget it. She'll forget him. If he hadn't written to her, she'd probably never have given him another thought.

Well, maybe she might have, once in a blue moon. Once a year at least, on every twentieth of every June.

'I forgive you,' she says, because he made her happy once. Let him have his absolution – and maybe it will help her too. Let there be no lingering resentment between them, no bitter aftertaste.

He reaches for her hand: she draws it back swiftly. 'Sorry,' he says, 'sorry, I just—' He gives his head a little shake. 'Thank you, Emmy. You're a far better person than I'll ever be.'

'I'm older now,' she says, 'and a bit wiser, I think. That's all.' She gets to her feet, the threat of tears long past, thankfully. 'I need to go. I have to prepare for the evening.'

'Sure.'

They walk together, retracing their steps, in sync like before. 'Can I ask you something?' he says. 'You needn't answer if you don't want.'

'What?'

'Have you met someone else?'

She could lie. She could tell him she's in love, and happier than ever – but where would that leave her? How would that help?

'No.' She wants to ask it back, but again her courage lets her down. They walk in silence to the gate. 'Well,' she says, and stops. What is there to say? It was nice talking to you? It was good to see you again? 'Good luck with the move to Dublin,' she says instead. 'Tell your mother I said hello.'

It might be a little easier in future when she and Sarah come face to face, now that Emily has met her son again and the sky hasn't fallen in.

'Maybe we could – I mean, I'll be back at weekends to see Mum,' he says. 'Could we meet up again, do you think? Just as friends.'

Just as friends. She wonders how that would go. She wonders if she wants them to be friends.

'Maybe. I'm not sure.'

'I'll give you a ring,' he says, and immediately flushes, and she realises the significance of what he's said. The ring he gave her on a rainy Sunday evening in March, the day before her twenty-fourth birthday, still lives in its little blue velvet box at the bottom of her sock drawer. Can't wear it, can't let it go.

'Goodbye,' she says, and turns away from him, and she feels his eyes on her as she walks off.

Could they really be just friends? Could they meet with no strings, no anxiety, no pressure to be anything more? It's hard to envisage – but she won't rule it out. He used to make her laugh: she remembers missing that. Surely nobody could object if they saw that she was in control of her feelings, that there was no chance of her being devastated by him again?

Therese Ruane can't be on the scene, or anyone

else. He wouldn't be looking to keep in touch with Emily, even just for friendship, if he was in a relationship. She can't see another woman happy with him contacting his old fiancée on his return to Ireland. No, he must be alone, as she was.

You're not in any danger? Heather had asked, and Emily had assured her that she wasn't. She isn't.

'You look pleased with yourself,' Mike says when she walks into the kitchen. Mike doesn't know where she's been, who she's met. Nobody apart from Heather knows.

'I'm not displeased,' she replies. She feels it went well, considering. He's going to ring again, and she's going to have to decide if she wants them to meet for a second time. She washes her hands and puts on her apron as Mike tells her about the copper cookware he saw on sale. 'You should have a look. I think it might be worth investing in.'

'I'll check it out.'

She separates eggs and whisks the yolks for the lemon tarts. She breaks chocolate into squares and sets them in a bowl over simmering water for the mousse.

Friends. Maybe. One careful step at a time.

Bill

Dear John,

Your email saddened me a lot. I didn't put it up on the page; I thought you might prefer me to respond privately.

It's clear you love your daughter dearly and wish very much to help her, but what the helpline people told you is sadly true: unless and until she is ready to accept help, unless she reaches out and asks you for it, you can't give it to her. I know that's horrible to hear, but it's the accepted reality.

Let me say this much to you, John. You have nothing, not a thing, to feel guilty about – and I feel certain that your late wife would say the same if she could. You haven't failed your daughter: on the contrary you did your best for her every step of the way. You hung back when you thought she needed space, and you tried to reason with her when you felt you should. You shared your concerns with your work colleagues, you enlisted your sister's help, you phoned what numbers you could find. You did everything you could think of, so please don't beat yourself up now. All you can do for her is what you're already doing: letting her know that she's loved, and that you're there and willing to help, and waiting for the day when she realises she needs you.

In the meantime, please look after yourself, and be kind to yourself – because if you don't, you won't be there when she comes looking for you. You may feel that the support groups aren't for you, and maybe they're not, but you might consider giving them a try before ruling them out. Sometimes simply sharing a problem with like-minded people can help.

Whatever you decide, I hope with all my heart that she finds her way back to the life she had with you, and that you both experience happiness again. I hope, too, that you get some peace while you wait for this – and if you really feel you can't sit down and talk with strangers, remember that you can write to me again. I'm always happy to listen, and offer what words of comfort I have.

Your friend,

Claire

Nothing new there, nothing to give him fresh hope. Not that he'd expected it – what could a newspaper agony aunt realistically know about addiction?

He pictured her as a well-meaning but ultimately ineffectual woman of sixty-plus – weren't they always that bit older? Never married, too busy trying to make the world a better place from the comfort of her computer.

She's wrong about the support groups: they're not for him. He did attend one in the month following Christine's permanent departure from the house, not that he'd accepted it as that at the time. Still listening every evening for her key in the front door lock, still searching, every time he went to town, for a glimpse of her, an opportunity to persuade her to mend her ways and come home. Still believing, or trying to convince himself, that it was possible.

And still trying to find help from wherever he could, so he'd gone along one evening to a group that advertised in the local paper. *Addiction support for those affected*, the ad said. *Join us for a chat in safe and discreet surroundings* – but after ten minutes of listening to a woman's tearful account of living with a gambling husband, and another woman's tirade against a drug dealer in her area, Bill walked out. What could they do for him, only pull him down further?

His finger hovers over the *delete* key. At least she responded. She sounds as if she genuinely cares. And it did feel good to get it all down in an email. He might drop her another, next time he feels at the end of his tether. Nice to feel someone's listening, even if she can do bugger-all to help. He saves the email and logs out.

The days pass. May becomes June and life goes on – and in the nursing home, it brings its usual mix of joys and sorrows.

Rosie Doyle slips away from them in her sleep one night, exactly the way she'd always said she wanted to go. She's buried in the town cemetery, with the son who rarely visited standing by her open grave in a good suit.

Eddie Martin moves into the home two days later to take possession of Rosie's room, and within hours of his arrival has found enough like-minded souls to organise a nightly poker game, much to Mrs Phelan's alarm, but so far they're only playing for matches.

Rory Dillon of the blocked sink wins fifty euro on a scratchcard his grandson gave him for his eighty-fourth birthday. He instructs his daughter to buy a tin of Quality Street for the day room, one a week until the money is used up, and everyone obeys the unwritten rule of leaving the green triangles for Rory.

Gloria McCarthy, their lead singer at the afternoon piano sessions, suffers a stroke that leaves her right side useless, and robs her of speech, and of song. Bill wants to call a halt to the sessions after it happens – it doesn't seem right to carry on without Gloria – but Kate Greene and Jenny Burke ask him not to stop. 'People would miss it,' they say, 'and Gloria might like to listen,' so they prop open her door, which is just up the corridor from the day room, and Bill hears her voice singing in his head as he plays.

The old minibus finally surrenders, leaving a group of residents stranded one Sunday at the community centre across town that offers afternoon dancing. Mrs Phelan puts the word out among her business associates, and within days they have a new bus, donated by the largest of the town's hotels. Well, not new, one from the hotel's existing fleet with a fair few miles on the clock, but in altogether better shape than its predecessor. More complicated under the bonnet too, but Bill does the best he can with that. He sprays over the hotel signage on the side of the vehicle, and lives in fear that Mrs Phelan will ask him to paint on the nursing home name in its stead, but so far it hasn't happened. He's never attempted it, but he strongly suspects that signwriting is not his forte.

Outside the home, life continues much as normal too. 'Changeable weather,' Mrs Twomey remarks, appearing on the other side of the hedge one evening as Bill is taking in the clothes he hung out that morning. 'You'll have to put those sheets through the spin again.'

'I will.' He won't chance the line a second time, more showers on the way by the look of that sky. He'll drape the sheets over the clothes horse, fill the utility room with the smell of pretend passion flower and ylang ylang.

'A week of June gone already.' Mrs Twomey, still there. 'Can you credit it?'

'I know.'

The year rushing by, like they all seem to do now. Betty's ninth anniversary approaching, Bill's forty-ninth birthday at the end of September. His and Astrid's birthdays occur close together: she's forty-four years and four days older than him. They've joked about having a joint party, but he's not much of a one for parties. Never was really, although Betty always insisted on making a bit of a fuss.

A cake from the Dutch bakery in town – the coffee one was his favourite – with candles stuck in that he used to let Christine blow out when she was still young enough to relish it. Make a wish, he'd tell her, and she'd wish aloud for a puppy, or a doll's house, or whatever she was hankering for at the time.

It was her birthday six days ago. She turned twenty-five. All that day Bill found her drifting around in his head, like she does on every one of her birthdays. He was reminded of his excitement when Betty announced she was pregnant, and the subsequent miracle of their daughter's arrival. He remembered the heart-stopping realisation – as he held her in his arms for the first time, as he marvelled at the tiny nose and ears and fingers, the tiny everything – that he and Betty had created a new life, and were now wholly responsible for another human being.

On her twenty-fifth he went into town after work, again as he did on every birthday. He walked the streets, went to the places where he'd spotted her before, kept going until his stomach growled with hunger. No plan in his mind, nothing but his urge to see her, to wish her a happy birthday and slip her some money, but he could find no sign of her. Did she even remember the significance of the day?

'Harry will be gone seven years tomorrow,' Mrs Twomey says, and Bill is brought back to the garden, and his sodden laundry, and his neighbour on the other side of the hedge with kitchen scissors in her hand. 'I'm picking a few dahlias to put on his grave.'

'Is it really seven years?'

He remembers Harry Twomey, decent man. Manager at the office-supplies shop in town, walked with a limp from a long-ago car accident, right heel not quite touching down when it approached the ground. Very dapper always, Harry. Pinstripes he favoured, the marks of the comb in his oiled hair. What was it he always said, some phrase he always used when he met you? 'Not a bad oul day', that was it. That was Harry's greeting, whatever the weather.

Poor Harry, came to a nasty end. Stumbled from a railway platform into the path of an oncoming train somewhere in Scotland – Glasgow, was it? Over visiting their son and his wife for a week or so. A new baby due, their first, the birth and Harry's funeral almost coinciding. One out, one in.

The rain returns just then, and Bill makes his escape. While the clothes are spinning he sticks a fork into potatoes that are boiling on the hob. He puts three fish fingers under the grill and opens a tin of garden peas. The kitchen still smells of the takeaway curry he had last evening. He eats his dinner listening to the rain hammering on the skylight, and he prays his daughter has a roof over her head.

And two evenings later, she shows up.

She has a cold. Her voice is thick with it. She refuses his offer of a hot lemon drink, and scratches at her scalp as she picks nubs of sweetcorn from the half pizza he placed before her. Head lice, he thinks, and tries not to imagine the places she spends her nights, or from whose head the lice might have migrated.

'Happy belated birthday,' he says, and the blank look with which she receives the remark tells him that she forgot it.

'… Thanks.' Beneath the table she rests her feet on Sherlock's flank. The dog continues to welcome her, and worship her.

'I looked for you in town, but I didn't find you.'

'Oh …' She sneezes twice, and swipes beneath her nose with the back of a hand, and gives a phlegmy sniff. Bill takes the box of tissues from the worktop behind him and places it next to her.

You're breaking my heart. You're breaking it. Of course he doesn't say it aloud. What's the point? She's past caring.

He lifts another slice from his half of the pizza and chews it doggedly. Pizza never did much for him, with all that melted cheese. He takes in the thin hunched shoulders of his darling child, his lost soul.

Every impulse in him yearns to gather her into his arms, to love her back to health, if that were only possible.

'Will you let me get help for you?' he pleads, as he always eventually does during their encounters. As he will continue to do until he has no breath left to do it. 'Will you please let me try, Christine?'

In response she moves aside her pizza. She's eaten precisely half of her three slices, and picked the sweetcorn from the rest of them. She plants her elbows on the table and sinks her head into her hands. Her hair is damp from the shower. She wears the clothes he washed after her last visit; the ones she arrived in are swishing about in the machine. The same sad routine as always.

'Will you please?' he begs again. He's not above begging. 'Christine, will you just help me out here?'

She shakes her head. 'No,' she whispers behind her hands. 'I can't.'

'You can, if you want to.'

'No.'

So once again he gives up. Instead he urges more pizza on her, and she takes another bite – purely, he knows, to shut him up. When she's eaten all she will, he insists that she dry her hair fully before she leaves, and gives her the usual things to take with her. He accompanies her to the front door and watches her walk away, his hand on Sherlock's collar to stop the dog going after her. He stands there long after she's vanished from view, and wonders how long it will be until he opens the door and finds two guards standing there with sombre faces and bad news, because this sort of story never ends well.

And it isn't until he's brushing his teeth later that he remembers Astrid asking if he knew anyone who might help restore her garden, and him telling her that he might. Is it daft to think Christine might be able to do something as normal as gardening? Is he crazy even to suggest it? He's missed his chance anyway now. He'll have to wait till she turns up again, and by then Astrid will probably have found someone else.

The following day he drops into The Food of Love at lunchtime, needing the sight of Emily, the comfort of her face. 'Bill, there you are,' she says, and as ever his heart melts at the sound of his name on her tongue, at the sight of her bright smile. He loves how delighted she always looks to see him, and he chooses to ignore the fact that everyone else gets the same warm welcome. A yellow dress she wears today, a pair of yellow and blue striped slides pushed into her hair. He loves her little fripperies, the pure delight of her.

'What'll it be?' she asks, and he chooses butter-nut squash and red pepper soup, and wishes he could tell her about Christine. He would love to pour it all out to her, to show her the sorrow that lives inside him, every minute of every day. It will never happen, of course. He wouldn't dream of inflicting it on her, or on anyone he knows. If he needs to vent he'll stick to his agony aunt, his anonymous listening ear.

His soup arrives. 'Bill,' Emily says, 'I need you again, I'm afraid. There's a loose floor tile in the corridor. It's in near the wall, but I'm still a bit nervous of someone slipping on the way to the toilet. Any chance you could have a look on Saturday?'

'Course I will – on one condition.'

She makes a face. 'You won't let me pay.'

'Not for such a small job. It'll take two minutes.'

'In that case, today's lunch is on the house.'

He demurs, she insists. 'I'll bar you unless you agree.'

'What's he done now?'

They turn to see Heather taking a seat across the table.

'We're doing a deal,' Bill tells her. 'She's bluff-ing about the barring.'

Emily laughs. 'He's impossible.'

'But we love him,' Heather replies, winking at Bill. 'You keeping well, William?'

'Can't complain.'

'What'll you have?' Emily asks her.

Heather orders mulligatawny; Emily vanishes.

'How're things with you?' Bill asks.

'Oh, you know. Same old, same old.' She reaches for a slice of bread. She takes pleasure in her food, makes no secret of it. 'It's Lottie's sports day at school tomorrow,' she goes on, spreading butter as generously as Bill himself does. 'She's planning to win the three-legged race. She and her buddy Amy have been practising hard in the park – have to say they're pretty impressive.'

Listening to how eagerly she speaks, hearing the pride that spills from her words, Bill feels a stab of jealousy, and is ashamed of it. He should be glad that her daughter is still hers, still innocent and unharmed, still the source of joy that Christine was for him. Mind her, he wants to say. Wrap her up. Lock her up if needs be. Do whatever you have to do to keep her safe, to keep the demons from getting her.

'She'll be eight in a few weeks. We've always gone off on a day trip for her birthday, just the two of us, but this year she's looking for a party in the house.'

'Good for her.'

They always gave Christine a party. A dozen or so of her friends, sausage rolls, chicken nuggets, an ice-cream cake – and when she was older, when her teens were approaching and she was casting off her childish preferences, the guests dwindled to three or four, and Bill was despatched with a takeaway pizza order. On his return, he and Betty would move into the sitting room, where they sat with the telly turned down low so they could hear the shrieks and giggles from the kitchen.

No more parties after Betty got sick. For Christine's sixteenth, just weeks before her mother's death, she asked Bill for money to have lunch in town with two friends. Her seventeenth was a very different affair, with the house filled with tension, and his daughter already embarked, if he'd only known it, on her dreadful journey. No birthday celebration that year, or since. He'd given her fifty euro on the day, wanting to mark it in some way: she'd pocketed it with mumbled thanks. Lined a drug dealer's pockets later, no doubt.

'How are they in the nursing home?' Heather asks – and glad of the change of topic, he tells her of Rosie's death, and Rory's scratchcard win, and Gloria's stroke.

'She loved to sing,' he says. 'I play the piano after work every day, we have a little sing-along before their tea, and Gloria was our singer. She loved all the old songs, knew all the words – well, most of them – but that's gone now.'

'How sad.'

'We still do it though. We leave her door open so she can hear.'

'Ah, that's lovely. Poor thing. I never knew you could play the piano, Bill.'

'I can't really. I mean, I can plink along. They're not fussy.'

Heather reaches for more bread, and they move on to speak of other things. And when a box with Gloria's name on it is delivered to the nursing home a few days later, they open it to find a brand new CD player, along with a selection of CDs – *Songs of Percy French*, *Old Irish Favourites*, *The Great American Songbook* – and no sender's name or address on it.

Gloria never married, never had children. She gets a once-in-a-blue-moon visit from a niece who lives in … Carlow, Bill thinks, or maybe Athlone, and a few cards at Christmas from other relatives, and that's it. He can't imagine which of them might be responsible for this gift.

Not that it matters who sent it: what matters is that someone took the time to do it, someone who knew the situation, and set about making the world a little happier for Gloria.

He brings it to her room. 'Now look what's come for you,' he says, setting it on her bedside locker, bending to plug it in. 'It seems you have a secret admirer, Gloria.'

He holds up the CDs, one by one. When she sees the Percy French, her mouth moves and she lifts her good hand, so he puts it on, and they listen to Columbus's sailing across the Atlantical sea, and Gloria settles back and looks at the ceiling and mouths along silently with the words, and before the first verse is over, a tear trickles from her left eye and runs into the pillow.

The world, he thinks, is full of silent, wonderful kindnesses. He must remember this, and take heart from it.

That evening, on impulse, he switches on his computer.

Dear Claire,

Thanks for your response. I didn't expect you to have a magic solution, but I appreciate your kind words. It's good to feel that someone has taken the time to think about my daughter's situation.

Not much has changed since my last email, except that I've had an idea and I wanted to run it by you. A woman I know is looking for someone to do some gardening for her, and I'm thinking of asking my daughter if she'd be interested. I figure there's nothing to lose – and isn't there a small chance that it might nudge her back on the right path? She used to like gardening, once upon a time. I'd be curious to hear your thoughts.

I went to a support group once. It wasn't for me.
Regards,
John
PS The world isn't a bad place; today I was reminded of that. I'll live in hope that things come right.

Astrid

SHE HAS A SUMMER COLD. IT'S DOING THE rounds, coughed out from one victim to drift through the air and settle on another. It began a few days ago as an itch in her throat, a minor annoyance that prompted a bout of painful dry hacking every so often. Within a day she was sneezing, and the cough had deepened, and her voice sounded like it was travelling through her nose. Now it has taken serious hold.

By night she must sleep, or try to, propped up with pillows that keep her airways tolerably clear; by day her head feels clogged and dull and achy. She sneezes often, and each sneeze hurts her chest, and feels like it's draining more energy from her. She adds Vicks and hot lemon drinks to her shopping list, and a small bottle of whiskey, and she stays away from The Food of Love, where she might pass her cold around the big table.

'You have a right dose,' Pat says when he delivers her frozen dinners on Monday morning. 'My wife is the same. Stay indoors, wrap up well' – but the sun has finally got some heat in it, so she ventures onto the patio with the velvety soft sky-blue throw that her nephew – well, her husband's nephew – and his wife gave her at Christmas. She sits swaddled, eyes closed, and listens to the chirruping of the birds as they flit and swoop in the sky above her bedraggled garden.

When the sun moves lower and the air grows chilly she returns inside, replacing the birdsong with music of a different kind as she riffles through the collection of long-playing vinyl records she and Cathal put together over the years: Beethoven, Schubert and Wagner, Pavarotti and Ella Fitzgerald, Mario Lanza and Billie Holiday. She selects a Schubert sonata and places it carefully on the turntable of the player that was a wedding gift from her parents-in-law, one of the few items of furniture she took with her when she moved into town.

It's too large to fit with ease in her small sitting room, but she appreciates its rich mahogany tones, and loves how its generous speakers flood the room with sound – and each time she regards it, and uses it, she is afforded some satisfaction at the thought of how her mother-in-law must have grudged every penny it cost, how she must have hated having to buy anything at all that commemorated her son taking for his wife a girl who was neither Irish nor born into the Catholic faith.

She lifts the arm and lowers it carefully to position the stylus on the vinyl, conscious of the permanent little tremor in her ninety-two-year-old hand. One small jump and down it goes, and she settles on the more upright armchair she bought four years ago, when hauling herself from the softer couch became too much of a struggle. All the adaptations, all the compromises old age demands.

But the music, the music, the music. Filling the little room, pouring into her soul, the music of her childhood, the music of her ballet classes, the music no war could kill, no devil in jackboots and a black uniform could destroy.

Later, before bed, she tips a measure of whiskey into a glass. She adds a teaspoon of brown sugar and drops in a lemon slice studded with cloves, and tops it up with boiling water. She sips, hacking weakly, throat burning, head aching. Sitting in bed, she pulls on thick socks and wonders if she will live to see her birthday in September. The thought is troubling – because life, for all its dark episodes, for all its trials and losses, can still throw up happiness, can still surprise and gladden her. Not ready to leave it, not yet.

'That cough sounds like it's gone to your chest,' Heather says the following morning, when she arrives for her monthly cleaning of the windows. 'I think you might need an antibiotic' – so Astrid makes an appointment that afternoon to see her doctor, who scolds her for not coming sooner. 'You could have got pneumonia,' she says, 'and then where would you be?'

Astrid says nothing to this. No response is required, she feels, apart from a remorseful expression.

The doctor writes a prescription. 'Bed rest,' she orders. 'Up only when you have to. Can you arrange for someone to cook for you?'

'I have wonderful neighbours,' Astrid replies, which isn't exactly answering the question, and not exactly lying either. Her neighbours, while they may indeed be wonderful – she doesn't know them well enough to confirm or deny this – are out at work all day: she has no intention of asking any of them to cook her dinner. Anyway, she doesn't need them, with Pat's meals waiting in the freezer.

'Ring me in a few days if you don't start to feel better.'

'I will, Doctor.'

She obeys instructions, staying in bed and taking her tablets, rising only to attend to calls of nature, and to make cups of tea or Bovril, to boil the occasional egg, and now and again to peel an orange, Pat's offerings after all proving too substantial for her compromised appetite, and the preparation of them, simple as it is, too much of a drain on her depleted energy.

The days drift slowly by as she drowses and dreams, and listens to the rain when it returns, and remembers a red cardigan with fat wooden buttons she had as a child, and Opa's teeth in a tumbler of water on the bathroom shelf at night, and the pattern of white seashells that danced joyfully around the hem of one of Mutti's blue summer dresses.

Heather phones. 'How are you feeling?'

'Better,' Astrid says, not sure if this is true, but wanting it to be.

'Really? Did you see the doctor?'

'I did. She gave me medicine.'

'Good. Can I get you anything? Groceries, magazines, bag of chips?'

'Thank you, dear. I'm fine. I have everything I need.' She hangs up and closes her eyes and falls into another doze. She sees Gerhard's model aeroplanes lined up on a shelf in his room, and the green bottle of Papa's hair oil sitting on the window-ledge of the bathroom, beside the cracked china saucer with its little muddle of Mutti's hatpins.

Emily phones. 'Heather told me you were sick. She gave me your number. Can I bring you any food? A little soup, maybe?'

'Thank you so much, Emily, but I can manage.' Emily has quite enough to do without tending a sick old woman.

'Well, please ring if you change your mind. It's really no trouble. And keep warm.'

'I will.'

And one morning she wakes feeling hungry. She inhales, and feels no catch in her chest. Her head is clear, her nose no longer stuffed. She removes her nightdress – how thin she looks in the wardrobe mirror, how worn out and pale! She steps carefully into the shower stall and stands beneath the warm water, taking slow grateful breaths. Not her time yet.

Afterwards, still fragile, she eats a slice of buttered toast and drinks two cups of tea, and watches a robin flit along her hedge. She *must* find someone to bring the garden back: who knows how much longer she'll have to enjoy it?

When she returns to the restaurant, almost three weeks after her last visit, Emily rushes to greet her as she steps inside. 'Oh great, you're up and about again! How are you feeling? Are you better?'

'I'm better,' Astrid says, but still Emily hovers and fusses – and when Bill shows up a few minutes later, he's equally concerned.

'You've lost weight,' he says. 'You need building up. I hope you took a taxi here instead of the bus.'

'I did.' Their concern is touching. She's glad she made the effort to come. As she does her best with the carrot and coriander soup, her appetite as well as her energy yet to return fully, she tells Bill of her renewed determination to find someone to reclaim her garden.

'You mentioned someone who might be interested,' she says. 'I don't know if you got a chance to ask her.'

Bill drinks water. He tears a piece from his bread but doesn't eat it. 'I didn't,' he says. 'At least, I did meet her, but ... I must admit it slipped my mind, sorry. I'll definitely ask, next time I see her.'

Astrid likes the thought of a woman resurrect-ing the garden, coaxing it back to life. 'I gave you my number and my address, didn't I?'

'You did. I'll let you know, as soon as I can.'

'I've called you a taxi,' Emily says, when Astrid is paying her bill. 'And take this,' she adds, presenting Astrid with a small white carrier bag. Astrid looks inside and sees something wrapped in tinfoil. 'Bread and butter pudding,' Emily says. 'It was on yesterday's menu. Reheat in the foil for ten minutes.'

She's lucky, so lucky to have people who care. That evening, she manages a few mouthfuls of the dessert, after a small serving of Pat's shepherd's pie. In the days that follow she tells herself that she feels a little less feeble each morning. She takes the tonic her doctor prescribed to rebuild her, and eats what she can, and walks slowly up and down the road, and no trace of the chest infection returns, for which she is deeply grateful.

At ninety-two she'll take what she can get. She has her music and her friends – and soon, hopefully, she'll have a garden to bring her joy again.

Heather

'MUM.'

'Yes, sweetie.'

'How come I don't have a granny or granddad?'

Heather looks up from the TV mag. 'You do. I've told you about them. They're my mom and dad, and they live in the States.'

'Well, how come I've never met them then? Why do they never come to visit?'

Heather sets aside the magazine. Here it comes. Might as well get it over with. 'Well, I guess we didn't always get along so well, honey. Not like you and me. So I figure it's best for them to live far away.'

She sees Lottie try to get her head around it. Not easy as an adult to figure out families, impossible as a seven-year-old.

'But maybe I'd get along with them.'

'Maybe you would.' Of course she would – because how could they not love her? What was it Emily said? Something about them deserving a chance to be grandparents.

She feels bad having lied to Emily about her dad buying the house for her. It just seemed easier than go into the whole trust fund thing, how it kicked in on her eighteenth birthday, how she's as rich now as a small country. Don't people treat you differently if they know you're rich?

'So maybe we could visit them,' Lottie says.

'Let me think about that one, sweetie.'

And over the following days she does think about it, as she's hosing the dirt from Brona McCarthy's car, as she's rolling a fresh coat of white emulsion onto Madge's kitchen walls, as she's shining her own mirrors and windows with balled-up newspaper.

Is it time they were told? With Lottie's eighth birthday approaching, should she finally come clean? What can they do only rant and rage, and refuse to acknowledge their granddaughter? She can't see that happening – can she?

She decides to go for it. She'll put it in a letter though – it's not something to be sprung on them in a phone call. That evening she waits till Lottie has fallen asleep. She opens her laptop and begins to type.

Dear Mom and Dad,
This letter has got some big news in it, so if you're not sitting down just now, you maybe should. Don't worry, it's good news, or rather it's got a

happy ending. For the longest time I've wanted to tell you, but the truth is I had no idea how you'd take it, so I chickened out.

She pauses to sip liquorice tea, trying to figure out what should come next.

So I guess I must backtrack a little. I told you about Gerry, the lovely man I looked after when I got here first, until he died. I know you were mad at the time that I didn't continue with my studies, but we've had that argument, so I'll say no more about it. You know I bought Gerry's house after my trust fund kicked in, and that I still live there. Well, all of that is true – but I left stuff out.

More tea, some head-scratching. The tricky part.

Here's what happened. A few weeks after I started working for Gerry I met a man – well, he was just two years older than me, and I was still a week off my seventeenth birthday, so I guess you could say we were just a couple of kids really.

Another pause. This is hard. Come on, she tells herself. Write the damn thing.

The truth is I fell in love. His name was Manfred, and he was from Germany, working in a bar in town. We met in a park, we struck up a conversation at an ice-cream van, and very quickly we began a physical relationship – my first, in case you're wondering. I thought he loved me too, I really did.

When I got pregnant – I'm sorry, we weren't as careful as we should have been – he told me no problem, we'd get married, but two nights later when I dropped by the bar where he worked, I was told that he'd gone back to Germany. I tried calling him, but I guess he'd got a new SIM card for his cell phone, because I couldn't get through. I had no address, no way to reach him.

Will they get this far without tearing it up? No way of knowing until they respond. If they respond.

So to cut a very long story short, I had a baby girl when I was seventeen, and I called her Lottie – well, she started out as Charlotte, but she's become Lottie. She's the reason I could never go home, even for a visit, because I couldn't find a way to tell you about her. But Mom, Dad, you should see her. First off, she's a lot prettier than I was as a kid – she's blonde like her dad, with the bluest eyes – but more importantly she's such a great kid. She's funny and clever and thoughtful, and just wonderful. She's the best mistake I ever made, and you're her grandparents, and I know I should have told you long before this, but I'm telling you now.

She lifts her fingers from the keys, suddenly drained. She rubs her face hard. Come on, nearly there.

She knows about you, because I've told her she has a grandma and a grandpa in the US. She'd love to meet with you some day, but that's up to you. I'm not sending a photo of her, not yet, not until you get used to the idea of her being there, and ask me for one. She'll be eight next week, on the seventeenth, and for the first time she's asked for a party at home rather than going on a day trip like we usually do. I'm going to fill our house with all her friends and make it a day to remember, because Lottie deserves the best celebration I can give her. It'll be a tight squeeze – I think I've told you that my house would just about fit into your living room – but we'll have fun.

You're digressing. Stick to the point.

So there you have it. Lottie is my big news. I hope you're not too disappointed in me. I never planned for this. I thought it would be years before I became a mom, but I'm not sorry about any of it. I don't regret meeting Manfred, even though he broke my heart, because he gave me the gift of Lottie, who mended my heart and brought happiness back into my life, more happiness than I thought anyone could ever fit inside them.

Maybe you'll call, after you've had time to get your heads around this. I hope you will. I hope you won't take it out on her if you're mad at me – but if I don't hear from you I'll take the hint, and I won't bother you again.
Your daughter,
Heather

She prints it out and reads it through, frowning, trying to decide if it's come out right. She imagines her mother taking it from the mailbox, wondering why her daughter is writing rather than calling. She sees her slitting open the envelope, standing in the kitchen, reading it just like this. Frowning like Heather too maybe, as she realises that there won't be a rich or titled son-in-law anytime soon, nothing for her to brag about at dinner parties.

She decides it will do. She folds the pages and pulls an envelope from the recycle bag, the one the gas company sent the last bill in. She's not a letter-writer – what would she be doing with envelopes? Writing their address brings a mental image of the house where she grew up, like it does every time she sends them Christmas and birthday cards.

She can see it, clear as anything – the white façade with its many windows, the blue shutters (are they still blue?) and wrought-iron balconies, the immaculate lawn in front – and all of it leaves her completely unmoved. It was, and undoubtedly still is, a beautiful house, but it never felt like a home, not in the way Gerry's little house does, not in the way Josephine's son's house felt, all those years ago.

She closes the envelope with the help of Lottie's glue stick, and slips it into her bag. She'll mail it on her way home from lunch at The Food of Love tomorrow – she'll come home the long way, by the post office. Emily will be happy when she tells her. Heather, on the other hand, won't be happy until – unless – she hears from her folks. Had to be done sometime, though. Had to lob that ball into their court and wait for them to lob it back, or walk away.

When she goes into the restaurant the following day she finds Astrid already installed at the oval table. Heather slips into a chair next to her. 'Hello, stranger. All better now?'

'Yes, all better – and thank you for your help.'

'I didn't do much, a few phone calls. You sure you're OK now?'

'Yes, I'm fine,' Astrid replies – but she looks so fragile. She's like the grandmother Heather never had – well, not that she didn't have them: she had two, still has one, but growing up she rarely saw them. Her Dad's mom spent more time in rehab than out of it, more interested in drinking the family wine than selling it, until it finally killed her before Heather's tenth birthday. Her mom's mom moved to Italy with her third husband while Heather was still a tot: Heather hasn't set eyes on her in years.

Her train of thought reminds her of the letter still in her bag. When Emily appears, Heather takes it out and shows it to her. 'You'll be pleased to hear I'm breaking the news to my folks.'

'About Lottie?'

'Yup.'

'Good for you.'

Heather looks at Astrid. 'I never told them I had a kid.'

Astrid stares at her. 'You never told them? How old is Lottie?'

'Eight on Friday.'

'You've kept her from them for eight years,' Astrid says wonderingly. No hint of judgement in her voice, but Heather suddenly hears how cruel it sounds.

She returns the letter to her bag. 'Listen, you guys don't know them: they didn't exactly win any parenting awards. I know I should have come clean at the start, but I had to get my own head around it. I was seventeen, far from home, deserted by the father.' She pauses, remembering the high emotion of the time. 'It was a hell of a thing to happen. And then, the longer I left it, the harder it got. At least now I'm making it right.'

A beat passes.

'I'm sure they'll be glad,' Astrid says.

'Wish I could be as sure. Fingers crossed.'

Emily takes her order and disappears. Heather wonders if there's been a follow-up to the meeting with her ex in the park. It went OK, Emily said, when she phoned Heather afterwards. We had a chat. He – explained a bit, and he apologised.

Are you going to see him again?

… I don't know. Maybe. He'd like to be friends.

And what would you like?

I'm not sure.

And that was nearly two weeks ago. She hasn't mentioned him since, and Heather hasn't pried.

Playing with fire, Heather would call it, having anything at all to do with the man who left her at the altar. Still clearly feels something for him, or she'd have torn his letter into pieces, ignored his phone call when it came.

Astrid leaves shortly afterwards, in a taxi that Emily phoned for. Heather passes the remainder of her time in conversation with the elderly man who takes Astrid's place, and who tells her that his wife is visiting her sister in England.

'She goes once a month,' he says, 'and spends a few days. I know it's great for them to get together, but I miss her when she's not around. The place is too quiet without her.'

'How long have you been married?'

'Forty-seven years in November.'

Forty-seven years. Almost half a century since he walked her down the aisle, and still he misses her when they're apart. Heather wonders if Manfred missed her at all after he scooted back to Germany, or if he ever thinks of the child he fathered.

'Heather.'

She turns to see Emily's brother taking a chair across the table. 'Daniel, hi there.'

They'd met on the restaurant's opening night, and several times since then. He seems to like variety in his female companions, rarely appearing with the same one twice. She regards today's, young and dark-haired.

And familiar.

'Nora,' she says. 'Fancy meeting you here.'

The girl offers a shy smile as she takes her seat. 'Hi, Heather. How's it going?'

The last time Heather saw her – saw her properly, as opposed to catching an occasional glimpse of her outside the school gates – Nora was a child of eleven or twelve. The face has since become a little leaner, the chubbiness shed, the hair cut in a new style, tight to her head on one side, longer on the other – but the eyes, and the soft, hesitant smile, are precisely the same.

Nora turns to Daniel, her hand moving to cover his on the table, as naturally as a wife might brush a piece of lint from her husband's lapel. 'Heather was my grandfather's carer before he died,' she tells him. 'We used to visit him.'

'Small world. You haven't seen one another since?'

'I've spotted you a couple of times,' Heather says, directing this to Nora, 'when you've collected Jack from school.'

'Oh, really? I didn't see you.'

She didn't see her because Heather took care to hang back, unwilling to engage. Not that Nora, an innocent child at the time, was to blame for any of it; she was just from the wrong family.

'I've met Lottie,' she says, 'at Jack's birthday parties. She's very sweet.'

'Thank you. I think so.' Probably wondering why Heather never showed up to the parties.

'I remember her as a tiny baby. You called her Charlotte then.'

'I did.' Heather recalls how enchanted the girl was with the new arrival. Can I hold her? she'd ask, and Heather would sit her on a kitchen chair and transfer Lottie carefully into her arms, as her parents sat upstairs with Gerry and pretended that Lottie didn't exist.

'I always loved Grandad's house,' Nora says. 'I loved, I don't know, the *feel* of it, or something. I used to imagine—' She breaks off, gives a half-laugh. 'Never mind.'

'You know I bought it, don't you?' Heather asks.

Nora stares at her. She appears genuinely astonished. 'What? *You* bought it? No, I never knew that. I can't believe it.'

She wasn't told. Of course she wasn't told. That little nugget would have been omitted from the family history, along with the fact that Gerry had originally left the property to Heather. When it came up for sale, around the time her trust fund dropped into her bank account, it was like a sign that couldn't be ignored. Heather could have afforded something a lot bigger, a lot grander, but that was the house Gerry had wanted her to have. That was where she and Lottie were meant to live.

'I used to wonder who bought it,' Nora says. 'I've never gone back to the street – I was afraid the house would look different, and I didn't want to see that. I'm so glad to hear it was you.'

Heather remembers walking into the estate agent's and pointing out the house on his list, and saying she was interested in buying it. You'd like a viewing? he asked, and Heather told him she would not. I know what it looks like, she said. I want to buy it. How much will it cost to take it off the market?

She waited while he made a phone call. She listened to his side of the conversation, which told her nothing at all. He hung up and told her that the owner would sell for ten thousand more than the asking price, which was still peanuts when she thought of how many zeros featured in her new financial bottom line. Fine, she said. How do you want to do it? He asked her for a deposit: she handed over her credit card. A week later, having expedited the legal pathway – money, she discovered, magically shortened waiting times – she paid the balance and signed the contract.

Fastest house sale in history, the agent told her, giving her the keys. I hope you'll be happy there.

I will, she replied, and she was. She is.

They must have been dumbfounded when her identity as the buyer was revealed. They must have been dying to know where she'd got the money. She imagined them trying to puzzle out how Gerry's young carer, who'd had the audacity to get pregnant while in his employ, had come up with the funds. It used to give her a kick, imagining their curiosity, and knowing that it would never be satisfied.

And of course Nora would likely have been

unaware too that Heather and Lottie had been ordered from the house in the immediate aftermath of Gerry's death. That information wouldn't have been shared with the children. Nora would have assumed, if she'd considered it at all, that they'd left of their own accord.

Heather is struck by a thought. 'Jack is invited to Lottie's birthday party on Friday.' Only because not issuing an invitation to Lottie's best buddy had been out of the question. 'You could bring him – and you'd get to see the house again.' And it would mean not having to face Yvonne – or worse, Shane. Heather had been bracing herself for an encounter, but maybe now it could be avoided. 'Three o'clock, if you're free.'

The girl's face lights up. 'I *am* free. I don't start work till six on Friday, and I'd love it – thanks so much!'

The perfect solution. Heather should have thought of it sooner. 'So where do you work?'

'Well, I'm part time at the cinema, but I'm doing a correspondence course in journalism. Nearly finished, actually.'

'Great. And you still live at home with your parents?'

Her smile dims. 'Well, not exactly. I'm still at home, but Mum and Dad split up last summer.'

'Oh – gosh. I'm sorry to hear that.'

Split up, which would explain why he was in The Food of Love on his own. So the happy couple – who never, now that she comes to think of it, seemed all that happy when she saw them together – have gone their separate ways.

'They share custody of Jack,' Nora says. 'Eoin and I … well, we generally stay put with Dad.'

Eoin, that was the name of the older boy. He's been at the school gates too. Heather would hardly have recognised him if she hadn't seen Jack running over to him, the small, freckly boy she remembered transformed now into a long-limbed teen in a leather jacket. Hair the same auburn shade, but longer and messier. 'How is he?'

'Good,' she says, brightening. 'He's doing really well, just finished Transition Year. He's had a paper round forever – he says he's saving up for a sports car. Dad says over his dead body.'

'I'm not surprised.' Interesting that the older children have opted to live with their father. Interesting, but none of her business. She gets to her feet. 'Well, time for me to disappear. See you Friday – tell Eoin I said hello.'

'I will. Say hi to Lottie.'

On the way home she posts the letter to her folks, and immediately puts it from her mind to focus on the party, just two days away. Roughly a dozen kids invited, along with whichever adult accompanies them. Judging by the parties she's attended with Lottie, some of the grown-ups will be delighted to have a couple of hours off, but others will hang around. A few of the neighbours might show too –

Heather has issued a general invite. The house will be bursting at the seams, but they'll manage.

They do manage. The sun comes out, allowing the younger guests to migrate to the small yard at the back, onto whose flagged surface Heather has chalked a wobbly hopscotch grid. 'Here,' she says, distributing more fat sticks of chalk. 'Draw on the walls – knock yourselves out.'

The adults spill between the tiny kitchen and marginally larger living room, on chairs and windowsills and radiators. Paper plates are passed around, followed by trays of catered fancy finger food that Heather in a million years couldn't recreate, or come close to. The kettle boils and boils again; borrowed teapots and coffee pots fill borrowed cups. Conversations are loud, and interrupted by laughter.

At four, they summon the children inside and light the eight candles in the centre of the giant chocolate cake. Lottie blows them out and closes her eyes – and her mother knows exactly what she's wishing for, and smiles to imagine her face when Johnny Cotter up the street appears later with a small cardboard box that has holes poked into it.

By five, most of the guests have taken off. 'Let me help you clean up,' Nora offers, Jack and Lottie having migrated back to the yard to cover the last square inches of wall with chalk.

'Leave it – it'll keep. Come and see the rest of the house.' So they climb the narrow stairs, and Heather opens the door of the room where Gerry spent much of his time while she looked after him, and where she herself now sleeps.

'It's smaller than I remember,' Nora says, standing in the doorway.

'I think things usually are, when we grow up.'

'He had yellow wallpaper, didn't he? With green flowers, or leaves or something.'

'He sure did. I left it up for a couple of years, but then it started to fall down.'

'They were his curtains.'

'They were. They're still perfect.'

She looks hesitantly at Heather. 'Can I go in?'

'Sure.'

She steps into the room and crosses to the window, and takes a fold of the navy curtains between forefinger and thumb. She looks out, her back to Heather, who leans against the door jamb. Emotional for her maybe, to revisit where he lived.

'He was such a sweet man, your grandpa,' Heather says. 'I loved looking after him. He was always so thankful for everything I did.'

There's a moment of silence before Nora speaks. 'Heather, would it be OK if I told you something?' she asks then, without looking around.

'Sure thing.'

Another brief silence. Heather waits.

'Mum, she, em—' She turns then, and Heather sees the shine of tears in her eyes. 'Sorry,' she says, thumbing them quickly away before they can fall. 'I've never told anyone this, not even Daniel.'

'You don't have to tell me. Not if you don't want to.'

But out it comes. Out it pours. 'She hit him,' Nora says, her voice trembling and low. 'Dad. She used to hit him. I didn't know, not for – I mean, I knew she used to get mad at him, I'd hear her shouting – but I never knew about—' She breaks off, the tears beginning now, rolling down her face, but she doesn't stop. 'I'd take Eoin away somewhere when she was in a mood – I didn't want him seeing her like that, so for ages I didn't know, I never knew, Dad never said – and then one day I – I saw—' She comes to another halt and clamps a hand to her mouth; Heather moves swiftly to wrap her arms around her.

'You poor love,' she says, feeling the shudder of her sobs. 'It's OK.' Palming circles on her back, comforting her like she comforts Lottie. 'It's OK, sweetheart.'

'I saw her punch him,' Nora says, weeping, her words muffled, but Heather hears. 'She punched him with her fist, right in the face, and he – he put his hands up, just to keep her away, and she – she kneed him, in the – and he – just doubled over, and she – she – she just kept on hitting him, and hitting him—'

'Shh.'

What a thing for a child to witness. What a thing for a wife to do to her husband. However dysfunctional the relationship between Heather's own parents, she'd never seen either of them strike the other. Their frequent rows, loud and angry, had certainly been hard to endure, and the hostile silences afterwards had filled the house with tension – but how much worse it would have been if violence, physical violence, had been part of it.

Shane was perfectly civil to her, Heather thinks, when Yvonne wasn't around – and even when she was there he was never mean, never made Heather feel like a servant the way Yvonne did. That carpet needs vacuuming, Yvonne would say, her face tight with disapproval. When was the bathroom sink cleaned? Gerry's hair could do with a wash. There's dust on that skirting board.

Yvonne was the one who rounded on Heather when she told them she was pregnant. You can pack your bags, she said – until Gerry intervened, and in his halting, post-stroke speech, made it clear that Heather was going nowhere.

Shane held back. He didn't get involved.

And when Gerry died it was Yvonne, not Shane, who called around with her ultimatum, knowing that there was nobody this time to defend Heather. And of course, Heather had assumed that Shane was behind it. She'd taken it for granted that he was in favour of her being evicted – but maybe she was wrong.

Maybe she was wrong about more, about all of it.

'I used to wish I lived here,' Nora says, drawing back, blotting her eyes with her sleeve, and Heather remembers her saying, *I used to imagine* in the restaurant the other day, and not going further. 'I wished Eoin and I lived with Granddad. I felt guilty wishing it, I felt I was being mean to Dad – but I hated what went on. I was always so scared, anytime Mum was in a bad mood.'

Why didn't he leave her? Why didn't he take the kids and go? Maybe he was afraid she'd get custody if they split up – wasn't the law often biased in favour of the mother? Wasn't she generally considered the default main carer when marriages broke down?

For whatever reason, instead of splitting up they had another child together. Yvonne was clearly pregnant by the time Gerry died. Nothing had been said to Heather, of course, but there was no mistaking that bump. Jack's birthday is in November, five months after Lottie's.

Was Jack a desperate attempt to heal things between them? Had Shane hoped a new baby would change her, soften her?

'He's been brilliant – Dad, I mean. After Mum left, he never once said anything bad about her. He changed his work schedule so he could be home earlier on the days he has Jack, and he brought the three of us to Austria at Easter because we had no summer holiday last year.'

How wrong you can be about someone. How hastily you can judge them, with no real evidence. I'm sorry about all of it, he'd said that night in the restaurant. None of it was my doing, he'd said, and

Heather had rounded on him, as much as called him a liar.

'I met him,' she says. 'He came to the restaurant one evening, not so long ago.'

'Emily's restaurant?'

'Yes. Emily put him sitting next to me.'

'I didn't know he'd been there. He never said.'

'I wasn't very nice to him,' Heather says slowly. 'I – well, let's say I blamed him for things that now I'm thinking were probably more down to your mum.'

Nora nods. 'Mum was the boss, for sure. It's not that Dad was weak – he just wanted to keep the peace, so he went along with her.'

Heather wonders which of them finally put an end to the marriage. 'Things are better now?'

Nora's smile is watery, but it's there. 'A lot better. Dad is actually not a bad cook. We take it in turns to do dinner, and Eoin pitches in too, when he's in the mood.' The smile fades a little then. 'Heather, don't tell him I told you – Dad, I mean, if you're talking to him again. Please don't tell him.'

'Of course I won't.'

Just then, the doorbell rings. Heather glances at her watch and sees a minute to half five. Johnny Cotter, right on time with his special delivery.

'Come with me,' she says. 'I got a kitten for Lottie: I think her reaction will be worth seeing.'

They go downstairs to let in Johnny and the kitten, and to set all the rest aside.

Emily

JULY. SOFT RAIN AND SUDDEN DOWNPOURS.
Snatches of sunshine that paint rainbows in
puddles, skies that turn in an hour from limestone
grey to cornflower blue and back again. The odd
thunderclap, umbrellas and sunglasses kept close to
hand. Gardens in full bloom, fresh-cut grass, flowers
spilling from suspended baskets and newly painted
window boxes.

The town has a different feel to it in July, with
families packed up and gone to mobile homes on
the coast, or apartments by more exotic shores. It
is full of clusters of European teens on the streets,
raincoated and backpacked, attending English
classes at the local comprehensive, and older tourists
who wander around churches and gaze at statues,
or sit at pavement café tables with opened maps.

More foreign faces than usual are to be found
around the big table in The Food of Love. Solo

travellers, couples, groups who happen on it by chance, or hear about it from others. 'It's like the United Nations in here today,' Heather says, upon leaving one lunchtime. 'I think we might be the only two locals in the room.'

She must be wondering if there's been any development with Fergal. She hasn't brought it up since Emily reported on their first meeting in the park. Are you going to see him again? she asked then, and Emily told her she didn't know. In fact, they *have* been in touch again but Emily has made no mention of it, still not sure that it's the wisest course of action.

What are they doing? What is happening here? On the face of it, nothing very much. A handful of phone conversations – twelve, to be precise. Another couple of walks in the park when he's back in town at the weekends. Twenty or thirty minutes they last, a few rounds of the perimeter, and that's it.

Well, not quite it. Somewhere over the course of the phone calls, she's slipped back into what she calls their comfort zone. They've grown easier with one another: she's cast off her wariness at renewing contact with him. It's *Ferg*, for goodness' sake.

And yes, she will admit to a small buzz of anticipation on the days when she knows a call is imminent. She does enjoy the laughter he can still evoke in her with some deadpan comment – and yes, she tends to replay their conversations afterwards, as she whisks egg whites and grates lemon rind and crushes digestive biscuits – but they're friends, still friends, nothing more.

He's expressed remorse, she's forgiven him: end of story. They've put their past to bed, and she's glad of it. Now they're moving on, like sensible adults.

He didn't phone on the anniversary of their wedding date. I've got meetings all day, he said, and it might well have been the truth – but it could also mean that he remembers. Maybe he thinks about it every year, like she does.

The only part of this that she's truly uncomfortable with is the secrecy – because she's still said nothing about it to anyone apart from Heather. Not to Daniel, or her other friends, or her parents. They wouldn't get it – none of them would. They'd be afraid for her, and furious that he'd dared to make contact again. She understands this completely. So for the moment at least, their re-acquaintance, their reconciliation and newfound … companionship must remain unshared.

She feels bad about keeping it from Daniel in particular – although these days, his sister's doings might not be high on his list of priorities. Every time Emily has spoken with him in the past two weeks, he's managed to manoeuvre the conversation around to one particular topic.

Nora taught herself to play the guitar. Nora has a nut allergy: she almost died when she was five. Nora's folks separated last year, her mum moved out to an apartment. Nora's father took her and her brothers to Austria at Easter. Nora's fluent in French and German.

Nora, not Nuala or Noreen. Nora, who caught his eye as she served him buttered popcorn in the cinema where she works. Emily doesn't remember the last time a girlfriend occupied his thoughts to this extent – did any of them?

He brought her for dinner again to the restaurant last week. They lingered until Emily was able to join them for coffee – and during a lull in the conversation she caught a look on her brother's face as he watched Nora tracing the embossed pattern on the tablecloth, and she sensed that he was about to entrust his heart, if he hadn't already done so. Be careful with it, she told him in her head. Be sure before you let it go.

She wants to tell him about Ferg. She wants to assure him that it's different now, that there's nothing for him to worry about. He and Ferg used to get on: surely he'll accept this new situation when she explains it.

He doesn't.

'I don't believe it. You're seeing that cretin again, after what he did? What are you thinking of, Em?'

'I'm not *seeing* him, not in the way—'

'You've met him. Isn't that what you said?'

'Yes, but we only—'

'And he phones you.'

'Daniel, it's not what you think, really it isn't.'

He folds his arms. 'Tell me what it is then, because

I'm finding this very hard to get my head around. What exactly is going on here?'

'I told you, we're just friends. We've got over what happened—'

'What happened? What *he* did, you mean. Easy for *him* to get over it.'

She shouldn't have said anything. She shouldn't have opened her mouth. 'Daniel, that's all in the past. If I can let it go, why can't you? I thought you'd understand.'

'Oh, I understand alright. I understand that he's muscling in again, and you're letting him. Em, he's hurt you once, he'll do it again.'

'He won't, honestly. He won't get the chance, because I'm not going to … get involved with him. I'm *not.*'

Daniel shakes his head. 'I should have binned that letter when it arrived.' Not listening to her, not believing her. He means well, she knows he does, but she changes the subject and vows not to talk about her ex with him again.

Later that afternoon her phone rings.

'I won't be down this weekend,' Ferg says. 'I have to attend a conference on Saturday.'

'Your mum will be disappointed,' she replies.

'Only Mum?' Laughing immediately after, sparing her the awkwardness of having to respond. 'But I have Monday off in lieu,' he goes on, 'and I was thinking you could come up to Dublin, just a day trip – or you could stay over. You're off Monday and Tuesday, right?'

'Well, yes, but … Dublin?'

'Why not? We wouldn't have to hide here.'

'Hide?'

'Oh, come on, Emmy – don't pretend you're not terrified someone will catch you out with me. Isn't that why we only meet in that grotty little park?'

She remains silent. How can she deny it when it's the truth?

'Look,' he says, 'I get it. They all hate me, I know that – and I hate putting you in an awkward position, but I like seeing you. So I thought we wouldn't have that problem if you came here. We could actually go out in public with no danger of me being lynched.'

She smiles. 'They'd probably stop short of lynching you.'

'I'm not sure about that. I'd say Daniel would cheerfully string me up, given half a chance.'

He would. 'Ah, well. Brothers, you know.'

'I know.'

Silence falls, not an uncomfortable one. They can do comfortable silences now.

'Think about it anyway. Just an idea.'

'I will.'

A day out in Dublin: ages since she's been there. Or two days, if she stayed over.

No. If she goes she won't stay over, won't complicate things. But she could do one day. She wouldn't drive – Dublin traffic terrifies her – but she could get the early bus and be there by ten. She'd have the whole day.

They'd have the whole day.

They could go to the Hugh Lane, her favourite gallery. Have lunch somewhere nice after that, and maybe a stroll in Stephen's Green if the weather obliged. On her way back to the bus she could nip into Marks & Spencer, pick up some Percy Pigs for Mike.

It could be lovely. She'll think about it.

'Has Astrid been in?' Bill asks the following day. 'Haven't bumped into her in a while.'

'She was here a few days ago. Saturday, I think, or maybe Sunday.'

'OK … I was wondering if she's got anyone to do her garden yet. Did she mention it at all?'

'No, she said nothing to me. Didn't you say you had someone in mind?'

'I did – but she's hard to get hold of.' He hesitates, and Emily notes the shadows beneath his eyes, the worry in them.

'It's my daughter,' he goes on, glancing up at her. 'Christine. She's … Well, we're not living together, she's left home, it's … a bit complicated. Anyway,' he says, turning to check the blackboard, 'I'll have the French onion soup, thanks, Emily.' And that seems to be the end of that particular topic, so she lets it alone.

Washing up after lunch, she thinks about the daughter she'd forgotten he had. He did mention her, a long time ago – must have been soon after he began coming here – but he never normally brings her up in conversation, never mentions her when he comes to do a repair. From his remarks today, and his apparent discomfiture, it sounds like there's been a falling-out of some kind. Poor Bill, must be rough if he's not on good terms with his only child.

'I'm thinking of going to Dublin on Monday,' she says, lifting a bowl from the water, handing it to Mike to be dried. 'Just for the day.'

'Yeah? Why not?'

She wonders if they could fit in a trip to the Botanic Gardens, where she's never been. They might have a gift shop where she could pick up a little pot plant for Astrid – and maybe something for Bill too, to say thanks for always being at her beck and call.

The week passes. 'I'll come up on Monday,' she tells Ferg when he phones on Friday. 'Just for the day.'

'Excellent. Let me know what time you're arriving, and we can make a plan.'

It's a step forward. It's an advance on meeting him here in the park. She feels like they're entering slightly different territory. It keeps her awake on Friday night.

What did Daniel say? He's hurt you once, he'll do it again. But he wouldn't have looked her up, wouldn't have made contact if he was just planning to hurt her again, would he? What kind of person would do that? Ferg isn't cruel or evil – he'd never deliberately cause her anguish.

She turns over, thumps her pillow. She'll go to Dublin. She'll enjoy the day with him, like she would with any friend.

The sun is shining on Monday morning as she walks the short distance to the bus station, which probably means it'll be raining by eleven. Who cares? She's packed a raincoat in her small rucksack; she's prepared.

She's not prepared.

'I still love you,' he says. Sitting on a bench in Stephen's Green, after the Hugh Lane gallery and a visit to the Garden of Remembrance and a sushi lunch. He tells her he still loves her as tourists stroll past, as ducks and swans glide across the pond in front of them, oblivious. 'I never stopped loving you, Emmy.'

She can't say, now that it's come to this, that she wasn't half expecting it. Waiting for it. Wanting it, if she's totally honest. She can't deny any of that, so she remains silent and watches the ducks, and she doesn't snatch her hand away as he reaches for it and encloses it in both of his.

'I was a fool, Emmy. You were the best thing that ever happened to me, and I gave you up. I made the biggest mistake of my life that day – but I really want to show you that I've learnt from it. I want you to give me a chance to prove it to you. I want us to try again.'

She turns to face him. Ask, a voice in her head demands. Ask him now. Don't chicken out.

'What about Therese Ruane?'

He doesn't flinch. His face doesn't change, apart from a tiny crease that appears between his brows. 'Therese? What do you mean?'

'She's in Canada. People said ... you went to her.'

'Emmy.' He's shaking his head, still cradling her hand. 'I'm so sorry if anyone said that to you. You know how people assume, and jump to conclusions. I chose Vancouver because I knew a few who'd gone out there, and Therese just happened to be there too. I didn't go because of her, I swear. You must believe me, Emmy. We were over before I met you, you know that.'

'Yes, but ... Therese finished it, not you.'

'I know that. What does that have to do with anything?'

You told me she broke your heart, she wants to say. Maybe it was over for her, but not for you. Maybe you never really got over her. But he looks so innocently at her that she can't bring herself to voice it.

'Listen,' he says. 'Full disclosure. I met Therese casually now and again – it was unavoidable, with friends in common, but there was nothing more between us.' He hesitates. 'I did go out on a few dates with other women while I was there, I can't deny that. I was trying to forget you, Emmy, but it didn't work.'

She tilts her head to the sky then and sees a bank of clouds settling in. They've had it dry so far; they haven't done too badly. And the rain might still hold off till she's back on the bus.

'So what do you think? Can we try again? Will you risk it?'

Her hand is warm in his. She thinks of the bleak days and weeks and months that followed his departure. Plenty more fish in the sea, Gran had said – but Emily hadn't ventured down that path again. She hadn't gone fishing; she was done with fishing.

And maybe, all along, she'd been waiting for Ferg to come back to her. Maybe, on some level, she had trusted that he'd return, and this was why she hadn't looked elsewhere. Was that it? Could that be it?

Nobody would be pleased if they got back together. Daniel would probably refuse to have anything to do with him, and her friends might well take the same stance. It could be Emmy and Ferg and nobody else – but time would change that, surely. When they saw things working out, when they realised he wasn't going to abandon her a second time, everyone would get over it, wouldn't they?

He's hurt you once, he'll do it again. If that were true, if you followed that logic, you'd never give anyone a second chance. One mistake, and you'd never forgive or trust or believe them again. So harsh, so final. So alien to everything she tries to live by.

She won't live by it.

'Emmy.'

She turns.

'Do you still have feelings for me?' he asks in a low voice.

Here. Here is where she must be careful. 'I ... I don't know. I'm not sure.'

He nods. 'OK. I get that. But you're willing for us to try again?'

'... Yes.' Is she? Yes, she is. Yes.

He smiles. 'Thank you. That's all I ask.'

'We must take it slowly,' she says. 'You mustn't rush me.'

He draws her hand to his lips. He turns it over and kisses the palm gently. 'I promise,' he says. 'I promise it'll be different, Emmy. Second time lucky.'

She'll say nothing to anyone for now – apart maybe from Heather.

Or maybe not.

You're not in any danger? Heather had asked, and Emily had assured her that she wasn't.

And now here she is, in danger of trusting him again. In danger of falling for him all over again.

He stands, still holding her hand. 'Let's go,' he says.

'Where?'

'Wherever you want. This is your day.'

This is her day. This is the seventh of July, the day that will forever be the one she agreed to try again.

'Let's just walk,' she says.

Baby steps. That's what they must take.

Bill

HE'S MADE A TOTAL MESS OF IT.

I might know someone, he said. That was his first mistake. He should have said, 'My daughter might be interested.' The reason he didn't – and of course he can see the nonsense of it now – was because he couldn't admit to Astrid that he can't contact his own daughter. So Astrid was given the impression that he was offering her some anonymous female acquaintance – which of course will come back to bite him on the behind if Christine actually ends up taking the job.

And now it's more complicated, because he's admitted to Emily that it's Christine he has in mind. There's something about Emily that invites you to share, and let your guard down. So she knows – and there's every danger that she'll mention it casually to Astrid. Has Bill's daughter agreed to work in your garden? she might ask – and then they'll get to talking, and Astrid will wonder, they both will, why he didn't reveal to Astrid the identity of the person he was proposing. And of course they'll also wonder why he can't just lift the phone and talk to Christine. What a God-almighty mess.

The thing is, he still wants to ask her. He remembers the entire days she could spend in the garden with her mother, weeding or planting or pruning, or moving shrubs from one spot to another. Betty was a great one for shifting things around. They need a new view, she'd say. They're tired of the old one.

Bill would be on lunch duty those days. He'd hard-boil a few eggs, cut slices from a loaf, put ham and halved tomatoes out on plates. He'd call them in when the pot of tea was made, and they'd come for just long enough to eat, soil under their fingernails even after they'd scrubbed their hands – neither of them could work with gloves on. Then off they'd go again, leaving him with the washing up, eager to get back out there.

Of course that was long in the past, long before everything went wrong – but his stubborn brain insists on clinging to the faint hope that being back in a garden, any garden, will work some kind of restorative magic on his daughter. He could say a friend of his was in need of someone to tidy up her garden. A small job, he'd tell her, just take a few days. He needn't say he'd put her forward already. He wouldn't put any pressure at all on her.

There'd be a few quid in it, he could say. Astrid would be generous, he thought, and money might be the thing that would make the difference to Christine. It would really help his friend out a lot, he could say.

He could suggest that she moved back in with him while the job was going on, just if she wanted. He wouldn't make a big thing of it, but he could put it out there as an option. It might be another bit of inducement, the idea of a bed with clean sheets for a few nights – and it would also mean that she'd turn up at Astrid's looking respectable.

Claire, his agony aunt, urges caution.

Dear John,
Thank you for your last email. I'm glad you feel you can talk to me.

It's difficult to know what to advise you on this occasion. I understand your great desire to help your daughter, and the notion of her getting involved in any sort of gainful employment must be so tempting – but please think carefully about this, John. Consider your friendship with the woman in question – have you thought about the repercussions if it all goes wrong, if your daughter fails to do the work, or disappoints in some way? You say there's nothing to lose – but maybe your relationship with your friend would suffer. Maybe, if it didn't work out, it would also push your daughter further away from you.

I'm sorry, John. I know this will be hard for you to hear, but I feel I must play devil's advocate, and point out the possible pitfalls. Of course you must do as you see fit – and if you go ahead with it, I sincerely hope there's a happy ending. Please don't despair if it doesn't work out – you are to be commended for not losing hope, and you must hang on to this hope despite disappointments.

Allow me to repeat what I said in my first message to you: when your daughter is ready, I'm sure she will ask you for help. In the meantime, know that I am rooting for you both, and wishing you all the best.

Your friend,

Claire

Not a lot of comfort there. Clearly she feels this would be a wrong move. He should leave Christine to her drugs, and wait till she's ready to be fixed – but he can't. He's sick of standing by and watching her destroy herself. He can't do nothing, not when there's something that might help.

Round and round it goes in his head, any spare minute he has. Going to work each day is a relief: he looks forward to the distraction of the nursing home, and the various continuing ups and downs of life there.

Eddie Martin, who replaced Rosie Doyle, is in trouble with Mrs Phelan about the card-playing. 'She said it's going on too late,' he tells Bill. 'She said

I have to stop at nine, before the milk and biscuits come around. She treats us like children,' he says, the frustration plain in his face, and there's nothing Bill can say to contradict that, and nothing he can do about it. So now the card games finish at nine, and a lot of the spark is gone out of Eddie.

On the happier side of things, Gloria is coming around a bit after her stroke, with some movement in her affected side. Bill looks in on her whenever he's passing her room. 'Music?' he asks, and she always perks up at that. He's found her a few more CDs, Maura O'Connell and Louis Armstrong and John McCormack. He holds them all up in turn until she nods, and he slots it in. The music fills her room, and she mouths the words, or as close as she can get to them. And sometimes she cries, but not out of sadness, he thinks.

He still does the sing-along at five o'clock. They'll never allow him to stop – not that he wants to. It's a bright spot in his day, a reminder of the good stuff, and a chance to stop wondering whether he'll get home to find her waiting outside. Wanting to see her, always wanting that, but dreading it too, because of how the sight of her as she is now stirs him up.

Today is different. Today there's someone else on his mind. After work, after the singsong, he returns to his cubbyhole behind Mrs Phelan's office and lifts the bunch of mixed flowers he bought at lunchtime from the bucket of water he placed them in. He wraps the damp stems in a few pages from an old newspaper, and pours the water down the adjoining toilet, and leaves the nursing home.

Eight years since he lost her. Eight years to the day since he last held the hand that had wasted to skin and bone in a matter of months. Eight years since he and Christine said goodbye to her, sitting on either side of her bed as she left them, quietly and without a fuss.

Was it that? he wonders, as he has wondered so many times. Was it the loss of her mother that set Christine on the wrong road, or would it have happened if Betty had lived, if cancer had chosen another victim and passed her by? He recalls his anger in the wake of her death, how he'd raged at God for taking her – because despite his rage, he had to go on believing in God, and heaven, and all that stuff. He has to believe that Betty is in a happier place now, or he may as well lie down and die too.

The day is dry and gentle; he slings his jacket over a shoulder. It takes twenty minutes to walk to the cemetery. Betty's grave, in the plot Bill bought a decade before, is located along the outer edge, next to Timothy Moran, fifty-six, and his infant grandson Thomas. A copper beech by the wall spreads its generous canopy overhead, sheltering both graves from the crueller elements.

He stands before Betty's black marble headstone, chosen by Christine. He'd have gone for a granite one if it was left up to him, but he figured it was a small price to pay if it gave comfort to Christine. By the time it was erected, almost a year after Betty's death, Christine had changed utterly from the tearful girl who'd selected it.

He closes his eyes and breathes in the soft calming sounds of the place, the gentle rustle of leaves, the calls of the birds that flit among them, the rumble of the traffic beyond the stone walls that surround the graveyard.

At length, he begins to speak. 'The Halpins next door moved out yesterday,' he says. 'End of an era. Gone to a bungalow, Caroline can't manage the stairs any more.

'John and Tina Foley are away to the Canaries again. This'll be their third time since Christmas.

'One of the little twins across the road – you wouldn't know them, they're after your time – he fell off a trampoline at a birthday party and broke his leg.

'There was a charity swim in the river on Sunday. Good turnout, I walked down to see it. I met Lucy Garvey, Dearbhla's mother. You remember Dearbhla? She used to be pally with Christine. Lucy's had to give up the taxi, her back is at her. She had Dearbhla's little baby with her, born just after Christmas. Conor, I think she said his name was, or Cormac.'

Dearbhla had been in Christine's class at school. The two had been friendly, in the days before Christine drove all her friends away. Lucy was the mother who'd called to Bill's door, more than a year after Betty's death, when he was already out of his mind with worry about Christine. She offered Dearbhla drugs, Lucy said. She wasn't angry with Bill, she didn't blame him. I just wanted you to know, she said. You need to know.

And after Christine left home, a long time after, he met Lucy in the supermarket, and she squeezed his hand and told him she'd seen Christine on the street, and how sorry she was, and you could tell she wasn't taking any satisfaction from it, the way others might.

He could be a grandfather now. He could be showing off a grandchild, like Lucy was.

He brings his mind back to his surroundings. *Beloved wife and mother,* he reads on Betty's headstone. She *was* beloved, by both of them. He'd loved her since he was fourteen and she was two years older, newly moved to the town and befriended by his sister Grace. Whenever she came to the house he would adopt an air of indifference, terrified that any attempt to interact with her would show him up for the gormless idiot he was.

I thought you didn't like her, Grace said four years later, after he'd finally found the courage to ask Betty if she'd care to go to the cinema with him, after she'd made his day by saying yes she would.

'I was thinking,' he says, 'of asking Christine if she'd like a few days' work, clearing a friend's garden. It's probably a long shot, the way she is now, but I thought it might be worth a try. I wonder would you think it's a good idea.'

What would she say, if she could still talk to him? Would she discourage it? Would she urge caution, like Claire has? He wishes there was someone else he could ask, but Grace, living in Cornwall now with her English husband, has washed her hands of Christine. I tried, she said, and she had: she'd made repeated attempts to talk to her when Christine was still living at home, when they still thought they could win her back. He can't involve Grace now. He's asked enough of her.

He could ring the helplines again: God knows he did it often enough. He began to recognise the different voices of the volunteers, he was on to them that often. But what if they give him the wrong answer to this particular question? Or maybe it's the right answer, but not one he wants to hear.

'Bill?'

He turns – and there is Emily, wearing a pale blue and white spotted dress. 'I thought it was you,' she says, holding a small bunch of pink flowers, her curls loose and glorious. She looks at the headstone. 'Is this …?'

'My wife,' he finishes. 'Eight years gone today.' The odd confluence, he thinks, of encountering the woman you love by the grave of the woman you loved. The sight of Emily is welcome, as it always is, but also strange on this occasion.

'Elizabeth,' she says, reading.

'She was Betty. I don't know why I put Elizabeth. Everyone knew her as Betty.'

'You do though, don't you?' She indicates the pink flowers. 'These are for my gran – she's buried further on. Everyone called her Bridie, but my father put Bridget on her headstone. I think people feel they have to do it properly.'

'When did she die?' he asks.

'Coming up on four years. She had a hat shop, where the restaurant is now.'

'I remember it,' he says. 'Betty got a couple of hats there, for weddings.'

'Did she?' Emily smiles. 'I could have met her. I used to go there a good bit after school.'

They might have met, Betty and the schoolgirl Emily. The thought is unsettling: he shifts it sideways. 'You were close, you and your gran.'

'… Yes.'

He could ask her, he thinks suddenly. He's already mentioned Christine to her in connection with Astrid's garden – he could fill in the blanks, ask what she thinks. Of all people Emily would be kind, wouldn't judge. Maybe they were meant to meet here.

But he doesn't get the chance. 'Bill,' she says, 'could I … would you mind if I asked you something?'

He's pulled up short. His brain slides onto a new track. 'No,' he says. 'I wouldn't mind.'

There's a pause. He sees her search for the right words, hears the careful way she eventually speaks. 'Would you think – a person deserves a second chance? Even if they really hurt you, should you trust them again if they tell you they're sorry, and if they promise not to … let you down again?'

The question, so unexpected, throws him further off balance. He decides not to consider its possible implications, and take it at face value. He casts about for the right response.

'I shouldn't ask,' she says quickly, seeing his hesitation. 'I shouldn't involve you. Forget I spoke, it's not important.'

'No, it's— I just …' He thinks of Christine, all the second chances he would give her without a thought. 'Yes,' he says. 'Yes, definitely. Everyone makes mistakes, everyone deserves a chance to come good.'

She smiles again, the sight warming him as it always does. 'Thanks, Bill.' Another pause. 'I should explain,' she says. 'Someone has come back into my life,' the colour blooming in her cheeks, and too late, he thinks, No, I don't want to hear this, but he has to hear it, 'and I – well, he wants us to try again, and … I've agreed.'

She stops. She's looking at him. Waiting.

'Right. Good luck,' he says, because of course it's what she wants to hear. 'I hope it goes well,' he says, as his heart folds and crumples. Not that he ever had a hope in hell with her, he *knows* that, he's well aware of that, but all the same the blow almost suffocates him. He makes a show of checking the time, but the numbers on his watch face may as well be hieroglyphics. 'I'm late,' he says. 'I'd better be off. Take care now.' Lifting a hand, moving away.

'Bye, Bill. See you soon.'

Her words drift after him. She'll wonder about his abrupt departure – or maybe she won't. Maybe it didn't register, because she's got better things to think about.

He wants us to try again, she said, and I've agreed. She's trying again with someone who hurt her badly. She's giving him a second chance, and he, Bill, told her to go right ahead.

At least he didn't bring up the subject of Christine – because he doesn't really want advice, does he? Not from Emily, not from anyone. His mind is made up. He's going to put it to her, next time he sees her. She can say no, she'll probably say no, but at least he'll have tried. He'll have done that, and his dithering will be over.

It's after seven by the time he turns onto his road. In the driveway of number three, Keith Flaherty is washing his car with his usual gusto, sending rivulets of sudsy water cascading onto the street. 'Hey Bill,' he calls, and Bill throws him a salute. Further on, the mother of the child with the broken leg pulls up in her Mini Cooper across the road. Bill waits while she gets out, and enquires after the patient, and is told he'll be coming home in the morning. He'll pick up a few of those easy-peeler oranges in the supermarket on his way home from work tomorrow, and drop them over.

And as he opens his gate there she is, waiting for

him. Grey woolly hat pulled low, despite the mild weather.

'Sorry,' he says. 'I was at the cemetery, saying hello to Mum.' He makes no mention of the anniversary. He lets her in, and they go through their usual routine. He scrambles eggs as water rushes through the pipes overhead. He opens a can of beans and heats them till small bubbles pop softly in the sauce. He fills the washing up basin with hot water and slides two plates in to warm. He scratches Sherlock's head and looks at the wall without seeing it as he waits for her.

'How are you?' he asks, when she's seated at the table, and she says fine. She always says fine, and never enquires how he is. He loads food onto a plate and places it before her: she accepts it with murmured thanks. He takes a can of Coke from the fridge and sets it down.

'There's bread,' he says, slicing it. 'Butter,' he says, adding the dish to the table. The running commentary he feels compelled to provide as the backdrop to their meals, tipping words into the chasm of all that is left unsaid between them. 'Your cold better?'

'Yeah, it's gone.' Popping the tab on the Coke and drinking. Forking up some egg, bringing it to her mouth. Trying.

The radio is playing – he has it tuned to Lyric. A choir sings a song he doesn't recognise. He's not that gone on choral music, but it's better than the offerings of other stations, the over-bright prattle of presenters, the pious spin of politicians, the irritating jangle of pop music. He's a fogey when it comes to the radio.

He butters bread. He ladles egg onto it and rolls it up. He always does this with scrambled egg. He remembers Betty and Christine teasing him about it. 'Look,' he says, holding it up to show her. 'Eggroll,' he says, and she gives a thin smile.

He takes a bite; some egg escapes and plops back onto his plate. He drinks from his glass of milk. Now. Say it now.

'There's something I wanted to run by you,' he says. Diving in before he can think about it. 'Something I thought you might be interested in.'

She scratches at her damp head before lifting her Coke and drinking again.

'I have a friend. I met her in a place I go to for lunch sometimes. She's old – she'll be ninety-three in September. Astrid, her name is. She's from Austria. Her family left it before the war, the Second World War, and came to live in Ireland. I'm assuming she's Jewish.'

He stops. He's babbling, shying away from the point. Christine takes up another minuscule piece of egg. The beans remain undisturbed. Too late, he thinks he should have put them on toast: she used to love that.

'She has a small house on the other side of the

canal, not too far from here.' He's never been to Astrid's home, but from the address he figures it can't be more than a fifteen-minute stroll.

'Her garden, her back garden' – did she say back? He can't recall – 'it's overgrown, and she needs someone to tidy it up. I thought you might be interested, since you and Mum used to like—'

A wave comes at him without warning, cutting off the rest of his words. He swallows. He blinks hard, twice. Across the table from him, Christine continues to pick at her food, giving no sign that she notices his rush of emotion. He sets down his makeshift roll and clears his throat, and scrubs a hand across his chin, over and back, to rid it of the tremble he can feel in it. The rasp of his stubble seems indecently loud. He drinks milk, tries again.

'I don't imagine it's a particularly big garden. I haven't seen it, but it sounds small.' Why hadn't he listened properly when Astrid was telling him about it? 'I wouldn't think the job would take too long, a few visits only. She says it's not strenuous work.' Did she? Did she say that, or did he make it up?

Christine pokes at the egg.

'She'll pay,' he says, watching her fork. 'She doesn't expect someone to do it for nothing.' He has no clue what the going rate is for gardening.

'You could sleep here for the few days the job would take – only if you wanted – and you could leave again straight after. I wouldn't put any pressure on you to stay if you didn't want to.'

The silence lengthens. He looks down at his plate, his appetite gone. He drains his glass. It begins to rain, drops pattering lightly onto the skylight, sounding like a polite little round of applause. He gets to his feet, needing to move.

He crosses to the window and sees a pale-coloured cat sniffing its way around the lawn. Belongs to the couple in the bungalow at the end – he's seen it sprawled on their gate pillar on sunny days, washing itself. Throwing him a disdainful look if he dares to interact with it. He has a respect for cats. He admires how they don't give a damn.

'OK.'

He turns from the window, not sure if he heard or imagined it. He regards the back of her head. 'Did you say something?'

She turns to glance up at him. 'I said OK. I'll do it.'

She's agreed.

She's going to do it.

He resumes his seat slowly. Go easy here. Don't get carried away.

'I'll get in touch with her so. I'll ask when it would suit her for you to start. I'll come with you the first day, to introduce you.' He's got holidays coming to him from the nursing home, he must have. He can't remember the last time he took a day off. He'll make the introductions, he might sit with Astrid for a bit while Christine gets started.

But she's shaking her head. 'Give me her address. I can sort it. I can go by myself.'

She doesn't want him to accompany her. She

doesn't want any reason to spend more time with him than she must. The only reason she comes here, the *only* reason, is that it's a convenience to her. All he's good for now is to provide hot water and clean clothes when she needs them. He tries not to let it hurt, but it does. It slices through his outer layer, pierces right to his core.

'Would you spend the few nights here?' he asks. Still trying, still unable to give up.

'No. It wouldn't work.'

He opens his mouth to argue, and shuts it again. He'll take what he can get, he won't push.

'Have you got her address?'

Astrid's address. Where? Where did he put it? He pulls out kitchen drawers, searches through the slips of paper attached with magnets to the fridge door. He empties his pockets: not there. He races upstairs and checks the rubbish on his dressing-table, opens more drawers, clatters hangers together in the wardrobe as he delves into other pockets. Where the hell is it?

And then, on the point of giving up, he remembers. He finds it on a shelf in the utility room, still neatly folded, the restaurant serviette with Astrid's address and phone number written in her small precise hand. He'd taken it from his shirt pocket before the shirt went into the wash, put it on the shelf for safekeeping.

He hands it over, along with the filled toilet bag and the bundle of tens. He hands them all to her, all his useless gifts.

'You'll need to ring her before you go,' he says. 'Make sure she's there, and that she hasn't already found someone – I haven't seen her in a while. Don't ring too early, she mightn't be up. Leave it till about ten.'

She gets to her feet. She tucks the serviette into a jeans pocket and pulls on her jacket.

'Won't you stay a bit longer?' he asks. 'It's raining again. Won't you just stay until it stops? You don't want to get another cold.'

But she pulls on her hat and says she must go, so he and Sherlock see her to the door as they always do, and she waves a hand to avoid having to hug him, and walks off into the wet evening.

And then, when it's too late to undo it, he thinks about what he's done.

She's an addict and he's sent her to Astrid, a frail, trusting woman. He's let his overwhelming desire to reach out and help her cloud his better judgement – and now he won't be accompanying her as he'd planned, to make sure things start off on the right foot .

He should have made a note of Astrid's phone number, and her address. Was it Cedar Terrace or Grove? He could ring her if he had the number. He could tell her on the phone what he hadn't been able to say to her face. He could say Christine had gone through a rough patch but was trying to sort herself out. He could let her know that much before Christine makes contact, but now he can't, unless he meets her by chance at the restaurant.

Then again, maybe it's as well that he can't. Maybe he should trust his daughter to do the right thing. He wants so much for her to do the right thing, to rise to this challenge he's set her.

What's the worst that can happen?

She won't turn up, or she'll turn up without phoning ahead, and Astrid will either accommodate her or she won't. She may already have got someone to do the job. Or Christine will be taken on, and she'll do the work but won't do it well, and Astrid will be disappointed but will pay her as promised, because she's Bill's daughter.

Or she might turn up and do a good job. She might astonish Astrid with her gardening know-how. A neighbour might see what she's doing and ask if she'd like more work. It might turn into —

No. Don't. Don't do that to yourself.

He closes the door and returns to the kitchen. He tips congealed egg and cold beans off her plate into the bin. He washes up as Sherlock whines softly beneath the table.

And later in the evening, on impulse, he sends another email.

Dear Claire,
I've done it. I've put it to my daughter, and she's agreed to take on the job. I appreciate your advice, but I can't be cautious here. This is something I have to try. We'll see how it goes.
John

And a day later, the reply comes:

> Dear John,
> I hope fervently that it works out. Let me know,
> one way or the other.
> Your friend,
> Claire

Astrid

'MY FATHER TOLD ME TO COME,' SHE SAYS, in a low-pitched monotone. She's wearing a jacket that is too large for her, all rolled-up sleeves and slipping-down shoulders. A child in her parent's clothes. 'He says you're looking for someone to work in your garden.'

So pale, her skin; an unhealthy pallor to it. Dark hollows beneath her eyes. Her face thin, too thin, sunken cheeks. Light brown hair pulled back into something. Twenties, Astrid thinks. Somewhere in her twenties.

'Forgive me – but who is your father?'

'… Bill. Bill Geraghty.'

Bill Geraghty? She's *Bill*'s daughter?

I might know someone, he'd said. Not 'My daughter might be interested.' How peculiar not to identify her – and how unlike him to send her around without a phone call beforehand to let

Astrid know. Perhaps he meant to ring, and forgot. They haven't met lately in the restaurant, although Emily did mention that Bill had been asking about the garden on his last visit there.

She studies the girl's face – and yes, now she can see the quiet dilution of his features. The eyes a shade lighter, but brown like his. The mouth, the chin, yes. Bill's daughter, in an oversized jacket, baggy corduroy trousers and scuffed brown boots.

I don't have a number for her, Bill had said, or words to that effect. Isn't that also a bit strange, not to have your child's contact details?

'What's your name?' Astrid asks, and is told Christine, and is not asked hers in return. She'll already know it, of course, from Bill – but still Astrid feels a proper introduction is called for, so she gives her name and extends her hand, which Christine, after the briefest of pauses, touches for an instant. The iciness of her fingers is a shock, although the day is mild. Something is not right here, something feels amiss. She wants to talk to Bill, ask him to clarify things, but without his number – why hadn't she thought to take it? – and with the girl on her doorstep, she'll just have to manage the situation alone.

She hasn't found anyone else to carry out the work. She stopped asking people after Bill said he had someone in mind. She pinned her hopes on him – and he has sent along his daughter, this strange, reticent creature. Is she robust enough for the work needed? So petite she is, so frail-looking. Nothing like the sturdy female gardener Astrid had been anticipating.

Still, she must at least give her a chance.

'Let me show you the garden,' she says, and leads the way through the hall and kitchen. 'I'm afraid I've let it go. I used to do it myself, but it's too much for me now. I should have got someone else long before this.'

She opens the patio door and they both step out. Bill's daughter regards the mess of weeds and overgrown shrubs, the mossy lawn, the hedge that straggles down the side.

'As you can see, there's quite a lot to be done,' Astrid says. 'It's all so overgrown. Have you done much gardening?'

'Yeah, a bit.'

Telling Astrid nothing at all. 'Some of the shrubs will have to go. They'll need to be dug out.' No reply. 'So what do you think? Are you interested? I'll understand if it's more work than you realised.' Giving her the option to back away from it. Hoping, she has to admit, that the girl will turn it down.

But she doesn't turn it down. 'I can do it,' she says, looking directly now at Astrid. 'How much will you pay?'

The question, posed so casually, so bluntly, catches Astrid off-guard. She hadn't thought as far as payment, has no idea what to offer. She would have done her homework, asked someone like Emily or Heather to advise her, if she'd had some warning of this girl's arrival.

'I'll have to check—'

'Twelve euro an hour,' Christine says. 'That's the minimum wage.'

Is it? Heather charges twenty in total to clean Astrid's windows – how long do they take her? Hard to say: she always stays for tea afterwards.

'You'll have to leave it with me. I'll need to—'

'Ten. I'll do it for ten an hour.'

It's almost harassment. Astrid prickles with annoyance. The girl appears to be plucking figures from the air. 'I do wish you wouldn't keep interrupting me,' she says, a little more sharply than she intended.

Silence. Christine continues to stare at Astrid with those pale brown eyes. There's something hunted in that stare, some hunger in it. It's almost, Astrid thinks, as if she's desperate for the work. But how can that be? How can Bill's daughter need a casual gardening job so badly?

'Are you working at the moment, Christine?' she asks.

A beat passes. 'Bits and pieces.'

No, this won't do. 'Christine, I must be honest. I don't think you are the right person for this work. It's quite physical. It will take rather a lot of energy – and forgive me, but you don't look all that able.'

'I *am* able,' she says. 'I'm stronger than I look.'

Maybe she is. She's certainly keen. And really,

how could Astrid face Bill again if she turned away his daughter without at least giving her the benefit of the doubt?

'Let's start with a two-hour trial,' she says. 'If I'm happy with your work, you can come back and do more. How does that sound?' Bill can't possibly object – and two hours might be more than enough for the creature.

'So will you pay ten an hour?'

'If I'm happy, I'll pay you twelve.' For outdoor physical work, she decides, it seems reasonable. 'So if we say—'

'I'll start now.'

Again, Astrid is brought up short. Again, she is conscious of a dart of irritation. Today is Wednesday, her day to visit the library – and even if it wasn't, she'd refuse. Bad enough that the girl turns up unannounced: she's certainly not going to dictate terms and conditions.

'Today is not convenient,' Astrid says firmly. 'I have plans. You can come back tomorrow, at ten o'clock.'

'OK. Can you give me an advance?'

Unbelievable. Astrid stares at her. The girl's expression doesn't alter – and again, Astrid senses a kind of desperation in the intense gaze. 'You want me to pay you before you've done any work?'

'I could use twenty euro. I'm a bit short.'

A new note in her voice now, a softening, a wheedling. Astrid's instinct is to say no – how cheeky to ask for money from someone she's only just met. Why can't she go to her father, if she's in such dire straits?

But there's some trouble between them, isn't there? There must be, if he has no phone number for her. And yet he proposed her to Astrid as a gardener, and gave her Astrid's address. The whole thing is mystifying.

She regards the girl, so wan – and frankly, malnourished-looking. For all Astrid knows, she might be badly in need of a square meal. 'I can give you ten,' she says. 'That's all the cash I have with me now. I don't like to keep it in the house.'

This is not the truth. She has sixty euro and some change in her purse – she always knows, almost to the cent, how much cash she has to hand – and some more in the locked drawer in her bedroom in case of emergencies, but ten is all she's prepared to hand over.

'One moment,' she says, and leaves the girl on the patio while she goes inside. In the kitchen she takes a tenner from her purse, and gets out her writing pad. *Received ten euro from Astrid Carmody*, she writes. She adds the date and tears out the page. Best to keep it official, no matter whose daughter she is.

'Would you sign this please?' she asks, setting the receipt on the patio table. The girl accepts the proffered pen and silently puts her name on the paper, and stuffs the money into her pocket with mumbled thanks. 'I'll let you out the side passage,'

Astrid says, and again leads the way. They walk in silence: the short distance feels longer than it is.

'Goodbye, Christine,' Astrid says. 'See you at ten in the morning.'

'See you.' Astrid watches as she scurries to the gate. Lacking in the social graces, none of Bill's warmth or humour about her. Then again, not everyone is blessed with good communication skills. Hopefully she's a better gardener than conversationalist. Hopefully she'll return wearing more appropriate clothing for the task in hand. Really, it's all a bit of a disappointment.

But she vows not to berate Bill when she meets him again: there's more to this situation than she can possibly know. She'll bide her time and see how the girl gets on tomorrow – hopefully the result will be gratifying, and she'll be thanking Bill next time they encounter one another.

But the disappointment continues. The following day, ten o'clock comes and goes with no sign of her, and by noon she still hasn't appeared. Astrid's collection of garden tools, retrieved one by one from her shed last evening, wait on the patio with nobody to use them.

She sits with a cup of tea and tries to puzzle it out. First, there's Bill's failure to identify her from the start as his daughter. Then there's her unannounced arrival, and the mystery of her, with her dishevelled clothing and her taciturn, almost sullen manner, and her blunt request – demand? – for money in advance.

Astrid will have to be honest with Bill, or as honest as she can be, when he asks – because of course he'll ask, next time they meet. She'll have to tell him that his daughter turned up unannounced, and didn't come back as arranged. She won't make any mention of the money that changed hands: poor man would die of mortification. He'd insist on reimbursing her, the last thing Astrid would want.

The girl must be unemployed. That may well be the bone of contention, the thing that drove them apart. A common enough theme, Astrid imagines, between parents and children. Bill possibly trying, like any concerned father, to get her some work, even if it's only a few hours of gardening. Christine resentful, seeing his actions as meddling, going along to Astrid's under duress, determined to be uncooperative.

But to take cash like that, to take a person's money given in good faith, and then to break her word. It's not the ten euro, it's the soulless, calculated element to the act that Astrid finds disturbing. And Christine must surely realise that there's a chance Bill will get to hear of it. Doesn't that bother her at all? Doesn't she care what her father thinks of her?

At lunchtime Astrid spreads peanut butter on crackers, and tips a spoonful of blueberries into a little dish of yogurt. She eats on the patio, with the kitchen door open so she can hear the radio. The news, as always, is bleak: yet another mass shooting in America, more bombs in Syria, an Irish tourist drowned while holidaying in Spain. So much tragedy, so difficult sometimes to hold fast to her belief in the goodness of the world, particularly today, but she must continue to cling to it. Every day she must remind herself of the many kindnesses, the many truly good deeds she's witnessed and experienced over the years.

After washing up she goes for the nap that has become part of her daily routine. Waiting for sleep, trying to keep her thoughts from the disappointment of Christine's actions, she visualises her mother's pearls, tucked safely in their locked drawer. She imagines holding them in her hand, tracing their cool smooth roundness with her fingertips. The exercise soothes her as it always does. She closes her eyes and surrenders.

The following day is Friday. She calls a taxi to take her to The Food of Love for lunch. Taxis continue to be her mode of transport since her illness; the thought has occurred to her that she may never again board a bus. Still, she didn't do too badly to keep going until now.

The route to the restaurant takes them past the town's nursing home: as the taxi approaches the building, Astrid sees a man emerge from it, and recognises him. Might as well get it over with.

'Please stop,' she tells the driver, and he pulls in. Astrid presses the button to slide down her window. 'Bill,' she calls, 'can I give you a lift? I'm on the way to lunch.'

'Astrid.' He crosses to the car, plants his hands on the window-frame. 'Actually, I've just eaten.' He nods back towards his place of work.

'Oh …' Didn't he say to her, not so long ago, that he loved escaping from there at lunchtime? She decides not to question it. 'Another time, then.'

'How are you keeping?' he asks.

'Very well, thank you.' She must say it. It sits between them; it must be spoken of. 'Bill, I met Christine. She dropped by two days ago.'

She doesn't miss the guarded look he instantly adopts, the small tightening of his features. 'Did she ring you in advance?'

'No,' she says lightly. 'She just turned up. Luckily, I was at home, so it wasn't a problem.'

His face drops. 'Sorry, Astrid. I asked her to phone beforehand. She must have forgotten.'

'You never mentioned she was your daughter,' she says, careful to keep her tone neutral.

Immediately she regrets the comment: the poor man looks hunted. 'I – it must have slipped my mind. Sorry.'

'It doesn't matter in the least. Maybe you did say it, and I forgot.' Be kind, when their battle is unknown to her. 'At any rate, it's of no consequence. We had a chat, and I showed her the garden, and we agreed that she'd come back the following day, which was yesterday, but …' How to put it? How to spare the man further distress? '… I'm thinking something must have come up, because, well, she didn't appear, and there was no sign of her today either. If I had a number for her, I'd have called, but she didn't leave one, and I didn't think to ask. I just thought you should know, Bill.'

He receives the news with no change of expression. Clearly, it comes as no surprise to him that she broke a promise. 'I'm so sorry, Astrid. She's not the most reliable.'

'Bill, it's not your —'

'I should never have put her forward,' he says, as if she hasn't spoken. 'I can see it was a mistake. There's been a - well, after her mother died, things changed. I see her only now and again.' He shakes his head. 'I'm sorry.' he repeats. 'I thought it might help if she had some … distraction. I was wrong.'

The absolute defeat in his voice is hard to hear. She places a hand lightly on his. 'Bill, I doubt there's a family in the world without some problem or another. Try not to worry too much - I'm sure it will sort itself out in time.' How trite it sounds - but it's the best she can do.

He shakes his head slowly. 'It's not …' He trails off.

'Christine is young,' she says, 'with a lot to learn.'

'She's twenty-five,' he says quietly. 'Not that young.'

While she's searching for a response he speaks again. 'Astrid, can I give you my number, just in case you need it?'

In case she needs it. What does he mean? She

opens her mouth to ask, but finds herself unable to frame the question. She takes out her phone and hands it to him. 'Will you add it to my contacts?' She can make calls and send texts, but anything more complicated takes her forever. He presses keys and returns the phone to her, and steps back from the car. 'I'd better let you go,' he says. 'Say hello to Emily for me.'

He looks so utterly forlorn. She regrets opening her mouth. She should have said nothing at all – or lied if he'd asked, told him nobody had been to see her. If ever a lie was called for, it was in this instance – but instead she told the cruel truth, and ruined his day.

'Try not to worry,' she repeats, once again hearing how useless the words sound. He makes no response, just lifts a hand and waves as the taxi pulls away.

She's not the most reliable, he said. I see her only now and again.

So sad, whatever the cause of their trouble. She'll give the girl a few more days to return. For Bill's sake, she'll give her a bit of leeway. If she doesn't reappear Astrid will put an advert in the local paper. She'll ask for a retired person to work in her garden – is she allowed to specify the age group, or is that regarded as discrimination? So difficult these days to avoid causing offence to someone or other. At any rate, she'll take out an ad – or perhaps she could ask at the local garden centre: they might be able to suggest someone reliable. Yes, that might be safer than taking on a complete stranger.

She puts it from her mind as they draw closer to the restaurant, but the exchange with Bill has unsettled her, and she realises that she's no longer in the mood for socialising. 'I've changed my mind,' she says to the driver. 'I think I'd like to go home.'

'No problem,' he replies, swinging into a side street. A banana sandwich she'll have, then the comfort of her bed, a few hours of dreaming and drifting. I'm old, she thinks, looking out at rushing shoppers and playing children and trotting dogs. I'm old and I'm tired and my energy is nothing like it was, but my mind is intact, and my hearing and sight are holding up. I'm not ready for the scrapheap yet.

'Going to stay fine all next week,' the driver remarks. 'We're getting a good run of it.'

'Indeed we are.'

'You going on any holiday yourself?' he asks, meeting her eye briefly in the rearview mirror.

'Oh no,' she tells him. 'I'm going nowhere.'

She's staying right here, for another while at least.

Heather

HER PHONE RINGS WHEN SHE'S AT GEORGE'S house, up a ladder with a sponge in her hand. The phone sits where she left it, on the windowsill a floor below. Two rings, three. Two more and her voicemail will click in. She'll leave it.

But it might be Madge, who's looking after Lottie this morning.

She drops the sponge and scoots down. She swipes her palms on her jeans and grabs the phone and presses the answer key, not stopping to check the caller ID. 'Hi,' she says.

A buzz, a click. Silence, followed by another click. It's one of those scammers from Outer Mongolia, ringing to tell her she's won a fortune on their lottery, and can they please have her bank details so they can lodge it. She'll hang on, give them one of her whistles.

'Heather?'

'... Mom?' She never calls at this hour. Isn't it the crack of dawn on the west coast? 'What's up?'

And then, abruptly, she remembers the letter. Jeez, how could she have forgotten it? She turns and leans her butt cheeks against the sill, waiting for whatever is to come.

'You have a daughter.' Her mother's voice sounds muffled. Maybe she's got a cold.

'Um ... yeah.' She shifts her weight while the silence lengthens. 'Mom? Hello?' Have they been cut off?

'You have a *daughter*.'

She's crying.

Her mother is crying, which could mean any number of things. 'Mom, listen. Are you OK with it, you and Dad? I need to know.'

'Heather,' her mother says – and then nothing again, and after that there's a fumbling, and a new voice. 'Heather, it's me.'

'Dad.'

'We got your mail. We're – well,' he says, and stops.

What is it with all this silence? 'Dad, can you please tell me? How do you both feel about it?'

'Well,' he repeats, and there's another pause, while Heather watches a bee buzzing around George's rhododendrons, or whatever they are. For crying out loud.

'Heather,' her mom again, 'we want you to come here, and bring your – bring Charlotte.'

'Lottie,' she says automatically. 'You want to meet her? For sure?'

'Well, of *course* we do!'

Wow. 'I'm glad to hear it, Mom. To be honest, I wasn't sure how you'd take the news.'

'Heather, we have a grandchild we've never met, a grandchild we didn't know existed. How could you keep this from us? How could you *do* that?'

'Mom, I was seventeen. I wasn't married. I didn't even have a boyfriend when she was born. I was afraid you'd cut me off, or at the very least bawl me out.'

'But to say nothing for eight whole years? Really?'

'I know. But—' She stops. She can't very well say, 'You were crap at being a mom, so how could I trust you as a grandma?' Who would it help? Not Lottie, that's for sure.

'Please come home, Heather. Please come soon, even just for a bit. Is she – is Lottie at school now, or on summer break?'

'School's out till the end of August.'

'Is she there with you? Can we talk with her?'

'No, she's with a neighbour. I'm working right now.'

It feels unreal. It feels a little weird. They want to be grandparents; they're excited to meet Lottie. Maybe they'll be better at it than parenting. Maybe they just needed to skip a generation. Maybe, after all, they don't know that they stank at being parents. Maybe they thought that was how it was done.

'So you'll come?'

They could go for a week, ten days maybe. She could take Lottie to meet Josephine's son Terry, and his wife and kids. The older brother whose name she's forgotten, the two little girls who aren't little any more. She wonders how they're all doing. She wanted to keep in touch after Josephine's death, but she was too sad to figure out how to make it happen.

She hopes they live in the same house. If not, she'll find them. She'll search the phone book, she'll call all the Terry Moloneys in California if she has to.

'We'll come visit,' she says. 'Soon as I can organise it.'

'When? When will you come?'

In the nine years she's been living here they've never been so keen to have her come home. They asked before, sure they did, but they never insisted like they're doing now.

She lets it go. 'Maybe a week or so? I'm not sure how often—'

'And can we call you later, so we can say hi to Lottie?'

'Sure. I'll be picking her up in a bit. Give us an hour.'

After she hangs up she finishes the windows, her thoughts darting about.

Wait till Lottie sees the big fancy house her mom came from. Wait till they hear their grandchild's Irish accent.

They're not mad. They want to meet her. They're excited to meet her.

She needs to book flights. Lottie's never flown before; it'll be such an adventure for her.

Lottie could do with new summer clothes, and with getting her hair cut.

'You look like you won the Lotto,' George says, paying her.

'Just happy,' she tells him. 'How about you, George?'

'Can't complain.'

He could complain. He has plenty to complain about. His wife Susie died last year, his only surviving brother two months before that. His children, every last one of them, live in New Zealand, and don't come home often enough. George has a dicky heart, and uncertain blood pressure, and pain in both his knees when it rains. But he soldiers on and never complains, and Heather brings a lemon drizzle cake each time she comes to do his windows, because he mentioned once that Susie used to bake them. Heather's aren't home baked, obviously, and probably not a patch on Susie's, but he seems happy to get them.

On the walk back to her street, just a few blocks away, she takes out her phone and scrolls through flight schedules from Ireland to San Francisco, remembering her sixteen-year-old self flying in the opposite direction, no thought in her head but to get to Ireland, to be in the country Josephine had loved.

'Oof!'

The collision, as she rounds a bend, knocks her phone from her hand, sends it skidding down the path.

'Sorry –' The man who crashed into her rushes to retrieve it: she doesn't recognise him until he's on his way back to her. 'Think it's OK,' he says, handing it over.

Stony-faced. Not surprising, given their last encounter.

'Thank you,' she says, beginning to move off – and then she halts. 'Hang on,' she says, but already he's vanished around the corner. Desperate to get away from her. She hurries after him. 'Wait!' she calls. He stops dead and turns. He watches warily as she approaches.

'Listen,' she says, 'I might have been a bit hard on you, that time we met.'

He shoves his hands into his pockets and makes no reply.

'What I mean is, I don't know the circumstances – I mean the situation. I shouldn't assume, is what I'm saying.'

Still no response. He could help her out.

'I'm trying to say sorry,' she says.

'Say it then.'

She stares at him. 'What?'

'Say sorry. If you really mean it.'

Annoyance rises. She takes a breath. 'Look, you could be a bit more – gracious about it.'

'Jesus,' he says, 'are you sorry or aren't you?'

She glares at him – and then, to her astonishment, he grins. 'You're so easy to wind up.'

He's winding her up? He can sing for his apology. She wheels and stalks off – but it's his turn to chase after. 'Heather, hang on, listen to me. Hang on, please –'

'I've got to pick up Lottie,' she says, not breaking her stride, but he catches up and walks beside her, giving her little choice but to hear what he has to say.

'Seriously,' he says, 'thank you. I did feel under attack the other night, but I can see where you were coming from. And in a way, you did have justification.'

She stops. He stops.

'Look,' he says, unsmiling now, 'like I told you that night, it wasn't my idea to chuck out you and Lottie, honestly it wasn't. It was the last thing I wanted, and I should have done more to prevent it.'

She has no quick response to this. Maybe he could have prevented it – but at what cost to himself, or his children? She can't blame him for wanting to protect them.

'Yvonne and I have split up,' he says then. 'You may have heard.'

'I heard something.' Things get around, particularly when children share classes. No need to say Nora had told her: it could as easily have been Lottie, or another parent in the class.

'I know it might sound like I'm blaming her now, when she's not here to defend herself—'

'No,' she says. 'Actually, it makes sense. She never took to me.'

'You made her feel guilty,' he says. 'You were doing what she should have done.'

'You mean looking after Gerry?'

'Yeah. I wanted Dad to come and live with us after his stroke, but she wouldn't hear of it. It suited her perfectly when you stepped in and took over, but it didn't stop her resenting you. You showed her up. Every time we went to see him you reminded her that she'd refused to take him in.'

'He wouldn't have been happy,' Heather says, 'having to quit his home.' Not to mention having to live with Yvonne, the daughter-in-law who just about tolerated him when they called to see him, who never had a genuinely kind word to say to him. 'It was best to leave him where he was.'

'Yeah, I can see that in hindsight ... Anyway, I'm the one who's sorry. I should have stopped her pushing you out – and I should have insisted you got the house in the will too, but I didn't.'

They're about the same height. He's – what? Fifty, maybe sixty pounds lighter than Heather. Slight frame for a man, not muscular. Yvonne isn't big: she's wiry, but she must be strong. Strong enough to push him around, strong enough to give him a thump whenever he didn't toe the line, whenever he attempted to stand up to her.

'Let's call it quits,' he says. 'On the sorry front, I mean.'

She tries not to smile at that, but a little one breaks through. 'Can I ask you something?' she says. 'Just out of curiosity.'

'Go on.'

'What did you think when you found out I'd bought Gerry's house?'

'I was glad,' he says, without hesitation. 'I thought it was right that you got to live in it. Surprised too, though – I'd assumed you had no money, but you paid over the odds for it.'

'My folks pitched in,' she says. True, in a manner of speaking. 'I don't imagine Yvonne was too happy when she heard who was buying.'

A wry grin. 'No. Not too happy.'

'But the money softened the blow.'

'Exactly.'

There's a pause.

'Well,' he says, 'I'm glad we cleared things up. I'd better let you get off.'

'I was sixteen,' she says.

In the act of turning away, he stops. Looks quizzical.

'When I started looking after Gerry. Not eighteen, like I said.' As long as they're telling the truth, she may as well go the whole hog. Not much he can do about it now.

He frowns. 'Sixteen? You're joking, aren't you? This is a wind up.'

'Nope. My folks put me on a plane for England. I was supposed to spend two years in a kind of swanky finishing school, but I … changed my mind and came here instead. They weren't exactly thrilled when they found out.'

'Jesus.' He shakes his head slowly. 'We employed a sixteen-year-old to look after my father. We probably broke the law.'

'I was mature,' she insists. 'I think I did a pretty good job.'

'So mature you got pregnant.'

He's mad. Now who's getting wound up? 'I did a good job,' she repeats. 'Didn't I?'

'You had no right to lie like that.'

'OK.' She turns away. She shouldn't have brought it up. Now she's gone and made things tricky between them again.

'I wish you wouldn't keep walking off.'

Here he comes again. No getting rid of him.

'Look, I'm not denying you did a good job – but you should have been honest.'

'Really? Like you would have employed a sixteen-year-old.'

'To look after my bedridden father? Of course I wouldn't.'

They reach Madge's house. 'Lottie's in here,' she says curtly, lifting the knocker. 'I think we have it all said, don't you?'

'I don't know. Any other lies you want to confess to?'

She lowers the knocker with a loud sigh. 'Why don't you let it go? It was over eight years ago, for crying out loud. I didn't kill your father, I looked after him as well as anyone would have – and for your information, he loved having a baby in the house. I would leave her in his room when I had to clean: he'd sit up in bed just gazing at her in her carrier. Sometimes I put her down for her nap in the bed beside him, and I'd sing them both to sleep. He was damn lucky to have me looking after him!'

He scratches his cheek, runs a hand through his hair. 'Don't push it,' he says.

'Well, he was – and I was happy to be there. We got on wonderfully – he was like a dad for me too, and a damn sight nicer to me than my own. Why do you think I bought the house? Because I loved living there, and because I knew Gerry wanted for it to be our home after his time.'

'OK,' he says. 'You're right. No point in getting mad now.'

'Thank God for that.'

'Just one more thing. Did you ever tell Dad your real age?'

'No way. I was afraid he might get nervous, being looked after by a kid.' She risks a smile.

His face softens slightly. Not a smile, but not far off it. 'The truth is, I always thought you were great,' he says in a rush. 'You were brilliant with him. I never thanked you properly for looking after him. So now you're what – twenty-four?'

'Twenty-five.' She remembers her parents, and the promised follow-up phone call. 'Listen, I gotta get going.'

'Right.' He extends a hand. 'Truce,' he says, and she shakes it.

'Truce,' she repeats. 'See you around.'

He turns from her again, starts to walk off.

'Hey,' she calls, an impulse coming to her, 'I wouldn't mind showing you the house sometime, if you ever wanted to see it again.' Why not? Why not let all that water run under that bridge? 'Not right now, there's a call I'm expecting – but maybe another time.'

He looks back. He wasn't expecting that. She can almost see the cogs in his brain pattering about, wondering what to do. 'That would be good,' he says slowly.

'How about Saturday afternoon?'

'I think I could manage that.'

'We go to the market in the morning but we'll be back around two. Why don't you swing by at two thirty?'

'OK,' he says, lifting a hand. 'Thank you. See you then. Say hi to Madge,' he adds, and it hits her only then that he'd know all the old neighbours, of course he would. This was where he'd grown up, where he'd spent his childhood and adolescence.

She was wrong about him. Her mind all made up until Nora, and now he himself, unmade it for her. She bangs the knocker at Madge's, and waits until the new kitten is installed in her carrier. Tinkerbell, Lottie's christened her, because the teacher is reading *Peter Pan* to them at school.

'Guess what?' Heather says, as they walk the short distance home with the carrier between them. 'I have a surprise for you.'

Lottie looks up at her hopefully. 'Chicken nuggets for dinner?'

Poor kid, such low expectations. 'Better than that. We're going to see your granddad and grandma. They want to meet you.'

The child's eyes widen. 'You mean – in America?'

'I do. We're going to fly in a plane.'

'Cool! Can Tinkerbell come?'

'I'm afraid not, honey. She'd hate it – cats don't really enjoy flying – but I'm sure Madge will be happy to look after her.' Hopefully. They'll bring her back a nice gift. 'Your grandma and grandpa are really looking forward to getting to know you. They're gonna call you on the phone in a bit to say hi.'

She'll book the flights this evening. Cost won't come into it. Hell, they can fly first class. Even though she has no interest in it, she can't deny that money comes in handy now and again.

'I hope they like me,' Lottie says, as Heather pushes the front-door key into the lock. 'Granddad and Grandma, I mean.'

Heather regards her child, her precious gift. 'They're gonna love you, sweetheart.'

They'd better. She'll really and truly kill them if they don't.

Emily

THEY'RE HAVING AN AFFAIR. EXCEPT, of course, they're not, with neither of them promised to someone else. But the secrecy makes it feel like that.

'I'll tell them,' she promises.

'When?'

'Soon.'

'How soon?'

'Soon.'

He pretends to be cross. He isn't cross. 'I've told Mum,' he says, winding one of her curls around his finger. She'd forgotten how he liked to do that.

'What did she say?'

'She's delighted.'

Will Emily's parents be delighted? Far from it. She'll have to win them over. And Daniel will definitely need to be won over. Daniel will most assuredly not be delighted.

She wishes it wasn't complicated. She wishes she and Ferg had just met for the first time, instead of reconnecting after a traumatic split. Not that reconnecting is all that bad, when every day brings a reminder of why she fell for him first time round.

He sends her flowers, gorgeous bouquets that fill her living room with scent and colour. He orders things online to be delivered to her: a white china teapot, so delicate she can almost see through it; prints of her favourite paintings; a baby-blue scarf in such a fine cashmere weave that she's sure he's sending her an empty box for a joke; a white-gold neck chain from which a slender wishbone is suspended.

He phones every afternoon, and sometimes at night too, after the restaurant is closed. They speak like the lovers they are, like the lovers they've become again.

'Miss you.'

'Miss you too.'

'Wish you were here all the time.'

'I know.'

'I want to wake up with you every morning. I want to fall asleep with you in my arms.'

'Me too.'

'Love you.'

'Love you more.'

She loves him more.

It's different, this time round. There isn't the

heady rush she remembers, when he filled her thoughts every hour of the day, when the prospect of seeing him was almost unbearably exciting. Now it's slower, it's gentler. They've done the fireworks, they've gone beyond them – and who needs fireworks anyway, at twenty-nine?

She takes the bus to Dublin every Monday afternoon, after the usual Monday shopping and sorting and cleaning are out of the way. She makes her way to his apartment, where she puts leftovers into his oven and pours herself a glass of wine and sits on his balcony that overlooks the Liffey while she waits for him to come home to her.

The following day they breakfast together. She walks with him to his workplace and keeps going to the bus station, picking up on her way a box of Ferrero Rocher or a scented candle for Maud Clarke, who lives next door to the restaurant and feeds Barney while Emily is gone. You had a good trip? Maud asks every time, and Emily tells her she did, and no more is said.

Spending that time in Dublin every week is tricky. It means getting up earlier the other mornings to keep on top of her second job – but she doesn't grudge it, particularly at this time of the year, when daylight hours are long and generous. Time enough to worry about winter – who knows where the next few months will take them?

They meet only briefly on Saturdays, when he comes to town to see his mother. With Emily working, a snatched walk in what she has come to think of as their park is all they can manage. He hasn't been to the restaurant yet. I know I have to wait, he said, until we go public – but she hates that he can't put his face in there, in case one of her friends spots him.

She must tell them. She must make it soon.

She decides to start with Heather. Heather can be her sounding board.

'I figured you'd get back together,' Heather says. 'I guessed that would happen.'

'Did you? Am I that transparent?'

'You're that forgiving.'

'… Do you think I'm making a mistake?'

Heather lifts a shoulder. 'Do you?'

Does she? 'No. I wouldn't do it if I thought that.'

'No, of course you wouldn't.' Heather searches her face. 'Are you happy, Emily? Are you really happy with him? Does he really and truly make you happy?'

'Yes.'

'In that case, I wish you the very best of luck. I hope it works out this time.'

'Thanks … Are you all set for the States?'

'Boy, are we ever. Lottie's already packed fourteen times – or that's what it feels like.'

'How are you getting to the airport?'

Heather picks at a thread in her sleeve. 'We have a ride organised. We're all set.'

'Safe trip. Hope it goes well.'

On impulse, when Astrid shows up the following day for lunch, Emily tells her too. Another sounding board, another who never knew Ferg.

'I've got back together with a man I was engaged to,' she says. They've opted to sit outside on the orange bench while they await Astrid's taxi, the rest of the lunchtime customers having departed, and the day being warm and sunny.

Astrid turns to face her. 'You were engaged to him?'

'Yes, a long time ago.'

'And may I ask, dear, what prevented you from getting married?'

It's kindly put, and it's a legitimate question. Emily must answer truthfully. 'He panicked, Astrid. He couldn't go through with it. He ... never turned up at the church.'

She sees Astrid digesting this. 'So you had no warning.'

'No.'

'And afterwards? Did he come and explain?'

'No, he left the country.' How badly it reflects on him. How cruel it makes him sound. 'But he's different now, really he is. It was four years ago, and he's apologised. We're both older – and we don't have to get married. Lots of people don't.'

She stops. Astrid lets the silence drift on. Has Emily offended her with implications of living as a married couple without the blessing of a church, or any institution?

A man walks past them carrying a stack of books. A jet-black cat sprawls in the dappled shade of a nearby rowan tree. Emily doesn't remember seeing it before, wonders if Barney has crossed paths with it. A small blue van pulls up outside the carpet shop: its driver gives them a cheery wave on his way in.

'But I think,' Astrid says, lifting her hand in a return wave, 'that you would like to be a bride. I think you would like to be a wife.'

Emily watches the cat as it rises unhurriedly, and stretches forelimbs and hind limbs in typical cat fashion, and settles down again. 'Well, I— Maybe some day. There's no rush.'

The truth is, she can't think about another wedding day, not when the first went so awry – but the truth also is that she would love that promise, that commitment. She would love the feeling of being entwined with someone, connected in that way with someone, for the rest of their days.

'Be careful,' Astrid says quietly. 'Look after your heart, dear.'

Yes, that's what they'll all say. Everyone will be concerned. Everyone will advise her to take care, to mind herself. But when it comes to love, there are no guarantees – so how can she be careful? What can she do but trust him not to run away again?

'I didn't love my husband,' Astrid says then. 'Or rather, I wasn't in love with him, I never fell in love with him. But he was a good, decent man, and I felt I'd be safe with him, and I was. And over the years, a kind of love grew in me, and I was content in our marriage.'

The first time she's spoken of him. Emily doesn't know what to say in response, so they sit in silence as the minutes tick by, as the driver of the blue van leaves again, as the cat dozes on.

'What about your garden?' Emily asks at length. 'How's that going?'

'The garden,' Astrid repeats, winding the handles of her cloth bag between her fingers. 'It's a work in progress,' she says, nodding. 'It will take a while.'

'Isn't Bill's daughter doing it, or did I imagine that?'

Astrid starts to speak, and catches herself. And then she starts again. 'Well,' she says, 'that was the plan.' She stops. 'This is in confidence, Emily.'

'Of course.'

'She called to the house. Christine. It must be more than two weeks ago now.'

Christine, yes. Emily had forgotten the name.

'So she's started?'

Astrid shakes her head. 'She said she would, and she was to come back the following day – but she never turned up.'

'Really? That's … odd. And she didn't ring to say why?'

'No.' Astrid lifts a hand, lets it drop. 'I feel,' she begins, and comes to another halt. 'I think there are problems,' she says, and Emily remembers Bill bringing flowers to his dead wife on her anniversary, standing alone by her grave in the cemetery, unaccompanied by their daughter, the child they had made together.

She shouldn't have talked to him about Ferg that day; it wasn't the time or the place. It's just that there's something lovely about Bill, something warm and sympathetic. He seemed the ideal person to confide in, when she was trying to decide if she'd done the right thing in getting back with Ferg. Would you think a person deserves a second chance? she'd asked, and Bill had said definitely, as she'd sensed he would. Like her, Bill would give everyone a second chance.

But he looked so downcast that day, and he left the cemetery right afterwards. He hasn't set foot in the restaurant since.

'I haven't seen him lately,' she says. 'Bill, I mean.'

'I met him not so long ago,' Astrid replies, 'outside the nursing home. I was in a taxi – on my way here, in fact. I offered him a lift, but he told me he'd already eaten.'

'Oh …' Could Emily have offended him in some way? Surely not. She replays their short exchange from the cemetery in her head, and finds nothing he could possibly object to.

'I'm guessing Christine is on his mind … You and I don't have children, Emily. It's hard for us to fathom what might drive a parent and child apart, but it must be something significant – and it must cause such sorrow when it happens.'

'Yes ...'

You and I don't have children. It's hard for her to hear it. But unlike Astrid, she has time. At twenty-nine she still has lots of time – and now she has Ferg again to make it happen. Four years ago, the notion of them having children was something they rarely talked about, a consideration they could push ahead of them into the future, but she remembers them agreeing that they'd like it to happen sometime.

There will be a child for them, more than one: she's certain of it. Eventually.

And eventually she summons her courage and tells her brother Daniel.

'I just hope you know what you're doing, Em,' he says, not showing much surprise at the news. Maybe guessing, like Heather had, that they were going to reunite, despite Emily's assurances that they wouldn't. 'You know I wish it hadn't happened – I wish you were with someone else – but I hope it turns out OK for you.'

'Fingers crossed,' she says lightly, and he doesn't return her smile.

'Will you be nice to him?' she asks. 'Or civil, at least?' He shrugs and says he will for her sake, and she has to be content with that.

Her old friends, the ones who went through the bad time with her, react in precisely the way she expected them to. 'How could you?' they ask. 'What were you thinking, Em? What on earth possessed you?' And she tries to explain, tries to convince them that he's changed, but she sees the doubt in their faces, and she knows none of them truly believes that this time she and Ferg will last. She'll just have to prove it, they both will, by staying together.

Sarah, at least, is pleased. I'm so very glad, she said, when Ferg phoned home last time Emily was in Dublin, and passed the phone to her. You're made for one another, anyone can see that. He's so happy now, Emily. Thank you for giving him another chance. You must come to tea, any evening that suits you.

I have some good news, she writes to her own parents. Better in a letter than on the phone. *Fergal is back in Ireland, he's working in Dublin now, and we're going to try again. We've sorted it all out, and we're making a fresh start. I wish you could see how sorry he is about what happened. I really feel it will work this time, and I hope you can both be happy for me.* She posts it and waits – and now it's three days later and her phone is ringing, as she's kneading dough in the early morning.

'Emily, I don't believe it,' her mother says without preamble. 'I can't believe you're having anything more to do with that man.'

'I just feel he deserves another –'

'He deserves *nothing*, not a thing from you!'

'But he's sorry, he really is – and if I can forgive him, surely you can.'

'Emily, please don't make us out to be the unreasonable ones here. Do you honestly not remember what he did, and how you were after it? You were heartbroken, the man broke your heart – and he didn't even have the courage to do it to your face!'

And on it goes. And her father, when he comes on the line, is no easier to convince.

'I'm very sorry to hear it,' he says. 'You might call it good news, but we certainly don't see it like that. We're worried for you, Emily, both of us.'

'There's no need to worry, honestly.'

But he will, and so will her mother, and so will everyone who recalls what happened, and there is nothing she can do about that.

'I have to go,' she says. 'I'm making bread.'

And tomorrow is Saturday, and she'll see him again – and now that everyone knows, they can meet wherever they want. No more secrecy, no more avoiding people who remember what happened. It'll take a while, there will be awkward encounters, but in time people will forgive him, like she's forgiven him.

She kneads dough, and counts the hours till three o'clock tomorrow.

Bill

'BILL, THERE YOU ARE,' MRS PHELAN SAYS, materialising as he's taking off his jacket, before he's had time to pull on his overalls. 'We've had an offer of paint from that new place on the Dublin road – I sent them a letter last week.'

He'll bet she did. She's coaxed free stuff from the most reluctant businesses in the town – and newcomers, eager to create a good first impression among the community, are particularly susceptible to her brand of pleading. 'That's good news. How much are they letting us have?'

'Enough to give the outside a facelift. I told them you'll be around this morning to pick it up.'

'Very good.'

'And I thought you might as well make a start on it today, as long as the weather's staying fine. I've got a young lad to help you, a neighbour of mine. He'll be here in an hour or so, after his paper round.'

'Right.'

He wonders how helpful a young lad who might never have lifted a paintbrush in his life will be, but he keeps quiet. Don't condemn till you try – a great phrase of his mother's, and often employed at the dinner table when Bill, a picky eater in his youth, was exhibiting a reluctance to sample an unfamiliar vegetable.

It's a good day for outdoor work, dry and calm. No sun, but no sign of rain clouds either. His kind of weather, always has been. He never was a fan of jetting off to places where the sun was waiting to scald you, never saw the attraction in laying yourself out on a beach like a joint of beef waiting to be roasted.

He drives the minibus to the paint shop and meets the manager, who shows him the large tubs he's set aside for the nursing home. 'Cream,' he said. 'That's what she asked for.'

Same as before, Mrs Phelan playing safe. Bill would go for a new look if it was up to him – a sky blue, or maybe a bright yellow. Probably just as well it's not his decision. He loads up and sets off again, choosing streets that will avoid the roadworks that held him up on the way. The new route takes him past the cemetery, and he thinks back to his encounter with Emily, and her question to him, and his response.

And now, stupidly, he finds himself unable to return to The Food of Love. Stupid, because what does it matter if she's with someone else, given that she was never going to be his? But it seems it does matter, this knowledge, this certainty, that there's another man.

Feels like months since he was at the restaurant, rather than just a couple of weeks. He misses her all the time, she's caused a constant ache to lodge underneath his breastbone, but still he can't bring himself to walk into the place again.

He misses the others too, the friends he's made there. He misses Heather's confidence and quick wit, and Astrid with her quiet wisdom and her positivity. But maybe after all he was never really the right fit for the place. No matter how many times he went there it never became altogether easy for him, walking in alone. He always had to battle against that edge of anxiety, the self-consciousness that urged him to turn and bolt – and when no familiar faces were to be seen, and he found himself among strangers, there was the added challenge of keeping back what he couldn't admit to, and making the rest sound interesting. If it wasn't for Emily and the other two, he'd probably have stopped going there long ago.

His mind turns to his other pressing concern, and again he gives himself a mental kick for ever having sent Christine to Astrid. What a monumental blunder that was. How mortifying that she had shown up unannounced at Astrid's, and then failed to return as agreed. How could she have done that, knowing Astrid to be his friend? How could she have so little regard for him?

She hasn't been home since but she will, as long as her father is fool enough to go on letting her in, as long as he keeps enabling her. He won't mention Astrid the next time she appears, and of course she won't either. They'll go on as they have done, as they'll keep doing till he ends his days, or she does.

But one thing will change. From now on he's vowed to stop asking her to let him find help for her. She'll never agree, he knows that now. The people who told him otherwise are wrong. This is her life and it won't change, and the sooner he acknowledges that, the better. He'll accept their occasional interactions, pitiful episodes as they are, and he won't look for more.

'This is Eoin,' Mrs Phelan says when he gets back to the home. The boy is lanky, with longish hair the colour of a conker, and a face dotted with freckles. Mid-teens, by the look of him. 'Just finished Transition Year,' he says, in reply to Bill's question.

Bill hands him a pair of overalls. 'Any idea what you want to do when you leave school?'

'Doctor,' he says, the word accompanied by a bashful grin as he peels off his leather jacket and climbs into the overalls. 'If I'm smart enough,' he adds, buttoning up. 'Something in healthcare anyway.'

Ambitious – and must have brains if he's considering a career in medicine. 'You ever painted before?' Bill enquires.

'Yeah. I helped my father do our house a few months ago – and I've painted my room a couple of times.'

Good, not a complete novice then. They start on the prep work, taking wire brushes to the old flaking paint, Eoin staying on the ground and Bill up the ladder. No great loss to anyone if Bill takes a tumble, but a future doctor needs to be kept safe.

The morning passes while the sun slides in and out of clouds, and the rain holds off. They chat, when they're in earshot of one another.

'Where's your paper round?' Bill asks, and Eoin names a few streets, and one is familiar.

'Do you deliver to a woman called Astrid? I'm pretty sure she lives on Cedar something.'

'I don't know first names, only last.'

What's her last name? Bill can't recall it. 'She's over ninety, a little frail but mentally very sound. She's Austrian, although she's lived here for years.'

'That sounds like Mrs Carmody in number twelve. She's nice. She always gives me biscuits or stuff when she's paying me.'

Carmody. It rings a bell. He wonders how she is, and if she's found someone to do what Christine couldn't, or wouldn't.

'You got kids?' Eoin asks later.

'Daughter. She's a gardener.' How quickly the lie comes, how easily it slips out. 'She's moved out of home, but she comes back every now and again for dinner.' The almost-lie, the nearly truth. He wonders suddenly if this boy, who seems pretty level-headed, has ever been offered drugs. Maybe it's a rite of passage for kids now; maybe they all get a chance to take the wrong path. Equal opportunities.

He wonders if there would have been a different outcome if he and Betty had had a son instead of a daughter. Would a son have coped better when his mother died? Would he have said no if someone, some scumbag, offered him something at the back of the bicycle shed, or wherever she'd taken the first step on the road to hell?

Enough, enough. He prises the lid from a tub of paint as Eoin sweeps up the flakes. 'You got brothers and sisters?'

'I have a little brother, and one sister. She works in the cinema. She lets me in free when her boss isn't around.'

'Handy.'

He and Betty used to go every Friday or Saturday night without fail. James Bond they liked, and Woody Allen. Bill loved the old black-and-whites, Laurel and Hardy, anything with Bette Davis or Victor Mature, all the early Hitchcocks. Betty was mad for a musical. Bill didn't share her enthusiasm: he thought it took the good out of a story when someone suddenly burst into song. Still, they went along to whatever was on offer until Christine arrived. They resumed when she was six months old, and they finally felt able to trust a babysitter to keep her alive till they got home.

At twelve, the lunchtime bell rings. 'Grub's up,' Bill says, and they down tools and head to the dining room, where they're served the roast chicken and carrots that's being dished out to the residents. It's not so bad, Bill has found. He's getting used to it. The meatloaf on Wednesdays is a bit bland, but salt helps – and why not take it when it's free, and he's entitled to it?

Glad you finally decided to join us, Mrs Phelan said when he first put his head around the dining-room door. She sat him at the staff table with Julie and Jean who clean the rooms, Maurice the secretary, Cathy the treasurer, Olivia the receptionist, and Maurice's nephew Andy, who comes on Mondays and Thursdays to pare corns and cut toenails, and generally attend to the ailments of ageing, tired feet.

Anytime you need a pedicure, he said to Bill, don't be shy, that's what I'm here for – and Bill, who'd never had a pedicure in his life, and who could never envisage a situation where he might feel the need of one, thanked him and said he was grand for the moment.

'Are you eating that?' Eoin enquires, and Bill surrenders his untouched bowl of stewed prunes and custard, thinking of Emily's warm chocolate tart with its crushed nut base and drizzle of berry sauce, or the glory of her gooseberry and pear cinnamon crumble.

It's approaching five o'clock when they finish the

first coat. 'You did well,' Bill says, as they shake out dust sheets and peel off overalls. 'You coming back tomorrow?'

'Yeah. I'll be here after my paper round again. Una said two or three days.'

A teenage boy calls her Una. Bill needs to get over himself. As he ties the laces on his shoes, a car horn sounds outside.

'That might be my dad,' Eoin says. 'He was bringing some people to the airport. He said he'd pick me up on the way back.'

'You head off so. See you in the morning.'

After rinsing the brushes and roller heads, Bill goes to the day room for the piano session. By now Gloria is well enough to be wheeled in for the proceedings, where she makes a valiant attempt to accompany Bill like before. Her voice has sadly diminished – even when Bill plays as quietly as he can she's barely audible – but her face is alight, and everyone chimes in heartily when the choruses come along. Buoying her up, it sounds like. Willing her to keep going.

It's gone six by the time he turns in at his gate. Nobody waits for him by the front door: he feels the usual mix of relief and disappointment. A shower, he thinks, to rinse away the grubbiness left behind after a day of painting. A bite to eat, and a quick trot around the block with Sherlock after that, followed by a read of the paper he picked up as usual on his way to work and brought home unopened, his flick through it after lunch missed today because of Eoin being around.

He steps into the hall, giving his customary whistle. Nothing happens. No eager tapping of claws across the kitchen floor, no scratching on the door.

He hangs his jacket on the banister. 'Sherlock?' he calls. Nothing.

He enters the kitchen and sees no dog. Fearful now, he steps into the utility room – and there is Sherlock, lying in his bed, giving a small whine at the sight of Bill, but making no effort to rise.

Bill crouches. 'What is it, boy? What's wrong?' He lifts paws and runs his hands along the animal's flank, searching for signs of injury that he doesn't find. He feels the scalp-prickle of anxiety.

Sherlock is ten, or thereabouts. Not a thoroughbred, far from it: he came to them as a rescue dog, when Betty got her diagnosis. Sherlock was her idea. I think we should get a dog, she said. I think it would be good for me – and Bill, wanting to do everything for her, ready to put himself in her place if he could, drove the three of them to the animal-welfare place, and there they picked out the scrawny little pup that had been found, trembling and terrified, on the side of a busy road.

It was only after Betty's death, when the anger and grief took up what felt like permanent residence inside him, when he and Christine started to draw further apart instead of closer, that he understood who the dog had really been for.

'OK,' he says, pulling a bath towel from the laundry basket. He bundles Sherlock into it and lifts the whining animal as gently as he can into his arms. The vet is open from six till eight on weekday evenings. May as well just go, instead of trying to describe symptoms over the phone. Hopefully it won't be too busy.

It's busy enough. A resigned-looking Alsatian sits silently by its owner's chair; a yapping terrier strains on its leash towards a cat that regards it disdainfully from the safety of its carrier. A pair of black-and-white pups huddle together in another carrier: hard to see where one ends and the other begins.

Bill checks in at the reception desk and takes a chair next to a small girl. Sherlock slumps on his lap, letting out an occasional whine. He'd outgrown his carrier within a year, and there never seemed a need to get another. Up to this, he was well enough to walk on the lead to the vet's for his shots. Up to this, he was never sick.

'It's OK,' Bill murmurs, stroking the dog's ears. 'You'll be OK, fellow.' You'd better be OK.

'What's his name?'

He glances up. The child, no more than four or five, is regarding Sherlock dispassionately. The woman accompanying her, presumably the mother, is distracted by her attempts to control the yapping terrier.

'Sherlock,' Bill says.

'Is he sick?'

'I think so.'

'Is he going to die?'

'Well, I hope not.'

One of the surgery doors opens. A woman appears with a poodle sporting a bandaged foreleg, and a cone around his neck. The Alsatian is summoned in.

'Our dog ate my dad's medicine,' the child pronounces, again exhibiting no evidence of concern.

'Did he?' Medicine. Could mean anything.

'Mum is afraid he'll die.'

'Who – your dad?'

'No, the dog. His name is Ollie.'

'Oh.' He regards the madly yapping Ollie. 'He seems OK to me.'

'But he still could die cos of the medicine. Dogs aren't supposed to eat people's medicine.'

'I suppose not.'

The main door opens. Bill turns instinctively – and in she walks, the sight of her, so unexpected, causing somersaults within him. Pale blue coat, jeans, blue shoes, hair loose and tumbling. Holding the handle of a carrier in which a plump grey cat crouches. Of all the vets in all the world.

She spots him on her way to the desk. He doesn't miss the beat that passes before she offers him a tentative smile. 'Hi Bill,' she says. She never hesitated before: her wide, happy smile came readily and easily, every time he walked through the restaurant door. He lived for that smile, and now it's diluted, and wary, and he only has himself to blame. She'll be wondering why he's stopped coming to eat in the restaurant. She'll be uncertain of his reaction now.

'Long time no see,' she says.

He must make some response. The best he can manage is a blurted, 'I've been busy.'

The smile, the half-smile, stays in place. 'Let me check in,' she says. He follows her to the desk with his eyes. I've been busy. Sweet Jesus.

'Your face looks funny,' the child announces loudly. Heads swivel to check out his funny face. He feigns deafness and turns his attention to Sherlock, who gives a feeble lick to his hand. 'Good boy,' he murmurs, willing the girl to direct her attention elsewhere.

Emily returns and takes the vacant seat next to him. 'It's good to see you, Bill.'

He gets a whiff of the scent he remembers. 'You too.' He wonders how she can be here at this hour – and then he remembers it's Tuesday, and the restaurant is closed. Her right hand rests on the carrier: she wears a silver ring he hasn't seen before, a small pale blue stone set into the band. From behind the second surgery door comes a sudden yowl, and the sound of something steel clattering to the floor.

The blasted child is still hovering, crouching to peer into Emily's carrier. 'Is your cat sick?'

Emily shakes her head. 'No, he's just here for his shots.'

'What are they?'

'Something to stop him getting sick.'

Short silence.

'Our dog ate my dad's medicine.'

'Oh dear. I hope he'll be OK.'

'His name is Ollie.'

'That's a good name for a dog.'

'What's your cat's name?'

'Barney.'

'My friend is Barney. He's a boy, not a cat. A crayon got stuck up his nose, and Mrs Furlong had to pull it out. Her face got all red.'

'Oh dear.'

Bill listens to the exchange, stroking Sherlock's ear. From the corner of his eye he can see Emily as she leans slightly towards the child, pushing curls behind a shoulder. Her hip is inches from Bill's.

He loves her. That hasn't changed. That remains a fixed and immovable state of affairs. He's a fool for love.

The first surgery door reopens. The Alsatian looks no less resigned. The noisy terrier is summoned in, along with mother and child. Almost immediately, the second surgery door opens to let out a man with a ginger cat in a carrier, and the entwined pups are brought in. Bill is next in the queue. He and Emily are left alone in the waiting room, apart from the receptionist who's tapping at her phone and taking no notice at all of them.

'What's wrong with your dog?' Emily asks.

'I don't know. He was out of sorts when I got home from work.'

'Poor thing.' She reaches across to lay a hand lightly on one of Sherlock's forelegs. 'Is he old?'

'Ten. About that.'

'He has the look of a collie about him.'

'He's a bit of everything, as far as I know. Not a lot of pedigree going on.'

She rewards him with a smile that doesn't last. 'Bill,' she says, in a new voice. 'I have to ask you something.'

No. Don't ask. Please don't ask me.

'Why do you not come to the restaurant any more? Was it something I said, that day in the cemetery?'

'No,' he lies. He's always been a useless liar. He can feel the heat in his cheeks. 'It's nothing you said. I've just been … busy with various … stuff. Work, and that.'

He can see the doubt in her face. An idiot wouldn't believe him. 'I'd hate to feel that I'd upset you in any way—'

'You haven't upset me.'

'You're not mad about anything?'

He finds a smile. 'Not mad, no.' If she only knew. If he could only tell her.

'Well, that's a relief.' She dips her head to focus on Sherlock again, causing her hair to tumble forward. She lifts a hand to sweep it back. 'It's just that, well, the thing is, I might not be here for … Well, there's a chance I'll be moving away,' glancing up, finding his gaze, 'and I'd hate for you not to come in again before that happens.'

He feels a swoop in his gut. 'You're moving?'

'Well, it's not … Nothing's settled, or anything. It's just a … a possibility. And it might not happen for ages. I just don't know.'

She's moving. She's leaving. Logic would say it was a good thing. Logic would point out that she'd be no more out of his reach than if she stayed in town, and having her move away meant there was no danger of bumping into her accidentally, like now.

But logic doesn't come into it. The thought of her not being around any more is unconscionable.

'Where?' he asks. 'Where are you moving to?'

'Well, it would be Dublin – but like I say, it might not be for a long time.'

Dublin. No. 'What about the restaurant?'

'Well, I'd have to sell it. I don't see how —'

'You can't,' he says.

She tips her head a fraction to the side. Says nothing.

'You can't move away. What about all the people who have nobody to eat with? You can't just – you can't just desert them.' Stop talking, his horrified inner self commands, shut your mouth – but he doesn't stop, he shuts nothing. 'They're depending on you. You can't just walk away from them.' Every word makes him sound more ridiculous and pathetic. He hears it: so must she.

He comes to a halt. They regard one another. A laugh floats out from behind one of the surgery doors. The receptionist sneezes. 'Pardon me,' she says, without looking up.

'I don't want to close it,' Emily replies then, in a small voice. 'Really, it's the last thing I want, but I have to … think of the future.'

The future. His future without her. Her future with someone else, with second-chance man.

'Bill Geraghty?'

He turns to see the vet beckoning him in, the owner of the tiny pups coming out without them.

'Will you come back?' Emily asks. 'To the restaurant.'

He gets to his feet with his bundle. 'Not much point,' he says, 'if you're moving on,' and her face changes, and immediately he wants to punch himself in the head. He walks away, his heart in his boots.

He tries and fails to push her from his mind while the vet examines Sherlock. He'd forgotten precisely how pretty she is, how beautiful her eyes, her hair, her everything. Why did he say that, how could he be offhand, so dismissive?

He becomes aware that the vet is speaking. 'Sorry?'

'Has he thrown up? Does he have diarrhoea?'

'Not that I saw, but I didn't check outside.'

'I'm guessing stomach bug. His vitals are normal and I don't feel anything iffy, but I'd like to keep him here overnight, see how he is in the morning.

If there's no improvement, we'll do an X-ray. That OK?'

'Fine.' He'd had no idea there were overnight facilities in the clinic. 'Will I call you, or …?'

'We'll give you a ring when we know more. Keep your phone near you tomorrow.'

He prays for her to be gone from the waiting area, and for once his prayer is answered. He drives home with his empty towel and lets himself into the darkening house. He stands in the hall for a second, listening instinctively for the clicking of claws on tiles before he remembers. The silence seems absolute, even though Sherlock, in the ten years that they've had him, has barked a total of about three times.

He flicks on the hall light. He catches sight of himself in the mirror. He frowns and steps closer – and discovers that his face is covered with tiny cream spots. Wonderful. The icing on the damn cake. Your face looks funny, the small girl at the vet's said, and he thought his broken heart must have been showing on it. Emily didn't comment, or Eoin, even though they must have seen the spots. The vet said nothing either. Everyone very polite, apart from the no-filter child.

His doorbell rings, startling him. Emily, he thinks, his heart giving a leap. He'll say sorry, he'll call himself a fool and beg her to forgive him. And then he realises that it couldn't be Emily, because she doesn't know where he lives. He opens the door to find Mrs Twomey on the step.

'Bill, I saw you earlier bringing your dog away, and now you're back without him. I hope nothing is wrong.'

She never misses a thing. She must spend her day positioned behind the net curtains. But she's concerned enough to leave her house and ring his bell. Tonight, that will do.

'He's being kept in. They think stomach bug.'

'Oh, that doesn't sound too—' She breaks off to peer closely at him. 'Bill, what on earth is that on your face?'

'Paint,' he says, stepping back. 'Come in.'

He makes tea and puts biscuits on a plate, despite her protests. She eats three, and tells him about the time Toto, an old dog of theirs, chewed in his puppyhood through the television cable just as they were about to tune in for the Eurovision. 'I wouldn't mind, but it was the year Johnny Logan won.'

'First or second time?'

'Second, I think.'

He tells her about painting the nursing home. She tells him of an aunt who, twenty years earlier, attempted to climb from the window of her nursing-home bedroom, convinced in her dementia that she was a teenage girl again, and bent on escaping to a dance.

He makes more tea.

'Tomorrow would be our fortieth wedding anniversary,' she says, halfway through her fresh cup, 'mine and Harry's', and the talk turns in that direction. Bill tells her of his own wedding day, when the rain never stopped, and of the upcoming nuptials of his nephew in England. Mrs Twomey tells him of a wedding in the town that never happened. 'A few years ago this would have been, just before I retired. A neighbour of a woman I used to work with, her fiancé didn't show up at the church on the day. Poor girl never saw it coming. Someone told me she's since opened a restaurant. I haven't been to it – I'm not much of a one for eating out.'

Bill drinks his tea. It's Emily, it has to be. Deserted on her wedding day: what kind of a man would do that to a woman? But now they're back together, and she's planning to move to Dublin, which means he must work there. She's giving up everything for him. Even if they really hurt you, should you trust them again if they tell you they're sorry? she'd asked Bill.

'I mustn't take any more of your time,' Mrs Twomey says, getting to her feet. 'This was nice, Bill. It gets quiet on your own, doesn't it?'

Later, scrubbing his face until it hurts, scraping paint from under his nails, the possibility occurs to him that Mrs Twomey is lonely. Does she have friends? He has no idea. She and Betty got on – they'd have regular chats over the hedge. Maybe she's still in contact with people she worked with, other nurses. Early sixties he seems to remember, when Harry died, so now she's close to seventy, if she hasn't already hit it.

What's her first name? Betty must have mentioned it, lots of times. It takes him a while, but he finally arrives at Carmel. Funny that he knew Harry as Harry, but she was always Mrs Twomey.

Funny too, how people can live side by side for years, for decades, how they can experience triumphs and endure tragedies in such close proximity, with just a few metres – a side passage, or sometimes nothing more than a shared wall – separating them. Funny how lives can run on parallel tracks, how they can intersect briefly every so often but never really connect on any but the most superficial level.

He thinks of how a father can yearn for the return of a lost child for weeks and months and years to no avail, how tears and pleas are equally useless tools when pitted against addiction.

He thinks of how a man can love a woman with his heart and his soul, and how she can be utterly unaware of it. He considers the two women who between them take over most of his waking thoughts, and the appalling truth that they are both out of his reach, both denied to him.

He steps from the shower and pats himself dry. He towels his hair roughly and pulls his fingers through it. He finds a T-shirt and boxer shorts and goes to bed. He thumps his pillow and turns onto his side and closes his eyes.

An hour later, still wide awake, he pushes back the bedclothes and fumbles for the switch of the bedside lamp. He sits on the side of the bed for a bit, yawning and rubbing his head, looking at his bare feet on the blue rug that Betty bought the week before she went to her doctor with a cough that wouldn't go away.

At length he goes in search of paper and a biro. He sits at the bureau in the corner of his room and draws down the hinged top.

He puts the biro to the page.

Dear Christine,
My only child, my precious girl. You lit up my life when they put you into my arms twenty-five years ago. I was unbelievably happy at the sight of you. I was also terrified I'd drop you and you'd break – but I didn't, and you didn't. It took over sixteen years for you to break, and when it happened, I broke too.
I'll always be your dad. You'll always be welcome in the house you once called home, but now I'm tired and I'm damaged, so I'm going to stop chasing impossible dreams, stop trying to fix my broken girl, and just go on loving her.
Dad

He turns to a fresh page. He writes again.

Dear Emily,
I'm writing to tell you that I love you. I've loved you from about my third visit to your restaurant. It might have been my fourth, I'm not sure. I just know that I walked in one lunchtime and you

smiled hello, and I knew that my bruised heart had surrendered again.

I understand that you don't love me back. I get that I'm too old for you, and that you love someone else. And even if those things weren't true I'd be no good for you, because I'm a mess, and pretty useless to anyone. And yet my feelings persist, and all I want is to see you, and be near you, and to watch you smile.

I hurt you tonight, and I hate myself for it. I also hate the thought of you moving away, but it's probably for the best. I'll try to forget you, but I'm making no promises.

I wish you a happy life.

Bill

He sets down the biro. He reads both letters once, and then rips them up and drops the pieces into the bin.

He switches on his computer, and opens his email.

Dear Claire,
You were right, I was wrong. It didn't work.
No need to answer this, just wanted to let you know.
John

He presses send, and off it goes. He returns to bed, and eventually he sleeps.

And the following morning, her answer is waiting in his inbox.

Dear John,

I'm so sorry.

Please don't lose heart. She will need you some day, I'm convinced of it.

Your friend,

Claire

Astrid

SHE'S SWEEPING THE BREAKFAST CRUMBS
from the kitchen floor when the doorbell rings. She
checks the time and sees nine fifty. Too late for the
postman, and Thursday is the wrong day for Pat,
and she's not expecting a supermarket delivery.

A meter reader maybe, or someone trying to sell
her a million television channels, or wanting her to
move her electricity account elsewhere. Or it might
be someone eager help her to find God, or Jehovah,
or whoever they believe in. She always says no, as
politely as she can, and still they keep coming. She
sets the brush and dustpan against the wall and goes
to answer it.

'Hello,' the girl says. Shoulders hunched, hands
thrust into her pockets. Same oversized jacket,
different trousers beneath, faded denim instead of
corduroy. Grey canvas pumps, might have been

white once upon a time. Hair ponytailed, not loose like before. Unsmiling.

'Christine. What are you doing here?'

'I've come to do the gardening,' she says. No intense stare today. Looking somewhere to the left of Astrid's elbow.

'You're over two weeks late. You didn't show up, and you didn't let me know why. I know you have my number. Your father told me he'd given it to you.'

'I lost it. Sorry.'

A lie? The truth? Does it even matter? 'In that case, you should have sent someone to tell me you couldn't come. It's not good enough. You really should have let me know.'

'… Sorry.'

She looks pitiful, so thin and pale. Should Astrid send her away? She's sorely tempted. But ten euro has already been invested – and she's here, she's come back. Astrid decides to focus on that, and let the rest go. Everyone deserves a second chance.

She steps aside. 'Come in,' she says. 'Better late than never, I suppose. You can do two hours, as we discussed.' Hard to imagine that she'll last two hours: she looks on the point of collapse.

They walk again through the hall and the kitchen to the patio. 'You can start by clipping that hedge. It needs a good tidy-up all round, top and sides. You'll find everything you need in the shed, clippers and a rake and a wheelbarrow. You can gather the clippings in the barrow and wheel them around to the brown compost bin at the side of the house. It won't all fit in, but do what you can, and I'll give you bags for the rest. There's a stepladder too, if you need it.'

Christine nods, her eyes fixed on the hedge.

'Is there anything you want before you start? A glass of water or a cup of tea?'

'No … thanks.'

'Right. I'll call you when the two hours are up. Please knock on the door if you need to use the bathroom, or anything else.'

'OK.' The girl moves off towards the shed, still wearing her enormous jacket. Go inside, Astrid orders herself. Leave her be. She'll do better when you're not watching her.

Back in the kitchen Astrid finishes sweeping the floor. After that she descales the kettle, washes and polishes the entire contents of the cutlery drawer, wipes down surfaces that don't need it, cleans the fridge. Avoiding the window and the patio doors, determinedly ignoring whatever may be happening beyond them.

As she replaces the fridge contents – milk, cheese and yogurt, the second half of the chicken stew she ate last night, jars of apple jelly and chutney – she decides she should offer some kind of sustenance when the two hours are up. The girl looks like she hasn't had a square meal in months.

She can have the remains of the stew that Astrid

was planning to eat this evening. It's no sacrifice: there are more of Pat's offerings waiting in the freezer, all of which can be heated from frozen.

She moves into the sitting room, leaving the doors open in case of a knock from the garden, and puts Wagner at a low volume on the record player. She finds her crossword book and makes a start on a new one, but her concentration fails her, and the clues she normally manages to solve remain impenetrable.

She takes her knitting from the basket by her chair and resumes the scarf in a burgundy shade that she started a couple of weeks ago for the nice boy who delivers the local paper. She thinks the colour will suit his red-brown hair. She's a slow, plodding knitter, her fingers not as cooperative as they used to be, but if she puts her mind to it he should have it by Halloween.

At length she returns to the kitchen and lights the oven and puts the stew in to reheat. Just before twelve, the savoury smell beginning to drift about the kitchen, she makes herself a cheese sandwich and plugs in the kettle, and sets the table for two. She opens the back door and steps onto the patio.

Oh no.

Parts of the hedge remain untouched, with the same wild straggling growth as before. Other sections have been hacked, attacked, with gaping holes where growth should be. The clippers sit on the grass as if flung there, blades open. Leaves and twigs litter the lawn. The rake leans crookedly against the hedge. There's no sign of the wheelbarrow.

Christine lies on her back in the centre of the garden, arms and legs akimbo. Her jacket has been tossed nearby, along with some kind of navy woollen garment. Her cheap-looking canvas shoes have been similarly discarded. The soles of her bare feet tilt outwards, and are dark. Her hair has come loose.

She could be a child, Astrid thinks, lying in such an abandoned way, surrendering herself completely to the earth. How stick-thin her arms are, exposed without her outer clothing, covered now by just a bottle green cotton top whose sleeves have been pushed above her elbows. How lean every part of her is, no breasts to speak of, stomach hollow, hip bones jutting beneath the light fabric of her jeans.

Could she be suffering from anorexia? Wouldn't it explain her undernourished appearance, and perhaps the trouble between her and Bill too? Anorexia, the deliberate denial of food to the body, would perplex and torment any father, would have him desperate to find a solution. But could Bill really have been so delusional as to consider Christine capable of physical work?

Astrid steps off the patio and crosses the lawn. As she approaches the prone figure, her eye is drawn to a red mark in the exposed crook of the girl's left inner elbow. Has she scratched herself on the hedge?

She stoops to get a closer look, and sees that it's not a scratch: it's a collection of small red dots, some scabbed, the skin beneath them patched with blue. She glances at the right arm, inside the right elbow, and sees the same mesh of dots peppering the skin there. Like puncture wounds, like the marks left behind after blood tests, a lot of blood tests. Or maybe caused by an allergy, or eczema.

Or …

And slowly, Astrid makes her way to the answer. Ah. Yes.

And everything makes sense then. Everything slots into place. Yes.

She knows very little of addiction, has had minimal contact with it. Over the years, at various social functions, she's noted people under the influence of alcohol, balance compromised, speech slurred. From time to time she has observed blank-eyed souls on the streets, removed from their surroundings. She's listened to tearful radio accounts of uncontrolled gambling, and the damage it can wreak. She has heard tell, through various means, at various times, of broken marriages, and destroyed families, and addiction-related deaths.

And here, lying in her garden this morning, is another addict, another slave to whatever poison she has been pumping into her veins. Moved out of home because of it, or maybe fell into wrong ways after she left the safety of her father's house. Living who knows where, begging no doubt for money to feed her habit. Asking for an advance so she could buy her next few hours of oblivion.

Astrid might have walked past her, might have dropped a few coins into her paper cup. You don't look into their eyes. You never look there, in case they look back, and show you too much.

She thinks of Bill, poor Bill, of his hunted expression at the mention of his daughter in their last conversation. All understandable now, his seizing his chance when Astrid mentioned needing someone for the garden. She feels no anger, no sense of betrayal, no fear. Pity is what she feels, for the father and the child.

'Christine,' she says quietly. 'Christine, wake up.'

The brown eyes flutter open. They look at Astrid. Do they see her?

'You fell asleep,' Astrid says. 'You're in my garden, Astrid's garden.'

A beat passes. They hold each other's gaze.

'Can you stand up? Can you do that?'

The girl gets clumsily to her feet, staggers slightly before finding her balance. Pulls down her sleeves, gives a slow shake to her head.

'Come inside,' Astrid says.

Without waiting for a response she returns to the house. In the kitchen she plugs in the kettle again. When it boils for the second time she makes tea and stands the pot on its trivet on the table. She takes the stew from the oven and ladles it into a bowl.

A sound makes her turn. Christine stands in the

doorway, her feet still bare, her hair pulled back carelessly into its ponytail.

'Let me get you slippers,' Astrid says. 'Those tiles are cold.'

'I'm alright,' Christine says – but Astrid goes anyway to her room and retrieves her slippers.

'Size seven,' she says, offering them. 'I have large feet, so you'll have plenty of room. Please put them on: you'll freeze otherwise.'

They're pink and cream check, and furry on the inside. Astrid bought them in the sales after Christmas, reduced from seventy euro – scandalous – to twenty-five. Christine regards them silently for a second before placing them on the floor and stepping into them. They're ludicrously big on her, but they'll keep her warm.

'Do you want to wash your hands?'

'I washed them outside, at the tap.'

'Oh, but that's only cold water – you should have used the bathroom.' No response. Conversation will be tricky. 'Have a seat,' she says, placing the bowl on the waiting table mat. 'Chicken stew,' she says. 'I hope you're not vegetarian.' Christine looks at it but makes no move to take up her cutlery.

'Don't you like chicken? I've made a cheese sandwich, if you'd prefer that.'

'No thanks. I'm not hungry.'

No wonder she's thin. Astrid opens her mouth to protest, and closes it again.

'Have you got any Coke?'

'I'm afraid not. I don't care for it.' Astrid pours tea without asking, and offers milk. Christine adds three spoons of sugar to her cup and sips, elbows planted on the table, stew pushed aside. Her fingers tap out a tattoo on the side of her cup. Astrid hears the soft scuff of her slippers on the floor.

Twenty-five, wasn't that what Bill said? She looks younger than that – and somehow, also older. Her frame is as slight as a young teen's: a school uniform wouldn't look out of place on her, but her addiction has stolen her bloom.

Her mother is dead. Astrid recalls Bill telling her that, sometime during their first conversation. Cancer, he said. The big C. Was that the catalyst? Was that where it had gone wrong?

'Christine, Bill told me about your mother dying.' The girl's hand stills.

'May I ask how old you were when it happened?'

'Sixteen.'

'That must have been very difficult.'

No response. Christine looks into her cup.

'I lost my parents when I was eleven,' Astrid says, studying the teapot. 'They died in the war – the Second World War, I mean.' The first time she's said it aloud in so many years. 'For a long time afterwards I was very unhappy. It's not easy, experiencing death when we are young. Especially the death of a parent.'

More silence. She listens to the gentle whirr of the electric kitchen clock, and more scuffing on the floor. A foot jiggling, she guesses, the girl unable to be still.

The teapot is sky blue and bulbous, with a chain of yellow and white daisies dancing around its middle, and a chip on the lid, a nick smaller than a baby's fingernail. Astrid found it in a charity shop, after she'd dropped and broken her bone china one, part of a set they'd been given as a wedding present. For years she'd used the good one on special occasions only: the rest of the time it had sat with its companions in a glass cabinet, until Cathal died and she sold the house and moved into town, and left the cabinet where it was. Left a lot of things where they were. The china teapot came with her – she'd been fond of it, and vowed to use it every day from then on, but she managed to break it before it had served a week in its new surroundings.

'My mum loved gardening,' Christine says then. Gaze still directed at her cup, hands clasped around it.

Astrid takes in the bowed head, the bitten nails, the unwashed hair. 'Did she? What a nice interest. I enjoyed it too, when I was younger. My husband loved peas, so I grew those every year. Along with other things, of course.'

'Mum grew flowers. She knew them all, all the names.'

'You must have had a beautiful garden.'

'We had.'

Astrid eats her sandwich while the untouched chicken stew cools, her mind taking her back once more to the darkest period in her life. She remembers, after her family's disappearance, waking in the middle of the night in the makeshift bed, the bundle of eiderdowns that Herr Dasler had set up in his attic for her. She would bolt upright, disoriented even after months of living in his house, clutching the bedclothes tightly, heart hammering, every muscle rigid with fear as she waited for the malevolent aftertaste of her nightmare to fade.

Her family didn't feature in those nocturnal terrors. They filled her waking moments; the loss of them took her over by day, but she never dreamed about them in the darkness of the attic, not once. It seemed as if her subconscious was afraid to let them in, for fear of what it might lead to. Eventually the memory of their voices faded. After that their faces blurred – how she wished for photographs! – and finally vanished.

But the months, the years in Herr Dasler's house! Creeping about by day, under orders to avoid the windows, not to run a tap or flush the lavatory, not to put on a light after dark unless he too was in the house. Scurrying up to the attic if anyone called. Reading his books, eating his food, wearing the clothes he bought when she outgrew her own. Using the flannels he tactfully provided to stem her monthly flow, scrubbing them clean in his bathroom sink, hanging them to dry on the rafters in the attic. Wondering, each endless day, each lonely night, if this was to be her life forever.

And when it was all over, when it was safe at last for her to leave the house, how glorious was the fresh air she'd been denied for years! She returned with him to her old street, clutching tightly to his arm, still afraid to trust that the danger was gone – but where their apartment block had stood, there was only rubble. No trace at all was left of them, no photo albums or letters, not the smallest item of clothing. Nothing to remember them by but the precious pearl necklace.

'Can I use the loo?'

She shakes her memories away and shows the girl to the bathroom. Following some instinct, she closes the door to the adjacent bedroom softly on her way back to the kitchen. Just being careful, she tells herself. Just staying on the safe side. In the kitchen she extracts a twenty-euro note from her purse: unearned, but needed to soften the blow. She slips the purse into a drawer as she hears the girl slopping back along the corridor in the borrowed slippers.

'Christine,' she says, as soon as she reappears, 'I'd like you to take this,' proffering the note, waiting until it's been pocketed, until thanks have been given for it. 'I think it's best,' she said then, 'if you don't come back.'

'What?'

She looks genuinely shocked. How could she

not have been expecting this? 'Christine, you didn't exactly do a good job today. You fell asleep – and my hedge looks worse if anything.'

'I can do better. I wasn't feeling good. I'll come back tomorrow –'

'No,' Astrid says swiftly and firmly. 'I'd prefer if you didn't.'

A beat passes. 'Just give me another chance.'

'No. I'm sorry. Christine, I really don't think you're well enough.'

'I'm fine, I'll come back –'

Astrid shakes her head. This is getting tiresome. 'Please, I'd rather you left. It's not going to work out, Christine.'

The girl doesn't move. Astrid feels a pinprick of alarm. Notwithstanding that she is Bill's daughter, she's virtually a stranger – and, given her actions this morning, probably under some kind of chemical influence right now. For all her apparent fragility, might she not possess strength when provoked? Might she lash out at Astrid at the thought of her income, such as it is, drying up?

She tries again. 'Christine, your father is a friend of mine, and a good man. I know he was hoping that this would suit you, but I really think he would agree that it's best for you not to continue here.'

To her relief, Christine turns abruptly and swings out through the patio door.

'Can I put the stew in a container for you?' Astrid calls. 'Will you take it with you for later?'

But no response comes. What does she eat? When does she eat? How long has she been living like this, from one day to the next, from one fix to the next? Did it come about from a combination of elements – the loss of her mother, lack of self-esteem, a desire to please, to fit in, whatever – or was it down to bad timing that put her in the wrong place at the wrong time? Was it as simple as that?

If Astrid's dance class had been on Wednesday instead of Tuesday; if the truck that took away her family had been delayed by fifteen minutes; if she hadn't found Herr Dasler's house that evening; if an Irish man, years later, hadn't asked to share her table in a crowded London tea room; if any of these elements had been different, who knows how life might have gone for her?

So many ways the dice can fall, so much depending on this decision or that, this or that course of action, this yes, that no.

Christine could be Astrid's granddaughter, or even great-granddaughter. How Bill must agonise, how he must despair for her. Where does she live? Where does she sleep at night? Who does she call her friends? How these questions must keep him awake, must torment him every hour of the day.

She steps out onto the patio, where the girl is shrugging on the jacket, having already replaced her shoes and sweater. How can she need so much clothing on such a warm day? Astrid stoops to gather up the discarded slippers. 'Christine, I'm sorry it didn't work out. If you would like to come back for a cup of tea anytime, please do.'

An expression, a grimace, passes briefly across the girl's face. 'Have you a plaster?'

'A plaster? Did you cut yourself?'

'I got a blister,' she says, showing her palm – and Astrid sees the welt, red and sore-looking, in the webbing between thumb and index finger.

'Oh, no – let me dress that for you. Please come back inside.' She hurries down the short corridor and retrieves her first-aid box from the bathroom shelf. On her return, Christine is standing just inside the patio door.

'I'm so sorry,' Astrid says, dabbing antiseptic cream on the blister, cutting a length from her Elastoplast roll. 'I should have given you gloves – I'm sure there's still a pair in the shed.'

'Doesn't matter.'

'Of course it matters.' Astrid presses the plaster carefully into place, noting again the thin wrist, the protruding knuckles, the bony, nail-bitten fingers. 'I'll give you some of this to take away, so you can change the old one when it gets dirty. Make sure to keep it covered until it heals.' She cuts two more lengths from the strip and hands them over. Christine pockets them and vanishes once more without a word. Astrid stands in the kitchen, listening to the soft sound of her footfalls travelling along the side passage until it too is gone.

She opens the drawer where she put her purse,

and finds it still there, and undisturbed. She tidies the kitchen, tipping the portion of stew into the compost bin. She could save it, untouched as it is, but her appetite for it is gone.

She returns the ointment and plaster roll to the bathroom. It is only when she turns on the tap to wash her hands that she notices the absence of the bar of lemon soap from its dish on the side of the sink. Easily replaced, she tells herself. Not a major crime.

She'll say nothing of the girl's return visit to Bill, next time she sees him. He won't ask, she won't say. And Christine, she's sure, will make no mention of it to him either, whenever they meet again.

The episode has left an uneasy flavour behind. She tells herself her actions were justified – how could she have agreed to let the creature continue, when clearly the work was beyond her? – and yet the vague edginess, and the regret, lingers.

Later in the afternoon the sun comes out. She walks to the end of her road and waits on a low wall for a taxi to pass by. She could phone but she likes the small bit of exercise, and taxis are plentiful at this time of day. Sure enough, one appears before too long and she flags it down. At her local garden centre she makes her way slowly between the aisles of plants, inspecting the various offerings and making a mental selection, an exercise she likes to indulge in from time to time.

A fuchsia and a red broom, definitely. A lavender,

and possibly a blue buddleia, although they can take over. A potentilla for its beautiful golden shades. A clematis, some variegated ivy, a Virginia creeper for autumn colour.

'I need someone to tidy up my garden,' she tells a staff member, stout and freckled. 'I need old shrubs dug up and replaced, and a few other things. I was wondering if you could recommend anyone. I'd prefer a mature person, someone reliable. I live alone,' she adds.

'I can put the word out, missus,' he replies. 'Want to leave us your number?'

'Thank you so much.' One of the bonuses of growing old, she has discovered, is that people are more inclined to be helpful. Perhaps she reminds him of his grandmother.

In the taxi that brings her home she searches the streets. She sees shoppers with carrier bags, and holidaymakers with their golden skin, and a young female busker strumming a green guitar, and a man pulling a squeegee across a shop window, and another tugging at the lead of a little sniffing dog. She counts three hunkered figures with their hopeful cups on the ground before them, but no sign at all of a thin girl in an oversized jacket.

She should have let her keep the slippers. Too big as they were, they might have afforded some warmth, some comfort, wherever she spends her nights.

The following day, Heather arrives to do the

windows. 'What happened to your hedge?' she asks, and Astrid tells her she got someone who didn't work out. Heather tuts and shakes her head and gets the wheelbarrow from the shed, ignoring Astrid's protests. She rakes up the clippings and deposits them in the compost bin, and promises to make enquiries among her neighbours for someone to finish the job. 'I wish I could do it myself,' she says, blotting her streaming eyes with her sleeve. 'You can see my problem.'

'I certainly can,' Astrid replies, pulling tissues from their box. 'I've asked at the garden centre and they'll find me someone, I'm sure. Now tell me about your holiday.'

Heather opens her bottle of cider vinegar. Best window-cleaner on the planet, she calls it, and it certainly works on Astrid's windows. 'It was good,' she says, pouring a generous measure into her bucket. 'It was kind of weird too, though. I mean, they were … pretty great with Lottie. Like grandparents should be, I guess – not that I'd know much about that. I never had a lot of contact with mine.'

She holds the bucket under the hot tap. 'They brought her out for pancakes and ice-cream, and they took her to the park, and to a drive-in movie, stuff like that. She had a blast.'

She turns to face Astrid as her bucket fills. 'And I don't know, I couldn't help it, but I found myself – resenting them a little. I mean, why were they never like that with me?'

She turns away again. 'They just passed me on,' she says, above the sound of the running water, 'from one nanny to another. They had no time for me. And now they have time for Lottie, and I'm finding it kind of hard to just accept it and be glad for her. I mean, I *am* glad, of course I'm happy that they like her, but I'm a little – well, I suppose, if I'm totally honest, I'm a little jealous too.'

She shuts off the water. She hauls the bucket from the sink and sets it on the draining-board, and gives Astrid a look that's hard to interpret. 'So what kind of a horrible person does that make me, to be jealous of my own kid?'

'Now stop that – you're probably the least horrible person I know.'

Heather laughs. 'Oh, come on – that can't be true!'

'It certainly can. It's also perfectly normal that you'd feel a little put out. You were their child, and they neglected you. But I think you must try to forget that now. Remember the good things, forget the rest.'

Heather nods. 'You're right. It's great that they're being good with Lottie. That's really all that matters.' Her face changes, softens into a real smile. 'I brought her to meet the son of an old Irish nanny I had. I used to visit with him and his family when— Well, anyway, that was cool, catching up with them.'

'I didn't know you had an Irish nanny.'

'Josephine.' Nodding briskly. 'She's the reason I came to Ireland.'

'Did you stay in touch, when you came over here?'

'Nope. She was shot dead in a mall by a crazy American with a gun.'

The words, so unexpected, stated so matter-of-factly, shock Astrid into silence. She watches Heather lifting the bucket, scooping up the waiting sponge, moving with her load to the patio. A second later, she pops her head back around. 'That might have come out a little blunt.'

'No—'

'Truth is, I can't dwell on it, or I'd fall apart, you know?' And Astrid sees the pain then in her face, hears it in the too-bright tone.

'Heather, I'm so sorry. What a terrible thing to happen.'

'Yup.' She vanishes again. Shortly after, Astrid hears the splash of water – and then, in a new voice: 'There's something else.'

'What's that?'

No response. Seconds tick by. Astrid steps outside.

Heather is standing on the little step stool she uses to reach the top of the patio door. She scrubs at the glass with her sponge, not looking at Astrid.

'You said there's something else.'

'Mm-hmm.' Still she scrubs. 'I think … Well, there's this guy, this man. Or there might be, I'm not sure.'

'What man?'

'Oh, well. It might be nothing.'

She hops down to dunk the sponge, squeezes it out, dunks it again. Astrid follows a small trail of water as it snakes across the tiles. 'What might be nothing?'

'Well, I guess he's just someone I got to know when I came here first.' Scrub, scrub, her sponge squeaking on the glass. 'He – well, I hadn't seen him for years, and then I met him again – met him twice, actually, first time in Emily's place – and then we just bumped into one another again. I don't know why I'm telling you all this.'

Astrid pulls a chair out from the patio table and sits. Waiting for more, because of course there's more, if she holds her tongue.

'I was his father's carer,' Heather says, now drawing a squeegee swiftly across the glass, pausing to wipe it dry after every swipe. 'I think I told you. It was the first job I got here.'

She slides the patio door closed and turns her attention to the unwashed side. 'I was young, and kinda desperate to start making some cash, in case my folks cut me off for coming here when I was supposed to be in England.'

Interesting, the hint of something – exhilaration, anticipation, nervousness, all of the above – that Astrid detects running through the chatter. Most interesting. 'You told me about the man you looked after, but you never mentioned his son.'

'Didn't I?' She scrubs and squeaks with her

sponge, sending more water splashing onto the tiles. Astrid lifts her feet to avoid an incoming drift.

'Well, that's the other thing. I never really liked him – although I didn't *dislike* him either. I really didn't know him, hardly knew him at all, but he used to come with his wife and kids. His wife was a real piece of work, I mean, she was a *real*—' She breaks off, glances over her shoulder at Astrid. 'Let's just say she was not a nice person. Anyway, like I said, I met him again out of the blue, just a little while ago.'

More scrubbing. More splashing. More squeegee.

'And?'

'And they've split up, he and his wife. Turns out …' setting the squeegee on the table, turning to face Astrid, still on her hunkers '… well, it turns out that they didn't have a good relationship.' She lifts her shoulders, gives a bashful smile. 'And … he's nice. I like him. He drove me and Lottie to the airport, changed shifts with someone at his work so he could do it.' She gets to her feet, pours the contents of the bucket into a drain. 'Collected us when we got back too. I'm not saying— Well, I don't know what I'm saying really. I mean, technically he's still married. Look, forget I said anything.'

She's all over the place. Confused about her parents, hurt that they're better grandparents, but glad too. A part of her still mourning the nanny she lost so violently. Developing feelings for this man, terrified to admit it. The first man she's ever discussed with Astrid: even Lottie's father barely got half a sentence, the only time Astrid recalls her mentioning him.

'Right,' Heather says, 'moving on,' and she refills her bucket at the kitchen sink and sets off to tackle the remaining windows, leaving Astrid to wash the breakfast dishes, and to pray that this man, who seems to have begun to creep into Heather's heart, has the sense to recognise what a treasure she is.

The next day, Astrid decides to take the bus to town for the first time in weeks. It's not a long journey from her house to the stop – even at her measured pace it takes under five minutes – but it feels like a real achievement. At the stop she sits next to a teenage girl, who makes space for her with a sweet smile and ignores her thereafter as she runs a fingertip along the screen of her phone.

When the bus arrives Astrid climbs the steps carefully. The driver's face is familiar, but she knows none of their names. 'Long time no see,' he says, and waves her on as she rummages for her travel pass, and watches in his mirror until she's seated before he moves off.

The walk from the main street to The Food of Love seems endless: she was a little ambitious, she decides. She reaches the restaurant with relief, and Emily, emerging just then from the kitchen, greets her with the usual smile.

'Good to see you, Astrid. All well?'

'Very well,' Astrid replies. 'I came on the bus.'

'Did you really? Well done.'

'I might take a taxi home.'

Emily nods. 'That would be wise, don't overdo it.' She pulls out a chair for Astrid. 'I don't suppose you have Bill's mobile number,' she says. 'I thought he might have a landline, but he's not in the phone book.'

'I do,' Astrid says, suddenly remembering. 'He gave it to me, last time I saw him.' She opens her bag, but her phone isn't to be found there. 'Sorry, I must have left it at home. I'll text it to you later.'

'Thanks. I just wanted a word with him.'

'Hasn't he been in?'

'No.'

She looks preoccupied. The smile might be a little over-bright, like Heather's the day before. She disappears with Astrid's order, and Astrid recalls their recent conversation about the man she had reconnected with. The man who had broken her heart, and then come back saying he was sorry. Strange that Emily and Heather had both come into contact with men from their past.

'Is everything alright?' Astrid asks when her soup arrives.

'Yes, everything's fine. I'm just a little tired, that's all.'

But Astrid doesn't think that's all.

When she gets home she searches for her phone, and doesn't find it. Not in any of the usual places, not by her bed, or on the coffee table in the sitting room, or next to the kettle on the worktop, or underneath the lid of the record player. Not fallen beneath the kitchen table, or left out on the patio. Where on earth can it be?

She tries to recall the last time she used it. Wednesday, wasn't it, to ring a taxi for the library? Yes, she didn't walk to the end of the road that day because it was raining.

She got the phone for emergencies, on her nephew's advice. She manages quite well without it most of the time, but the loss of it now is annoying. Without a landline either she feels adrift, cut off from the rest of humanity, which is quite ridiculous.

When it still hasn't turned up by Monday she returns to the library and the supermarket, but it hasn't been handed in at either location. She travels on to the garden centre, where she finds the man she spoke with on her previous visit, and she tells him of the loss. 'I don't suppose I left it here?'

'I haven't come across it, I'm afraid.' He asks the others; they shake their heads. 'I've found you a gardener though, if you're still looking. I passed your number on to him on Saturday, but that's not going to be much good if your phone is gone. Hang on.'

He riffles in his wallet and finds a folded slip of paper. Astrid reads *Markus Nowak* and a number. 'Do you know him?' she asks.

'Haven't met him myself, but he's done work for my sister, and she was pleased. He's Polish, she said. Nice lad, and not too dear.'

A lad isn't a retired person. A lad is young, or at any rate younger than Astrid had been hoping for, but she thanks the man and slips the note into her bag. 'One more stop,' she tells her taxi driver, and fifteen minutes later she's bought a replica of her old phone. Her new number will have to be memorised, and her contacts, all fourteen or so, are gone.

She thinks of Emily, waiting for a text with Bill's number on it. When the new phone has charged she calls directory enquiries and is given the number for the restaurant.

'Sorry,' she tells Emily, and explains the situation.

'Thanks, Astrid. Thank you for trying. Shame about your phone.'

Has Bill given up coming to The Food of Love? Such a pity if he has. Astrid hopes it has nothing to do with Christine, hopes it's not guilt about sending her to Astrid that's keeping him away. So difficult, such a sad situation.

She places a call to Markus, whose accent she has some difficulty with, but she gives him her address and manages to elicit a promise from him to call later that day to see the garden.

And life goes on, as it tends to do.

Heather

HER PHONE RINGS ON TUESDAY EVENING at seven o'clock precisely. She presses the answer key and says, 'Hi Mom,' and 'Yes, she's here,' before passing the phone to her daughter. 'Grandma,' she says, but Lottie already knows it's Grandma.

Heather clears the table of dinner dishes, picturing her mother on the other side of the Atlantic, all the way across the huge landmass of the States to the west coast, where it's eleven in the morning. She sees the fresh cup of coffee that will have been poured before the call was placed, the sun that's probably streaming in through the big kitchen windows, the white-tiled floor that has almost certainly been mopped once already by Anita, whom she and Lottie met when they visited.

She fills the sink with water and half listens to Lottie's side of the conversation, which consists mostly of yeses, and uh-huhs, and giggles. In the two weeks since their trip to the US, Grandma has called at seven o'clock on Tuesday and Friday – and Heather, feeling her way in this new family dynamic, says hi and passes the phone to Lottie, and tries not to feel too left out.

But like Astrid said, she must focus on the positive. Their trip to the US was a success. After an initial awkwardness – to be expected – she and her folks got on pretty much as well as she could have hoped for. Nobody yelled, nobody threw stuff – and Lottie now has grandparents who care about her.

The visit to Josephine's son and his family was as bittersweet as she'd known it would be. Lovely to see them, to catch up with their happenings – the little girls she'd played with in the yard both in high school now, the son a pet groomer. Sweet to reconnect with them, and also sad. Josephine's ashes were sent back to Ireland at her sister's request, so there was no grave to visit. Just as well: Heather isn't big on graves.

And on a completely unrelated note, there's Shane.

He brought flowers when he came to revisit his father's house. Big colourful daisies that made Heather's nose itch just looking at them, but it was nice of him. She wondered if Nora had suggested it, or if it had been his own idea.

She introduced him to Lottie and gave him coffee, and afterwards she walked him through the handful of rooms in the house where he'd grown up. He was nervous at first, didn't know what to do with himself, kept folding and unfolding his arms, stirring coffee that had already been stirred to death – but he relaxed a bit as the visit went on.

It's strange, he said, standing on the threshold of his father's room. That you live here now, I mean.

Strange good or strange bad?

Not bad, he said. I told you I was glad when you bought it. In the tiny front bedroom that used to be his, and that's now Lottie's, he pointed at the house directly across the street. Delahuntys, he said.

That's right. Just Jim there now. The kids are living overseas. His wife died a couple of years ago.

Teresa. I was at her funeral.

Heather had gone to the removal, had lined up with the other neighbours to pay her respects to Jim and the kids. She and Shane might have come face to face then, but they hadn't.

We're going back to the States for a week, she said as they returned downstairs, so I can introduce Lottie to my folks.

He didn't ask why it had taken eight years for Lottie to meet her grandparents. Heather was waiting for it, but he didn't.

When are you off?

Tuesday.

From Shannon?

Yup.

I could run you, he said, getting into the jacket he'd left on the banister. I could bring you to the airport.

Shannon was an hour away. Wouldn't you be working? she asked.

I can switch shifts, it's not a problem – so he'd picked them up on Tuesday and driven them all the way to the airport. And when he was dropping them at Departures he'd said, I can collect you when you get back if you want, so that had happened too.

And after he'd been so nice to do that, Heather felt it was the polite thing to invite him to dinner. To say thanks, she said, and so three evenings after they'd got home from the trip she cooked shepherd's pie from a recipe she found online – she'd never in her life owned a cookbook – and he came and ate it.

And at the end of that night, after Lottie had gone upstairs to get into pyjamas, he asked if Heather would like to go to a movie sometime, so they went to the new Will Smith two evenings later, and left Lottie with Madge.

And tomorrow, which is a Saturday, the three of them are meeting in the park for a walk and an ice-cream.

And she has no idea where it's going, or if it's going anywhere at all.

He's older. He's at least fifteen years older than her. He must be still married to Yvonne. Her name hasn't come up between them since their conversation on the street, but it takes a lot longer than a year to ditch a spouse in Ireland.

And apart from his marital status, the idea of anything developing between him and Heather is still a bit weird. Since Lottie started school, and Heather saw him bringing a little boy into the classroom that first frenetic day, she'd become expert in avoiding him. When they'd both responded to the call for parents to accompany the class on the senior-infant school tour, she'd engineered it so she was never once close enough to him that they'd be forced to acknowledge one another. When he'd turned up to the cycle bus she helped organise in first class, Heather again made certain that they were well separated along the line of little cyclists.

At school concerts and parent-teacher meetings, and any other occasion where they might coincide, she was careful to give him and Yvonne a wide berth. Never, she vowed, would she voluntarily have anything to do with them.

And now things are changing – and she's not one bit sure how she feels about that.

Nothing has been said that would give her reason to think he has any romantic interest in her. They haven't even held hands, for goodness' sake. He hasn't gone further than a silly little goodbye wave when he leaves her. Maybe he's just looking for a friend – and maybe that's all she wants too.

Is it hell.

'Done,' Lottie announces, setting down the phone.

'Good girl. What did Grandma say?'

'Nothing much – except she'll see us at Christmas, her and Grandpa.'

Heather turns from the sink. 'What?'

'She said she'll see us —'

'Where? Where will she see us? We're not going there for Christmas.'

'No, they're coming here.'

'They're coming *here*?'

Don't be a stranger, her mother had said when they were leaving, and Heather, trying to swat away battling emotions, had said something noncommittal like See you soon. The kind of thing you say to people when you're parting from them, even if you have no idea when you'll see them again.

Don't be a stranger means come visit us again at some vague time in the future. It definitely does not mean we're coming to see *you*. They didn't once hint that they might be considering a trip in this direction. Lottie must have picked her up wrong.

'What exactly did Grandma say? Tell me her exact words.'

'I *told* you. She said that she and Grandpa are coming here for Christmas.'

'Here, to Ireland?'

'Yeah, Mom – cos we live here, remember?'

'Don't be a smartass.'

Sounds like there's no mistake. Christmas in the big house of her childhood meant more parties than usual, which also meant more rows, before and after. The house professionally decorated from top to bottom, eggnog in the refrigerator, dishes of brightly wrapped candy around the house that

Heather would stuff into her pockets and eat in her room.

She hated Christmas movies, where everyone started out sad or lonely, but always, always, ended up happy, just in time for Christmas Day. Oh, she knew they were just movies with make-believe characters, but even in the real world it seemed that Christmas worked its magic on everyone else, and passed her by. Even when Josephine was around she got a week off at Christmas like all the other nannies, so Heather had no ally.

She and Lottie have a Christmas Day routine. They spend the morning doing the rounds of the neighbourhood, distributing a scented candle and a box of mince pies to each of the households, and staying for tea or lemonade or whatever's on offer. When they get home they exchange gifts, and Heather professes herself delighted with whatever Madge and Lottie have picked out with the twenty euro Heather will have handed over a week earlier.

Later, the two of them share a turkey and cranberry sauce pizza in front of whatever festive movie Lottie selects from Netflix – Heather doesn't mind them so much now. Afterwards, if the weather's OK, they walk to the park to throw broken bits of leftover pizza crust to the swans. It's the perfect day.

'Grandma said they'll go to a hotel, but I think they should stay here.'

'Do you now.'

'Yeah. We've got lots of room.'

Lots of room, in a tiny two-bedroom house. Her folks would die of claustrophobia in five minutes. 'And where do you think they'd sleep?'

'Well, you could move to the couch, and they could have your bed. It's big enough for two.'

'Right.'

Heather turns her head to hide the grin. For as long as she can remember her parents have slept apart – not just in separate beds, but in entirely different rooms, on opposite sides of the house, with a staircase, two bathrooms, a guest room and Heather's old room between them. The thought of them climbing together into Heather's very modest double bed – not a king, not a queen – is the stuff sitcoms are made of. 'Let's worry about sleeping arrangements later, OK?'

Will they come? Time will tell. Was her mother testing the water by saying it to Lottie? She looks down at the part in her daughter's golden hair. She bends to deposit a swift kiss on it.

'What's that for?'

'Just for being you, kiddo.'

Let them come, let them see how her life is here. Let them experience the things she holds dear now. Let them come to The Food of Love and be introduced to Emily, and eat dinner at the big oval table. Let them meet Madge and the rest of the neighbours, let them sit in Victor McCarthy's kitchen and listen to his father Ernie, an exile from rural County Clare, belt out manic tunes on his fiddle while Victor accompanies him with a pair of dessertspoons that clatter and dance against his thigh.

Who knows? They might even enjoy it.

After the dishes have been done and the floor swept she tries calling Astrid, as she does occasionally in the evenings, but Astrid's phone must be dead because she gets nowhere, no ring tone, no voicemail. She'll try again in the morning,

Later that evening, Lottie already in bed and reading aloud to Tinkerbell, Heather casts a critical eye on the contents of her wardrobe, and decides an overhaul might be in order. She can't remember the last time she wore anything but Levi's, teamed with a shirt or sweater. Emily is always trying to get her into dresses: maybe she could give one a try, if only for the laugh.

She has no idea what style to go for. Nothing with a waist. Nothing that might highlight the fact that she hasn't had a waist since she was twelve. Nothing frilly or fussy, nothing that would add bulk to the bulk. Emily, she decides, will have to accompany her on a shopping trip.

Shame she's got nothing cute for tomorrow's outing to the park. Something with a bit of a swish to it, something that would make her feel pretty, or pretty-ish.

It's not a big deal. It would just be nice, that's all.

Emily

IT MAKES SENSE. SHE KNOWS IT MAKES perfect sense. He works in Dublin and he wants her with him. Four years ago she would have been more than happy to make the move. Leaving the hair salon wouldn't have cost her a thought, plenty of salons in Dublin – but that was before Gran died and left her the shop, before Emily took a deep breath and opened The Food of Love.

'It's hard to explain,' she says. 'This restaurant is more than just a job, it's my calling. It's what I was meant to do.'

'I get that, sweetheart, honestly I do – but you don't have to give it up. I mean, obviously you'll have to give up *this* one, but what's to stop you opening another? I know it would take time to find the right premises, and of course it costs a fair bit more to run a business in Dublin – but you'd have money from the sale of this one, and I'd be happy to help out.'

'But Ferg, this one is special. This one is like ... Gran's gift to me. I know that sounds silly, but —'

'It's not silly, it's sweet – but we have to be practical here. I can't move back home – it simply isn't an option with my work – so if we want to be together you need to come here. Wouldn't your gran have wanted you to be happy?'

'Yes, of course, but ...' But still she can't bear the idea of giving up the restaurant. 'I might let it, for a while anyway.'

'Let it? If you did that you'd have no capital – but hey, baking is your thing, right? Why not look for work in an established bakery instead? Do you really want the responsibility of running your own place again? Wouldn't you prefer to be taking home a steady wage, and being able to forget about it when you clock off?'

'I like the responsibility. I love being my own boss.'

'In that case, you'll have to sell up, Em. But look, the important thing is that we'll be together, right? Isn't that all that matters?'

He doesn't get it. Of course she wants them to be together, but it's not all that matters. He wasn't around at the start. He doesn't know about all the nights she lay awake, wondering if she was crazy even to consider opening a restaurant with one table. He didn't see the long hours she and Mike put in, testing and tasting and tweaking recipes; he wasn't there on the days she spent trawling through charity shops for what she could find to save a fiver here, a tenner there.

He didn't witness her agonising over a shade of paint for the walls, and the tiles for the floor, and the font for the name above the window, after she had finally, finally, decided what that name should be. He'd missed all that because he was miles away. He was an entire continent away when she'd opened her doors for the first time, heart in her mouth, and one diner had shown up.

He doesn't understand how precious it is to be able to live and work where Gran lived and worked. He doesn't see how attached she has grown to the small room with the big oval table, and how she loves meeting the different people who come to eat there every day. He doesn't know how much she values the friendships she's made with Heather and Astrid and Bill.

Well, maybe not Bill. Not any more.

What happened? She has no idea. Why did he seem almost angry that time they met at the vet's, and she told him about moving to Dublin? Why hasn't he come back to the restaurant?

She called an electrician last week, when a socket stopped working. It killed her. It should have been Bill.

She misses him. She misses his easy grin, his hopeless jokes, the lost look she catches on his face sometimes. She misses how he always sweeps his breadcrumbs from the tablecloth into his empty soup bowl. She misses the hair that's as unruly as her own, and the dark eyes, and the nose that's too big to call him handsome. He's not handsome, but he's lovely.

She has to sort things out with him. She can't leave them as they are, can't move to Dublin with unanswered questions, with the uncertain feeling there is between them now. She has no number for him, no way of getting in touch unless she rings the nursing home, which she's reluctant to do. Instead she's planning to call there this afternoon, once the post-lunchtime tidy-up is done.

And in the meantime, there's her brother Daniel.

Come and meet him, she said, just for an hour. Come to my place on Saturday afternoon for coffee. Bring Nora, she said, thinking it might make him more inclined to be nice, but it didn't. Daniel managed to convey all too clearly, from his curt responses and charged silences, that the past hadn't been forgotten, that Ferg hadn't been forgiven. Was he never going to let it go? Was Emily forever to cringe when the two of them were in the same room?

Ferg ignored it. He concentrated on Nora and Emily, and was careful never to interact solely with Daniel. I'm sorry, Emily said later, he was rude – but Ferg told her not to worry: he'd expected as much from a loyal brother. He'll get over it, he said, and Emily nodded, and hoped, and wondered how her parents would be when they came face to face with Ferg, as they inevitably would. At least they're separated from him by an ocean, unlike Daniel.

It will be strange after she makes the move to Dublin, not having her brother down the road from her. They've never lived further apart than they are now; there's never been more than a short walk from her door to his. That will take some getting used to.

But she must focus on the bigger picture, the reason for all the change. They'll finally be living together. She loves him, and he loves her – it's a natural progression to live under the same roof.

Is it a bit soon to be considering it though, just a few weeks into their new relationship? He doesn't think so.

Emmy, it's not like we're starting from scratch here. We had two years together. We know what we're doing, and what we want. I know it's what *I* want.

And she wants it too. And Dublin is vibrant and bustling, and she'll love it once she gets used to it.

She must tell Mike. She's been putting it off, but as her employee he should know so he can think about finding another job. She hates the thought of them not working together any more. We're the perfect team, he's said more than once, and she has to agree.

Stop it. Stop being so negative. Think of the upside. Be happy.

'I *am* happy,' she says aloud.

'Glad to hear it,' Mike replies, tipping bread crusts into the compost bin.

She drops a bundle of clean spoons back into their tray. Might as well get it over with. 'Mike, there's something I've been wanting to talk to you about.'

'What's that?'

'It's about me and Ferg.'

'Right.'

They've met, briefly. The day Ferg came to have coffee with Daniel and Nora, Mike was leaving as Ferg arrived. Introductions were made. 'You know he lives in Dublin.'

'Yeah.' He takes up the brush and begins sweeping the floor. 'Don't tell me you're moving.'

She waits until he looks up.

Her expression stills his brush. 'You're not moving, are you?'

'I probably am, Mike. I mean, it looks like things are heading that way. We've talked about it.'

'Are you serious?'

'Dead serious.'

'Crikey.' He resumes sweeping. 'Look,' he says, 'tell me to mind my own business, but is it not … a bit soon?'

She smiles. 'We've got history, Mike. We go back a while.'

'… Oh.'

'We went out for two years. It didn't last, and he went to Canada, but we're both older now and … well …'

'So you're picking up where you left off.'

'Kind of.'

He props the brush in a corner. 'So when is all this happening, then?'

'I'm not sure. I'll have to put the restaurant on the market.'

'You're selling up?'

'I … Yes, I'm afraid so. I'd much rather not. I hate the thought of letting it go, but I don't see what else I can do.'

He unties his apron, chucks it aside. 'Maybe I could rent it from you. Maybe.'

The look on his face. The hope in it. 'Mike, there's nothing I'd like better, but I'll have to sell. I'll need capital if I want to buy someplace in Dublin.'

'Yeah. Right. Course you will.' Taking his jacket from behind the door. 'I can see that.'

'I wish I could sell it to you,' she says, but they both know that's not an option. He hasn't got the cash to rent it, let alone buy it. 'Look, nothing is going to happen right away. I just wanted to tell you, so you have a bit of warning.'

'OK.' He takes his keys from the drawer where he stows them. 'Let me know when I need to start looking. And good luck, by the way.'

'Thanks.'

Where will they be, both of them, by Christmas? Will the restaurant still be hers, or will there be a new owner, with maybe very different ideas about what to do with the place? She wishes she could pack it up, brick by brick, and carry it with her to Dublin, and find the perfect spot there to reassemble it.

When the kitchen is sorted she pulls on a jacket and leaves by the back door. The nursing home isn't far, up to the main street, through the indoor market, around by the boys' primary school, the library, the fire station. Ten minutes, twelve at the most.

The leaves on the trees outside the library have started to turn, the new school year beginning next week, another summer coming to an end. Little did she imagine at the start of this one what changes lay waiting for her.

Walking past the big double doors of the fire station, she thinks about the many times Bill would have made this same journey on his way to and from the restaurant. She remembers the first time she saw him, the wary expression on his face as he stood on the threshold, ready to turn and bolt. Bill, he'd said, when she enquired, just Bill – and right away, she'd warmed to his tentative smile.

He might not appreciate her showing up without warning at the nursing home, interrupting him in the middle of his working day – but with his continuing absence at the restaurant eating away at her she must have it out with him, get to the bottom of it.

She approaches the metal gates and regards the two-storey building beyond them. Well maintained, on the outside at least. Recently painted, by the look of it – and abruptly she remembers the tiny dots of paint all over Bill's face, the night they'd met at the vet's. She takes a breath and walks up the short driveway.

The heat hits her as soon as she steps inside. The receptionist – shining brown hair, red-framed glasses, blue fingernails – regards her dubiously when she asks for Bill. 'Is he expecting you?'

'No. I just need a quick word, if I can.'

'He could be anywhere.' She lifts the receiver of the phone on her desk. 'Who will I say?'

She hesitates. Should she give her name? Might he avoid her like he's avoiding the restaurant? 'Maybe you could just say it's a friend of his. I'd like to surprise him.' She tries to smile, but it feels stiff.

The receptionist doesn't smile back. She taps a single button with a blue nail and says, 'Is Bill around? Someone is looking for him.' She listens. 'OK,' she says, and hangs up. 'Have a seat,' she tells Emily. 'They'll try to find him.'

Three chairs are lined up in a row in front of a window, in the kind of functional design that doesn't encourage loitering. Emily chooses the middle one. 'It's warm in here,' she says, slipping off her jacket.

'Old bones. They need the heat.'

'I suppose so.'

She turns to look out the window. She sees a white minibus, a paved path winding through a neatly mown lawn, unpainted wooden seats. She wonders if Bill cuts the grass, or if they have a gardener.

A man appears around a corner, tapping his

way along the path with a knobbly stick, a flat cap on his head, a blue scarf knotted around his neck. Something, a book she thinks, pokes from a jacket pocket.

He settles himself on the first seat he encounters. He pulls out the book and then fumbles inside the jacket until he finds spectacles that he doesn't immediately put on. Instead, he lifts his face to the sky.

'Emily?'

She turns. Bill is in navy overalls, which throws her for a second. He isn't smiling. He looks like he thinks she might be bringing him bad news.

'What are you doing here?' he asks.

She gets to her feet. 'Bill,' she says, 'sorry to bother you. I would have rung, but I don't have your number.' She darts a glance at the receptionist, who isn't looking in their direction but who can't avoid hearing every word. 'Maybe we could go outside. It won't take long, honestly.'

In response he moves to the door and holds it open. She steps past him, glad of the cooler air. 'Here,' he says, and leads her around the corner of the building, away from the man on his bench, to a little flagged courtyard. Steam issues from a vent on a wall. Three big bins stand near a door that's propped open across the way. The kitchen, she guesses, hearing a clattering from within.

Bill stops. He slips his hands into his pockets and waits. She tries to gather her words, tries to figure out how best to come at it. She had the conversation in her head last night, but it's slipped away from her now.

'Bill,' she says, her jacket held like a shield between them, 'the truth is, I'm worried. I know you said I hadn't done anything to upset you, that time we met at the vet's, and I hope that's true, but I still feel there's something up. I feel you're ... not being completely open with me.'

He stands mutely before her. Isn't he going to help her out?

But maybe he *is* helping her. Maybe his silence is letting her know that she's right.

'I think there's something you're not telling me,' she goes on. 'I could be wrong but – I have this ... Look, I would really like to sort this out, Bill. Can you please help me? I don't want to go away feeling there's stuff – unresolved between us. If I've done anything, I'd really prefer to know, so I can fix it.'

His gaze slides from her face to rest on something over her shoulder. He clears his throat. He takes a hand from a pocket and runs it through his hair. 'You didn't do anything,' he says. 'Not a thing. But I can't come back to the restaurant, and I wish you wouldn't ask me why.'

She considers this. 'So there *is* something.'

He dips his head – is it a nod of acknowledgement? Why won't he open up? What is there to hide between them?

She frowns. 'Let me get this straight. I haven't

done anything to upset you, but you still won't come back, and you won't let me know why.'

He gives a shrug. 'Emily, I can't.'

It's not good enough.

'It's not good enough!' It comes bursting out of her, the force of it taking her by surprise. 'It's not *fair*, to just – turn your back on me, with no explanation!'

'You're the one who's leaving,' he points out mildly. 'You're the one turning your back on everyone.' Hands dug into his pockets, still refusing to meet her eye.

'What? That's got *nothing* to do with it – you stopped coming in before I told you about that!' Her face feels hot. Her breath catches in her throat. She must drag it out. 'Look at me!' she demands, and he does, he looks straight at her. 'I thought we were friends, Bill Geraghty, but this is *not* how you treat a friend!'

She wheels away, giving him no chance to respond. He could call after her, he could make some attempt to defend himself – but he doesn't. Let him off so. Let him stay away, if that's what he wants. She'll manage fine without him.

It takes her a few minutes, it takes her until she's marching past the library to realise that her face is wet. She blots it with her jacket, not breaking her rapid stride. She shouldn't have lost her temper. He wouldn't intentionally hurt her, he's too kind for that – but she *does* feel hurt by his refusal to explain.

She feels let down, abandoned by someone she was fond of. *Is* fond of.

She crosses Main Street, setting her face into neutral, refusing to let more tears fall. You're the one turning her back on everyone, he said. How could he be so cruel? How could he hurl that at her like an accusation, when all she's doing is following her heart?

Except that her heart is being pulled in two opposing directions.

'I had a row,' she tells Heather that evening, when the American comes in for dinner. 'With Bill.'

'With *Bill*? Our Bill? I don't believe it. Was he here?'

'No, I went to the nursing home – and it wasn't so much a row as me getting mad with him.' And then someone at the other end of the table needs her, so she has to stop.

'I'm trying to see it,' Heather says, when she gets back. 'You being mad with Bill. I can't imagine it.'

'I know, it's awful—' And then someone else needs her, so in the end she and Heather wait until much later, and talk on the phone.

'I just wanted to know why he doesn't call in any more. It's bugging me.'

'So did you ask him?'

'Of course I did. I said I thought I must have upset him.'

'And what did he say?'

'He said I hadn't, but that he couldn't come back, and he couldn't tell me why.'

'So you got mad. Did you yell at him?'

'Kind of.' She sighs. 'Bill, of all people. I feel terrible.'

'So tell him,' Heather says. 'Write him a letter.'

'A letter?'

'Why not? Tell him you're sorry. If you write it down, you can make sure it comes out right.'

'I can't write to him. I don't have his address.'

'Send it to the nursing home. Tell him we need him back in the restaurant. Tell him I miss him too. I'm sure he *will* come back, when whatever's bothering him now is in the past. You'll still be here.'

'That's the thing, though,' Emily says. Might as well break the news to her too.

Heather doesn't take it well. 'What? You can't be serious. You can't move to Dublin – you can't close the restaurant. I won't allow it.'

'Believe me, I hate the thought too, but I want to be where Ferg is.'

'What about him wanting to be where you are? Why do you have to be the one to move?'

'Because he wouldn't get as good a job here in town. He'd have to take a serious cut in his salary.'

'Oh for crying out loud, what has money got to do with it? Your heart and soul are in that restaurant – it's your passion. What part of that does he not get?'

All of it.

'Look, nothing's sorted, we're just talking. Anyway, it's late and I'd better go – but thanks for listening.'

'Thanks nothing. I know I'm giving you a hard time here, it's just that I don't want to see you go – but I guess you've got to look at the bigger picture, the happy-ever-after one. Just make sure you don't spend your life doing what he wants, and forgetting about your own stuff, OK?'

'Of course.'

'Oh, and I need you to come shopping with me, for a dress.'

'You want to buy a *dress*? What's the occasion?'

'No occasion, just figure I need a change from the jeans. Will you come?'

'Of course I will. I'd love to.'

'Great, we'll set it up. And hey, write to Bill. Take it from me, it feels good to get things off your chest and down on paper.'

So the following afternoon, she does.

Dear Bill,
In the time you've been coming in to The Food of
Love, you've become one of my most valued

Dear Bill,
We've known one another now for quite some
time, and I thought

Dear Bill,
You have always been one of the people I look
forward to

Dear Bill,
I shouldn't have got angry with you yesterday. I
feel very

Dear Bill,
I'm not quite sure how to

Dear Bill,
I'm sorry. It's just that I miss you.
Love, Emily

Bill

SHE WROTE TO HIM.

Two short sentences, twelve words from start to finish, counting her name and his name. Dear Bill, she wrote. I'm sorry, she wrote. It's just that I miss you, she wrote. Love Emily, she wrote.

The wallop in the gut he got when he walked into the lobby and saw her, turned in her chair to look out the window at Rory Dillon. The very last person he'd been expecting to see. Not that he'd had a clue who to expect: nobody ever called to his work.

Of course the first thing he'd thought of was the guards, coming with bad news about Christine, so Emily was a relief after that. But it had stopped him in his tracks all the same, the sight of her. He'd had to take a second to gather his scattered wits, to inhale a bit of calm before he said her name. Olivia behind her desk pretending not to notice, but no doubt taking it all in. Putting two and two together, and getting a wrong answer. Passing it on to Julie and Jean, next time she met them. Bill and his lady friend.

Emily's face though, in the courtyard. Blotched with pink as she pleaded with him to tell her why he'd stopped eating at the restaurant. Clutching her jacket tightly, looking so bewildered and upset. It killed him, knowing he'd put that look on her face.

It's not good enough, she said. It's not fair. Every word piercing him like a dart, and him helpless to defend himself – because what could he say without giving the game away? The one thing he did say, about her turning her back on everyone, was out before he could stop it, like that time at the vet's.

Fool, with his big mouth and his talent, his absolute genius, for putting his foot in it. And her parting shot: I thought we were friends, but this is not how you treat a friend. On the point of tears, and he'd sent her there with his thoughtless remark.

And then, two days later, the letter. Post for you, Olivia said, the first letter he could ever remember getting at the nursing home. The envelope plain and white, the handwriting on it unfamiliar. He should have guessed, but he didn't. He brought it to his cubbyhole and opened it, and read it and read it and read it. He folded it and put it into his top pocket, and spent the rest of the day pulling it out again and crucifying himself again.

For the first time since he'd begun it, he skipped the singsong at five o'clock, completely unable

to face it. He told them he was sorry but he had a
headache, and he'd see them tomorrow. He picked
up a burger on his way home, and he opened a bottle
of beer and sat on the back step with Sherlock, who
had recovered from his bug, and he tried to think of
nothing at all as he drank beer and gave most of the
burger to the dog.

And now it's the next night and Christine is here,
her first appearance since he sent her to Astrid. And
despite his determination not to bring up the subject
he has to, because it's been picking at him.

'Astrid tells me you called to her without ringing
beforehand. She said you just turned up.'

'I didn't think I needed to ring.'

'I asked you to,' he says, 'so she'd have a bit of
notice.'

'… Sorry.'

'And then you never went back.'

'I did go back. I cut her hedge, but she didn't like
it.'

Oh God. 'You went back? When?'

She looks at him. 'A few days ago.'

'Why didn't you go when you said you would?'

'I was sick.'

Sick. High. Away with the fairies. He swallows
the words, not having the stomach for a full-blown
row.

'I cut her hedge,' she repeats, 'like she asked me
to.'

'And why didn't she like it?'

A shrug that causes a twitch of annoyance in him. 'She said it wasn't good enough. She said don't come back.'

Bloody hell. Astrid had sent her packing. The shame of it. The mortification.

He remains silent until she drains her can of Coke and pushes her beans on toast aside, and then he gets to his feet and goes into the utility room. He takes the filled toilet bag and hands it over. He doesn't add the money he always adds. He asks nothing of her. He says nothing more, but waits silently for her to leave.

'I went,' she says, 'like you told me to.' Pulling on the jacket he has washed and dried. 'You shouldn't have sent me,' she says.

He makes no response. She's right, but he's damned if he's going to agree with her.

He sees her out silently, his hand on Sherlock's collar. He waits until she's out of sight, trying to remember what Eoin the paper boy had told him was Astrid's house number. Ten it might have been, or twelve. He can ring both doorbells; he can find her.

She has his phone number, but she didn't ring him when Christine finally returned. She didn't ring because she didn't want to admit that she'd had to send her packing. Sparing his embarrassment, even though he was the cause of all that disturbance.

He has to make amends.

After work the next day he crosses the canal and asks a man with a buggy for directions to Cedar

Grove, which turns out to be a small narrow road with just a dozen houses, bungalows on one side and two-storeys across from them. Numbers ten and twelve are both on the bungalow side, divided from one another by the same style of low wall that runs between Bill and Mrs Twomey. Number ten has a red motorbike parked in the driveway, so he walks up the path to the front door of number twelve, the last of the houses on that side, and presses the bell beside the blue door.

'Bill,' she says in astonishment. She wears the familiar cardigan and skirt combination that he's accustomed to seeing her in, but on her feet is a pair of pink and cream slippers. 'What are you doing here?'

'I've come to explain,' he says, 'and to apologise.'

She steps back to let him in. She closes the door and leads him into a little room that's dominated by a large mahogany thing on legs, some sort of old music player, he suspects, for vinyl records, a turntable nestling in all likelihood under that hinged top – and yes, there on the shelf behind is a collection of vinyl.

The only other furniture in the room is a small tweed couch, an upright padded chair with a basket full of wine-coloured knitting on the floor beside it and a low table. No television, no knick-knacks, no photographs or any ornamentation on the mantelpiece above the fireplace.

'Take the couch,' she says. 'I've gone beyond it. Shall I make tea?'

'Not for me, thanks.' He sits and opens his mouth to speak, but she, settling herself into the chair, gets there before him.

'First of all,' she says, 'you have nothing in the world to apologise for, Bill. You were trying to help your child, and for that, no parent should be criticised.'

He attempts once more to speak, and again he's beaten to it.

'And as for an explanation, I don't think that will be necessary either.' She looks at him, her face softening. 'I know, Bill. I know about Christine. I have seen the marks on her arms.'

She knows. The humiliation of it causes him to bow his head. 'I shouldn't,' he says. 'I should never have let her come to you.'

'Please, you mustn't blame yourself, I won't have it. You saw a possibility for her, and you reached for it. Nothing bad happened.'

'She told me you sent her away.'

Astrid nods. 'She was not in a state to work. I had no option.'

'Astrid, I'm so sorry,' he says. 'I wish I could turn back the clock.'

'Well, you cannot do that, so put it out of your head.' She pauses. 'On a happier note, I found a man to work in the garden, and he is marvellous. He is Markus, from Poland, and he is making such a difference – would you like to see?'

He can hardly say no, so he follows her into the

kitchen and through to the patio, and there he takes in the long, narrow garden with its neatly trimmed low hedge and clipped lawn, its shrubbery and presumably newly planted flowers, its climbers just beginning their ascent of the end wall. I cut her hedge, Christine said: he prefers not to know the full story there.

'Bill.'

He turns to regard her.

'I am sure, knowing the kind of man you are, that you were the best of fathers.'

He looks away again, folds his arms. 'For all the good it did.'

Astrid sighs. 'Bad things happen,' she says quietly. 'We do nothing wrong, we do our best, and still bad things happen. This is the way of the world. It is sad, but it is so.'

'I sent an email,' he says, his gaze still on the garden that the Polish man has brought back to life. 'I wrote to that agony aunt in the paper. Claire. I asked her for advice.'

' … And what did she say?'

'The same as everyone else, that nobody can help Christine until she wants it herself.'

'Yes, I believe this is true. It must be so heartbreaking for you.'

He makes no response. A bird alights on the hedge, flits away again. The flowers in the bed are bright like jewels, pinks and reds and yellows, and smaller, softer ones whose petals are mixes of yellow and purple and blue. Betty would have been able to name every one.

'Can I ask,' Astrid says then, 'if you will return to Emily's restaurant? You don't have to tell me why you stopped going there, that's your business. I'm simply enquiring if you're planning to come back.'

It's unexpected, this change of subject. He casts about for something to say. He thinks of the letter, the words Emily wrote. *It's just that I miss you.*

'I don't know, Astrid,' he admits. 'I don't know if I'll be back.'

'She misses you,' Astrid says. 'Emily.'

He's startled at the echo of his thoughts. Has she guessed? Can she have guessed? Was it written on his face every day he sat at the oval table? Did he give himself away without knowing it?

'We all miss you, of course – but Emily ...' She lets it drift away.

'She's leaving,' he says. 'Did she tell you? She's selling up, moving to Dublin.'

'And you feel betrayed,' Astrid replies, in the same thoughtful tone. 'You feel abandoned.'

'Don't you? That she could just—' He breaks off, afraid to let the rest out. He sets his mouth and goes back to looking at the garden.

'Bill, she's trying to do what's best. She's torn – anyone can see that. She doesn't want to go—'

'Then she shouldn't! He doesn't deserve her! He left her on her wedding day! Did you know that? Did she share that with you?'

Too much: he realises before he's got to the end of it. If she hadn't guessed before, she knows now. Time to go.

'Sorry,' he says, 'I'm just a bit— Look, I have to get going. You have my number if you need me.' If Christine shows up again, he means, now that he's given her access.

'Actually,' Astrid says, 'I'm glad you mentioned that. I mislaid my phone and had to replace it, so I lost all my contacts. Let me get my new one, and you can add yourself again.'

She leaves him on the patio, leaves him kicking himself once more. *He doesn't deserve her* – how could he blurt out something like that about a man he's never met?

Astrid returns and hands him a phone that looks exactly like the old one. He inputs his number and hands it back, and then he puts hers into his own phone. 'Don't mind me,' he says. 'Take no notice. I'm a bitter, messed-up creature.'

'You're nothing of the sort,' she says sharply. 'I won't have you talking like that, Bill. You're a good, decent man and I'm proud to call you my friend. I can see you're under pressure now, but stay strong. Everything passes. Everything passes,' she repeats, looking intently at him.

Does it? He wonders what she knows of suffering. She escaped the war with her family, she got married, and she lives in apparent comfort now. No children to break her heart, no major trauma – at least, none that she's ever spoken of, or even hinted at. On the face of it, she's got off pretty lightly.

She walks him back to the front door. 'Emily told me,' she says. 'About the wedding, I mean, the one that didn't happen. I think it's brave of her to try again.'

He says nothing. He can't agree, not without sounding insincere. Best to keep his trap shut.

'I know she'd love you to come back, even just once. Just so she knows you're not angry at her for leaving.'

But he *is* angry. He's hurt and dejected and miserable, and thoroughly fed up with everything. 'I'll see,' he says, and leaves it at that. It's not until later, when he's pulling the lawnmower from the shed after his dinner of bangers and mash, that her comment about her phone being mislaid comes back to him.

Mislaid.

He walks behind the mower as it slices through the grass, and thinks of Christine taking money from his wallet while he slept, after what had turned out to be her last night under the same roof as him. Could she have stolen from Astrid? Wouldn't a mobile phone be easy to hock for a few euro, even one as uncomplicated as Astrid's?

Let it not have been her. Let the damn phone have fallen from Astrid's bag in a taxi, or wherever. Let it not have been pocketed by Christine.

He finishes the lawn and empties the cuttings

into his compost bin. As he closes the shed door, Mrs Twomey emerges from her house. 'Bill, isn't it a lovely evening?'

It is. He hadn't noticed. The sky is slashed with red and pink and orange, the late summer air redolent with the scent of newly mown lawn. The birds have retired for the night, leaving peace behind them.

'I've just put the kettle on,' she says, 'if you fancied a cuppa. We could have it out here in the garden.'

A hundred excuses rise up in his head. He tamps them all down. 'Sure. Let me wash my hands and I'll be over.'

As good a way as any to distract his head for half an hour.

Astrid

'MY WIFE,' MARKUS SAYS, PASSING HER HIS phone. 'Her name Amelia' – and Astrid sees a smiling fair-haired woman holding a small baby. 'Our boy,' Markus says, and follows with a word that seems entirely made up of consonants, presumably the child's name, so Astrid smiles and pours more coffee – he likes it so strong – and makes no attempt to repeat it.

Markus is working a slow miracle in the garden, plant by plant, flower by flower. On his first visit he repaired the hedge with his own electric trimmer. Because of Christine's hacking he was obliged to lower the entire thing by about a foot, which somehow makes the whole place seem bigger. He borrowed his brother-in-law's trailer and loaded up every bit of what he'd removed, and took it to the recycling centre.

On his subsequent weekly visits he treated the lawn, and raked up the moss when it died and went black, and planted new grass seed in the bare patches – and already, just a couple of weeks later, Astrid can see tiny green pins popping up. He reclaimed what he could of the shrubs and dug out the rest, and replaced them with fuchsia and lavender and broom, all her favourites. And then he fed and watered and fed.

He put in new clematis and a climbing rose against the wall at the end. They're small and unassuming, but she can visualise them ascending and spreading. She can see them in her mind's eye, blooming and magnificent.

He emptied the flowerbed of weeds and debris. He rejuvenated the earth with fertiliser. He took Astrid to the garden centre where she invested in trays of cheerful cyclamen, and violas and pansies that were a little past their best, but she needed something instant, and the reduced price made up for their lesser glory. They're planning an array of mixed bulbs – snowdrops, tulips, daffodils, hyacinths, crocuses – to bring fresh colour to the bed in the spring, and after the threat of frost is past she'll get him to plant out the seedlings that she's going to coax into being indoors, like she used to do every year.

Everything is coming back, it's all coming back, and it thrills and delights her to see it. Now that the bulk of the work has been done, Markus will come every two weeks for a couple of hours to keep it on course, to steer it safely to full glory.

But Bill. Bill is on her mind, in her thoughts. She

wishes she could have convinced him that no harm was done – except to the hedge, and that was fixable, and had been fixed. No harm has been done to their friendship, no harm to the trust she placed in him, the esteem she holds him in. But she could see that her reassurances weren't reassuring him.

And of course she knows how he feels about Emily. She'd have to be blind not to notice how he lit up whenever Emily appeared, the way his eyes followed her around the oval table. His voice when he spoke to her; his face when she addressed him, when she said his name. Anyone could see how he felt, if they thought to look for it.

And they would be so perfect together, Bill and Emily. He would be so good to her; she would be so good for him. What a cruel streak Fate must have, ordaining that A fall in love with B, who has eyes only for C.

'I've been to an estate agent,' Emily tells her. 'He's going to come around next week and have a look. You're the only one I can say it to, the only one who's not cross with me for leaving. Mike is devastated to be losing his job, Heather clams up if I mention it, and Bill, well …'

She shrugs as if it's nothing, but Astrid knows it's not nothing. 'Bill is going through a difficult time,' she says. 'Don't be hard on him.'

'Have you been talking to him?'

'I have, about Christine.' She doesn't elaborate. 'I feel so sorry for the poor man.'

Emily makes no response. It's not like her to be unsympathetic.

'And of course I'm not cross with you, but I am sad. This place will be a big loss to a lot of people.'

'I know. I know.'

'Have you begun looking in Dublin yet? For a possible premises, I mean.'

'Not yet, no rush with that. Time enough when I move there.'

Astrid doesn't ask when that might be. She wonders who would be interested in this small space. Would anyone care to keep it on as a going concern? Doubtful. She doesn't imagine there's a whole lot of income from one table, however large. Not for the first time, she marvels at the way Emily can sustain it, and pay Mike a wage. She must live very cheaply.

'I can't talk to her about it,' Heather says, cleaning Astrid's windows. 'I just can't imagine the restaurant not being there any more.'

'Yes, it will be strange. Perhaps you could buy it,' she suggests. A joke, of course – where would Heather get the money? – but her friend doesn't laugh.

'You know she had a row with Bill, don't you?'

Astrid frowns. 'Who – Emily?'

'Yes. She won't mind my saying it to you. She called to the nursing home to ask him why he'd stopped coming to the restaurant, and they ended up rowing.'

'Oh no.' She recalls Emily's shrug, her apparent lack of empathy with Bill's predicament. Astrid should have known there was more to it.

So there is feeling on both sides, on Bill's and on Emily's, with Emily being compelled to seek him out, and their exchange somehow becoming heated. Is she sure of what she's doing? Has she chosen wisely? Is she giving up too much for this man in Dublin?

'Looks like my folks are coming for Christmas,' Heather goes on. 'They were threatening to, and I didn't think they'd follow through, but now they're asking me to recommend a place for them to stay, so it looks like it's going to happen. I'm thinking about Park Lodge, which is the only possible place in town I can imagine them being happy.'

Park Lodge, located not in the town but on the edge of it, is more a country house than a hotel. Stone façade, ivy, sash windows and balustrades. Astrid was there once with Cathal, a few months before he died, for the golden wedding anniversary celebrations of a couple they'd known for years. *Won't feel it till it's our turn,* Cathal said, but they'd never got there.

Old grandeur was Astrid's impression of the place. Proper china and good glasses for the meal, wallpaper and sideboards, a drawing room with a piano and a large fireplace. Little black and white tiles on the floor in the entrance hall, cobbles in the courtyard to the rear, where old stables had been converted into bedrooms. Yes, the Americans will find it charming.

'It will be lovely for Lottie to have them around,' Astrid says. Pause. 'And for you too.'

'Yes, we'll see how it goes. Will you be spending Christmas with your nephew and his family again?'

'Oh, I expect so.'

She won't, of course. She has a standing invitation to his house, located in a town fifteen miles from Dublin, but each year she assures him that she has local plans. She has no problem being alone on the twenty-fifth of December. To tell the truth, a quiet Christmas is a relief, after all the years she had to endure the company of her in-laws on the day.

She recalls with a shudder the false jollity as presents were exchanged and opened before the dinner. A cookery book once for Astrid, inside whose cover she read *Merry Christmas Mary from Judith*, a passed-on gift that her mother-in-law hadn't bothered to open – or maybe she had.

A glass of sweet sherry she didn't want, and carols playing in the background that always struck Astrid as a dig at the Jewess. The turkey that her father-in-law made such a performance of carving, always too thickly. The crackers with their cheap, childish trinkets, their silly paper hats. The overcooked Brussels sprouts, Astrid's least favourite vegetable; the stodginess of the plum pudding. The hour or so in front of a television turned up too loud before she and Cathal could decently take their leave.

Kind souls like Heather would be bothered, of course, if they knew Astrid was spending Christmas Day alone, so she simply pretends otherwise, and everyone is happy.

She wonders about Christine. Where will she spend the day that traditionally brings families together? Any thought of her is accompanied by a sense of disappointment, a feeling of failure on Astrid's part – but what could she have done for the girl, if her own father can't help her?

And Bill. Will he be alone at Christmas, or does he have other family to take him in? She thinks he made mention of a sister once. Perhaps Astrid could get in touch with him closer to the time, now that she has his number again. She could sound him out, see what his plans are. If it transpired that he had none, she could ask if he'd like to come to her for dinner – because whatever about her being happy to spend the day on her own, she doesn't like to think of Bill in a similar situation.

The following day is Wednesday, her library day. After lunch she calls a taxi and gathers her books. The sky is uneasy, rain on the way – and sure enough, she's barely in the car before a shower starts.

'You're a great reader,' Judy at the library says. 'I'm looking forward to the time when I can sit and read all day,' and Astrid thinks, but does not say, that she would happily trade places with the librarian in return for the energy to do more than turn the pages of a book, or work a few rows of knitting. Much as she appreciates her content life, there was so much more that she loved to do, so much that is denied to her now in old age.

She tells Judy of the improvements to her garden, and Judy asks for photos, which Astrid doesn't have. 'Take a few with your phone,' Judy suggests, and a promise is given, although Astrid will ask Markus to take them. Once she's chosen her new books, she makes her way to the pretty little café two doors down for a pot of herbal tea, her usual practice on library days. As long as she's out, she may as well make the most of it.

The rain continues to fall: she watches it drizzle and roll down the window, blurring the passing pedestrians into moving blots of colour. She lingers longer than she normally would as she waits for it to pass, but when it shows no sign of letting up she calls a taxi, instead of walking a small part of the way home and hailing one en route.

'Going to be a wet night,' the driver remarks, and Astrid thinks of the ones who live on the street, the rough sleepers as they're called now. No bed, no comfort, no heat – and again her thoughts turn to Christine, who may have nowhere to hide from the elements tonight.

'Mind how you go,' the driver says, and she thanks him and gets out, and turns to see her gate open. She always closes it when she leaves: someone must have slipped a leaflet through her letterbox, and neglected to close the gate.

But there is no leaflet on the hall floor. No note, no money-off coupons or laundry detergent samples. Nothing but a series of pale brownish marks on the off-white tiles that she mopped earlier.

She bends to peer at them. They're smudged, but they look very much to her like the marks that wet shoes would leave behind. Not hers: the rain didn't start until she was on the way to the library.

She feels a prickle of uneasiness. She stands in the hall and listens intently, and hears nothing but the whisper of the continuing rain as it falls on the path outside.

'Hello?' she calls, and again, more loudly, 'Hello? Who's there?'

Someone was here, in her house. Someone might still be here. What if he or she appears? What if the kitchen door or the sitting-room door is flung open and a person marches out? Should she leave right now, before that has a chance to happen? Should she ring Will Flannery's bell next door and ask him to come in and have a look? No – it's too early: he'll still be at work. What then? Should she knock at other doors on the road? Should she keep trying until someone answers?

She looks about the small hall, checking for any sign of disturbance other than the footprints, and finding none. The walking stick she bought on the advice of a friend three years ago, and has used precisely once since then, stands propped in its usual corner behind the door – reminding her, each time she sees it, of Papa's umbrella that always stood just so, in just such a spot.

Her coat rail with its six metal hooks, lowered by her nephew a few years ago to accommodate her diminished reach, looks as it always does. There are her blue scarf and grey winter coat, and the navy poncho she never wears, hanging precisely where they were this morning. The Turner print she treated herself to when she moved into the house is still on the wall by the sitting-room door.

She looks down once more at the footprints and tries to make sense of them. They imply that the intruder came in through the front door, but it shows no sign of damage, no indication of forced entry.

The only one with a front-door key, apart from Astrid herself, is Heather. Just in case you lock yourself out some day, she said. All you need to do is give me a call, and I'll be right with you. There's a third key, hanging on a hook just inside the patio door: Astrid keeps meaning to find a secure place for it outside, in case Heather isn't nearby if and when she's needed. Keeps meaning to, and keeps forgetting.

She should call the police. That's what she should do. She should call them and wait right here until they arrive, instead of going out in the rain to find neighbours who may or may not be there.

And then she thinks: No. I will not call the police. I will face unafraid whatever there is to face.

She leaves the front door ajar and advances

slowly, every sense alert for rogue sounds. She moves along the hall, avoiding the footprints, her steps barely disturbing the silence. Feeling, it must be said, a little afraid, or a little more than that. She reaches the kitchen door and puts a palm to it, and pushes it in.

Her hands press to her cheeks. Oh, my.

Disorder. Mayhem. Drawers pulled out, contents scattered. The cutlery tray upended, forks and spoons everywhere. The sugar bowl toppled, a fan of white on the table. Fridge and freezer doors thrown open, yogurt spilt, a puddle of milk. Pat's ready meals tossed about the floor, their foil lids ripped off. The saucepans she no longer uses scattered across the tiles. Plates, cups, all smashed.

She lowers her hands, which have begun to tremble. She advances carefully into the room, picking her way through the destruction. She has never experienced burglary, never had her home, her refuge, violated like this. She looks at the hook where her spare key hangs – and sees, with a new lurch of dismay, that it has disappeared.

Who? Who could have taken it? Who has been in the house? Pat, bringing in the meals each Monday morning. Eoin the paper boy, whom she brings into the kitchen on Fridays while she gets his payment. Markus. Heather. Christine.

Christine.

Going in and out a few times through the patio door, the day she attempted to cut the hedge. Left alone in the kitchen when Astrid went to get slippers for her bare feet, and again when Astrid got the first-aid box to treat her blister. Christine, the only possible culprit.

But could the key really have been missing since then? Astrid tries to gather her scattered wits, to recollect when the girl was here. She rewinds through the days, the weeks, to Markus's first visit, her call to him prior to that, Christine's second and final appearance at the house a handful of days before that. Four weeks ago, around then. Could she really not have missed the key in all that time?

Yes, she could. Unless she'd gone looking for it, there was no reason for her to have noticed its absence. Something so familiar, so invisible in its familiarity, could have been taken at any time. But if Christine was indeed responsible for its disappearance, why would she have waited so long to use it?

And then Astrid remembers the two weeks that passed between Christine's first and second times to show up at the house, after she'd promised to return the following day. Maybe time loses its meaning when addiction moves in; or maybe it is reconfigured, elongating or condensing in response to whatever chemical changes are taking place in the mind. Christine may have slipped the key into her pocket and then forgotten about it, and only come across it again by chance.

But what of this calamitous scene? Why cause

so much damage? Could it have been prompted by resentment at Astrid's sending her away – or was it a search, a frenzied hunt for money, or anything that could be sold to feed a hunger that food can't satisfy?

And then, with a fall of her heart, she thinks of her most treasured possession. More precious, far more, than the emergency cash in her bedroom. Dearer to her even than the letters her saviour Herr Dasler wrote in the dozen years that passed between her leaving Austria and his death. She thinks of the one thing she would most hate to lose in the world.

She must look for it. She must go to her room and see if it's still there.

She can't.

She stands in her vandalised kitchen, unable to act. She stands, surrounded by broken things and spilt things and thrown-about things. She lets time travel on while she summons the courage to face the possibility that it is gone.

Finally she turns and leaves the kitchen, and makes her way down the corridor. The fear that she might not be alone has abated, has moved aside to accommodate the greater apprehension. Let it be safe, she prays. Let it not have been found. Let it still be there.

She enters her room to find the same disorder. Pillow and bedclothes in a tumble on the floor, mattress half on, half off the base. Lamp knocked sideways, book splayed open, wardrobe door gaping, clothes pulled from hangers, and—

No.

No.

No.

'No!' she wails, stumbling to her knees before the wrenched-open drawer that had been locked, the wood around the lock splintered and cracked now, the kitchen knife that must have been used to hack at it tossed onto the rug by her bed.

Trailing from the drawer is her old soft red scarf; she knows without lifting it that it will be empty of the pearl necklace she had enfolded so carefully within it. 'Mutti, Mutti, Mutti,' she moans, pressing the scarf to her face, rocking, lowering her head to the floor, prostrating herself in her grief, 'liebe Mutti, liebe Mutti,' her last reminder gone, nothing left of her now.

After a time – an hour, half that, more than that – she clambers slowly, stiffly to her feet. She shuffles to the door, feeling every one of her ninety-two years, scarcely able to see for the tears that run along the creases and runnels of her face, that trickle past her throat and soak into the neck of her cardigan. She makes her way back along the corridor, pressing a hand to the wall for support, for guidance, her breath coming out in sobbed gulps. Mutti, Mutti.

She must check the sitting room; she must see what the state of play is there before alerting the police to the burglary. She opens the door and steps inside, not seeing in her distress the album cover on the floor that slides forward as soon as she places her foot on it, pitching her off-balance. Her arms fly out as she crashes to the floor.

Her eyes close. She lies without moving among the broken shards of her beloved records.

Heather

'WHAT'S YOUR FAVOURITE COLOUR?'

'Blue,' he says, without stopping to think. 'You?'

'Green, ever since I came to Ireland. Does that sound like a load of schmalz?'

'Kind of.'

'Don't care. Lottie's is gold. Madge says she's got notions of grandeur.'

He laughs. 'Long time since I heard that one.' He tips chopped lettuce into the salad bowl and reaches for a cucumber. 'Madge used to be my babysitter – she must be over a hundred now.'

'She's sixty-eight, and as hale and hearty as myself. You're not as ancient as you'd like to think.'

He's thirty-seven, which is only twelve years older than Heather. He married Yvonne at nineteen when Nora was on the way. Yvonne was twenty-one, his older woman. They'd been together for four years.

Heather was a kid of seven when he married Yvonne. Heather was in grade two when he walked down the aisle with his new pregnant wife. Nine years later, he and Heather came face to face for the first time when she lied about her age so she could look after his father.

He finishes the salad and begins separating a garlic bulb. 'How's that sauce coming along?'

'Good. Do those bay leaves stay in?'

'Yes, until it's done. Has the wine cooked off?'

'No idea.' Who knew white wine was an ingredient in spaghetti bolognese?

He looks into the saucepan, gives it a stir. 'OK, now you can add the tin of tomatoes. Stir them well in, bring it up to a simmer, then lower the heat and cover the pan.'

'Yes, sir.'

They're making dinner in his kitchen. They're cooking for five: him and her, his two older kids, and his daughter Nora's boyfriend, Daniel. Lottie is home with Madge: too soon for her to be part of this – and anyway her buddy Jack is with his mother, in the rented apartment she's been living in since the marriage split.

Heather is on her second glass of red, because she's in this house for the first time. She's in the kitchen where Yvonne put meals together for years, and she's making dinner with Yvonne's husband. And even though nothing will be said aloud – hopefully – Yvonne's children are bound to wonder what precisely Heather is doing here. Comparisons, she feels, will be inevitable.

The sauce bubbles. She turns down the flame, finds a lid for the pan. Yvonne's pan, Yvonne's lid. 'What's next?'

'Check if there's cream in the fridge. We can do without, but if we have it, we'll chuck it in later.'

She loves the we. It's so long since she's been part of a we. She opens his fridge, which is considerably better stocked than hers. Wedges of cheese, eggs, cooked meats, sausages, butter, yogurt, jars of pesto and olives, a tub of hummus, another of potato salad, bottles of fish sauce and sweet chilli sauce, milk and juice. She shifts things around and locates an opened carton of cream, and sets it by the stove.

'Can you cut a few slices of that bread? Eoin likes to mop up his sauce.'

'Thick or thin?'

'Medium.'

'Like this?'

'Perfect.'

She's told him about Josephine. He's told her about being bullied at school because of the milk-bottle glasses he ditched as soon as he could afford contacts.

She hasn't mentioned Lottie's father.

He's said nothing of the abuse Yvonne meted out.

They have time.

They have time.

I used to enjoy meeting you, he said. You were always so cheery.

I wanted to talk to you, he said, every time I saw you at the school. I felt bad about everything, but you made it kind of plain you didn't want me to come near you, so I left you alone.

You were the enemy, she said. You and Yvonne.

After we met in the restaurant that evening, he said, I couldn't get you out of my head. Everything you threw at me was justified, but I honestly never wanted any of it to happen.

I know.

I hated myself for going along with Yvonne, but I had the kids to think of. I had to try to keep the peace for their sake.

I know.

I was dreading Lottie's party, he said. Given how badly our meeting in the restaurant had gone, I mean. I knew I'd have to bring Jack – he'd never have forgiven me if I didn't, and there was no way Yvonne was taking him – and then Nora told me she was going, and I was so relieved.

And then, he said, we met on the street.

We did.

I knew we'd get on, he said, if we were given a chance.

Would you like to come to my place on Thursday? he'd asked, after the walk in the park. Nothing fancy, Jack will be with his mum so it would just be dinner with the older two. Nora might ask her boyfriend.

So here they are. Here she is, about to give love another try, like Emily. Here she is, getting a little tipsy on wine, because when it comes to love she's very much out of practice, and because on paper he's still married, and his kids might resent her muscling in, and it's all a bit terrifying.

She hears the opening of the front door. 'That'll be Eoin,' Shane says, mincing garlic into a small bowl. 'He might be quiet. He had a bit of an upset this morning.'

'What kind of an upset?'

The kitchen door opens. A teenager walks in, shrugging off a backpack.

'Eoin, this is Heather,' Shane says. 'She used to look after your granddad – you mightn't remember her. She's mum to Lottie, Jack's friend.'

'Hi Eoin,' she says. 'I've seen you at the school gate a couple of times.'

'Yeah,' he says, just that. He's distracted, she tells herself. It's not that he doesn't want her there.

He turns to his father. 'How is she?'

'I checked just before I went off duty. She was gone to surgery.'

'But she'll be OK?'

'Hopefully. It's early days.'

Heather looks from one to the other.

'A woman on his paper round,' Shane explains. 'She was broken into. Eoin found her this morning.'

'Oh no – that's awful.'

'He called me – I was on the early shift. My crew

took her to the hospital. She's ninety-two, poor creature.'

A tiny bell pings in Heather's head. 'Where was this?'

'Cedar Grove.'

Cedar Grove. Astrid.

'Mrs Carmody?' she asks Eoin. He nods. He looks at his father.   'You know her?' Shane asks.

'She's a friend.' Her stomach clenches. Astrid, burgled. Astrid, injured. 'You said she's had surgery.'

'Yes, a broken hip—'

Heather pulls down sleeves, grabs her bag from the worktop. 'I have to go to her.'

'I'll take you,' Shane says, setting down the garlic crusher. 'Eoin, will you keep an eye here? Just turn that sauce off in about half an hour. Cook some spaghetti if you want to eat before we're back.'

'Let me know how she is.'

'Will do.'

'She was very confused when we got to the house,' he tells Heather on the way to the hospital. 'Normal after a shock. She was lapsing into another language – German, I think.'

'She's Austrian. Was she able to say what happened?'

'Nothing that we could make sense of. It's a good job the front door was open or Eoin would just have put the paper through the letterbox and gone away again. He called her, and when he got no answer he went in.'

'What time was this?'

'Eight, around that.'

Eight o'clock in the morning. 'Where was she?'

'Front room.'

She closes her eyes, opens them again. 'Who would attack an old woman?'

He glances at her. 'That may not have happened, Heather. She might not have been at home. She could have fallen afterwards. Everything was up in a heap – she could easily have tripped.'

Everything in a heap. Astrid's little house, neat as a new pin anytime Heather had seen it.

'We won't know for sure what happened until she comes round.'

Until. Unless. She tries not to picture it, but all she sees is someone, some man, raising a hand to Astrid. Astrid, who would blow away in a stiff breeze. 'Will she be alright?'

He darts a glance at her. 'Let's wait and see, OK?'

His training kicking in, she thinks. 'Don't give false hope' must be one of the first rules. You can see it in his driving too, keeping to the speed limit even though she wants to yell at him to hurry up, to put his foot down hard on that damn gas pedal.

'What about her house? Is it secured?'

'It is. The guards are investigating.'

Another invasion, on top of whoever trashed it. Guards taking photos, dusting for fingerprints, or whatever it is they do. 'I have a key,' she says. 'She gave me one in case she ever locked herself out. I can fix up the house, when the cops are done.'

'That would be good.'

'Ninety-two,' she says, her hands clenching and unclenching, her gut churning with worry. 'Ninety-two.'

He takes a hand off the steering wheel to squeeze hers briefly. 'They'll do everything they can, Heather.'

She clutches at the words, even as she recognises them for the cliché they are. She pictures Astrid opening her door with a smile, always happy to see Heather with her window-cleaning kit. Always looking on whatever bright side she could find.

They approach the hospital. 'She has a nephew,' she says, remembering. 'I've never met him, but he needs to know.'

He nods. 'She's on file at the hospital – he's probably listed as her next of kin so he'll have been contacted.'

Next of kin. She's never liked that expression: it has death sewn into it. They enter the hospital gates, and Shane pulls up at the main door. 'She's in Intensive Care,' he says. 'I'm not sure if they'll let you in, but tell them you're with me. I'll park and follow you in.'

'Intensive Care,' she says to the man at Reception, and he points her in the direction. She wonders, as she hurries along corridors, if he could smell the alcohol on her breath. Not that it's any of his damn business – but thank the Lord she was just halfway through that second glass.

'Astrid Carmody,' she tells the nurse who comes in answer to her summons at the double doors that lead to Intensive Care. 'I was hoping to see her.'

'Are you family?' The nurse definitely smells the alcohol, by the sour look on her face.

Can she say niece? Better not – might come back to bite her. 'I'm a good friend, I'm here with Shane Gillespie. He's parking the car ...' and here he comes, slightly out of breath. Must know a shortcut.

'Críona, I'm glad to see you. Heather is a close friend of Mrs Carmody's – is there any way you could let us in, just for a minute?' Tucking a hand into the crook of Heather's elbow as he speaks. Making a statement, it feels like. 'We'd really appreciate it.' That we again.

There's a short pause, during which Heather shifts slightly, forcing his hand to release its hold – and allowing her to grab it with hers, and hang on to it.

'A minute, that's it. She needs her rest.'

'Bless you,' Shane says, and they follow her across the tiled floor, past machines and cubicles and an empty bed stripped of its linen, around a partition wall and into a little curtained-off area, where Heather has to work very hard not to burst into tears at the sight that awaits her there.

Astrid lies unmoving under a sheet, a bruise in shades of red and purple staining the entire left side of her face. Her head, and both arms from elbow to wrist, are bandaged. There is a tube in her nose, another going into the back of her left hand. She wears a blue hospital gown. Her eyes are closed.

She looks tiny, the size of Lottie.

Heather approaches the bed, touches the hand that doesn't have a tube in it. She runs a thumb to and fro along the wrist bone, strokes the swollen knuckles, feels the rise of the veins that look like they could break through the papery skin at any time. Cold, so cold, despite the heat that's causing beads of sweat to pop on Heather's forehead.

She cradles the hand, she strokes it, tries to send warmth into it. 'Astrid,' she whispers, 'Astrid' – and the eyelids flutter, and the eyes open, and immediately Heather's own eyes fill with the threatened tears. She blinks hard: not yet. 'Sweetheart, don't try to talk. I heard what happened, and I'm just here to see that you're OK.'

No reaction from Astrid, nothing to indicate that she's heard. Nothing but the open pale blue eyes, pupils flickering about Heather's face, so she keeps on talking in a low voice because Astrid's silence must be filled with something. 'I'm here with my friend Shane. He's a paramedic. His son Eoin delivers your paper – he's the one who found you. He called his dad, who came in the ambulance and picked you up. You're in good hands here, nothing for you to do but concentrate on getting well. And don't worry about your house – I'll keep an eye on it. I have a key – remember?'

Something, some agitation, chases across Astrid's face then. Her mouth opens, and a sound issues from it, so tiny that Heather misses it. She leans closer. 'What was that, honey?'

'Key.' Just the word, nothing else. And again, 'Key.'

'Yes,' Heather says. 'You gave me a key. Don't worry, sweetie, everything's under control.'

'You need to leave.' The nurse's voice behind her. 'She has to sleep now.'

'Sure,' she says, not turning around, giving the hand she still holds a gentle squeeze. 'I'll come see you again tomorrow. Get some sleep now.'

She'll bring hand cream, she'll massage it into the skin, and a comb for the hair that's lost its way. And she'll bring a nightdress, a pretty one. She'll go to Dillon's, where she never shops because the prices are crazy, and she'll get the best they have, and it will be soft and fabulous.

'I had a quick look at her chart,' Shane tells her on the way back to the car. 'She suffered a head injury, and she has lacerations on her arms, and the damage you saw on her face. That, and the hip. All consistent with a fall. There may not have been violence.'

They stop for a red light. She watches a man walk past the car with a small perky dog on a lead. She asks again the question she asked on the way to the hospital: 'Will she be OK?'

She doesn't miss the pause. 'They'll know more

after the night,' he says. 'If her general health was good before this—'

'It was. She had a cold, flu, something, a little while ago, but she was better.'

'Well, that's a good thing. That'll help.'

They drive along Main Street. She looks out at shops, and sees only Astrid with her bruised face and bandaged head. 'Will you take me home?' she asks. 'I'm not sure I can handle a family dinner tonight.'

'Of course I will. Whatever you want.'

She shifts in her seat to face him. She takes in his profile, the regularity of his features, the general *tidiness* of him. The pale brown hair streaked with blond that frankly could do with a decent cut.

'You're a good man,' she says. 'You're a credit to your father.'

He turns and gives her a smile that makes her insides flip over. 'You're not so bad yourself,' he says.

Emily, she thinks, as they cross the canal. She must let Emily know.

Emily

IT'S THE FIRST DAY OF SEPTEMBER, GREY and drizzly. She rubs butter into flour for shortcrust pastry, thinking about how much she hates the estate agent, who has just left.

It's compact, isn't it? he said, measuring walls with his fancy gadget, tapping numbers into his iPad. Few enough businesses it would appeal to – size-wise, I mean. His hair stiff with some product or other, suit trousers straining across stout thighs, top button of his white shirt undone. The toes of his black shoes coming almost to a point, which she always feels looks daft on a man.

It's plenty big enough for my restaurant, she told him. I don't have a problem with the size.

You have only one table, he pointed out, with a smile that made Emily want to mess up his silly hair.

My grandmother had a hat shop here for years.

Well, he said, nudging his designer glasses up

a notch, I don't imagine hats would take up too much room. Even if someone were to knock the dividing wall and incorporate the kitchen, it would still be fairly bijou. No, I'd say we're talking niche positioning here, but we'll see what we can do.

Bijou. Niche. Codswallop. She adds sugar to the bowl and mixes it through. She makes a well in the centre and drizzles in iced water. She works the dry mixture into the liquid, her touch light, her movements practised and automatic. The Food of Love is a proposition to him, a possible sale, that's all. He sees none of its charm, none of the hard slog that went into its creation, none of the satisfaction she experiences at the end of every working day. It's just square metres and location to him.

Don't take it personally, Ferg tells her, he's just doing his job – but how else can she take it?

He doesn't care. He has no idea what it means to me.

Emmy, he's not paid to care, he's paid to sell.

She can't argue with that, but it's all so cold, so without feeling. No sign, she told the estate agent. I don't want you to put up a sign. She couldn't bear the thought of it, a constant reminder every time she looked out.

He wasn't happy about that. A sign will boost interest, he said. Signs always help – but she wasn't budging. No sign, she said again, and he had to put up with it.

Daniel and Nora appear at the restaurant that

evening. 'We've eaten dinner, but can we have dessert?' Daniel asks, so Emily brings them bowls of Eton mess and a plate of ginger snaps.

'You've heard about Heather and my dad,' Nora says.

'She told me,' Emily replies, pouring coffee.

I can't explain it, Heather had said.

But you had a row with him! You made him leave the restaurant!

Well, I didn't exactly make him leave – but yes, we did have a row. And now we're not rowing. What can I say? Feel free to laugh.

'How do you feel about it?' Emily asks Nora. She imagines a parent's new partner takes some getting used to, whatever the circumstances. And the fact that Heather is closer in age to Nora than to Shane must count for something too.

'Fine, actually. She's lovely.' Nora pauses. 'Anyone who makes Dad happy is OK with me.'

It was a bad situation, Heather told Emily. He'd stayed with her for the kids, he didn't want to leave them – and in the end she was the one who walked out. No more details were given, and Emily didn't ask.

'We were all to have dinner together tonight,' Nora goes on, 'but they went off to see someone in hospital before we got there, so we ate without them.'

'Oh, no. Who was it?'

'No idea. Some woman Eoin delivers a paper to.

Heather knows her too: I think she might do some work for her.'

'Heather works for everyone.' Emily takes a seat, the restaurant having all but cleared out, the last two diners on coffee and cookies at the far end of the table.

'So did the estate agent call?' Daniel asks.

He's dead set against the move. How can you sell Gran's place? he asked when Emily told him of her plans, which upset her so much that he ended up apologising. He's trying to make up now by feigning an interest, but she wishes the topic hadn't been broached.

'Yes, he was here earlier.'

'So what did he say?'

'Well, he didn't seem that taken with it. He basically said it's too small for most businesses to bother with.'

'That's ridiculous,' Nora says immediately, and Emily wants to kiss her. 'Plenty of people would be interested, I'm sure. You could have any number of businesses here – a little bakery or a delicatessen, or maybe a jewellery shop, or a gift shop. Loads of possibilities. The kitchen would make a perfect store room – and they'd have all the upstairs too.'

'Yes …' But Emily doesn't want to think about anyone else here, stacking magazines in racks, or sliding a tray of cookies or watches into a display cabinet. She wants nobody else to live in her apartment either, looking out on her garden, cleaning her bathroom.

She dreads to think about what will become of the big table, where two years' worth of friendships have been forged, and stories exchanged. Who will want it, when she no longer has a use for it? She might have asked Bill if the nursing home could use it, but that's not going to happen now.

He didn't respond to her letter. She pushes away the hurt and returns to the estate agent.

'He says the location isn't great either.'

'Well, that's just nonsense!' Nora again. 'It's not five minutes from the main street, for God's sake!'

'I know. We'll just have to wait and see.'

The conversation turns to other things. The series of black-and-white movies the cinema is planning to run for the month of September; Daniel's invitation to ghost-write a novel for an old school friend who's now a national sports personality; the weekend trip to London they're planning for Daniel's birthday next month.

'I'm throwing a surprise birthday party for one of my regular customers,' Emily tells them. 'She'll be ninety-three at the end of this month. It'll be at lunchtime, because she doesn't go out in the evenings. You might come, both of you.'

It was to be a joint celebration for Astrid and Bill, since their birthdays are so close together. Now it's a party for one, in this sad new world that doesn't include Bill.

After saying goodnight to the others and closing up, Emily clears the table and brings her tray into the kitchen, where Mike is scrubbing pots.

'Why don't you head off?' she says. 'I can finish up here.'

'Sure?'

'Sure.'

'OK, then.' He finishes the pot he's working on and dries his hands. 'See you in the morning, boss.' Pulling on his jacket, zipping it up.

'Goodnight, Mike. Thanks.'

He's been quieter since she broke the news of the move to him. She's glad he wasn't here this afternoon when the estate agent called. She feels so guilty about him. She's had a few quiet words on his behalf with other restaurateurs: she thinks, hopes, it won't be long till he's invited into another kitchen.

As she's rolling up her sleeves, her phone rings. She takes it from the shelf where it lives during opening hours, and looks at the display. Fergal's name surprises her – she called him earlier, after the agent had left. Why was he ringing again?

'Hi, Ferg. What's up?'

'Emmy. You can talk?'

'Yeah, Mike's just gone home, so I'm on my own.' Silence.

'Hello? Ferg?'

'I'm here. I need to—'

He breaks off. He sounds funny. Something's up. She leans against the sink, crosses one foot over the other. 'Ferg, what's wrong? Has something happened? Is it your mother?' Sarah hadn't been well at the weekend, a sore throat, a headache. Emily had meant to ring her, and had forgotten. 'Is she worse?'

'No, it's not Mum. Look, Emmy, there's no easy way to say this.'

He stops again. No easy way? 'What are you on about?' Has he lost his job? Crashed the car? 'What is it, Ferg?'

'Oh God,' he says. 'I – I don't know –'

'Tell me, for goodness' sake. You're scaring me. Say it.'

'Look,' he says, 'I got a— I spoke with Therese Ruane today. She – she called me.'

She frowns. 'Therese Ruane? Why would she ring you? Has something happened in Canada?'

And in the long silence that follows, her mind slides pieces quietly together, and she gets it.

She gets it. She finally gets it.

The room begins to swim. She lowers herself slowly to sit on the floor. She bends her knees, wraps her free hand around them. Her heart is thudding so hard it hurts.

'Emmy?' His voice sounds far away.

'What are you saying? What are you *saying*?' She shouts it as loudly as she can – she fills the kitchen with it. 'What are you saying to me?' Heat spreading in her face, a pulse pounding in her temples. 'Say it! Say it!' Squeezing the phone so tightly her hand aches.

'I'm sorry, I'm so sorry –'

'Did you go back with her when you went to Canada? *Did* you?'

'Yes. I – I didn't plan it, you must—'

'You didn't *plan* it? You didn't *plan* it?' Her rage, the strength of it, frightens her. She wants to hit him, to hurt him in any way she can, to break him in pieces. 'You went to *Canada* – you left me on my wedding day and you went straight to where she was! Don't tell me that wasn't planned – don't tell me that! Did she ring you that time too? Did she beg you not to marry me?'

'No, I mean – no, it's not—'

'So you went crawling back to her, *you* were the one who begged, and she took you back.'

Silence.

'Did she? Was that what happened? Tell me!'

'Yes.'

She might throw up. She sinks her head onto her knees, inhales deeply. 'Why did you come home? Why did you write to me?'

'We fought – she didn't want to come back to Ireland—'

'So you split up, and you came home to your big job, and just decided to – pick things up where we left off. God, I'm a fool, I'm such a fool!'

'Emmy, it wasn't—'

'Don't *call* me that!' she shouts. 'Don't ever call me that again!'

'Sorry – no, it wasn't like you said, I really did want to see you again—'

'Because you couldn't have her! Only because of that!'

'No, no, I swear to you, it wasn't like that.'

But she doesn't believe him, because he's not to be believed. She loved him once, and he ran away from her without looking back, without a second thought. And she picked herself up and recovered, and then he came back and did it all over again.

How could she have been so gullible? Why hadn't she listened to Daniel, to everyone? Why hadn't she torn up that letter, had nothing more to do with him?

'So she's coming home now, is that it? She's decided she can't live without you, is that it?' The words opening a wound in her but she must let them out: they insist on it. 'Is that what's happening? Is it? *Tell* me!'

'… Yes.'

And with that one word, it's over.

She ends the call while he's still talking, still telling her how sorry he is. She lets the phone clatter to the floor, feeling everything shaken up in her, everything whirling and crashing and colliding in her. Alone in the kitchen she wails, she moans, she rocks, she pulls at her hair – she abandons herself completely to her grief. How could she have been so blind? How could he have done it to her, not once but twice?

She was his rebound person. Therese Ruane broke his heart, and along came Emily to mend it. He used her to heal, to make himself feel good again. I still love you, he said. I never stopped loving you, he said, but the truth was that he'd never loved her in the first place. The despair, the desolation she feels threatens to drown her.

And then her phone rings again.

She jumps at the sound.

It was all a joke: he's ringing to tell her it's not true. She'll kill him. She'll bloody kill him.

She wipes her trembling damp hands along her dress and picks up the phone and blinks tears away so she can see the display.

It's not him.

She presses the answer key. 'Heather.' Her voice sounds rusty, her scalp stings, her throat hurts. She attempts to steady her breathing.

'Emily, I know it's late,' an urgency to her words, 'but I wanted to make sure you were closed. I have news about Astrid.'

'Astrid?'

She listens, her face changing. She tries to take it in, tries to focus, to push the other aside. Her back aches. She pulls herself up to standing while Heather is still talking. 'Is she – will she be OK?'

'She was still confused when I saw her, but I'm hoping that was just after the surgery. We'll know more tomorrow – I'll go in first thing. They mightn't let me see her, but I'll do my best. Shane will keep me posted too.'

'Let me know, as soon as you have news.'

'Sure.'

It doesn't feel real. Astrid injured, Astrid lying

in a hospital bed. Emily pictures her sitting in the restaurant, small and neat and always smiling. 'Does Bill know?'

'Not yet. I don't have his number.'

'I'll tell him,' Emily says. 'I'll drop by his work tomorrow morning.'

It will give her something to do. It will occupy her head and keep the other from destroying her. 'Heather,' she says then, the sorrow rising again, tightening her throat, 'there's – something else.'

'What's that?'

And then she finds she can't say it. She simply can't get the words out.

'It's nothing,' she says. 'It can wait. I'll talk to you tomorrow.' She hangs up quickly and places a call to the hospital, swallowing a fresh desire to sob. 'Astrid Carmody,' she says. 'I'm wondering how she is.'

She's put through to Intensive Care, and is asked by a clipped voice if she's family. 'Grand-niece,' she says without a thought.

'The patient is resting,' she's told. 'We'll know more in the morning,' which tells her nothing at all. She says thank you and hangs up. She feels as weak and fragile as a convalescent. She empties the sink of the water Mike was using. Her watch shows five minutes to eleven. She said goodbye to Daniel and Nora half an hour ago, and sent Mike home directly afterwards. It feels like a lifetime has passed.

She finishes cleaning up in silence, numb now, spent now, focusing on the task in hand and nothing else. She turns off the light and climbs the stairs, her legs dragging on every step. She undresses and brushes her teeth and washes her face, avoiding the mirror that would be no friend to her tonight.

She pulls open drawers. She finds his postcards and his letters and his photos. She rips them up, every one. She piles them into the bathroom sink, and puts a match to them. Afterwards she washes away the remains and scrubs the sink clean.

She slips off the white-gold ring with the aquamarine stone that he gave her, a week after she agreed to try again. She'll take it to a charity shop on Monday. She'll tell them it's worth a bit, and not to let it go too cheap.

She takes out the box with her engagement ring inside. Imagine if she'd married him, and then found out – because she would have found out, sometime – that he was in love with another woman. She closes the box and places it in her handbag. She'll call to his mother in a few days and ask her to return it to him. Sarah will be upset and embarrassed to see her, but there is nothing Emily can do about that.

In bed she tries to sleep, and fails. She'll have to tell everyone, her parents, Daniel, her friends. They'll all be very sympathetic, and they'll try not to look satisfied that they were proved right, and she'll try to pretend she doesn't see it.

She won't be moving to Dublin. She won't be selling the restaurant. It's a good thing, she knows that. It's the one positive thing to come out of this

– but for now, the knowledge brings her no solace at all.

She'll never trust a man again. She'll never fall in love again, never know the joy of children. She'll live alone, grow old alone.

She endures the endless, unbearable night, tearful and miserable. Her eyes smart with weariness, her head aches with it, and still her brain refuses to allow sleep. At first light she leaves her bed, an hour earlier than her normal rising time, and goes down to let in Barney.

'I've been very stupid,' she tells him, but he burrows his head in his food bowl and ignores her. She showers and dresses, choosing a pair of soft grey chinos and a loose pink shirt. Comfort clothes. She boils the kettle and makes tea, and then finds herself unable to drink it. She sits at the upstairs window for a while as the morning gets underway in the street.

Back in the restaurant kitchen she starts her bread. Granary and dark rye loaves today, to accompany the pumpkin and spicy chicken soups on the menu. Life goes on. Each time the memory of last night's bombshell hits her – and it keeps hitting her – she wants to curl in a tight ball and cry some more. She thinks of Astrid too, but is afraid to ring the hospital for fear of what she might hear. She can't take more bad news.

While the dough is proving she washes her hands and returns upstairs. It's still too early to go to the nursing home. She stretches out on the couch, afraid to close her eyes in case sleep comes – and Barney hops onto her stomach and settles there, purring. Does he know? Can he tell that her world has tumbled over again? She strokes his soft coat; he nuzzles into her palm. He knows.

At length she lifts him off and gets her jacket and sets out. Her eyes burn with tiredness, her bones ache with it. She thinks of seeing Bill again. What will he say? How will he be when they're face to face?

He's not there. 'You just missed him,' the receptionist tells her. 'He went home sick, ten or fifteen minutes ago.'

Bill, sick too. Coming on top of Fergal's treachery and the news of Astrid, this is a fresh and most unwelcome blow. 'Do you have his address? It's very important that I speak to him.'

'I'm sorry.' She doesn't look sorry. 'We can't give out that information.'

'How about his phone number then? Can you let me have that at least?'

'I'm not supposed to –'

'Oh please. It's really important. A friend of ours has been in an accident. I have to tell him – he needs to know.'

The number is handed over, grudgingly. Emily thanks her and leaves the building. She calls him and gets no answer. Three times she tries, and three times it rings and rings and eventually goes to his voicemail. On her third attempt she leaves a message. 'Bill, it's Emily. I have news about Astrid.

Please give me a call.' So much else she wants to say, to ask, but it's not the time for that.

She returns to the restaurant, where the loaves are ready to be knocked back and left to rise again. She paces the kitchen floor, her head pounding, her insides knotted with tension. It feels like everything is breaking apart, everything familiar changing and disappearing, leaving her spinning in confusion, leaving her struggling to breathe, to survive.

The bread is in the oven when her phone beeps to signal a new text. She opens her inbox and reads, *Thanks for calling. I know about Astrid – Bill.*

He can't even talk to her, can't even address her by name any more. What did she do that he cut her off so absolutely? How wrong she was to think he was a good man. In the end he has shown himself to be no better than Fergal, turning his back on her without explanation when it suited him.

She's taking the bread from the oven when Heather phones.

'She'll be OK. She had a good night and she's eaten a little breakfast. They let me in for a second, literally – I barely got to give her a hug and tell her we're thinking of her – but it looks like she's out of the woods. I have a few jobs to do now but I'll go back in a few hours, and Shane will see her later too, and get a proper update.'

'That's wonderful.'

'It sure is. She'll outlive us all. Did you tell Bill?'

'Not in person.' She fills her in.

'Oh no – poor Bill. Text me his number and I'll

call him later. So what were you going to tell me last night?'

Emily closes her eyes. 'It's over,' she says, her heart again dropping. 'He broke up with me. He's gone back to his ex.' No details. She hasn't the heart for details – and thankfully, Heather doesn't look for them.

'Oh Jeez, I don't believe it. Oh, Emily, sweetheart. Are you OK?'

'Not really.'

'Want me to come around? I can cancel a few jobs. I could help with lunch – I mean, not cook, obviously, but I could lend a hand, just be there.'

'Thanks, I appreciate it, but Mike is due soon.'

'I'm so sorry, honey. We'll talk later. I'll call you this afternoon.'

Shortly afterwards, Mike arrives. Emily tells him, haltingly, that her plans have changed. 'I'm staying put,' she says. 'I'm not moving to Dublin, not selling up. I hope you'll stay too,' she says, her voice trembling, every ounce of willpower needed not to break down in front of him. 'I really hope so.' Her eyes swimming.

'Emily,' he says, regarding her with such concern on his face that she can't bear it.

'Don't – don't be nice to me, or I'll make a fool of myself.' Pressing a tea towel to her eyes, doing her best to smile.

'Listen,' he says, steering her to a stool, pushing her onto it, 'here's what I think. I think you should take the day off.'

'Oh no, I can't—'

'Of course you can. When was the last time you had a break, apart from the days we don't open?'

'Never – but that's—'

'Exactly. Never, not one single time. And – sorry, but by the look of you, I'm guessing you didn't get a whole lot of sleep last night. Am I right?'

'Well …'

'So here's what you need to do. You need to get me a sheet of paper so I can write a note and put it on the door, and then you need to turn off your phone, and go to bed and sleep. OK?'

'But the bread is done.'

'I'll make stuffing from it tomorrow. Anything else?'

She shakes her head, out of energy, and feeling now an overwhelming urge to sleep. 'I'll get you a page.'

The note is written, and pinned to the door. *Closed due to unforeseen circumstances*, it reads. *Sorry to disappoint. Back tomorrow.*

'Thank you,' she says, hugging him.

'Not a bother. I'm glad you're staying – for purely selfish reasons, of course.' He smiles; she tries to smile back.

Back upstairs she finds fresh pyjamas and climbs into bed. Everything can wait. Everything will still be there in a few hours.

She switches off her phone and closes her eyes – and this time, sleep comes rushing in.

Bill

'I HOPE YOU DON'T MIND ME RINGING YOU at work,' the man says. 'My son asked me. He met you a while ago, when he went to help you paint the nursing home.'

'Eoin,' Bill says, wondering where this is going. Conscious of Mrs Phelan, into whose office he has been summoned to take the call, hovering outside in the corridor. Able to hear every word, whether she wants to or not.

'Eoin, that's right. And he says you mentioned that you were a friend of Mrs Carmody's, so he thought you'd want to know.'

Mrs Carmody. Astrid. Eoin delivers her paper; she gives him biscuits.

'Yes, I'm a friend. Is something wrong?'

And then Eoin's father tells him what happened to Astrid. And as he listens to the account, Bill feels a cold fear oozing up from the soles of his feet and travelling into every square inch of him.

Christine.

No. It wasn't Christine. It couldn't have been Christine.

'How is she?' he asks, and the man, who says he's a paramedic, tells him she's in Intensive Care, but that her injuries aren't thought to be life-threatening.

Not thought to be life-threatening. Jesus Christ.

He thanks the man and hangs up. He stands for a second, two seconds, the fear still worming its way around him, a sheen of sweat on his forehead that he swipes away with his overall sleeve.

The door is pushed open. He attempts to gather his wits.

'Bill, are you alright?' Mrs Phelan, frowning at him. 'You're terribly pale.'

'I – I might head home,' he says. 'I think I'm coming down with some bug.' In the three and a bit years he's been working in the nursing home he hasn't taken a single sick day. The white lie will be forgiven.

'Of course you must go. Get yourself back to bed. Will I call you a taxi?'

'No, I'll pick one up on the road. Thank you.'

He hurries from the room, his only thought to get away, to marshal his scattered thoughts, to rid his mind of its horrible suspicions. In his cubbyhole he pulls off his overalls and gets back into his jacket, praying he's wrong. She wouldn't. She couldn't.

'I'm taking off,' he says to Olivia in Reception. 'Not feeling too good,' he says, and keeps going before she can quiz him. He walks home, he half runs home, and searches for a photo of his daughter that doesn't make her look like a different person from the one she is now.

The best he can find is a snap of Christine and Betty sitting side by side in some café, cups and buns and a teapot on the table before them. He vaguely remembers taking the photo. It was during a weekend they spent in West Cork, he thinks, about a year before Betty died. Christine, in a red sweater, leans into her mother's side, an arm around Betty's shoulders. She's unsmiling, with her hair caught up at the back of her head.

It's not ideal. She looks too healthy, too young and fresh, but it will have to do. He folds it so Betty is hidden, and slips it into his pocket.

He's halfway to the main street when his phone rings. He ignores it, knowing it won't be Christine, and she's the only one he wants to talk to now. Twice more it rings, and after the third call, he hears the ping that announces a voice message.

He pulls it out then and sees three missed calls from the same unknown number. It occurs to him, belatedly, that it might be an update on Astrid. It could be Eoin's father again, having got Bill's mobile number from Mrs Phelan. He presses the voicemail key and waits – and then, with a heart lurch, he hears the last voice he was expecting.

'Bill, it's Emily. I have news about Astrid. Please give me a call.'

Emily, having got his number from someone – Astrid, maybe. Emily asking him to call her, wanting to tell him what he already knows. He can't talk to her now. He can't think about anything else until he finds his daughter.

For the next hour he trudges the network of streets around the centre, crouching to speak to anyone who looks like they might know Christine. 'My daughter,' he says, showing them the snap. 'I need to speak to her, it's urgent.'

Heads shake, nobody can help him – until finally, an emaciated youth with an empty beans tin on the ground in front of him says, 'Yeah, I know where she is.'

Bill takes a tenner from his wallet. 'Bring me to her,' he says, 'and I'll give you this,' but the boy shakes his head.

'I can't bring you, but I'll get her. For twenty,' he says, gambling on Bill's desperation.

'OK.'

He waits, leaning against a shop window. People pass without glancing at him. He searches faces and sees preoccupation, everyone headed somewhere, everyone busy with life. Is this what it's like for Christine? he wonders. Everyone rushing past, nobody looking at her, apart from the odd few who toss her a coin.

After a while he takes out his phone and listens

again to Emily's voice. He can't ignore it. He must at least acknowledge the message. He opens a text box and types, *Thanks for calling. I know about Astrid – Bill*. It sounds so cold. He should put her name on it. He's about to add it when a movement catches the corner of his eye. He looks up to see Christine and the youth advancing in his direction. He presses *send* and pockets his phone, and walks towards them.

'Christine,' he says. Her padded coat is unfamiliar, green and grubby. She doesn't meet his eye. 'I want to talk to you.'

'My money,' the lad says, and Bill fumbles a twenty from his wallet and hands it over before turning back to Christine. 'We need to talk.'

'What about?'

'Let's go somewhere quieter.'

She shrugs. He takes her arm and brings her down the street and towards the canal. They walk in silence. In his head he frames questions. Stay calm, he tells himself. Stay focused. Don't get angry. Don't accuse.

He sees a bench. 'Here,' he says, and they sit. Following a sudden impulse he pulls the photograph from his pocket. He smooths it out and offers it to her.

'You and Mum,' he says, and she looks at it wordlessly but doesn't take it. He watches her profile and sees no reaction, no hint of feeling.

He returns the snap to his pocket, never taking his eyes from her. 'My friend Astrid,' he says then –

and he senses rather than sees a sudden stillness, a new alertness in her. 'You remember Astrid.'

'Yes.' She's looking at the water, her face in profile. She blinks rapidly.

'She lost her phone,' he goes on. Watching her, watching her. 'Did you know that?'

She turns. 'No.'

'You took it,' he says calmly. 'Didn't you?'

'No. I didn't.'

'You took it and sold it for drugs.'

'I didn't,' she repeats, more forcefully. 'I didn't take it.'

'I know you did,' he says, in the same even tone. 'You stole from her like you stole from me.'

'No!' She makes as if to get up. He puts a hand on her arm to keep her there.

'I haven't finished. You stole her phone when you were in her house, and then, the day before yesterday, or maybe in the middle of the night, you went back for more.'

'What? No.' But this denial is less vehement.

'You broke in. You attacked her—'

'No! I didn't! I didn't touch her!'

'You put her in hospital. She's in Intensive Care.'

'That's *not* down to me! She wasn't even—'

She breaks off. She bites her lip, looks sharply away from him. Tries to tug her arm from his grip, but he holds on tight.

'She wasn't even what?'

No response.

'She wasn't even what, Christine? We can stay here all day if we have to.'

She mutters something he doesn't catch.

'What was that?'

'I said she wasn't *there*.'

He digests this. 'So you did break in.'

'No – I had a key. I took a key.' Sullen now, head bowed. 'I wasn't going to use it, I just wanted – I was mad at her for telling me to go. I saw the key and just … took it.'

'And you did use it.'

Silence. A teenage couple walks by, hand in hand. He waits until they're out of earshot.

'You let yourself in with her key. You attacked her and robbed her.'

'No – she left! I saw her going away in a taxi.'

'So she came back while you were still there. She walked in and found you, and that was when you attacked her.'

'I didn't! I did *not* attack her!'

'She's in hospital. She's badly injured. She was found lying on the floor, the morning after you robbed her. She's ninety-two years old, Christine.'

'I didn't do it! I didn't touch her!'

He bows his head. Enough. He can't.

'Christine,' he says, his voice low, his words measured, 'I have to let you go. I can't deal with you any more. I can't take it. I can't take your lies. I can't bear what you've done with your life. I can't watch you destroy yourself any more. I don't want you to come to the house again. I don't want to have anything more to do with you.'

'Why won't you believe me? She wasn't there!'

'I don't believe you,' he says. 'I can't believe you. You've forgotten what the truth is.' He gets up. 'Don't come home,' he says. He turns on his heel and walks blindly away, swerving around people on the path, almost tripping over a dog lead in his haste. He has just told his daughter goodbye. He has just disowned her.

At the end of the path he stops and looks back. The bench where they sat is empty. There's no sign of her.

The hospital. He must go there. He must find Astrid. He walks rapidly past shops and offices and roadworks, his face set, his mind racing.

Christine will be caught and arrested and put away – and if Astrid dies, Christine will become a murderer. The thought makes him want to retch. Waiting at an intersection for the green man, he pulls out the photograph of mother and daughter again. He looks from one face to the other, seeing the similarities that used to delight him. Same mouth, same chin, same hairline. The green man beeps: he pockets the snap and moves on.

He turns through the hospital gates, wondering if he'll be allowed to see Astrid, if she's in any condition for visitors. Wondering what reception he'll get, if he does manage to see her. Will she remember who attacked her? She might already, if she's well enough, have given Christine's name to the guards. She might refuse to speak to Bill, refuse to let him near her – and who would blame her?

His fault, all of it.

'Bill?'

It's Heather, coming down the driveway towards him. 'You're here about Astrid?'

'Yes.'

'They won't let you in, I tried just now. I got in earlier, but there's a new nurse on duty and she's like the Gestapo. Astrid had a good night and she managed some breakfast.'

'Is she – will she be OK?'

'They think so.'

He took a breath. 'Do they know who – attacked her?'

'She wasn't attacked,' Heather says. 'She told the nurse. She slipped and fell on some smashed records, or something. They caused cuts to her arms, and she banged her head, and fractured a hip … but whoever burgled the place was gone when she got home.'

Relief, gratitude, floods through him. Christine is not out of the woods, not by a long shot, but she didn't hurt Astrid. That much, at least, is true.

'Hang on – I thought you were sick. Emily told me.'

He thinks of the three missed calls. 'Not sick – more of a day off.'

She takes his arm. 'Come on then,' she says. 'I'd

kill for an espresso,' so they cross the road to a café, where she orders the coffee and an apple Danish.

'Tea for me,' Bill says to the waitress, and it arrives in a pot with an accompanying little biscuit.

He tells her of the phone call from a man he didn't know. 'His son helped me to paint the nursing home a few weeks ago. Astrid came up in conversation – he has a paper round, it's a long story.'

'Shane,' she says, stirring sugar into coffee. 'He's my new boyfriend – that's a long story too. You just missed Emily.'

He frowns, trying to keep up. *It's just that I miss you.* 'What do you mean?'

'She called to the nursing home this morning. That's where she got your number.' Heather pulls her Danish apart and dunks a piece in the small espresso cup. 'I said I'd go and tell you, but she said leave it to her. I'm guessing she was hoping to make things up with you. She told me you'd had words.'

He says nothing.

'And you haven't been to the restaurant in forever. I don't know what's going on, Bill, and I know it's none of my business, but for the life of me I can't figure how you two could have fought about anything. I mean, it's plain that you worship the ground she walks on—'

'What?'

'Oh, come on – you can't deny it.'

He can't. He lets it go. 'Listen,' he says. He looks into his teacup, but finds no inspiration there. 'It's just – I'm going through some family stuff right now. I need time to sort it out.' Weak – he can hear how weak it sounds, even though it's true. Mostly.

Heather signals to the waitress. 'I'll have another espresso, honey. Bill, how're you doing with that tea?'

'I'm fine.'

'You going to eat that biscuit?'

'No.'

'Look,' Heather says, when the waitress has disappeared, 'I'm sorry if you're having problems – and believe me, I know all about how families can mess you up. But honest, Emily could do with all her pals around her now.'

'What do you mean? She's moving to Dublin. She doesn't need us.' It shoots out, a little stronger than he meant it to.

Heather nods. 'I'd better fill you in on that,' she says. 'I guess she won't mind.' She halts as her fresh coffee appears. She smiles her thanks and waits till the waitress is out of earshot again. 'The thing is,' she says, dropping a sugar cube with a plop into her cup, 'she recently took up again with a creep who did the dirty on her a few years ago.'

Bill tops up his tea. Say nothing. Keep your trap shut for once.

'Well, as of last night, that's all finished. He's getting back with an old girlfriend – and turns out it's not for the first time. He sure sounds like some piece of work.'

Bill digests this news in silence.

'And can you believe he did it over the phone? Hadn't the guts to face her.'

'So she's not moving?'

'For sure she's not.'

'And the restaurant?'

'Well, I think it's a fairly safe bet that it's not closing. She'll be happy about that, at least. The thought of having to sell it was killing her.'

So she's staying put, going nowhere. The man who got a second chance has thrown it back at her. The Food of Love will continue to open its doors, five days a week. It's all good news, on the face of it. 'How is she?'

Heather grimaces. 'Pretty miserable.'

He thinks of the voicemail she left on his phone. Even though she'd just been dumped, she'd taken the time to go to the home to tell him about Astrid. And maybe, like Heather said, to make her peace with him – and how had he responded? With a curt text that didn't even have her name in it. And he'd ignored her earlier letter, completely ignored it.

Heather finishes her coffee and gets to her feet. 'I've got errands to run before I collect Lottie from school. I want to get a killer nightdress for Astrid, for one. Please think about coming back to us, Bill. Promise me you'll consider it, for Emily's sake.'

'I will.'

After she's gone he finishes his tea and wonders

what to do next. It's a quarter past noon, and he has an afternoon to kill.

He could go to The Food of Love for a bowl of soup.

She might not want to see him – it would be nothing more than he deserves. But he could thank her for her letter, and for calling to tell him about Astrid. He could do that much, at least. The more he thinks about it, the more he wants to see her. Aches to see her.

He'll go. If he doesn't he'll be left wondering, and kicking himself. If she makes it clear that he's ruined things between them, he'll take the hint and stay away for good.

It's ten to one as he approaches the street. The place will be full enough: Fridays are generally busy. If there's no space at the table, he'll wait.

But it's not full, it's closed. For the first time that he can remember, the restaurant is closed on a Friday. He reads the short note on the door.

Unforeseen circumstances. Another way of saying she's too sad to open up today. It's too impossible for her to be cheerful today.

He steps back to look at the upstairs windows. She sleeps at the front because she likes to hear the sounds of the street when she wakes. He knows this because she said it once. Now the curtains are closed.

He takes out his phone and listens again to her voice. *Bill, it's Emily. I have news about Astrid. Please give me a call*. Should he place a call to her now, and risk waking her if she's asleep?

No. He'll leave her alone. He'll go home and paint the front garden wall, which he's been threatening to do for ages. The paint has been sitting in the shed for at least two months. He'll bring out the radio; he'll turn it up loud. It'll blot out thoughts of Astrid and Christine, and Emily.

But none of that happens.

He spots the green jacket from three houses away. Waiting by the front door, like she always does. He stops on the path, uncertain whether to turn back or face her. Why is she here? What does she want from him now? Did she not understand what he said to her?

He resumes walking, more slowly. He must make it clear; he must stay strong. He will not allow her into the house; he will stick to his resolution. Even though she didn't cause injury to Astrid, she robbed her. She betrayed Astrid's trust, and her father's too.

She doesn't wait for him by the door. As soon as he opens the gate she hurries towards him. 'I brought this,' she says, thrusting something, a necklace, at him. 'I took it from your friend's house. I got money too, but that's gone.'

He regards the string of pearls, cold as stone in his hands. He looks back at his daughter. Stay strong. Claire said that in her last email, but she meant it differently.

And then, and then, and then, her face collapses, he sees everything in it soften and fall, and then, and then, and then, she says the words he has waited for so long to hear.

'Dad, I'm sorry. I want to – I want to get well. I don't want to be this person any more. I'm so sorry about that lady. Will you help me?'

And without stopping to think, without checking to see if anyone is looking, without even being aware of what he's doing, he slips the necklace into his pocket and reaches out and pulls her towards him. He lowers his face to bury it in her unwashed hair, and holds her close.

'I will,' he says, full of elation and terror and hope. 'I will.'

Dear Claire,

Quite a lot has happened. I won't go into it all. I just wanted to tell you that my daughter has asked for help. She spent last night in her old room for the first time in over eight years, and I've managed to find a place that will take her in. I'm afraid to think this might be the turning point, but at least it's a step in the right direction. Thank you for your support.

Please wish us luck.

John

Dear John,

I am so happy to hear this news, thank you so much for letting me know. You are right to be cautious. There's no guarantee that your daughter's life will now turn around, but as you say she has taken that first important, precious step, and I know you will do everything in your power to help and support her. You ask me to wish you luck, and I do with all my heart. I wish you both all the luck and courage and strength in the world, and my hope, my fervent hope, is that things will work out, and all will be well, and you'll both be happy again.

Do let me know how it goes. I'll be waiting to hear, with fingers tightly crossed. You are not alone in this.

Your friend,

Claire xx

Astrid

AS THE DAYS PASS AND SHE WAITS FOR her body to heal, lying in her hospital bed, people tell her things.

'I'm doing OK,' Emily tells her. 'After the shock wore off, I realised it would never have worked out. We would never have made it, not with him feeling he was settling for second best, and I don't want to be someone's second best. And it means I won't be leaving here, I won't be selling up, which I'm really happy about.'

And because she sees the loneliness and disappointment and resignation in Emily's face, Astrid tells her about the person who cares very deeply for her, and for whom she would never be second best. 'He thinks he's not worthy of you,' she says. 'He thinks he's too old, and too troubled – I told you about his daughter. And maybe he's right, maybe he's not the one for you, but he's a good man, and he deserves someone like you.'

'Bill?' Emily says. 'Bill doesn't have those kinds of feelings for me. We were friends, but he walked away with no explanation.'

'He is your friend,' Astrid insists. 'He walked away because he couldn't bear the thought of you with someone else. He walked away because he didn't want to burden you with his problems.'

'Bill,' Emily repeats, her thoughts going somewhere Astrid can't follow. Enough to have planted the seed in her head. Leave it there, let it put down roots – and maybe, in time, it will bloom.

'It was Christine,' Bill tells her quietly, the following day. 'She was the one who burgled your house. She took your key and let herself in. I tracked her down because I – well, I thought she might have done it, and I was right. I told her I didn't want any more to do with her, but she came to the house later and gave me this—' and Astrid gives a cry of joy as Mutti's necklace finds its way back to her.

'She took money too,' Bill says. 'That's gone, but I'll repay it. It's the least I can do. It would never have happened if I hadn't sent her to you.'

'The money isn't important,' Astrid replies. 'She returned all I need,' and because she sees his shame and wants to take it away, she lays a hand on his and tells him the truth about her family, so he can understand how much the necklace means to her, how precious the gift he has just given her.

His face changes as she speaks. It fills with compassion, driving the shame from it. 'My God,' he says quietly, when she finishes, 'such a burden for a young child to bear,' and they sit in silence for some time while he digests it.

'Astrid,' he says then, 'she's trying to get well. Christine. They've taken her into a centre in Galway for twenty-eight days.'

'Bill, that's wonderful news. I'm so glad to hear it.'

'Yes … maybe … Could I ask you to wait until she comes out before you give her name to the guards? Could you do that for me?'

Oh, poor man. Poor man. The entreaty, the worry in his face, when he should be concentrating all his efforts on hoping for a good outcome. 'Bill, I won't be reporting her. If the guards ask me, I'm going to say I don't want to pursue it. I'm going to put it behind me, and you must try to do that too. Let it go, let all of it go now.'

And he thanks her with a catch in his voice, and she sees the fragile hope in his eyes. And she hopes too, hopes that the girl will be able to stay strong, and fight the addiction when it torments her.

'When will they let you home?' he asks.

'I'm not allowed home,' she replies. 'Not immediately. They're looking for a respite place for a few weeks. They say I can't be alone in the house. It's not safe, not till I'm fully recovered.'

Do you have family you could go to? the doctor asked, and Astrid thought of her nephew who wasn't really her nephew, and his wife and three small children, and his house with no spare room, and she said no. The thought of moving into an institution, however efficiently run, does not appeal in the least. At almost ninety-two she's afraid, she's terrified, that once installed there she will never get out, never live again in her little house, feeding her soul with the renewed beauty of her garden.

She voices her fears to Bill. She tries to make a joke of it – 'Once they have me, they might decide to keep me' – and the following evening he returns with a woman Astrid has never met.

'My next-door neighbour,' he says. 'Carmel Twomey. She wanted to come and see you.'

The woman, short and sturdy, her brown hair sprinkled with grey and cut in a blunt bob, smiles at her. 'I hear you might need somewhere to go for a few weeks,' she says. 'I'd be very happy to have you stay in my house. I was a nurse in my day but I'm retired now, with too much time on my hands. I'm a widow, and my son lives with his family in Scotland, so I'd be glad of the company. Just something for you to consider.'

And Astrid understands that this is Bill's way of saying thank you, so she tells Carmel that she would be delighted to accept her generous offer, and she marvels once again at the kindness of strangers.

When Bill appears again the following evening, she enquires, as innocently as she can, if he's been back to The Food of Love.

'I called a few days ago,' he says, cheeks going pink, 'but it was closed.'

'Yes, poor Emily. You heard about her romance finishing?'

He nods. 'Have you spoken with her?'

'She visits me when she can in the afternoons. She's sadder and wiser. She needs her friends around her now. Do drop back again, Bill. I know she'll be glad to see you. She's very fond of you, you know.'

Planting a seed in another head, doing her best to bring happiness to two good people.

'I've cleaned up the house,' Heather tells her the next day. 'It's all set for you to move back in when you're able. I've taken the liberty of replacing a few bits and pieces in the kitchen.'

'Thank you so much,' Astrid says, reaching for her purse, but Heather tells her to stop right there, in a voice that causes the heads of Astrid's three roommates to turn simultaneously towards her.

'Listen,' Heather goes on, at a more reasonable volume, 'I don't generally mention it, and you can keep it to yourself, but I'm actually stinking rich, a trust fund my folks set up' – flapping it away with a careless hand – 'probably to ease their guilty consciences. So I can well afford a new teapot and a few cups. And what's more, I've replaced your record collection too, so there.'

'My – music?'

'Yes. I had all the sleeves so it was easy, and it

gave me a total kick to source them all on the net, so please don't be too proud to accept them.'

More kindness, more than she deserves. 'And this beautiful nightdress too. You're too good, Heather.'

'Ha – far from it! When are they letting you out?'

'The day after tomorrow.' She tells Heather of Bill's neighbour's offer, and Heather claps her hands and declares herself delighted. 'Everything's working out!'

And then, the night before she's discharged into the care of Carmel Twomey, she has another visitor.

'You mightn't remember me. I'm one of the paramedics who came on the scene and brought you here. My name's Shane, and my boy Eoin delivers your paper. I just thought I'd say hi, and glad to see you're on the mend.'

Eoin's father. She has seen his face before. She searches about in her memory until it releases the information.

'You've taken out your earring,' she says, and he looks at her in bemusement.

'We shared the table at The Food of Love one lunchtime,' she says. 'A few months ago. You overheard me saying I was from Austria, and you told me you'd been there on holidays. You said you didn't like the memorial.'

She watches the change that comes into his face. 'I remember,' he says. 'I knew it upset you, when you left straight after. I'm sorry. I don't always think before I speak.'

She shakes her head. 'You just stirred up a few things. It wasn't your fault, you weren't to know. Thank you for looking after me.'

'Heather asked me,' he says then, 'to lose the earring, I mean,' and Astrid realises that this is the man who has brought the recent glow into Heather's face, the man who took time off work to ferry Heather and Lottie to and from the airport. This is the man who visited Lottie's classroom to tell them what a paramedic does, and who brings food for Lottie's kitten whenever he calls to take her mother out.

'Heather looked after your father,' she says, putting all the pieces together.

'She did. He was very fond of her.'

His son Eoin is polite and friendly, and his daughter, according to Heather, is a sweet girl, and may just be the making of Emily's brother Daniel, who by all accounts – well, mostly Heather's – is a terrible womaniser, and needs to find someone to stop all that.

'Your marriage,' she says, because when one is almost ninety-three one can take such liberties, and Shane tells her that he has begun the process of ending it. 'I'm glad to hear it,' she says. 'Heather is a dear friend.'

'She's safe with me,' he promises, and she is inclined to believe him.

'I hear you met Shane,' Heather says the next morning, as they wait for the doctor to sign Astrid's discharge form and let her go.

'I think he just might deserve you,' Astrid tells her, and Heather squeezes her hand.

The doctor gives her the crutch she's been using for her hobbles up and down the corridor. 'Keep up the short walks,' he says, 'a few times a day. Your GP has been put in the picture and will be in touch, and we'll have you back here for a check-up in a few weeks.'

'Will I walk again without the crutch?' she asks.

He regards her over his spectacles. 'I suspect that you could do anything you put your mind to,' he replies. 'I've met few people with your resilience and your positive outlook, and they're what count. Your mobility will come back. Just take it slowly.'

Take it slowly, as if she has a choice. 'Thank you,' she says to him, and 'Thank you' to the nurses who tended her, and 'Thank you' to the porter who puts her into a wheelchair and pushes it to Heather's car, and 'Thank you' to Heather who ferries her to Carmel's house. She is thankful for so much.

'Now,' Carmel says, ushering her into the warm kitchen, 'I've made a tea brack, so you can have a slice of that with a cuppa, to keep you going till lunch. You'll be pleased to hear that you're sleeping downstairs – I got Bill and another neighbour to bring down one of the spare beds and set it up in the dining room. Well, I call it a dining room, but I haven't dined there since my Harry died, and even then we only used it if we had company. Have a seat while I make the tea.'

Astrid hasn't heard a word. 'Your garden,' she murmurs, gazing through the window.

'Oh, do you like it? I must say I'm rather proud of it.'

Astrid takes in the patio paved with limestone slabs, a little cast-iron table and pair of chairs perched in its centre; the three large pots by the wall holding wisteria and azalea and begonias; the raised bed of herbs that cascade over their wooden border; the rockery, full of clambering dianthus and aubrietia and campanula; the little stone-edged pond, dotted with lilies and flanked by a trio of fishing gnomes; the curving path that leads down to the Japanese Acer, with its blaze of red foliage. 'It's beautiful, just beautiful.'

Carmel comes to stand beside her. 'You're a gardener.'

'I am – well, I was. Now I have a man who comes.'

'Would we take our tea outside?' Carmel asks. 'I could get you a blanket.'

'That would be really lovely, thank you.'

She may never go home.

The Party

THEY HAVE A CAKE EACH, ON HEATHER'S insistence. Nobody should have to share a birthday cake, she declared, so Emily obediently made two. Astrid's is a spiced rum and raisin log, dark and rich and topped with bitter chocolate frosting; Bill's is a simple lemon sponge, sandwiched with citrus buttercream and dusted on top with icing sugar.

The September day is chilly, a hint of winter in the breeze, so Emily turns up the heating as she spreads the oval table with a cream linen cloth and sets out plates and forks and napkins. She's serving a wild mushroom tart that Mike prepped yesterday, and a squash and barley salad with elderflower balsamic dressing that's all her own work.

What'll we do about candles? Heather asked, and they quickly decided that forty-nine on one cake and ninety-three on another was out of the question, so

Emily has stuck a single thin white candle into each cake. One candle, one wish.

She knows what both of them will be.

The doctor says another week or so and I'll be able to manage alone again, Astrid told her. Carmel is so thoughtful, and so attentive, but …

But you'd love to be back in your own place.

I would.

And Bill? Bill's wish is easy.

In another week or so his daughter's stay at the rehab centre will come to an end. After that, he's taking her to Cornwall for a short holiday. It's close to where his sister lives but he wanted them to have their own place, so he's booked a small house by the sea.

Bill told her all this, during their talk.

I want to explain, he said, if you have a few minutes. Turning up one afternoon out of the blue, catching her all unawares so she became flustered, remembering their last encounter at the nursing home, and the letter she wrote in its aftermath that was ignored.

Come in, she said, because what else could she say? And in he came, and after that she didn't know what to do with him so there they remained, standing by the big empty oval table as he stuttered out the story of Christine, looking over Emily's shoulder and above her head, and somewhere to the left of her elbow, looking anywhere but into her eyes.

It started after her mother died, he said, or maybe before. When I found out what was happening, I –

I tried to stop it, but I couldn't. I did everything I could think of, but … it wasn't enough. She moved out of home, she left school, she slept rough. She became – someone else.

He stopped. She waited for more.

And more came.

She was the one who burgled Astrid's house. She took a key when she was there – you might recall I sent her to Astrid to fix up her garden. I thought if she had something to do, something to aim for, it might … I was wrong. I went looking for her when I heard about Astrid. I found her, and she admitted it. I was angry, I was so angry with her.

He stopped. Emily waited for more.

And more came.

She's getting help now. She's in a treatment centre. I haven't been allowed to see her, but she phoned me last night – they can use the phone once they're halfway through – and she sounded … Here he paused, and Emily could see the struggle and the fear and the hope all tangled up together in his face. She sounded like the girl I remember, he said at last, and Emily wanted to hug him because he looked like a man desperately in need of a hug, but she didn't. Instead, she waited for more.

And more came.

I had to stop coming here. I – I wasn't fit company, I thought I'd only – I didn't know what I was thinking really – but it was badly done, and it wasn't fair to you – not to let you know, I mean.

And Emily simply nodded, and waited for more. And more came.

You asked me about – giving someone a second chance, he said, that day I met you in the cemetery. You said you wanted – and I – I – well, I— It's just that I didn't realise what you were asking …

It's OK, she said, seeing that what Astrid had told her was true. Seeing it in his face, hearing it in his falling-apart words. I know, she said. It's OK, you don't need to say any more. You just need to start coming back here.

He smiled then, a weak kind of a thing, but it was there. I came a few days ago, he said, the day after Astrid, but – you were closed. He snapped his mouth shut then, and she understood that he'd heard about her and Fergal.

I'm staying put, she said. I've taken this place off the market.

Yes. I heard. I'm really glad. And he finally met her gaze. I'm glad, he said again. I – we wouldn't want to lose you. None of us would.

She didn't trust herself to speak, so she said nothing. They stood there while the seconds ticked by, while life went on in the street beyond the window.

Thank you, he said then.

For what?

I don't know, he admitted – and the silliness of this made her laugh, and when he saw her laughing he laughed too, and it got easier.

He knows nothing about the party. He's not aware that he's being brought here today, and neither is Astrid. The plan is for Heather to collect Astrid and Bill's neighbour Carmel, and then to swing by the nursing home and pick up Bill. They think they're going to Heather's house for lunch. Astrid's birthday is still four days away, and Bill's is later again, so neither of them will suspect a thing.

It's Monday. It's nearly three weeks since Emily picked up the phone and heard Fergal telling her it was over. She's spoken to her parents; she's broken the news to Daniel and her friends. Everyone is predictably outraged on her behalf; everyone is being extra kind to her.

Heather wanted to stake out his mother's house until he showed up, and then to let him have it. Eggs, she said, or maybe rotten tomatoes. Nothing life-threatening, just enough to express my disgust.

Daniel wanted to visit him at his workplace in Dublin. Put the frighteners on him, he said, although precisely how he intended to do that was unclear. Her parents invited her to Portugal for a holiday. I'll stand you the airfare, her father said.

She turned down all the offers. I'm fine, she told everyone – and oddly, she is. Once the shock subsided, once it sank in, she saw it all clearly, saw *him* clearly. Their second attempt should never have happened. She did love him first time round, but going back to him, she now realises, was more an act of hope than of love, more an attempt to show everyone that she'd been right all along, that he'd come good – but she hadn't, and he hadn't.

Therese Ruane is welcome to him.

And Bill, well …

It's early days. It's too soon after Fergal. She needs to let all that go. She needs space and time for a bit. And Bill needs time too, to reconnect with his daughter, to be there for her now more than ever.

And after that, who knows what might happen?

She certainly won't rule it out. No, definitely not.

She polishes glasses. She smiles.

She's such a good liar.

An anniversary, she told Astrid and Bill separately. I'll be ten years in Ireland on Monday. I wanted to mark it in some way, so I thought I'd prepare a little lunch for my friends. Will you risk my cooking? I can come and pick you up – and Emily will join us too.

It's not ten years, it's just gone nine, but she doesn't think they'll do the math. Anyway they both said yes, so she's on her way to pick them up. Carmel will accompany them, because it seemed mean to leave her out. Barring emergencies, Shane will meet them if he can at the restaurant and Daniel and Nora are coming too. They'll be a merry little crowd.

She's also a good planner.

I'd like to make a donation, she said. I'm friendly with Bill, and he always speaks so highly of the place, and I imagine you don't get half enough funding. Can you take a credit-card payment now over the phone? And once that was all sorted, and Bill's boss had run out of thanks, Heather brought up the other topic. I wouldn't ask only it's a special occasion, she said. A surprise early birthday lunch for him, and it will more than likely run on a bit. Would you mind awfully if he was a little late back to work on Monday?

Bribery is so effective.

She hums as she drives. These days, she finds herself humming quite a bit.

We'll be happy to welcome you at Christmas, she wrote to her folks. *Lottie is excited to see her grandma and grandpa again. I'm not sure if I said it while we were there, but thank you for being so kind to her. I really do appreciate it.*

I've met someone, she wrote too. *He's a man I got to know when I first came here but we lost touch, and recently we met up again. He's a paramedic and I like him an awful lot. He'll be around at Christmas, just so you know.*

They're going to have Christmas dinner in his house, she and Lottie and Shane and his kids – and maybe Daniel, and maybe Emily too. My folks are coming to Ireland, she reminded him, and he said the more the merrier, so she'll ask them along.

Should be interesting.

She turns onto the road where Bill lives, and Carmel. She finds the green door that Astrid said to look out for. She parks the car and walks up the driveway, and taps out a jaunty rhythm on the knocker.

❖

'Hello!' Heather says.

She looks happy. Her hair has been released from its usual ponytail: how shiny it is. She wears a red dress with swirls of orange, and chunky red boots that Astrid would have said were more suited to a trip on a motorbike, but that's the difference between ninety-two and twenty-five.

'Ready to go?' Heather asks. She settles Astrid into the passenger seat of her little car while Carmel locks up. 'Not long now,' Heather says, 'till you're going home.'

'No – the end of the week.'

Her birthday on Friday – what better present could anyone have given her? She's considering a small belated party when she has settled in again. Nothing fancy, just a little afternoon tea perhaps, with the people she loves.

And as for Christmas Day, she's been invited to spend it with Carmel. My son and his family are coming home, she told Astrid. They have two little girls, so Santa will be stopping here. I'd love for you to join us. I know I'm biased but the girls are little dotes, not a bit spoilt. You'd love them.

What luck, meeting Carmel. In the time that Astrid has been sharing her home, they have bonded over gardening, and music, and literature. So many shared interests. How clever of Bill to bring them together.

Carmel appears. 'Isn't this lovely?' she declares, getting into the back seat. 'Such a treat. What have you cooked for us, dear?'

'It's a surprise,' Heather replies, starting the car. 'You'll have to wait and see. Is everyone warm enough?'

Bill is waiting for them outside the nursing home: Heather pulls up and he gets in beside Carmel. Astrid is glad he could join them: with Christine coming out of rehab soon it will be an uncertain time for him. He could do with a little distraction, even if only for his lunchtime hour.

She's happy that Emily is coming too. Since her relationship ended she's grown quieter – but not, Astrid thinks, broken-hearted. Not so much sad as resigned. Maybe she recognises the ending for the blessing it was – or maybe she hasn't got that far yet. Maybe it will take a little longer to realise what a lucky escape she had, and to turn her thoughts in a new direction.

'Right,' Heather says, pulling up outside the restaurant. 'Let's hope Emily's ready to go, or my lunch will be ruined.'

'I'll get her,' Bill says, climbing out.

Astrid watches him walking to the door, ringing the bell. Can't wait to see her. So sweet.

❖

She appears quickly, before he's expecting her. She's a little flushed, in an orange and white check dress he hasn't seen before.

'Hi Bill.'

'Hi. Are you all set?'

'I am,' she says, looking past him to wave to the others. 'Come in.' She takes a step back, waits for him to enter.

He stays put. 'We're going to Heather's.' Doesn't she know this? Has there been a mix-up?

'Actually,' Emily says, a smile dimpling her cheek, 'I think we're staying here.'

Behind him a car door opens: he turns to see Heather getting out.

'Slight change of plan,' she says. 'New venue.' Opening Astrid's door. 'Why don't you go in, Bill? We'll be right there. Come on, Carmel, you too.'

So he goes in, not knowing what to expect – and what he sees are balloons hanging in bunches, and strings of lights running along the wall, and the big table laid, and a gift-wrapped package at two place settings.

What he sees, standing by the table, are Emily's brother, and a young woman he doesn't recognise, and a second man he doesn't recognise. 'Happy birthday!' they chorus, and while Emily is making introductions the others enter, and more introductions are made, and glasses of homemade lemonade are handed around, and it's a surprise party for him and Astrid, and the girl he didn't know is the girlfriend of Emily's brother, and the man he didn't know is her father and Eoin's father, the paramedic who attended Astrid at her house, the man who rang Bill to give him the news, and also the new man in Heather's life.

And Heather apparently has had a word with Mrs Phelan, and he's not expected back to work till at least three.

'A toast,' Heather says, raising her lemonade, 'to two good friends. We've had many lunches together, and hopefully we'll have many more, now that The Food of Love is staying open. I know we're a little early, but happy birthday to Bill and Astrid.'

'Happy birthday to Bill and Astrid,' they all chorus, and after that the gifts are opened, and Astrid's is a set of garden lights, and Bill's is a scarf that's the colour of the sky on a perfect day.

They eat a tart with mushrooms in it, and a salad whose ingredients he's not familiar with, but like every other dish in this restaurant it tastes good. Afterwards two cakes are produced, and he and Astrid blow out their respective candles, and he offers up a silent wish for his daughter to be well again, and to stay well.

On Friday he'll drive to Galway and take her away from the rehabilitation centre that's given her twenty-eight precious drug-free days. They'll travel on from there to Dublin airport for their flight to

Exeter, where his sister will pick them up and drive them to the small cottage in Falmouth, Cornwall, he has rented for five days. There, he will simply let her be. He'll walk with her if she wants it, and listen if she talks. He'll take her out to dinner, or eat at home if she'd prefer. He'll light the fire if the evenings are chilly – or they might sit out at night, wrapped up, to see the stars.

They'll take it a day at a time, a minute at a time.

'More cake?'

He lifts his head to see Emily at his side. He smiles at her, and she smiles back. In that handful of moments they may as well be alone in the room, for all the sense he has that anyone else is there.

He takes more cake. He has hope, in a lot of directions.

Emily

EMILY FEENEY, TWENTY-NINE AND STILL
in pyjamas, sits down to tap out a letter on her
computer.

My dear faithful readers,
This week I'm stepping off my usual path to address
you all together. I'm doing this because there are
two things I want, and need, to say to you.

When I was asked, just over two years ago,
to stand in for the person who'd been taking
care of this page before me, I was thrown. I
felt inadequate, unqualified to help others, and
terrified that I might give the wrong advice, and
make things worse instead of better.

But then I remembered sitting down each
week with my grandmother when the newspaper
was delivered, and opening this page with her. I
would read out the problems, and she would give

the advice she thought best before we read the printed response, which never differed greatly from Gran's. Every now and again we'd switch roles, and she'd read the problems out to me, and I would attempt to respond to them, asking myself, 'What would Gran say?' This, I realised, was my training ground. Gran was wise, and she was kind, and she employed her wisdom and her kindness in every response she gave.

So I said yes to the offer, and I became Claire, and each week since then you have put your trust in me and sent me your problems and your worries and your hurts, and every week I have attempted to help you by asking myself, 'What would Gran say?' And even though I lost her before I started doing this, I honestly believe that she's still helping me, still guiding me, still showing me the best way to help you, dear readers.

As you know, some of your letters appear on this page, along with my advice. Other responses are returned to you privately, in the envelopes you enclose with your letters, or to your inboxes if you choose to contact me through email. I answer every single piece of correspondence I receive, publicly or privately, and I always try to give the kindest possible response to each. The most important thing Gran taught me was to be kind.

So today I want to say thank you. Thanks to all of you who have shared your stories with me, and looked to me for advice. It's an honour and a privilege, and I don't take it lightly for a second. I hope I have been of some help.

I want to say something else.

Like many of you, I have been in love. Like many of you, I have been rejected. I know the pain of being betrayed, not once but more than once. After the first time, I stopped believing in love. I turned from anyone who might offer it. I shut myself away from the possibility of love. And then, after a long time, I found the courage to give it another chance, and again I was disappointed.

But the second time, I learnt something. I learnt that love is not the problem. Love is never the problem. Sometimes, out of fear or out of loneliness, we make wrong choices. We see what we want to see, and close our eyes to what we don't. We persuade ourselves that all is well, we paper over cracks, even when we know, in the deepest parts of our hearts, that something is not right. We try to fool love, but love won't be fooled, and sooner or later, our wishful-thinking relationships drift away and are lost.

Love, real love, is faithful. Real love never disappoints. What disappoints are our wrong choices, and we can't blame love for those. We must not become bitter or disillusioned. We must stay open, we must give love every opportunity to find us – and when it does we must embrace it, and hold tightly to it.

Dear readers, we must trust in love, and we must be kind wherever possible, to ourselves and to others. That is my advice to you this week, and my advice to me. If Gran were here, I think she would say the same.
Your friend,
Claire xx

She reads it over, deleting a word here, adding another there. She imagines them reading it, the people who open the paper each week and turn to her page, the people whose letters find their way to her, either by courier each Friday from her uncle in Dublin in a large padded envelope, or into the specially created email address that only she can access.

It terrified her in the beginning, all that hope. Who was she to advise anyone, she who had made such a wrong choice in her own life, she who lived without romantic love, who told herself each day that she didn't need it? But she had Gran, and Gran helped her. Even when the problems seemed insurmountable, Gran gave her the words and helped her to arrange them on the page, and slowly she grew in confidence, and she began to look forward to the letters and emails.

She tries to help them all, friends and strangers alike. Reading their words, putting herself in their shoes, imagining the best strategies for the best outcomes. And now, finally, she is about to put her own advice to the test. She is about to place her trust in new love, which feels very much like it might be real love, and the right choice at last.

She is about to choose Bill, who is also John. She wonders how it took her so long to realise that they were one and the same person, to fit the clues together and match them up. She'll have to tell him, sometime into the future, that she and Claire are the same person too. She'll figure out the best way to do it, when the time comes.

She closes her computer. She goes off to begin her day.

Acknowlegements

To all at Hachette Books Ireland: Ciara D, Joanna, Ruth, Siobhan, Elaine, Breda, Bernard, Jim and Ciara C. Thank you for your excellent attention any time I come looking for it and for your occasional lovely surprises. After fifteen books together, I think we can safely say we're an item.

To my enthusiastic and invaluable agent Sallyanne Sweeney, I'm so glad we got together! Thank you for all you do.

To Geraldine Exton and Philip Gleeson, always so generous with your time and expertise. Thanks a million.

To Mam, Dad, Treas, Tomas, Colm, Ciaran and Aonghus, thank you for the ongoing support and encouragement.

To my many great pals whom I won't name in case I leave anyone out – you know who you are. Thank you, I salute and love you.

To book bloggers who play such a vital role in writers' lives, a big thank you for your support, it's much appreciated.

To readers who pick up this book wherever – bookshop, charity shop, library, pal's house, holiday accommodation – and decide to take a chance on it, thank you. You have my deep gratitude.

Thank you all. xx

*It's their twenty-year school reunion but the Plunkett
sisters have their own reasons for not wanting to attend ...*

Caroline, now a successful knitwear designer, spends
her time flying between her business in England
and her lover in Italy. As far as she's concerned, her
school days, and what happened to her the year she
left, should stay in the past.

Eleanor, meanwhile, is unrecognisable from the
fun-loving girl she was in school. With a son who
is barely speaking to her, and a husband keeping a
secret from her, revisiting the past is the last thing
on her mind.

But when an unexpected letter arrives for
Caroline in the weeks before the reunion, memories
are stirred.

Will the sisters find the courage to return to the
town where they grew up and face what they've
been running from all these years?

The Reunion is a moving story about secrets,
sisters and finding a way to open your heart.

Also available as an ebook and audiobook

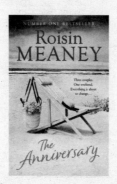

It's the Bank Holiday weekend and the Cunningham family are escaping to their holiday home by the sea, as they've done every summer for many years.

Except that now, parents Lily and Charlie are waiting for their divorce papers to come through – and have their new partners in tow.

Their daughter Poll is there with her boyfriend and is determined to make known her feelings for Chloë, her father's new love. While her brother Thomas also has feelings for Chloë – of a very different nature …

And amid all the drama, everyone has forgotten that this weekend also happens to be Lily and Charlie's wedding anniversary.

Will any of the couples survive the weekend intact?

Also available as an ebook and audiobook